ROGUES

THE OMEGA SUPERHERO BOOK 4

DARIUS BRASHER

Special thanks to Michael Hofer and Paul Krause, higher lever supporters of Darius Brasher's Patreon campaign. Michael and Paul, your support is much appreciated!

PART I

1

Rogue
noun /rōg/

A person with superpowers who uses those powers without a license granted by the Heroes' Guild and the United States Department of Metahuman Affairs in violation of the federal Hero Act of 1945—i.e., a supervillain.

UWant Online Dictionary, 2017

I strode through a sea of unconscious henchmen toward Amok. As I advanced on the superpowered terrorist, the arms and legs of his henchmen moved out of my way due to slight gestures of my hands. Since the prostrate men wore crimson armor, it was like parting the Red Sea. Maybe Moses had been a telekinetic like I was.

I glanced at the giant digital clock that hung from the old warehouse's rafters like a scoreboard. Obviously installed by Amok and his men, it was as out of place in the abandoned toy warehouse as a cockroach in a bowl of soup. It was tilted so the hostages kneeling at Amok's feet could see it and their fear could mount as the seconds ticked away. A little over fifteen minutes remained until the dirty bomb Amok had hidden here in Astor City exploded, killing everyone in the warehouse and untold citizens in the rest of the city.

Other licensed Heroes, including my friend Isaac Geere—the Hero Myth—were trying to evacuate the city. As Astor City, Maryland was one of the country's largest urban areas with a population in the millions, there was no way the other Heroes would get everyone out in time. Not when Amok had only given the city an hour's notice of the impending explosion.

I had already scanned this sprawling warehouse with my telekinetic touch. There were lots of mice, enough bugs to give an insectophobe nightmares, and bits of broken and unfinished toys. No bomb. Amok must have hidden it somewhere else in the city. I'd have to get the bomb's location straight from the horse's mouth.

Since Amok's Metahuman powers let him literally feed on fear, I tried to tamp down the fear mounting in my chest as the seconds slipped away. My hands burned with my powers as they always did, feeling like they were over a warm fire. Waves of energy pulsating out of them that were invisible to everyone but me. It was hard to not rush through the warehouse to where Amok stood on the raised platform with the hostages. I forced myself to approach Amok slowly. Calmly, deliberately, without fear. Fake it until you make it. The fear was more for the others in the city than for myself. Most days, me getting killed felt like it would be a blessed relief.

Amok was a Rogue. Rogues were people with superpowers who used them despite not being licensed to do so. Non-

Metas often called them supervillains. I called them pains in the ass. There were five general categories of Rogues: the money-hungry; the power-hungry; the fame-hungry; the ones whose bats in their belfry were hungry—that is, the ones who were batshit crazy; and the ones who were a messy medley of the other four. Doctor Alchemy was a prime example of the fifth category—a greedy, power-mad, spotlight-loving Rogue who was also loony tunes. He was the father of Smoke, the Heroic name of my friend and lover Neha Thakore whom I had let the Sentinels kill a couple of years ago.

Though Amok was not as powerful as Doctor Alchemy, Amok was still an infamous terrorist whose fiendish attacks had gotten more elaborate and deadly over the years. This latest plot of his was to plant a nuclear bomb in Astor City, tell everyone about it through social media and the local news, and for him and his death cult followers to feed on the resulting panic and fear like hogs at a trough thanks to Amok's powers until they and everyone else in the city were vaporized in a nuclear fireball.

So yeah, Amok was definitely in the batshit crazy category of Rogues. What he lacked in raw Metahuman power he made up for with sheer nuttiness and reckless disregard for human life.

"Where did you find these knuckleheads? Hapless-R-Us?" I said to Amok about his unconscious henchmen. I spoke with a forced glibness. *Who's scared he's going to fail like he did with Neha and get everyone in the city blown to radioactive bits? Not me. No fear. No doubt. I've got this.* Not even I believed my internal pep talk. Hopefully lack of fear was like The Secret—if you believed it hard enough, it would manifest. "Is that the same place they get *Star Wars* Stormtroopers from? They look intimidating and make a lot of noise, but pose no real threat to the hero. That would be me, by the way. The fancy duds and the cape are what give it away. These jerks barely slowed me down. Must be hard to find good help these days. Now be a good little Rogue and tell me where the bomb is before I'm forced to beat it out of you."

My cape rustled softly behind me as I got closer to Amok and the kneeling hostages. Amok glared at me. The hostages quivered in fear. I wore my full Omega suit: a full-body, dark blue costume that moved with my body like the second skin it was despite the fact it was tough enough to deflect knife thrusts and low caliber gunshots. A cowl hid my features except my eyes, nose, and mouth. A silver white omega symbol was on my chest; a cape of the same color billowed out from my neck. As I advanced toward Amok, my shoulder still hurt from that brutal fight with the Rogue Grendel a few days ago. I barely felt it. The pain was like bad background music—faintly annoying, but I was only vaguely aware of it in the face of the threat Amok posed. Nothing focuses the mind like imminent death does.

Amok was mostly bald, with a fringe of iron gray hair ringing the back of his head. He wore a charcoal robe and leather sandals. He was of medium height, thin-limbed, with a slight belly. His feet were dirty, his skin pale white, his face chubby and unlined. He would look like a monk who spent too much time cloistered in his monastery if it weren't for the assault rifle strapped to his body. Also, his eyes. His irises were as gray as his robe, but the whites of his eyes were anything but white. They were as green as a leprechaun's suit. The bizarre color was not a side effect of his Metahuman power. Rather, his eyes were tattooed. At some point he had undergone a procedure known as sclera staining, in which needles injected ink into the whites of the eyes.

Yeah, like I said—Amok was batshit crazy.

He stared at my approach with the glassy eyes of an addict. His drug was no narcotic, though; his drug was the fear his terrorism caused. "I can taste your fear, Omega," he said. He spoke with a pronounced lisp, making his voice the hiss of a snake. "Fear you will fail. Fear everyone will die because of you. Your fears are justified. And delicious." He licked his lips, like he was savoring a meal.

So much for willing my lack of fear into existence. I always suspected The Secret was a load of crap.

Less than thirty feet away now. As calmly as I could, I said, "Where's the bomb, Amok? I'm not going to ask nicely again."

Amok reached out to snatch the badly dyed red hair of the nearest hostage, a white woman in a large, shapeless shift dress. He yanked her toward him. She yelped in fear and pain. Amok jabbed the barrel of his gun into the side of her head. Her eyes rolled back, like those of a frightened horse. "Oh Jesus, Jesus, Jesus," she prayed. Some of the other hostages gasped; others gibbered in fear, their eyes darting from Amok to the countdown. They cowered where they knelt despite the fact the guns of Amok's henchmen were no longer pointed at them. I did a quick count. Maybe twenty of them. They were scared. So was I.

"Stop where you are or the fat bitch gets it in the head," Amok hissed. There was no anger in his voice. Only intense pleasure. His face looked almost orgasmic. Though Amok could sense the fear of everyone in the city, the closer the source of the fear, the more acutely he felt it. It was probably why he had taken hostages and forced them to watch the countdown to their personal Armageddon.

I reached out with my powers, running my mind over the gun pointed at the woman. Screws unscrewed, metal and plastic peeled apart. In the blink of an eye, the gun disintegrated in Amok's hand. Its parts clattered on the concrete floor. Amok was left holding only the gun's stock and trigger. Both his and the woman's eyes widened in astonishment.

"You were saying?" I asked. I hadn't even broken stride. *Don't be afraid*, I told myself. *Keep calm. Don't feed his hunger. You'll find the bomb in time. You have to. You won't fail this time. Not again.*

Now that a gun no longer threatened to blow her brains out, the look on the face of the woman in Amok's grip changed. Fear disappeared, displaced by rage. Her face red, she rammed her head backward, directly into Amok's crotch. I winced merely seeing the force of the blow. Amok gasped in pain, doubled over, and fell to his knees, clutching his privates. The woman twisted around, pulling off one of her high heeled wedges. She started pounding on Amok with the thick shoe. Her fleshy arm rose and fell like a hammer that had found a nail. I guess she didn't need Jesus' help after all. God helped those who helped themselves.

"Who's the fat bitch now, huh bitch?" she screamed as she pummeled Amok. "Who's the fat bitch now?" Hell hath no fury like a woman called a fat bitch.

I sprang into the air, flying the remaining distance to Amok and the woman. He covered his head with his arms, trying to protect himself from the woman's blows. I grabbed her arm and pulled her away from Amok. She went sprawling, her dress sliding up and bunching around her waist. I had yanked more roughly than I meant to in my haste to stop her before she clocked Amok on the head and knocked him out. I needed him conscious.

"Jeez lady, calm down," I said. I averted my eyes from her exposed thong and ivory flesh. The last thing I needed was for her to attack me too for ogling her. "Don't you know who I am? I'm Omega. I've got this under control."

"Really? Cause it kinda doesn't look like it." She jabbed a

finger at the countdown overhead. Less than fourteen minutes left.

The lady had a legit point.

I scanned the room with my powers again, this time locking onto all the weapons of the unconscious henchmen. Most of them I disassembled just as I had Amok's. The sound of countless gun parts hitting the cement floor filled the air. The few guns I left intact I levitated over to the platform the hostages and I were on.

"Take these and cover Amok's men in case they wake up," I ordered the hostages. "I'll take care of Amok and the bomb." The hostages slowly got to their feet. Everyone but the chubby lady looked dazed by all they had been through. They grabbed the floating guns as I commanded. In my Omega suit and cape, I was an authority figure, just as my Hero Academy training had promised I would be. If I had just been in regular clothes as 23-year-old Theodore Conley, the hostages, most of whom were older than I, likely would have thought, "Who the hell is this kid to give us orders?" I was careful to disable the firing pin of the gun I gave to the heavyset lady. She clearly had anger issues. I didn't want her losing her cool and shooting Amok in the head before I extracted the bomb's location from him.

Amok still lay on the floor, making no effort to get up. Though his face was now bloody thanks to the chubby lady's wedge of vengeance, there was a blissful smile on his face. His teeth were rotting, spotted brown and black. I could smell his breath as I stood over him. It reeked like a rotting corpse. Terrorism clearly was higher on his list of priorities than oral hygiene.

"Fear swaddles the city like a baby's blanket," he said, his green-haloed gray eyes looking heavenward in a hazy, unfocused way. "So warm and delectable. I've never felt the like before."

I looked down at him with disgust. Endangering all these lives just to feel a high. I wondered where this nutjob had gotten the fissionable material for the bomb. I pushed the thought aside. An issue for a later time. Assuming there was a later.

I examined Amok's body clinically. I kicked him on his right side, under his ribcage. He moaned gutturally and curled up like a poked caterpillar. I said, "That was a liver shot. Right now it feels like you've been kicked in the balls, had the breath knocked out of you, and like you want to throw up. As bad as it feels, the next blow will be worse. Where is the bomb?"

Despite his ragged breathing, Amok still smiled, as if he was listening to beautiful music only he could hear. He shook his head no.

Of course it wouldn't be that easy. When was this job ever easy?

I shoved my foot out and rolled Amok over a bit. I punched him hard twice, this time near his back. His body straightening out like he was being electrocuted. He howled, the pain I had inflicted now enough to pierce the fear-fueled euphoria he was experiencing. I said, "Those were kidney punches. Now it feels like you have lava diarrhea shooting through your guts. You'll likely be pissing blood for a while. You're obviously willing to die, but I doubt anyone is willing to live through the hell I'm going to put you through the next few minutes if you don't tell me what I want to know." I put my boot on his already tender genitals. I pressed down and twisted my heel. Amok howled again. "Now where is the bomb?"

"Stop it!" one of the hostages cried out. "You're hurting him."

"Shut up," I snapped irritably, not taking my eyes off Amok. Amok had taken these people hostage and was about to blow them and everyone else up, yet this birdbrain was still sticking up for him. Some people were too kindhearted for their own good. Not me. I'd learned my lesson the hard way. I would pull Amok's toenails out through his penis and worse if I had to. Dad, Hannah Kim, Neha . . . I'd be damned if more people died because of me.

Amok softly said something, still smiling happily despite the pain he was in. He was crying. Tears of pain, or of joy? I couldn't tell. I leaned closer, thinking maybe he was saying where the bomb was.

He wasn't. He was singing. I recognized the words. It was the Nine Inch Nails song *The Day the World Went Away*.

Crap. That settled it. I could subject him to more pain, but I knew Amok wasn't going to tell me anything. Not now, not like this, while he luxuriated in the citywide fear and panic his ticking time bomb caused. Getting him to tell me what I needed to know while he was in this condition was like trying to get someone tripping on heroin to focus on a quadratic equation. I needed to detox him and quick.

I glanced up at the countdown. T minus thirteen minutes and counting until the city blasted off into nothingness. Thirteen? I wasn't superstitious, but that did not seem like a good omen.

Inspiration struck. Amok felt people's fear more intensely the closer he was to it. If I got Amok away from all the people he had terrified in Astor City and I roused him from the fear-fueled euphoria he was basking in, maybe my fists could then talk some sense into him.

I started the stopwatch on my wrist communicator, the one

Amazing Man had given me years ago. This would be the worst possible time to lose track of time. I raised a force field around me and Amok. Carrying Amok with me, I shot up, toward the ceiling of the warehouse.

"Omega, wait! Where are you going?"

"Don't leave!"

"Come back!"

"Save us!"

The cries of the hostages trailed me, making me feel like a rat leaving a sinking ship. I felt guilty even though I knew I wasn't abandoning them. If there was one thing I was really good at, it was feeling guilty. Being raised Catholic had made sure of that.

I punched through the roof of the warehouse with a crash. The sun was bright overhead. It was midday. The warehouse was in the industrial part of the city, not too far from the gym where my fellow Hero Truman Lord worked out. I rose high enough to avoid slamming into any nearby buildings. Then I sped off toward the north with Amok floating beneath me.

Everywhere I looked below, the roads leading out of Astor City were snarled with bumper-to-bumper traffic. The sound of thousands of car horns filled the air, as if the city itself wailed primally. How many people had gotten out of the city? How many more would get out before the big kaboom? A tiny fraction of the population, no doubt. A densely populated city couldn't be evacuated in less than an hour. Not even close. How many would die? Thousands, certainly. Millions, maybe.

I just had to find that bomb. Even if I had to wring Amok's neck to do it.

I increased my speed. Sonic booms went off in my wake as I broke the sound barrier. The landscape below became a blur. I normally did not fly this fast near population centers, but this was an emergency. Some busted windows and ruptured eardrums were better than countless incinerated bodies.

The further we got from Astor City, the more alert Amok seemed, as if he was reluctantly waking from a deep dream. He twisted, looking around, wincing in pain from my earlier blows.

"Where am I? Where are we going?" he demanded. He didn't sound out of it like he had before.

"I'm taking you far enough away from Astor City so I can beat the crap out of you and you'll actually care," I said.

Even though the scenery was a blur, it was obvious how high in the sky we were. Amok gulped, looking wild-eyed and panicked as he looked down. I didn't think it was the beating he was afraid of. I had picked up and flown with a lot of people over the past few years, and I recognized the look on Amok's face.

He's afraid of heights, I thought.

Interesting.

Change of plans. I altered my trajectory. I now moved straight up into the sky instead of in a straight line away from Astor City. Amok's green-rimmed eyes looked like they were about to burst right out of his head the higher we went. He gibbered something. I couldn't understand what he said, but it didn't sound like "This is fun!"

I finally slowed to a halt. We were up so high that the features of the geography below couldn't be made out. Everything was geometric patterns, like what you saw when you looked out of an airplane window at cruising altitude.

The air was cold and thin here. What there was of it whistled in my ear. Amok clawed the air, but I kept him far enough away that he couldn't touch me.

"Please . . . down. Let me down. Let me down," he croaked pleadingly.

"Sure thing," I said. I put my closed fist in Amok's face dramatically. Then I opened it, simultaneously releasing my power's hold on him.

Screaming, flailing, Amok plunged toward the ground like a dropped bag of trash.

2

_____

With my powers locked onto him so I would not lose sight of him, I let Amok free-fall for several seconds. The way he sawed the air with his limbs, it looked like he was trying to learn how to fly on the . . . well, fly.

I dropped like a stone with my arms folded. I caught up with him, matched his speed, and slowed both of us to a halt. We were still very high up.

"Where's the bomb?" I asked again. I yelled to be heard over the rushing wind.

Flecks of vomit spotted Amok's face. The front of his robe was soiled. I wondered if he was peeing blood as I had predicted when I had kidney punched him. Rogues were a lot less scary with vomit on their face and bloody pee in their pants. Amok gasped, sucking in air like a bellows. "I'll tell you. I'll tell you. First just let me down."

"Nope. Tell first, down second." I made a big show of lifting my closed fist again, then opening it. I released my hold on him again. He plunged down once more, screaming like a banshee all the while.

I waited a few more seconds. I glanced at my watch. About ten minutes left. If I couldn't get an answer from Amok, I'd fly back to Astor City and try to locate the bomb on my own one last time. If I couldn't, when it detonated, maybe I could contain the explosion in a force field and minimize the deaths, devastation, and fallout. Even with my powers augmented by the Omega suit, I didn't know if I could contain such an explosion once it had already begun. There was a decent chance I'd die trying.

As plans went, that one blew. Literally. I didn't have a better one.

I dropped again, slowing and then halting Amok's descent when I was abreast of him. He hung upside down. I left him that way. We were close enough to the surface that I could make out the features on the ground now. We were over a wooded area. I was sure we were no longer in Maryland. Pennsylvania, maybe.

"The clock is ticking. Last chance," I said. "Where is the bomb?"

Amok's eyes bulged down at the trees far below. From up here, the forest looked like a giant green pincushion. There was no way Amok would survive the fall.

"You're a Hero. You're not going to let me die if I don't tell you," he said. I couldn't tell whom he was trying to convince: me, or himself. Apparently the prospect of death was a lot less appealing if a fear-fueled orgasm wasn't blinding one to the horror of it.

"Sure, I'm a Hero. But I'm also the Hero who's world-famous for killing Mechano. If I'd kill a fellow Hero, I'll certainly have no problem killing terrorist trash like you."

Amok shook his head, stubborn despite his fear. "You're bluffing."

I shrugged. "Suit yourself." I raised my closed fist again. "Thanks for flying with Omega Airlines. Next and final stop, Splatterville." I started to open my fist.

"Wait!" Amok cried.

I paused with my hand partially open.

"The Cantor Building," Amok said, the words rushing out in a torrent. His tattooed green eyes rolled in his head like a slot machine display. "The bomb is on the fifth floor of the Cantor Building. I swear. Just let me down." The Cantor Building was in downtown Astor City, not too far from Star Tower and the UWant Building. It was closed for renovations that were set to begin next month. Empty. If Amok was telling the truth, it was the perfect place to hide a bomb. It felt like he was being honest, but there was no way to know for sure.

"How do I disarm the bomb?" I asked.

"It can't be disarmed. That's how I designed it." Wonderful. The day kept getting better and better. What was up next, a planet-busting asteroid slamming into us?

Amok was of no use anymore. I released my hold on him and let him fall.

"Nooooooooo!" he shrieked. The cry trailed after him like a streamer. He screamed all the way down. He thought I would let him die despite him telling me about the bomb.

Tempting, but no.

I parted tree branches out of the path of Amok's fall. I slowed him down before he slammed into the ground. Gradually, to avoid turning his internal organs into pâté. He was out of sight now, but my telekinetic touch was all I needed. I ripped open a man-sized crevice in the forest floor. I lowered Amok inside of it. I covered him with dirt. It was like burying the world's worst time capsule. The soil was moist but firm, like semi-set cement. I packed it in tight around Amok's body.

When I finished, he literally could not move a muscle. Unless he magically developing super strength, there was no way he was getting out. I didn't cover his head, of course. I wasn't trying to kill him, as tempting as the notion was. Amok had hurt a lot of people over the years, and would hurt a ton more today if I didn't do something about that bomb. If a pack of coyotes or a bear ambled along and made an hors d'oeuvre of his head before I came back to retrieve him—assuming I was alive and not bits of radioactive ash—I wouldn't lose sleep over it.

Nine minutes left. It had only taken a few seconds to drop Amok and secure him in the ground, though they were precious seconds I hated to waste. However, I didn't want to drag Amok back to Astor City with me. I wouldn't reward his bad behavior by giving him a further taste of all the fear and anxiety he had created in the city.

The instant Amok was secure, I zoomed back toward Astor City. I retracted my cape into the Omega suit with a thought as I flew. It slid back into my neck like a retracting tongue. I had only worn it to seem more authoritative to the hostages and Amok, like when a judge dons her robe or a doctor his white coat. Though they looked impressive, capes usually just got in the way.

As I accelerated toward Astor City, I thought about using my communicator watch to tell Myth what I'd learned. I dismissed the thought as soon as I had it. He already had his hands full helping with the evacuation. Call Truman instead? The problem was, with the roads blocked by people fleeing the city, as a non-flying Meta Truman wouldn't be able to get to the Cantor Building in time. And even if he could, what would he do to the bomb when he got there? Shoot it? Quip it into submission?

No. I'd take care of it myself. Though I trusted Truman and I especially trusted Isaac, I trusted my abilities and powers as Omega to take care of the bomb more than I did Isaac's or Truman's. I wasn't going to call any other Hero for help, either. After what had happened with the Sentinels, I trusted most other Heroes as much as I'd trust a snarling dog that had already bitten me.

Besides, if you want something done right, do it yourself.

I flew as fast as I could, which was pretty bloody fast these days. The world became a blur. I had hidden an electronic beacon on top of the UWant Building almost a year ago after I had gotten lost on the way back to Astor City while flying from San Francisco in the middle of the night. Embarrassing. Getting lost would be more than merely embarrassing now.

Using my watch to hone in on the UWant Building beacon, I slammed to a stop in the air above the emerald green glass building, the city's tallest. My pulse pounding, I twisted in the air, anxiety and adrenaline making me burn even more precious seconds while I got my bearings.

There. The Cantor Building, a gray and red rectangular structure, a midget compared to Star Tower and the UWant Building, both of which towered over it.

I flew to the smaller building, and dropped down to what I estimated was the fifth floor. The streets were packed with honking cars, bumper to bumper, like rush hour on steroids. At least the people stuck here at ground zero would be killed instantaneously, unlike people on the periphery of the city and in the surrounding suburbs who'd probably die a long, lingering death from radiation poisoning. Every radioactive cloud has its silver lining.

I scanned the floor with my telekinetic touch. Lots of junk, trash, and construction supplies. Nothing that looked like a bomb. Shit! Had Amok been lying? Wait. I counted a column of windows from the ground up. One, two, three, four, five, six. Damn it! I was one floor too high. So much for my estimation. What a time for such a stupid mistake.

I scanned the floor below the one I had just swept.

There! That had to be it.

With a spherical force field around me, I swung out and down, like a wrecking ball. I crashed into the wall of the fifth floor, slamming through it with an inward spray of metal, cinder block, and drywall.

Since I had a lock on what I had found with my telekinetic touch, I didn't have to wait for the dust to clear before striding through the empty office I had burst into, down a hallway, and into an area that appeared to be an employee break room. An open, unplugged refrigerator was against the wall. An unrecognizable piece of food rotted and stank on one of its shelves. Flies buzzed around it. A nearly empty vending machine was next to the fridge, with two bags of potato chips inside of it that looked lonely and forlorn.

A second vending machine, this one for the Blast brand of sodas, was overturned with its back facing up. Resting on top of the soda machine was a device a bit shy of the length, width, and depth of the vending machine it rested on. Looking like something an auto mechanic and a mad scientist might join forces to create, the device was a rat's nest of tubes, large cylinders, and wiring. On the top of it was a glowing digital display. Its countdown matched the countdown on my watch. Two thick iron chains crossed over each other on top of the device. The chains were bolted to the floor, securing the device and the vending machine in place.

I didn't need Amok to paint me a picture to know this was the bomb. And putting it on top of a Blast vending machine? Amok must have had quite the chuckle over that one.

Five minutes left. Fuck! I'd been cursing a lot the past few minutes, something my devout churchgoing parents wouldn't have approved of. Then again, if there ever was a time for profanity, this was it. There might not be time for profanity— or anything else—later.

I had trained in the use and defusing of explosives when I was Amazing Man's Apprentice. I had used that knowledge to help me defeat Iceburn. Nothing I had learned from the Old Man prepared me for something like this, though. Looking at the bomb and its maze of wires and components, I didn't know where to even begin to deactivate it. If I started tinkering with it, I might set it off. If I had advanced degrees in mechanical engineering, nuclear physics, and supervillain douchebaggery, I might have taken a stab at it. But as it was, I didn't dare. Too risky.

Okay, trying to defuse the bomb was out. Could I instead throw a force field around it and contain its explosion? Maybe. I had absorbed the massive amount of energy that had resulted when I destroyed Mechano, after all. But I had no idea what kind of explosive yield the bomb would produce. Maybe it would be small enough for me to handle. Then again, maybe not. I couldn't take a chance on all these maybes. Not when so many lives were at stake.

With my heart in my throat, I walked around the vending machine and bomb, bending over to examine them as quickly yet as thoroughly as I could. I didn't see any pressure or dead man switches. I gently probed the setup with my telekinetic touch, paying special attention to the underside of the bomb, halfway expecting the thing to blow up in my face as a result. If you hadn't heard of a booby trap before, it would sound awesome, especially if you were a dude. But I had stumbled into enough booby traps since becoming a Meta to know the name was misleading—they were not at all awesome.

However, if there were any booby traps in place here, I didn't recognize them as such.

The first good news of the day. This meant I could move the blasted thing. *Blasted thing.* Definitely no pun intended.

Two minutes left. No time left to be delicate or pussyfoot around.

With my powers, I snapped the chains securing the bomb in place. I flung them aside. They clanged to the floor. I latched onto the bomb with my mind, enveloping it in a force field.

With my personal force field up and the bomb in tele-kinetic tow, I slammed through the break room ceiling, shot through the floors above, and punched through the roof of the Cantor Building.

No time to figure out where to go other than straight up.

I rose faster than a rocket. The bomb dangled behind me like a scarf blowing in the rushing wind. Soon I had left Astor City far behind. Even so, I kept rising. I did not dare let the bomb detonate in the atmosphere. Even if a high-altitude detonation didn't kill anyone immediately, the wind would carry the radiation God only knew how far to sicken and perhaps kill countless people. A slow death was still death. I needed to make it to the Karman line, the boundary sixty-two miles up that was between the Earth's atmosphere and outer space.

I screamed up, higher and higher into the sky. Through the clouds of the troposphere, past the stratosphere, into the mesosphere. The sky transitioned from blue to violet to almost black. Little time remained according to my watch.

Here would have to do.

I released my hold on the bomb. I moved slightly to the side and slowed down, but not too quickly or else the forces at play would tear my body apart.

The momentum of the bomb sent it rocketing past my decelerating body. Though the air was mighty thin this high, the speed of the bomb was such that its air wake sent me tumbling. I spun, end over end, out of control. Even so, I had the presence of mind to track the bomb as it continued up, up, and away.

The bomb shot into the blackness of space. It exploded without a sound in the dark vacuum. I didn't see it, but I felt it with my telekinetic touch.

I righted myself and slowed to a complete stop. My breathing was labored and my heart raced. I felt like I had just completed a race. I guess I had. My trophy was an intact Astor City and still living citizens.

I'd done it. It wasn't saving the entire world as apparently I was destined to try to do as the carrier for the Omega spirit, but this was far better than nothing. First save the city, then the world. Hopefully. The saving of a thousand cities begins with a single city. Or something like that. I was no good at riffing on clichés when I'd just averted a disaster and my heart was still pounding a mile a minute.

There wasn't much breathable air left in the force field surrounding me, but I couldn't help but linger to admire the beauty of the planet below. I never tired of looking at it. I hoped I was up to the challenge of dealing with the threat to it the Sentinels had warned was looming. I had worked my fingers to the bone over the past couple of years to prepare myself.

As I feasted on the sight of the world below, a question that had been nagging the back of my mind this whole time came to the forefront, waved at me insistently, and demanded my attention:

When I had dangled Amok in the air earlier, would I really have dropped him a third and final time to let him fall to his death if he hadn't told me where he had stashed the bomb?

I mulled it over as the world turned.

As someone who was supposed to be a Hero, I didn't much like the answer.

3

I stood on top of the emerald green UWant Building in my Omega suit. It was the tallest building not only in Astor City, but in the entire country. From up here, I could survey almost the entire city with my powers. I was capeless because, being alone up here, I did not need to impress anyone with my Heroic authority. Intimidating terrorists and bossing around hostages was not on tonight's agenda.

I perched on the edge of the roof's observation deck with my arms outstretched. Even after all these years, I still needed to move my hands and fingers to use my powers. Athena, one of my Academy instructors, had unsuccessfully tried to break me of the habit; unfortunately, moving my hands and fingers seemed necessary to trigger my powers.

The UWant Building's thin spire was behind me. Flashing airplane warning lights mounted near the top of the spire blinked off and on, supplementing the light of the full moon overhead. Isaac said I looked like a gargoyle when I stood up here like this. A shame he didn't think I looked like a were-wolf. With the moon hanging so low and bright in the night sky, the temptation to howl at it was almost irresistible.

It was a few hours after midnight. I was wide awake despite the early hour. Ever since absorbing the Omega suit, I did not need much sleep. I would grab some shut-eye for a few hours after I finished doing this final sweep of the city with my telekinetic touch. I came to the city's tallest building to do it because, from up here, there were fewer things in the way to obstruct my telekinetic touch. Thanks to my Omega suit augmented powers, I did not have to always physically patrol the city like I used to. As that old Yellow Pages' commercial said, I often let my fingers do the walking. Maybe referencing outdated television commercials was manifesting as a secondary superpower.

My telekinetic touch brushed past several minor crimes in progress. Car break-ins, vandalism, prostitution, illegal dumping, that sort of thing. In a sprawling big city like Astor City, crime was a twenty-four hour a day, seven days a week enterprise. But the crimes I sensed were nothing terribly serious the police could not handle. So, I kept my nose out of the criminal brush fires and let the cops deal with them. I would only intervene if something big happened or if someone was in physical danger.

My hands-off approach to being a Hero was relatively new. In the immediate aftermath of Neha's death, I had jumped on all wrongdoing, no matter how big or small. I'd done that partly to train myself in the use of my newly augmented powers to prepare for the world-threatening crisis supposedly on the horizon, and partly out of the desire to help and protect people. However, another reason I instantly transformed into a one-man anti-crime spree was to drown myself in work to keep from dwelling on Neha's death. Mission most definitely not accomplished on that last part.

I had soon realized, though, that the city and the surrounding area were coming to rely on me and my crime-fighting efforts too much. It was a like a parent spoiling a child by giving him everything he wanted and doing everything for him. When the parent died, the child would be up a creek without a paddle because he was too reliant on the parent. I didn't want the same thing to happen to Astor City if I bit the bullet. Being a Hero was a dangerous vocation. I wasn't going to live forever. Frankly, I would not want to even if I could. After all the deaths I had seen and caused, life had lost most of its luster.

I sensed a presence behind me. Isaac?

No.

I lowered my hands and turned around. Shadows cast flat geometric patterns all over the surface of the roof. I didn't see anyone. Not with my eyes, at least.

"I know you're there, Ninja," I said, looking into the dark gloom of two converging shadows. "You're not fooling anybody. Why are you skulking in the shadows? You're not Batman."

Ninja's lithe black-garbed form melted noiselessly out of the darkness. If I had not known she was there, it would seem like she appeared out of thin air like a restless wraith. A scabbard sheathing a katana was slung across her chest; the hilt of the sword poked over her right shoulder.

Ninja was a licensed Hero. She was the current chairwoman of the Sentinels. Though tradition and the Sentinels' charter mandated there be seven Heroes on the group roster, the team had been decimated. Avatar had been murdered. Mechano had been destroyed by me. Seer was imprisoned at MetaHold. Millennium was nowhere to be found, presumably on the run from the authorities. Ninja, Tank, and Doppelganger were the only Sentinels who remained. They had tried to recruit replacement Heroes, but public opinion, once adoring, had turned against the team when I had exposed

Mechano's, Seer's and Millennium's crimes against me and others. Most Heroes had no interest in associating with the Sentinels' once glorious but now tainted name.

"Of course I'm not Batman," Ninja said. Her voice held a whisper of an accent. Only her narrow Asiatic eyes were visible through the black cloth wrapped around her head. "Batman is not real. Plus, my boobs are bigger than his."

My eyes flicked to her slight chest. "Only marginally," I said acerbically. The Sentinels' hero worship I had grown up with had died with Neha.

"We Japanese tend to not be a busty people."

"Sneaky though."

"That racist."

"First Pearl Harbor, now you creeping up behind me tonight. Facts aren't racist. I stand by my statement."

"If I really had been creeping up on you, you never would have known I was here." Ninja then said something in Japanese. It didn't sound complimentary.

"What did you just call me?" I demanded.

"There's no exact English equivalent. Roughly translated, I referred to you as a fish belly white barbarian."

"Now who's the racist?"

The cloth around her mouth twitched. She was smiling under her mask. "Takes one to know one," she said.

Despite myself, I almost smiled back at her. I twisted my mouth's movement into a scowl instead. It was hard to not like Ninja, though I didn't want to since she had the murderous stink of being a Sentinel on her. Unlike the other Sentinels, she did not take herself so seriously. And, unlike Seer, Millennium, and Mechano, she was not a murderous criminal camouflaged as a Hero. Truman had gone through the Trials with Ninja, and vouched for her. I had also investigated her on my own, and she had checked out okay.

Though I did not know Ninja's real name, her loose-fitting jet-black ninja garb could not hide her appearance from my telekinetic touch. She was slim but muscular, like a ballerina. She had to be at least middle-aged based on how long she had been on the Sentinels and her exploits over the years, but she didn't look it. In addition to having the body of a woman decades her junior, her face was unlined, with a timeless quality many Japanese women were blessed with. Her Metahuman powers were twofold: she had a sixth sense for her opponents' weaknesses, and she could surround the various weapons she carried with an energy field that allowed her to cut through literally anything.

I said, "Let's exchange schoolyard taunts some other time. I'm too busy protecting the city. Something you and the other Sentinels woefully failed to do."

"I hate to admit it, but I deserve that."

"Damn right you do."

"How many times do I have to apologize for what the bad apples on the Sentinels did to your family and friends?"

"I'm not sure I can count that high."

The roof fell silent. A cloud crossed over the moon, darkening the roof. Ninja became nearly invisible in her black clothing. If I took my eyes off her, I doubted I would be able to find her again, at least not with my naked eye.

Ninja glided soundlessly closer. I got the impression she could walk on eggshells without cracking them. "I understand we have you to thank for taking care of the bomb Amok terrorized the city with a few days ago. You saved the city."

"Again," I corrected her. "I saved the city again." I wasn't bragging exactly, more like rubbing her nose into the fact that I was doing what the Sentinels were supposed to. Though apparently Ninja, Doppelganger, and Tank did not have anything to do with the other Sentinels' nefarious activities, it was hard to be chummy with someone associated with the team behind the deaths of your father and the only woman you had ever loved.

"You saved the city again," she amended. "You've been quite the busy bee since you exposed the corruption in the Sentinels. I read that Meta-related crime in the city is down over eighty percent since you took up being a Hero full-time. Violent crime in general is down over thirty percent. What was it Mayor Stone called it the other day? Oh yeah: the Omega Effect." The cloth around her face crinkled again. "I'm sure your action figure sales are through the roof."

My face got hot with embarrassment. The truth of the matter was that my action figure sales *were* through the roof. As someone raised to believe that modesty was a virtue, the fact I even had action figures embarrassed me. The public loved me, and anything my name was on sold like hotcakes. After Seer confessed to the crimes she, Millennium, and Mechano had committed, overnight I went from the despicable monster who had partially destroyed Sentinels Mansion to the daring Hero who had exposed the rot at the heart of the Sentinels. Public opinion was so fickle that watching it gave me whiplash.

One good thing about suddenly being seen as the second coming of Avatar, Elvis, and Jesus combined was that State's Attorney Willard Flushing, who had at first charged me with murder for destroying Mechano, dropped the charges with great fanfare. Flushing was an elected official, and he had seen which way the Omega wind was blowing. When he had announced the charges against me, he had used words like "monster," "reckless," and "no respect for due process or the rule of law" to describe me. When public opinion shifted after Seer's full confession, Flushing then proclaimed that not only was my destruction of Mechano completely justified and entirely legal, but that I was a Hero cut from the same cloth as icons like Omega Man and Avatar. By the time Flushing finished gushing about me, if I hadn't known better, I would have thought Flushing had been at Sentinels Mansion with me when the whole thing had gone down and he had fought valiantly at my side. Or at least held my cape for me. Truman said Flushing was positioning himself to run for governor, and that he already had his eye on the White House. God help us.

Even after the criminal charges were dropped, the Heroes' Guild had kept me on probation for several months until Ghost finished his probe into whether I should retain my Hero's license. Ghost was the Guild's chief investigator. During my probationary period, Ghost turned up unexpectedly from time to time to observe me in action, looking like a restless spirit in his off-white costume that covered him from head to toe. There were not even holes in his mask for his ears, eyes, and nose. I didn't know how he didn't suffocate to death. The grim reaper was probably too scared of him. A giant man who was seven feet tall if he was an inch, Ghost's mere presence was terrifying. Every time he had shown up to observe me, it felt like a surprise rectal exam performed by a doctor with extra-large hands and no lube. I had been very careful to mind my Ps and Qs until Ghost cleared me and lifted my probation. It was a good thing Ghost did not discover I had cheated during the Trials and had illegally imprisoned Mad Dog in The Mountain, Avatar's former lair. If Ghost merely observing me felt like a rectal exam, I shuddered to think what him punishing me might feel like.

Another good thing about transforming overnight into an international superstar was that it enabled me to become a full-time crime-fighter. At the suggestion of Laura Leonard, the attorney who represented me when I was charged with Mechano's murder, I had leveraged my newfound fame to make a few bucks. I had only gone along with it because having the money to quit my job at the *Astor City Times* would mean I could devote my efforts full-time to mastering my augmented powers so I would hopefully be ready for the major crisis Seer, Mechano, and Millennium had told me was coming.

Thanks to Laura's legal and business savvy and a boatload of licensing deals, I now had more money than I knew what to do with. Among other Omega brand merchandise that flooded the market, there were Omega comic books, games, posters, tee shirts, Halloween costumes, underwear, and, as Ninja had alluded, action figures. I even had a book coming out in a couple of months. Though my publisher marketed it as an autobiography, in reality the professional author Abby Ackers had ghostwritten the book. Abby had gotten the material for the book over the course of numerous interviews with me. Abby told a few whoppers in the book and made me seem a lot more heroic and fearless than I was, but mostly she stuck to the facts. I had been careful to not reveal to her anything that would compromise my secret identity, of course. The book's title was *Zero To Omega Hero: My unbelievable journey from a license to till to a license to kill.* "It'll sell books," my publisher had assured me when I protested the idiotic title. I certainly did not have a license to kill, nor did I have a license to till when I lived on the farm in South Carolina. Not that there were such things anyway. I wished I had been savvy enough to negotiate the right to approve the book's title. Publishers were trickier than Rogues.

I had not jumped at every money-making offer, though. For example, I had been offered an absurd amount of money to star in a series of pornographic films. I turned that proposal down. There were limits to how far I would go in prostituting myself, like when asked to literally prostitute myself. Unfortunately, there were some unscrupulous people who capitalized on my fame without my permission. Some enterprising soul was selling an Omega brand dildo. "The next best thing to Omega actually being there," read the ad for the sex toy. Isaac had gleefully pointed it out to me after discovering the toy for sale on the *Hero Hags* website. It was doing a brisk business with the cape chasers who frequented the site. I was not at all pleased about having my name associated with it. Laura told me that a certain amount of trademark infringement was to be expected, and that I should ignore it. Easy for her to say; she had not seen the damned thing. Out of morbid curiosity, I had. Once seen, it was impossible to ignore. The very long box it came in assured the consumer it was anatomically correct. It most definitely was not. I had heard of penis envy, but suffering from dildo envy had been a new low.

Irritated, I tried to shove thoughts of action figures, pornos, and dildoes aside. Easier said than done once you've seen the monstrosity that was the Omega brand dildo.

"I wonder if vibrators think dildoes are lazy," I said.

"What?" Ninja's puzzlement at the non sequitur was obvious.

"Never mind. A friend of mine seems to be rubbing off on me."

"If she's handling dildoes and vibrators, you should get her to wash her hands first."

"He's a he, not a she." I shook my head at thoughts of Isaac. "Shouldn't you be out looking for Millennium instead of stalking me and piggybacking on my stupid jokes?"

"I'm an experienced Hero. And a woman. I'm a master multitasker. I can do all three."

I was curious despite my irritation. "Any new leads on Millennium?"

Ninja shook her head. "The Sentinels and the investigative

arm of the Heroes' Guild are looking for him. So far, nothing. I'll let you know if that changes. Right now, it's as if he's dropped off the face of the Earth. Since he's capable of both time travel and dimension-hopping, maybe he has."

Isaac and I had looked for Millennium too from time to time since Neha's death. We hadn't been able to find him either. In addition to me wanting to bring him to justice, it made me uncomfortable knowing there was an Omega-level Meta out there somewhere with an ax to grind against me. I had chopped his hands off, after all. I had the feeling I had not seen the last of him.

"If you aren't here to tell me you've apprehended your teammate, to what do I owe this intrusion?" I asked. "Looking for Hero tips, maybe? Here's one: Don't associate yourself with a bunch of psychopathic killers."

"You know why I'm here."

I rolled my eyes. "This again? I admire your persistence if not your tastelessness. For the thousandth time, I'm not going to join the Sentinels. Ask some other schmuck whose father and friend weren't killed by your team. Weren't you listening to the tip I gave you? I'm going to follow my own advice. I wouldn't join you guys if you were literally the last Heroes on Earth."

"I'm not here to ask you to join the Sentinels. We've disbanded."

I was struck dumb with surprise for a moment. The Sentinels were the oldest team of Heroes and admired world-wide, or at least they had been until my confrontation with them. Them breaking up was the Heroic equivalent of The Beatles breaking up.

"What? Why?"

"The public doesn't trust us anymore. And I can hardly blame them. Without the public's confidence, we can't be as effective as we should be. Plus, we haven't been able to recruit a single new Hero to replenish our ranks. We had hoped to turn public opinion around, but we're as reviled now as we were when you first exposed what Mechano and the others had been up to. Tank, Doppelganger and I took a vote yesterday. We agreed to go our separate ways."

"So if you aren't here to again ask me to join the Sentinels, why are you here? To ask for my autograph? To have me run a 'How to be a non-murderous Hero' seminar for you and the other former Sentinels? Talk to my publicist Margot Barron." The fact I even had a publicist still blew my mind.

"Mechano didn't have any family. Consequently, in his will, he left his vast fortune to the Sentinels. Since Tank, Doppelganger and I are the last members standing, all that money plus Mechano's intellectual property rights and royalties are being divided equally among us. We're now among the richest people in the world. Doppelganger is retiring. He says he's going to buy an island somewhere and, I quote, 'Get all the tropical tail money can buy.'" Tank doesn't know what he's going to do yet. As for me, I'm going to use my newfound fortune to start a new team. I'd like a chance to make up for the fact so much nefarious activity went on right under my nose without me being aware of it. I can still do a lot of good in the world." Ninja paused. "And I want you to be the first member of the new team."

Ninja's offer took me aback for a second. Then I laughed.

"Though I get you didn't have anything to do with my father's or Smoke's death, I'm not interested. Remember the Omega Effect? It's not called the Omega and His Amazing Friends Effect. I'm doing just fine on my own. Besides, why do I get the feeling you're only asking me to join to help scrub you of your Sentinels stench? 'If Omega is willing to join forces with Ninja, then she must be okay,' you're hoping the public will think." I shook my head. I left out the fact that I was afraid to get close with anyone. Dad, Hannah, Neha . . . people associated with me had a nasty habit of getting killed. I had even stopped fighting crime alongside of Isaac a few months after Neha's death. I didn't want a single other person hurt or killed because of me. "No thanks. I'm not going to be your public relations prop."

"Your presence on the team would elevate its stature and help me rehabilitate my tarnished public image. I'm not going to lie and say that isn't a consideration. But you need me as much as I need you."

"And how do you figure that?"

"You've been a licensed Hero for what, around three years now? Even though you're one of the most powerful Metas I've ever seen and you seem to be a good man, you're still relatively green."

Ninja slid even closer to me. She was now close enough to touch. I couldn't help but be suddenly hyperaware of the curves of her athletic body despite the looseness of her black costume. I had not been with anyone romantically since Neha, and that seemed like forever ago. There was a slightly seductive sashay in Ninja's walk as she approached that I suspected was no accident. But if Ninja thought she could use her femininity to bend me to her will, she had another thing coming. My genitals were not the boss of me. Maybe they would be if they were the size of that Omega brand dildo, but they weren't.

Ninja said, "You've got a lot to learn still. I can help you with that. It's the least I can do to make up for what the Sentinels did to your father and Smoke. Plus, even the most powerful Heroes need help from time to time. A team can provide that. Though your powers are godlike, you're not a god. You're just a man. And no man is an island."

"Wrong. I am," I said firmly, studiously ignoring how close

Ninja's body was to mine. She was just a hair shorter than I. If she wore the towering heels so many other female Rogues and Heroes inexplicably seemed to favor, I would have to look up to meet her eyes. "I don't need you. Or anybody else. Anything that happens, I can handle it by myself."

Ninja's right leg shot out without warning. She swept my legs out from under me. I fell backward. I barely caught myself with my powers before the back of my head smacked against the roof.

Ninja's katana was out. Its tip almost kissed my Adam's apple. I hadn't even see her draw the damned thing. The razor-sharp blade glowed faintly pink with Ninja's powers. When lit up like this, it could cut through anything. Including my force fields and the Omega suit.

Barely breathing, I followed the path of the curved blade up to Ninja's eyes. They looked amused.

"If you can handle everything by yourself, Island Man," she said, "how come you're flat on your back right now?"

Before I could respond, she laughed out loud. It sounded more good-natured than mocking. She sheathed her sword with a practiced motion. She held her hand out to help me up. I waved her away and stood up on my own. I didn't want to touch her. Maybe she'd try to throw me off the roof to further emphasize her point. I wouldn't put it past her. I in turn considered using my powers to throw her into outer space. She could keep Mechano and the atoms of Amok's detonated bomb company.

Ninja laughed again at the look on my face. She stepped to the side, toward the edge of the building.

"Think about what I said, Omega. Even the best of us get knocked down and need help back up."

Embarrassed by having been so easily caught off guard, I didn't want her to have the last word. "No man is an island," I said, repeating her words. "Not only are you a sneak attacker and a stalker, but you're a plagiarist, too. You stole that phrase from the poet John Donne."

"Wrong again. Donne used it after hearing me say it."

"No, he didn't," I scoffed. "He died in the seventeenth century."

The fabric around Ninja's mouth twitched again. "Time travel," she said. "I get around."

She stepped off the edge of the roof. She plunged from view.

Alarmed, I hastened to the spot where Ninja had fallen. I peered over the roof's edge. The city's lights reflected off the mirror-like facade of the UWant Building, making me squint. Ninja was nowhere to be seen. I couldn't find her with my tele-kinetic touch, either.

I knew she could not fly or teleport. I wondered how she had disappeared.

Huh.

Maybe she *was* Batman.

4
———

Isaac pointed an accusing finger at me.

"You got knocked on your ass by a girl," he exclaimed. His brown eyes danced with delight.

"First of all, lower your voice," I wheezed. I was breathing hard. I had just finished my final set of bent over barbell rows. This was back and chest day. Isaac and I were working out at Apex Fitness, our gym in downtown Astor City. There were plenty of people around. I did not care if they overheard that I had been knocked down by a woman; I did care if they overheard I was Omega. "Second of all, Ninja's not a girl. She's a woman. And that woman is one of the best martial artists in the world, if not the best." I was both embarrassed and defensive about getting knocked down. What a rookie thing to let happen. What if Ninja had not been friendly?

"That'll be how you tell the story. When I tell the story, she'll be an itty-bitty girl in pigtails." Isaac turned to look at a small group clustered around one of the nearby squat racks. He raised his voice, saying "Hey, did you hear about how my friend here got knocked on his ass by a girl?"

They all looked at us.

"It's not appropriate to refer to females that way," one of them said huffily. She was a short blonde in sweatpants and a sports bra.

Isaac raised his hands placatingly. "Sorry, you're quite right. My bad. What I meant to say was that my friend got knocked on his ass by a Vaginal American. Better?"

The blonde sniffed. She pointedly turned her back on us. She whispered in an outraged tone to one of her friends. Isaac shrugged and turned back to me.

"You try to be politically correct," he said, "and that's the thanks you get. There really is no pleasing some people."

"It's tough being you. Nobody knows the trouble you've seen. Nobody knows your sorrow."

Isaac pointed at me accusingly again.

"That's from a Negro spiritual. You're appropriating my people's culture again. And before you jump on me for saying Negro like you did when I said girl, that's what those types of songs are formally called, so stay in your lane Captain Caucasian." Isaac shook his head in mock disgust. "Now I'm even more glad you got knocked on your ass."

As Isaac was fond of reminding me, he was a black man. His skin was the color of pale leather. He was both a couple of years older and a couple of inches taller than I. His freshly shaved bald head shone dully under the gym's bright lights, making the lightning-shaped scar on his temple from our fight with Iceburn years ago stand out more than usual. I was so used to him being bald that if he grew his hair out, it would probably look like he was wearing a disguise. Glossy straight black hair covered his legs and arms. He wore white athletic shorts, white sneakers, and a black wife-beater sporting white letters that read *I flexed and the sleeves ripped off*. As for me, I wore what appeared to be a plain tee shirt, shorts, and tennis shoes, but they all were really manifestations of the Omega suit. I never took it off. I made it withdraw into my body when I showered and slept, and had it assume the form of whatever clothes I needed when I walked around as a civilian. Laundry was a thing of the distant past. Dry cleaners would hate me if they knew.

Though he had been relatively slender when I had first met him at the Academy, Isaac was jacked now, with the lanky yet muscular build of a competitive sprinter. The men in the group with the blonde had avoided making direct eye contact with Isaac when he had spoken to her. Though a couple of them were huge meatheads and much bigger than Isaac, I had noticed more and more over the years that something about the way he carried himself made other men tread carefully around him. He was developing the same faint air of menace that people like Truman and Athena wore like a second skin. An occupational hazard of being a Hero, maybe. I supposed I had it too, but it was hard to accurately assess how intimidating others might find you when you were the one wiping the morning sleep out of your eyes and pulling your underwear out of your butt crack.

Isaac and I moved to a different part of the gym floor. Music thumped from overhead speakers, weights clanked, and people grunted with exertion. We had a standing workout date three times a week. It had been pounded into our heads during the Academy and later as Amazing Man's Apprentices that physical fitness was as important to an effective Hero as being adept in the use of his superpowers was. I enjoyed working out, something I would have never thought possible when I was a scrawny kid who grunted when I picked up a thick dictionary or when I had puked my guts out during the Academy's intense training sessions.

I especially looked forward to these workouts because they gave me a reason to hang out with Isaac. He was one of my few friends, and the only close one. Ever since I had decided to fight crime by myself in the interest of not getting someone else I cared about injured or killed, I did not see Isaac nearly as often as I would like. We didn't even live together anymore as I had moved out right around the time we stopped fighting crime together.

Isaac loaded a bar with plates at one of the incline bench press stations. He plopped down heavily on the bench. He stretched and yawned. He looked tired. One of his roommates had just moved out, and I knew he was having trouble making ends meet, even with working a bunch of overtime at his job. Astor City was an expensive place to live.

"Between holding down a full-time job and your," I glanced around to see if anybody was nearby, "um, nocturnal activities, you're pulled in way too many directions. You look like you haven't slept in a week. I wish you'd take me up on my offer to give you enough money so you can quit working, or at least cut back on your hours some." Isaac had worked as an illustrator at Pixelate, the movie animation company, ever since we moved to Astor City after the Trials. He was a very talented artist. "You wouldn't even have to pay me back. I won't miss it. I'm printing money these days."

"Rub it in, why don't you?"

"You know that's not what I'm doing. I'm just trying to help. Think of it as me repaying a debt. You've help me more times than I can count."

"I appreciate the offer, but no. I'm not taking a handout. From you or anybody else. The fact we're even talking about it has my father rolling over in his grave. In addition to self-reliance and standing on your own two feet, he taught me to never trust a white man who wants to give a black man something for free. Y'all showed up in Africa centuries ago giving away free cruises to America. Problem was, it was a one-way trip." Isaac smothered another yawn. "Once I land a berth at one of the major Hero teams, I'll be all set." That was Isaac's dream. Most such teams required a minimum of three years of Heroic experience. Isaac had just submitted applications to several of them. I had no doubt some team would snatch him up—as someone who could turn into a wide variety of mythological creatures, Isaac was a powerful Hero. The problem was that Isaac being accepted by a Hero team meant he would have to move away from Astor City; there were no such teams in the area now that the Sentinels had disbanded. The thought of Isaac leaving made my stomach hurt. Though we weren't biologically related, Isaac was my brother in all the ways that mattered.

Isaac grinned. "Besides, I'm not going to let you be my sugar daddy. Whenever someone offers someone else money with no strings attached, the offerer secretly has an exchange of bodily fluids in mind. I see the way you look at me."

"With disdain, dismay, and disgust?"

A pretty Latina in pink yoga pants who looked like she did a lot of squats walked by. Isaac's eyes lingered on her as she climbed the stairs to the aerobics area on the second floor. With his eyes still on her, Isaac said, "No. Sometimes I swear you look at me the way I'm looking at that cutie with a booty over there." Isaac cocked his head slightly to the side as he stared at the woman. He whistled softly. "Whoever invented yoga pants deserves a Nobel Prize."

I waved a hand in front of Isaac's staring eyes. "Hello! Don't you already have a girlfriend?"

"I have a girlfriend, not a blindfold. My eyes still work."

"They won't work for long if Sylvia catches you looking at another woman like that."

Isaac blinked, tearing his eyes away from the Latina. He shuddered. "Oh God, please don't tell her." Sylvia didn't put up with any nonsense. She was just the kind of person Isaac needed. I liked her.

I grinned. "I can make no promises."

"Oh," Isaac began casually, "speaking of girlfriends—"

"No," I interjected firmly.

"You don't even know what I was going to say."

"You were going to say that Sylvia has a friend who is just dying to meet me and that you think I should go out with her, fall in love, get engaged, make you my best man at the wedding, and name you godfather to all our vanilla babies. The answer is no." Under the theory that the best way to get over someone was to get under someone, Isaac had pushed various women on me since shortly after Neha died. His matchmaking efforts had gotten worse after he met Sylvia— the two of them had started double-teaming me. Single women outnumbered single men in Astor City by almost two to one. As a professional party planner, Sylvia got around a lot, seemed to know every man-hungry woman in the city, and was all too eager to sic them on me. I often wondered if her girlfriends paid her a bounty each time she hooked one of them up with a man.

Isaac looked abashed. "Okay, maybe you did know what I was going to say. At least let me tell you about Viola before you reject her."

I made a face. "Viola? Who's named Viola these days? Is she ninety-years-old? Should I pick her up in a horse and buggy for our first date?" I waved my hand dismissively. "No, never mind, don't tell me. I don't want to know because there won't be a first date."

"Well, first of all, you're saying her name wrong. It's Viola, like the flower. Not the instrument viola." With the former, he said her name with a long *i*; with the latter, he said it with a long *e*.

"A viola is a flower?"

"Yeah. They're in the violet family. You were raised on a farm. How do you not know that?"

"We grew fruits and vegetables, not flowers."

"Well I'm fresh out of girls named Rutabaga and Cantaloupe."

"And you're fresh out of luck if you think I'm going to go out with Viola, or Pansy, or Chrysanthemum, or whatever other flower child you come up with."

"C'mon man, when have I ever steered you wrong?"

"Two words: Candace Helwig."

Isaac looked embarrassed. "I'd almost blotted her out of my mind."

To get Isaac and Sylvia off my back, I had reluctantly agreed to go out on a blind date with Candace five months ago. "I haven't. How could I forget about someone who asked to drink my blood on the first date? Not that asking on the thousandth date would be any less creepy."

"Maybe she was thirsty."

"Or maybe she was crazy. To be honest, I only have myself to blame. When I walked into the restaurant to see her green and orange hair, septum piercing, cat eye contacts, and a tattoo of a vampire on her neck, I should have turned around and walked out."

"Your parents raised you with too many Southern manners to do that."

"Unfortunately." I shook my head at myself and the memory of Candace. "Never ignore aposematism."

"Why you gotta drag the Jews into this? First cultural appropriation, now you're bad-mouthing Jewish people. Apparently you brought racism up North along with your Southern hospitality."

"Not anti-Semitism. Aposematism. It's the term describing

how animals often warn you they are poisonous or otherwise dangerous by their coloration. How someone as well-read as you doesn't know that is beyond . . ." I trailed off, seeing the amused twinkle in Isaac's eye. "Oh. You did know. You were pulling my leg."

"Yep. Remember, I'm an Academy graduate. Second in my class, as I recall. I know lots of words. Like *viola*. And *duped*, and *gullible*, and *simpleton*."

"Why do I always fall for your foolishness?"

"Because I'm convincing. Just like I'm going to convince you to go out with Viola. Look, I know how you felt about Neha. She was my friend too. I hate that she's gone. Not a day goes by that I don't think about her. But life goes on. She wouldn't want you to waste your life away, mired in guilt and self-pity."

"I'm not wasting my life away," I protested.

"Don't interrupt when I'm in the middle of straightening your life out. All you do is train, fight crime, and then sleep for a few hours, rinse and repeat. You live the life of a warrior monk. I know you want to make sure you're ready for the looming crisis the Sentinels warned about, but the way you're going about it, you're on the express train to Burnout City. Like you said, I'm pulled in too many directions myself. I know a little something about burnout. You're taking it to the next level. You might be the poster child for it. For depression too, come to think of it. I'm worried about you. You need some fun and frivolity. You need a life that has nothing to do with masks and capes." Isaac took a swig from his water bottle. He wiped his mouth with the back of his hand. "Ranting is thirsty work. Look, I'm not saying you have to marry Viola and have a bunch of babies and name them all after me. Though that last part's not a bad idea. All I'm saying is that you need to stop moping about the past, freaking out about the future, and start living in the present. Going out with Viola can be the start of that. Candace was a mistake. That's on me. If I had met her before letting Sylvia pawn her off on you, I would've known it was a bad fit. But in Sylvia's defense, you're so straitlaced she thought someone as out-there as Candace might balance you out. You know, be the yin to your yang."

"The Mister Hyde to my Doctor Jekyll." I doubted Isaac would think I was so straitlaced if he knew I had cheated during the Trials and had imprisoned Mad Dog in The Mountain. I still had not told him. If I did, there was a chance Isaac would report me to the Guild. I had too many things to worry about already without the Guild watching my every move again. More importantly, I didn't want to tarnish the image Isaac had of me. Having him think ill of me would be more than I could stand. I felt pretty guilty about keeping secrets from my best friend, though. I would have to add it to the long list of things I felt guilty about. As I looked down on Isaac's open, friendly face, it made me feel like the world's biggest dick to hide things from him.

Then I thought of the Omega brand dildo. No, I was the world's second biggest dick.

"I wonder if Tony Robbins gets interrupted this much when he's dropping self-help knowledge," Isaac muttered about my Dr. Jekyll crack. "Anyway, I learned my lesson from Candace and not taking the time to vet her. I've actually met Viola. Told her a bunch of tall tales about you. Like you, she fell for my lies, and she wants to meet you. She's smart, funny, nice, the whole package. She's a sweetheart of a person. I think you'll like her."

"'Sweetheart of a person' is another way of saying she has a great personality. So great that I'll probably not even notice her hunchback or her lazy eye."

"You haven't been with a woman in how long? Over two

and a half years? Beggars can't be choosers. Besides Shallow Man, Viola's cute. She's got all the right body parts in all the right places. Because I'm such a good friend, I risked getting the stink eye from Sylvia by taking a nice long look and making sure. The sacrifices I make for you. You're welcome."

"It's a wonder the Pope hasn't canonized you."

"He probably would if I stopped creepily staring at women. And if I was Catholic. Wait. Does money come with sainthood? Because I could convert."

"I don't think so."

"A shame. The church is a tax-exempt money-making enterprise, yet it can't break a piece off for the saints? Seems unfair. The saints need to unionize. Anyway, can I tell Viola you'll give her a call?"

"No."

"But—"

"No," I said even more firmly. "I'm not interested in fun and frivolity, as you put it. I get all the frivolity I need from talking to you. All I'm interested in is making sure I'm ready to face whatever crisis is coming down the pike. I failed Neha. And Hannah. And Dad. I won't fail again. Or have someone close to me get hurt simply because they're close to me. If I must live the life of monk to avoid all that, then that's what I'm going to do."

Isaac sighed in resignation.

"I can't say I'm surprised to hear you say that. The phrase 'stubborn as a mule' was probably coined to describe you. But try to keep an open mind about going out with Viola. If not her, then someone else. At least think about it. And I wouldn't be so quick to dismiss what Ninja said to you, either. She has a point—you can't do everything by yourself. If you won't let me help you, you should let *someone*. As powerful as you are, you're not omnipotent. I've seen you often enough in your underwear first thing in the morning to be certain of that."

He lay down on the bench under the suspended barbell. I moved behind his head to spot him. He looked up at me and said, "You can't carry the weight of the world on your shoulders alone. If there really is some major crisis in the works like the disgraced Sentinels told you, you'll need all the help you can get. Plus, I'm pretty sick of your brooding loner impersonation. You see how you're standing there to spot me in case I need help lifting the weight? That, my friend, is a metaphor."

Isaac was quiet for a while as he did three sets of ten reps each, with a brief rest between each set. If this was what it took to keep Isaac from nagging me, I would use my powers to tie a barbell around his neck.

I felt eyes on me as Isaac started a fourth set. I looked up from watching Isaac's barbell rise and fall to look at the mirrored wall in front of us. Through its reflection, I saw a pretty blonde woman languidly riding a stationary bike behind us. She noticed me looking back at her and smiled. I gave her a slight nod of acknowledgement. I turned my attention back to Isaac, dismissing the woman from my mind. A few years ago, a pretty woman smiling at me would have made my week. Who was I kidding? It would have made my year. Now I found it faintly irritating. Women threw themselves at me all the time when I was dressed as Omega. They weren't attracted to the man under the mask; they were attracted to Omega's fame and power. The way they behaved around Omega versus the way girls had behaved around Theo most of my life showed me how mercenary and superficial most people were. It made me miss Neha even more. She had liked me for me.

After Isaac's final set, we switched places, with me lying on the bench after taking some of the plates off the suspended bar. Though I was far from the scrawny kid I had been when my powers first manifested, I was still not as strong as Isaac. When Thomas Jefferson wrote that all men were created equal, he had not been talking about bodybuilders.

Today I was doing descending pyramids—starting the first set with the heaviest weight I could manage, then dropping in weight with each successive set. By the end of them, I was benching the empty bar. I was so spent that my arms and chest shook as I completed my last set, though the bar only weighed forty-five pounds. I did the last set quickly, trying to maximize the pump.

"You really should slow down when you do those," came a woman's voice. My eyes darted to see the blonde woman who had been on the stationary bike. Now she stood at the foot of my bench. I refocused on completing my set, and re-racked the bar. I sat up and got a good look at the woman. Like an impressionist's painting, she looked better from a distance than close-up. She was probably about my age, though tanning beds had prematurely aged her. Her eyelashes were fake, and her hair looked brittle from being bleached too often. Her caked-on makeup made her look a little clownish under the harsh gym lights. Her outfit was expensive, revealed more than it concealed, and looked like it had never been sweated in. She was slender, but more skinny-fat than fit. She had the all the earmarks of someone who came to the gym to hook up more than she did to work out.

"Excuse me?" I said, annoyed at the interruption. Talking to someone when they had a weight overhead was bad gym etiquette, not to mention dangerous.

"I said you were doing those all wrong. You were going too fast. I can show you how I do them, if you'd like." Her tone and body language implied she wanted to show me a form other than just proper form.

I looked her up and down. I said, "Tell you what—if I need to learn how to slather on eye shadow so that I look like a racoon, you'll be the first person I ask. As far as workout advice is concerned, I'm all set."

The woman was taken aback. She looked like I'd just slapped her.

"I was just trying to help," she huffed once she'd recovered. She stomped off.

Isaac looked at me as if he had never seen me before.

"I take back everything I said before about your Southern charm and manners," he said. "I've never seen you be so rude to someone. What the hell is wrong with you?"

I shrugged. "She's just some dumb cape chaser."

"You're not wearing a cape, jackass, or a sign that says 'Super-powerful Meta,'" Isaac said in a low, earnest voice. "She doesn't know who you are. She came over here because she was interested in you. Though I can't imagine why." Isaac shook his head at me in disbelief. "This is what I mean. You're in costume so much that it's consumed you. You don't know how to take the mask off. It's why I've been saying you need to get a life."

I didn't feel like arguing, so I didn't respond. But I knew the truth:

I didn't need people like Ninja. Or Viola. I certainly didn't need Miss Clown Face. I didn't need anybody.

It was safer for everyone that way.

5

I was flying late at night in a routine patrol of the city when I saw a man standing on the side of the Avatar Memorial Bridge. He was perched on the narrow outcropping on the outside of one of the stone balustrades. A fall would be lethal.

I swooped down. My cape sprouted from the neck of the Omega suit. Clothes make the Hero.

"Is everything all right?" I asked the man once I was level with him. I floated in mid-air several feet from the bridge's side. My cape flapped loudly behind me, the sound mixing with the patter of a gentle rain. Water trickled down the invisible force field around me.

"Jesus!" the man cried, startled by my sudden appearance. He nearly slipped off the edge of the bridge before catching himself by grabbing the bridge's thick stone side.

My mouth twisted wryly. "Hardly. Is everything all right?" I repeated. The man's eyes were wild, rimmed with red. I suspected tears mingled with rainwater on his face.

"You scared the shit out of me." He did a double take. His head moved forward as he looked hard at me in the dim glow from the streetlights that soared over the bridge. "Oh my God! You're Omega. You're famous. My, um, little cousin wears your underwear."

A car approached, its headlights illuminating one side of the man. Reddish-brown skin, prominent broad nose, high cheekbones, troubled dark eyes. Mexican descent, or maybe Native American. He was older than I. Early thirties maybe. Wet black hair clung to his skull like seaweed. His blue shirt, tan khakis, and brown loafers were drenched.

The passing car made a sound like frying bacon on the wet bridge. It was after 2 a.m. There weren't too many cars on the road now in this part of the city. Right inside city limits, the bridge was on one of the major thoroughfares running from the Deerwood suburb to the northeastern quadrant of the city. A city park was far below the bridge, shrouded in darkness.

I waited until the car zoomed by.

"Tell your cousin I appreciate it," I said. "Can I help you with something?"

"No, I'm good." His voice was ragged, like he hadn't slept in a while.

"Sir, clearly you're not. You're standing in the rain on the edge of a bridge in the middle of the night. Why don't I help you back over the railing and we can talk about what's troubling you?"

"Come any closer and I'll jump!" he exclaimed. I froze. Only the tips of one hand's fingers on the stone railing kept the man from toppling into the darkness below.

I said, "If you know who I am, you know what I'm capable of. You're not going to fall unless I let you fall."

The man's eyes narrowed.

He said, "All right, I guess you can stop me from falling. But what are you going to do, follow me around day and night from here on out? If I don't off myself tonight, I'll do it tomorrow. Or the day after that." He sounded and looked like an educated man. How had a guy like this wound up here? Regardless, he had a point. Even if I forcibly removed him from the bridge, I couldn't become his personal shadow to make sure he didn't hurt himself later.

I didn't know what to do. I wasn't a crisis counselor. I had no experience with literally talking someone down from a ledge. The Academy's class in Hero Psychology, Strategy, and Tactics hadn't prepared me for this.

"What's your name?" I finally said after hesitating.

The man looked reluctant, like it was a secret he didn't want to divulge. "Angel," he admitted. He pronounced the *g* in his name the Spanish way, like it was a harsh sounding *h*. Mexican descent then, not Native American.

"Tell you what, Angel," I said, saying his name the way he had, "I'll make a deal with you. You tell me what's bothering you and we'll hash it out. Maybe I can help somehow. If you decide you want to jump after we talk, then I won't stop you."

Angel looked surprised. "Really?" Other than the way he had said his name, his voice was accentless.

"Really. You're a grown man. It's your life. You can do what you want with it."

Angel mulled it over.

"All right," he said. He barked out a humorless laugh. "Besides, I've got some time to kill."

I laughed, though not amused by the pun. In reality, I was scared. Scared I wouldn't be able to talk this guy into not jumping. Scared I would fail and get someone killed again.

I floated over to the stone railing. I sat, but not too close to Angel. I didn't want to spook him. I pulled my cape from under me and let it hang on the other side of the balustrade. After a moment's hesitation, Angel hoisted himself up on the thick railing as well.

There we sat, just a few feet from one another, with our feet dangling into a dark void. Rain sprinkled down, providing a sound almost like background music. Just two guys shooting the breeze, one of them praying the other wasn't about to plummet to his death.

"I'm listening," I said. I wished I had something more profound to say, but I was no psychiatrist.

Reluctantly, after a few fits and starts, Angel began to tell me his story. Once he got rolling, though, the words spilled out of him in a torrent, like he was a dam under stress that had been ready to burst.

Angel was a lawyer. His parents had illegally immigrated to the United States from Mexico, but Angel was born in Texas. His father was a roofer and his mother a housekeeper. They had sacrificed, scrimped, and saved to give him, their only child, the best education they could, which to them meant sending him to private Catholic school. He worked hard in school, got a full scholarship to a good college, and was the first in his family to graduate college. He followed that up with graduating from law school, and then passing the bar. He moved to Astor City, taking a job with one of the prestigious white-shoe law firms here, making more money than God. Despite rolling in money, he soon tired of helping rich people get richer. He quit his big firm job, opened his own practice, and was poorer but much happier representing the little guy he had screwed over when he was at the big law firm.

Several years passed uneventfully as Angel slowly built his legal practice. Then, his father fell off one of his roofing jobs, seriously hurting himself. As he did not have medical insurance, it was a financial disaster for the family. Angel helped his parents out as much as he could, but his practice was not generating enough income to make much of a dent in his father's hefty medical bills. Angel had more than enough money to help his parents, though, in his attorney trust account, which was the bank account in his name in which all the retainers his clients paid him were deposited. He was not supposed to take any money out of that account until he had earned it and billed his clients for it.

Knowing dipping into that account for personal reasons was both unethical and illegal, Angel resisted the temptation to do so. But when his father needed an expensive medical procedure, Angel could resist no longer. He took enough of his clients' money out of the trust account to cover the cost of his dad's procedure. He planned to replenish it as soon as he could. Rather than replenish it, though, over the course of several months as his father needed more and more procedures, Angel almost completely wiped out the money in the account.

One of Angel's few corporate clients demanded its sizable retainer back once it became clear to the company that Angel was too distracted with his family's problems to provide the level of service it had come to expect from Angel. There was not enough money in the trust account to give the client its money back. Angel tried to stall the client, scrambling to scrape the money together so the corporate client wouldn't learn that Angel had stolen it to help his father. Angel faced losing everything he had worked for and his parents had sacrificed for.

Eventually the client grew suspicious. It reported Angel to the Maryland State Bar Association, the body that licensed and regulated attorneys in the state, much like the Heroes' Guild licensed and regulated Heroes. Three days ago Angel got a letter from the bar, demanding that he explain why he had not returned his client's money. For the past couple of days, Angel had been in limbo, not knowing where to turn or what to do.

He decided to do this.

"I don't understand," I said when Angel had finished. "Why not just tell the bar what you did and why you did it? It's not like you took the money to buy drugs or you squandered it gambling. You took it for a good cause. Besides, it's just money. You can always make more and pay your client back."

His eyes pained, Angel shook his head. "Taking a client's money without earning it is an express train to disbarment, regardless of why you took it. Being a lawyer is all I ever wanted to do. Swearing the lawyer's oath in the Court of Appeals in Annapolis was the proudest moment of my life. I can't stand the thought of not being able to practice law anymore. On top of that, practicing law is all I know how to do. If I can't practice law anymore, how in the world will I make the money I need to pay my clients back? Clean toilets alongside my mother?" Angel snorted derisively. "There aren't enough toilets in the whole country. Plus, what I did is a crime. It's no better than breaking into someone's house and stealing their wallet. Worse actually, because no one is surprised when a burglar steals something. I'm a lawyer my clients trusted. I breached the fiduciary duty I have to properly handle money entrusted to me. There's the very real possibility I'll wind up going to jail." He shook his head again. "I can't stand the thought of that either."

Angel let out a long breath. "What I wouldn't give for an ice-cold beer right now." He smiled mirthlessly. "Confessing crimes makes me thirsty."

Angel fell silent. I didn't know what to say. I was afraid that if I opened my mouth, the wrong thing would pop out. I just wanted to keep Angel talking. If he was busy talking, he wasn't busy jumping.

"You know the one thing worse than being disbarred or going to jail?" Angel added.

"No, what?"

"The look on my parents' faces when they find out I'm a criminal and not their golden child." Tears mingled with the rain on his face. "They're devout Catholics. Salt of the earth. Aside from coming into this country illegally, they've never done anything wrong their entire lives. And the only reason they did that was so I would be born American and have a shot at a better life than they had. They raised me right. Work hard, be nice to others, tell the truth, and don't take anything you didn't earn. The fact I took money that didn't belong to me will make them absolutely sick. I can't face them. Not after all the sacrifices they made for me. I won't."

"Surely they'd understand you only did it to help your father," I said gently.

Angel snorted.

"You haven't met my parents. With them, there's a right thing to do, and a wrong thing to do. Black and white. It will shame them to their core to know I've done this. I can just hear my father now." Angel effortlessly slipped into a Mexican accent: "I'd rather have died falling from that roof than see the day my son's a thief."

"How's your dad doing, by the way?"

Angel smiled, the first genuine one I had seen from him. "That's the one silver lining in this whole disaster. He's on the mend. The doctors say he'll be as good as new with a little rehab."

Angel's eyes got wide as a six-pack of beer abruptly glided in from the gloom to hover in front of me. I pulled two of the bottles out, uncapped them with my powers, and leaned over to offer one to Angel. Angel looked at the proffered bottle like it might explode.

"Did you conjure that out of thin air?" he asked incredulously.

I smile. "No. I'm not a magician. There's a convenience store two blocks north of here. I levitated the beer from there. I'll go there afterward and pay for it."

Angel took the beer from my hand. "You're a handy person to have around. Can you turn water into wine too?"

"I'm still working on that one."

"Maybe skip that trick. Look how the first guy to figure it out wound up." Angel glanced at the bottle's label. "Corona. A Mexican beer. Huh. You racially profiling me, amigo?" It was the second genuine smile Angel had given me. I hoped it was a good sign.

"A happy accident," I said.

We drank.

Angel wiped his mouth with the back of his hand. "Though this is the first time I've ever stolen anything, it's not the first time I've been accused of stealing something."

"Is that so?"

"Yeah. When I was about to start the second grade, my parents moved us from Texas to Iowa. There were better job opportunities for my parents, plus they had heard of a Catholic school there they thought would be good for me. The community we settled in was about as white as you could get without living in the Arctic Circle. No racial diversity. Hell, we *were* the diversity. My second day in the new school, a kid in my class told our teacher somebody took his Mickey Mouse watch. Since I was the new kid and the only brown kid, the teacher accused me of taking it. I denied it, of course. She didn't believe me. Said I had to stand in the corner as punishment, and that she would tell my mother when she came to pick me up. Janis Worley. As long as I live, I'll never forget that ugly bitch. Face like the surface of the moon. Tits like deflated tires. Breath like a Gila monster. I'll also never forget her calling me a 'thieving spic' under her stinky breath as she dragged me into the corner.

"I had to stand in the corner the rest of the day, furious, crying, and yet determined to not let anyone see that I was crying. First time anybody ever called me a spic. It wasn't the last." Angel drank more beer. "As it turned out, not only had I not stolen that kid's watch, but nobody else had either. The dumb kid had taken his watch off and forgotten he had put it into his lunchbox. He didn't find it until he got home from school that night. He told Miss Worley the next day. She didn't even have the decency to apologize to me. What she thought of me was written all over her pockmarked face: 'Even if you didn't steal that watch, you're going to steal something else. People like you are just no good.'"

Staring off into the darkness below, Angel tapped the tip of his beer bottle against his chin. Almost to himself, he said, "I think that's why I worked as hard as I did, pushed myself like I did, to try to make something of myself. To prove to all the Miss Worleys I've run into that they were wrong about me. About people who look like me."

He was crying heavily now. It was as if the years had rolled back, and I was looking at the face of that second grader crying in the corner.

Angel jerked his head back up like he was waking from a dream. He lifted his beer in a toast. He said, "Well, here's to you Miss Worley. Congratulations. You were right. I'm nothing but a thieving spic." He drained his beer. He dropped the bottle. "A litterbug too." The bottle disappeared into the darkness below. I did a quick scan of the park below with my telekinetic touch. Nobody was down there to get brained by the glass bottle. After a few seconds, I felt the glass smash on the asphalt trail that cut through the park.

Angel stared at where the bottle had disappeared. It

looked like he was steeling himself to push off the railing. "Hey, that reminds me of a joke," he said. "What do you call a thousand lawyers who jump off a bridge?"

I shrugged, afraid Angel was about to do his best beer bottle imitation.

"A good start. Gimme another of those beers. I need all the liquid courage I can get."

I floated another beer to him. While he was drinking, he wasn't jumping.

Angel drank. "Hey, how far down do you suppose the ground is, anyway? I didn't even hear that bottle break."

My mind had already reflexively crunched the numbers. "A shade over two hundred and fifty-six feet," I said.

Angel looked at me like I was a wizard again. "How do you know that?"

I shrugged. "Simple math. It took the bottle a hair over four seconds to hit the ground. Plug that into the acceleration due to gravity formula, and there's the answer." Angel looked at me as if I had split the atom. "There's more to being a Hero than flying around and delivering beer to people, you know."

"Apparently. I for one certainly hadn't been counting how long it took the bottle to hit the ground."

"I pay attention to small details like that. You never know when a detail is going to save your or someone else's life. I learned the importance of noticing details at Hero Academy. It gave me a grounding in the math I just used, too."

"Tell me about that. The Academy, I mean."

"I'd rather talk about you."

"Dude, I'm sick of talking about me. I want to hear about you. I'm a fan."

So, I told Angel about my time at the Academy. Angel was a good listener, interrupting only to ask clarifying questions. I imagined he was a pretty good lawyer.

Talking about my Academy days must have loosened my tongue. The beer probably helped. Plus, if Angel was listening to me, he wasn't listening to the whistling of the wind as he plunged off the bridge. Regardless of why, before I knew it, I also told him about Mom dying from cancer, how I had been bullied much of my life, Dad's murder, how I finally found a sense of belonging when I met Neha and Isaac, my fight against Iceburn, how Amazing Man had not thought I was tough enough to handle the Trials, the attempts on my life before and during the Trials, Hammer's death during them, me cheating during them, me swearing the Hero's Oath, Hannah's death, my confrontation with the Sentinels, Neha's death, and the fact that now I spent every waking hour preparing to defend the world against the major crisis the Sentinels had warned about. I even told him how I had imprisoned Mad Dog in The Mountain. It was the first time I told anybody that. I did not tell him my true identity, of course, nor that of Isaac and Neha.

"Jesus!" Angel said once I had finished. "That's quite a story. You've been through a lot."

I shrugged. "It is what it is." I drank more beer.

"You obviously feel bad about a lot of the things you've done. You've gotta love Catholic guilt. We have that in common."

"It's not merely Catholic guilt," I said. "The guilt I feel is for good reason. Dad would still be alive if I had left the farm with Amazing Man to learn to use my powers. Hannah would still be alive if I hadn't confronted Mad Dog. Smoke would still be alive if I had handled things with the Sentinels differently or if I had been more adept in the use of my enhanced powers."

"I don't know, man. It sounds like you did the best you could. I won't pretend that I know what the life of a Hero is like. I sit behind a computer most of the day. The most dangerous thing I do is risk a paper cut. But it seems to me that's all you can do—the best you can with what you have, and let the chips fall where they may."

I twisted to look Angel in the eye.

"And is this the best you can do, sitting up here screwing up the courage to kill yourself? What about your parents? What about the clients you're abandoning? They need you."

Angel held my gaze for a moment, then looked away. "Of course this is not the best I can do. Don't you think I know that? But I'm too afraid to face my problems. I'm not brave like you."

"Brave? Me?" I laughed out loud. "I'm scared all the time."

Angel looked surprised. "Really? Of what?"

"I'm scared every time I get into a fight with somebody. Scared I'm going to get hurt. Or killed. Scared an innocent will get hurt or killed because of me. Scared that someone else I care about will get killed. I'm scared that when the crisis I told you about comes, I won't be ready for it." I hesitated. "But, right this second, mostly I'm scared that you're going to jump. And, to be perfectly honest, I'm scared that I'll follow your lead and jump too. Another person dying because I've fallen short again is more than I think I can stand."

Angel was quiet. He just stared at me. Another car zoomed by, illuminating both of us.

I said, "Let's make a deal. If you'll climb down from here and face your fears, I'll do what I can to help. My lawyer Laura Leonard is one of the best in the city. She can help you deal with the bar. Maybe she can keep you out of jail, too. If anybody can do it, she can."

"I don't have the money for a high-priced attorney." Angel snorted softly. "I don't have the money for an any priced attorney."

"You don't need money. I'll pay her for you."

"I can't ask you to do that. You've got enough things to worry about without taking on a charity case."

"Believe me, it's not a problem. Thanks to my newfound fame, I've got more money than I know what to do with." I smiled slightly. "Remember, I'm raking in all those underwear royalties."

Angel hesitated. Clearly, he was wavering.

I said, "I think the reason you feel so terrible is because you know you're running from your problems. Like I did, you took an oath. In your case it was to put the interests of your clients ahead of your own. You know you're breaking it by coming up here and trying to end it all. I'm willing to bet that if you jump your last thoughts will be of how you wish you hadn't left your clients in the lurch. I know it's hard and I know it's scary, but you have an obligation to something bigger than yourself. You have to try to live up to it. You have to face the consequences of what you've done, and then move on. If a dumb hick like me can do it, I know you can."

"I don't think you're a dumb hick," Angel said slowly. "Seems to me you're pretty smart. How else could you do all you've done?"

"Believe me, I've had a lot of help. Let me return the favor and help you now."

The rain lessened, turning into a fine mist. It gave the headlights of an oncoming car an otherworldly glow.

"All right," Angel finally said. "If you can do what you need to do despite your fears, then I guess I can too. I'll tell the bar what I've done and face the consequences." He swung a leg back over the railing. "C'mon. I'll walk back home and get the ball rolling. Before I change my mind. As Macbeth said, if something unpleasant has to be done, then 'twere well it were done quickly."

It seemed like a bad time to remind him that Macbeth had died at the end of the play, so I didn't. "Hold on a second," I said instead.

Angel paused. His legs straddled the railing.

"Can we stay and talk for a while?" I asked. "Not too many know my story. Not all of it, at any rate. It's good to be completely honest with someone for a change." The loneliness I usually suppressed with frenetic activity pressed on my chest like a weight.

"Sure, man, sure." Angel swung his leg back over. "It would be an honor."

Despite saying I wanted to talk, for a little while, we didn't talk at all. We just sat there and drank beer in companionable silence.

Angel broke the quiet. "If I ask you a question, will you give me an honest answer?"

"Sure. Why not? As long as I get to ask you one too."

"Deal," Angel said. "You go first."

"Your cousin isn't the one who wears Omega underwear, is he?"

Angel blushed and looked sheepish. "Guilty as charged. Matter of fact, I've got a pair of them on now. It was the only clean underwear I had left. Laundry hasn't been much of a priority lately." Angel shook his head. "Like I said, you're no dummy."

"Me? You're the one who casually quotes *Macbeth*."

"I've got the nuns of my Catholic school to thank for that. Those ladies didn't play around. You'd get smacked with a ruler if you weren't up to snuff. I can speak Latin like a Roman centurion because of them. Fat lot of good that's done me. Not a lot of demand for a thieving lawyer who's fluent in a dead language. Alright, my turn."

"Shoot."

Angel looked at me earnestly. He said, "If I had jumped, would you really have let me fall?"

I thought of Mom, Dad, Hannah, and Neha. About how I understood despair and the temptation to end it all. About how I understood feeling utterly alone. Who was I to stop someone from doing something I had half a mind to do myself?

"Yes," I said.

6

I walked aimlessly around my apartment. I was drinking an aggressive cabernet sauvignon. That was how the salesman at the wine shop had described it: *aggressive*. If he thought a bottle of fermented grapes was aggressive, clearly he had never dealt with Rogues.

It was the day after I had sat on the bridge with Angel. I drank straight from the wine bottle as I went from room to room. I didn't need no stinkin' glass. Glasses were for guys with friends and family who might think he was a wino if he didn't use them. I had no family, and few friends. Besides, no need to stand on formality when I was alone. I was almost always alone. Nobody here but the Three Amigos: myself, me, and cabernet makes three. That was usual. Well, outside of the cabernet part. What was unusual was for me to drink this much in such a short period of time. First the beers with Angel, now this bottle of wine, my second one of the day. As Truman was fond of saying, alcohol and superpowers did not make for a good combo. What the hell did Truman know, anyway? Nothing but a spoilsport gumshoe who liked to ruin my good time, that's what he was.

I belched, covering my mouth like a gentleman. True grace was observing the niceties even when no one was around. Huh. That was a great line. It was a wonder no one had offered me my own etiquette column. I'd have to call Stan Langley, my old boss at the *Astor City Times*, and demand an explanation for the oversight.

I was tipsy, and rapidly becoming more than tipsy. Perhaps this was how alcoholism started. I hoped I skipped the vomiting and blackout phase and went straight to the hooking up with random women phase. *Dear God: I'd like to skip the cirrhosis phase as well. Please and thank you.*

My place was the penthouse apartment on top of a mid-rise, mixed-use building on the edge of downtown Astor City, within walking distance of Apex Fitness. Retail stores were on the bottom floors of the building; residential apartments were on the top floors. I owned the building. I bought it months ago after assuming a substantial mortgage using my income from Omega merchandise as collateral. Well, I should say that a corporation owned the building, with a series of shell companies between it and me. But pierce all the corporate veils and slice through all the legal mumbo jumbo, and I was the owner. Laura had set the whole legal house of cards up. I only vaguely understood it. It likely would have taken the combined efforts of Clarence Darrow and Learned Hand to unravel all the companies and legal fictions that hid the connection between the corporation whose name this building was in and Theodore Conley. Learned Hand was a famous judge and legal thinker, not a Metahuman as his name would make one think. A waste of a perfectly good superhero name.

My apartment was much bigger than the mobile home Dad and I had lived in when he died. It made me feel guilty that I lived high on the hog in this big place while Dad moldered in his grave. But, Dad had been the one who had emphasized the value of owning real estate. He often said real estate was a solid investment because God was not making any more of it.

My dark hardwood floors felt cold against my bare feet as I wandered around. I grabbed the edge of a door, stopping myself from falling. No, *stumbled around* was more like it. If Mom were still around, she would say I needed to put shoes on before I caught cold. Little did she know her little boy had grown up to be the possessor of the Omega suit, which not only reduced my need for sleep, but apparently made me immune from minor illnesses as well. I had not gotten so much as a sore throat since the suit had become a part of me. However, since one can never be too careful about catching cold, I took another swig of wine. It warmed me from the inside, starting in my stomach and radiating outward. Nature's antifreeze. I wondered if the Centers for Disease Control and Prevention knew about it.

I ambled from room to room, restless, feeling as though I was looking for something, though I knew my apartment and its contents like my tongue knew the inside of my mouth:

Floor to ceiling windows on one side of the apartment afforded a stunning view of the twin giants of Star Tower and the UWant Building. Parts of the glass could swing open, letting me fly out of here when I needed to. There was a kitchen, library, living room, bathroom, and a large bedroom. The huge walk-in closet in the bedroom was a quarter of the size it had been when I moved in. Three-fourths of it, walled off and concealed thanks to the carpentry skills I had picked up from Dad, contained my Heroic paraphernalia. Stored there were my red Academy graduation cape, the white cape I received with my Hero's license, my license, and the huge gold ring with the masked man on the face of it that had come with the license.

The portal to The Mountain was also in my hideaway. With Avatar gone, The Mountain was my lair. Since the Omega spirit had passed from Avatar to me when he was murdered, I guess I had as much right to The Mountain as anyone else. I didn't go there much, though. Seeing Mad Dog there reminded me of Hannah and how I had failed her. I pretty much only went to The Mountain to replenish Mad Dog's food and water and to clean his cell. It was about time to go see him again. I did not look forward to it. Mad Dog's name was descriptive—he was like a rabid dog I had adopted that I didn't want. Sometimes I was tempted to turn him over to the authorities. That temptation passed when I thought of how I had found Hannah after Mad Dog killed her—with a hole blasted through her body and the smell of human waste mingling with cooked flesh. Then I resolved anew to keep Mad Dog imprisoned until kingdom come.

Also in the hidden area in the closet was a computer system I had paid Hacker to set up. Hacker was a Hero I had gone through the Trials with who now worked for a tech firm in Seattle. With her ability to control computers, she was the star of the firm, and made even more money than I did. One might think that, considering our history together, Hacker would have set up my computer system for free. Whoever thought that did not know Hacker.

The computer system was named Augur. It constantly monitored the Internet, radio, cell phone traffic, cable, broadcast television, and police and other government broadcasts for signs of trouble Omega might need to deal with. If I was not home, Augur alerted me where the trouble was via my communicator watch.

Tonight, Augur was quiet as a mouse. That was a good

thing. Thanks to my drinking, I was in no condition to get into a fight with anything. Except maybe a breathalyzer.

I was not even in my mid-20s, yet I already had a high-tech early warning system, a teleporter to my own personal lair, and I owned a building near a major city's downtown. I had more money in the bank than I could shake a stick at, and more flooded in from my various licensing deals by the day. The hefty sums of money I donated to various charities barely made a dent in the piles of money I was accumulating. And how could I forget—I was one of the most powerful Metas in the world. Famous to boot.

By the lights of a lot of people, I was successful.

I did not feel like a success. I felt terrible.

I paused my aimless wandering. I found myself in what was usually my favorite room—my library. Dark wood and heavy furniture adorned the room, like you might find in a men's club a century ago. The shelves groaned under my ever-expanding book collection. One good thing about having money fall out of my ears was I could afford to buy lots of books for the first time in my life. As had been the case when I was a kid, these days most of my free time—what little there was of it—was spent reading. Books were my friends. Due to the dangerous life I lived, I was too afraid to make new human ones. I didn't want what I had let happen to Neha and Hannah happen to someone else.

There was a price to pay for that. My talk with Angel had reminded me of what it felt like to form a personal connection with someone new. I had forgotten how good it felt. Getting a taste of it with Angel and then being without it again in my normal life was like walking back into a blizzard after warming up over a cozy campfire.

I stood in front of the library's mantelpiece. I looked with sadness at the pictures there of my parents and Neha. Every time I looked at Neha's picture, I felt sick that I had not reconciled with her before she died.

Above the mantel hung a framed sketch of James, my and Neha's son who was named after my father. He had my hair and eyes, but Neha's coloration and gently hooked Indian nose. I knew he was not real. But, thanks to the dreamworld I was in when the Omega spirit tested me to see if I was worthy of possessing the Omega suit, I had lived an imaginary alternate life in which I had been happily married to Neha and we had a son together. Though it had not *been* real, it had *seemed* real. My memories of our lives together were as concrete as the memory I had of getting out of bed this morning. More so, actually, because those memories were infinitely more precious. Thanks to that other life I remembered with Neha, when the Sentinels killed her, it had felt like losing her for the second rather than the first time.

Shortly after defeating the Sentinels, I had gone to a police sketch artist Truman had recommended. I had described James, dredging under the artist's expert guidance small details out of my mind that I had not even known were there. The sketch above my mantle was the result. It was the spitting image of how I remembered James.

Other than my memories, the sketch was all I had of James. I missed him desperately. Seeing his birth, seeing him take his first step, hearing his first word, teaching him to throw a ball, reading to him at night, watching him grow . . . I missed it all. I also missed Neha, Dad, and Mom. To a lesser extent as I had not been as close to them, I missed Hannah and Hammer.

I took another swig of wine. I swallowed the dregs of the bottle. I did not feel the warmth of the alcohol anymore as I stared at my loved ones who were gone forever. The cold weight of loneliness pressed against my chest, making it hard to breathe.

Cold fury suddenly possessed me. I was sick of this being my life.

I flung the empty wine bottle with all the force I could muster. It shattered against the wall with a smash. My fists were clenched. My chest heaved. My hands burned even hotter than they normally did as I struggled to not lash out with my powers at something, anything. I wished there was a Rogue I could punch. I hated that Dad, Hannah, and Neha were dead because of my mistakes. I hated my life, which seemed empty, tasteless, and gray.

I hated me.

When Neha died because of me, the only thing that had kept me going, the only thing that kept me from flying into space and going until the vacuum sucked the life out of me was the Hero's Oath. I had sworn to use my powers to protect people. I had refused to give up and violate my oath the way the Sentinels had. Learning I was the Omega, charged with protecting the world against a gathering crisis, had only enlarged the scope of my Heroic responsibility. I had assumed back then the crisis would hit soon. Days, weeks, maybe a few months at the most. But here it was, years later, and everything was exactly the same, with no crisis on the horizon. Natural disasters, street crime, alien invasions, Rogues . . . those I could deal with. But the waiting for the promised crisis, the loneliness, the isolation, the keeping secrets, the being afraid of getting close to anyone, the fear of failing again, of not being enough again . . . I didn't know how much more of all this I could take. It was like being a lonely little kid again, only with the added responsibility of superpowers and saving the world. I felt like a pressure cooker about to explode.

I once read that sustained loneliness was as bad for your

health as smoking was. I believed it. I wanted to pick up a piece of the broken bottle and use it to slit my wrists. It was not just the wine talking, though maybe the alcohol had ripped the scab off my darkest emotions. In vino veritas. I felt fragile. As if I would break like the wine bottle. I was held together only by duty, obligation, and promises to keep. I feared I'd fall to pieces if someone came along and jostled me the wrong way.

I looked down at the broken glass mess I'd made. I was suddenly disgusted with myself. Had I drunk wine, or whine? I needed to calm myself before I did something worse than breaking a bottle. I was no good to myself or anyone else like this. I was tempted to fly around the city and clear my head, but I was too afraid of what might happen if I ran across someone to take my frustration and anger out on.

I needed to sit tight and wait for my emotions to calm and my alcohol buzz to fade. I reached for a book. I pulled from a shelf the book of poetry Neha had given me when we were the Old Man's Apprentices. Though I've always been a big reader, I had not appreciated poetry overly much. When I told Neha that, she had bought me this poetry anthology. "Maybe this will class you up a little," she had written inside the front cover above a big smiley face. I often read this book when I felt particularly lonesome for Neha and James.

I settled into the black leather recliner I normally did my reading in. I flipped the book open at random. I started reading the first thing my eyes fell on. It was the 1897 poem *Richard Cory* by Edwin Arlington Robinson. It read:

> *Whenever Richard Cory went down town,*
> *We people on the pavement looked at him;*
> *He was a gentleman from sole to crown,*
> *Clean favored, and imperially slim.*

And he was always quietly arrayed,
And he was always human when he talked;
But still he fluttered pulses when he said,
"Good-morning," and he glittered when he walked.

And he was rich—yes, richer than a king—
And admirably schooled in every grace;
In fine, we thought that he was everything
To make us wish that we were in his place.

So on we worked, and waited for the light,
And went without the meat, and cursed the bread;
And Richard Cory, one calm summer night,
Went home and put a bullet through his head.

A chill ran down my spine as I closed the book. Sometimes clarity washes over you gently, like baptismal waters. Other times it bashes your head like a falling anvil. This was one of those latter times.

I was Richard Cory. The parallels between me and him were obvious. As Omega, I was famous; people admired me; women wanted to be with me; I had plenty of money. On the surface, I was the American Dream personified. And yet, like Richard Cory, I was miserable behind closed doors.

I had been serious when I had told Angel I was afraid that if he jumped, I might jump too. I was at my breaking point. Like Richard Cory, would there come some calm night when I came home and put a bullet through my head?

Despite what my Catholic upbringing had taught, I did not think there was anything inherently wrong with suicide. If my life was not my own to do with as I chose, then what was? Killing myself had occurred to me years before when I was a kid, usually when some bully at school made my life miserable. I had not gone through with it because I had known taking my life would devastate my parents, especially Dad after Mom died and it was just the two of us. When I was a kid, I had more people to think of than just myself.

Despite Mom and Dad now both being gone, I still had more people to think of than just myself. I was the Omega, charged with protecting the world. I didn't want the responsibility. Want it or not, however, I had it. If one day I gave in to despair and killed myself before dealing with whatever the threat was the Sentinels had told me about, then I would have failed the world just as I had failed Dad, Hannah, and Neha. I was bound and determined to not fail again.

Something had to change. I needed to do something about the crushing loneliness I felt before I succumbed to a dark impulse and did something to myself the entire world might come to regret.

Due to what had happened to Hannah and Neha, I was still afraid of what might happen if I became friends—or more —with someone. But, I was starting to become even more afraid of what might happen if I didn't.

I got up and found my smartphone.

Had a change of heart, I texted Isaac with unsteady hands. *Can you give me Viola's number?*

_____

7

"**I** saac says you're a real superhero," Viola said.

I choked on my latte. I started coughing and sputtering. Viola's blue eyes widened in concern. "Oh my God, are you all right?" she said. She started to get out of her chair. I waved her back down. After all I had been through the past few years, it would be mighty embarrassing if a pumpkin spice latte was what did me in. Saint Peter would call me a basic bitch when I arrived at the Pearly Gates.

I reached for my glass of water and cleared my throat.

"Isaac said what now?" I asked once I could.

"He said you're a real superhero. Because of all the money you give to charity."

"Oh. That," I said, relieved that Isaac had not blown my secret identity. I should have known better. Despite the fact Isaac loved to talk, he would never violate a confidence. "An uncle died a couple of years ago and left me a bunch of money. So much that the only job I have now is managing my investments. Since I didn't earn it, I figure giving some of it away is the least I can do." It was my go-to cover story when someone asked what I did for a living. I was so good at lying these days that it might as well have been my backup superpower. My chances at getting into Heaven were likely slipping away. My chances of getting into Congress were probably rising exponentially.

"You're being too modest," Viola said. "I think it's great that you're so generous."

I shrugged. "To whom much is given, much will be required." I felt like a pretentious jackass as soon as the quote was out of my mouth.

"Luke 12:48," Viola said immediately.

I was surprised again, this time without choking on my drink. Progress. Next up, solid foods. "You know your Bible."

"Of course. The Bible is where the voices in my head get their marching orders. They had me slaughter a ram and sprinkle its blood on an altar just the other night." Viola saw the look on my face and paused. "That was a joke."

"Oh, I know."

"Your mouth says you know, but the rest of your face says otherwise."

"It's just that if you really did have voices in your head, it would be par for the course. I've had bad experiences lately with blind dates and blood."

"There's no way I'm letting you say that without telling me the story behind it. Spill it. The story, not blood."

I told Viola about my ill-fated date with Candace Helwig. As I spoke, classic jazz music played softly under the hum of other conversations. The smell of roasted coffee hung in the air. We were in a Perk Up coffee shop in Astor City, not too far from my place. I had learned my lesson from meeting Candace for dinner. I had felt obligated to stay for the entire meal even though I knew when I laid eyes on Candace that she wasn't my type. I read a newspaper article a while ago about a guy who had a boulder fall on his arm while he hiked alone in the woods. To free himself before he died of dehydration, the hiker had sawed his arm off with his pocketknife. Dinner with Candace had made me appreciate the desperation the hiker had felt.

So, instead of meeting Viola for a long dinner at night, we sat in a coffee shop in the middle of a Saturday. If Viola proposed to drink my blood as Candace had, asked to harvest my organs, spoke in tongues, tried to get me to join a cult or run for office, or did something similarly nutty, I could make a quick escape after only dropping a few dollars on coffee.

Fortunately, Viola had done none of those things so far. She seemed as different from Candace as it was possible to be. Instead of having green and orange hair, multiple face piercings, a neck tattoo, and the air of someone who hated herself and was looking for a reason to hate you too as Candace had, Viola looked and acted like a normal, well-adjusted person. She was a hair shorter than I in her high-heeled boots. She had thick golden blonde hair worn in sausage curls that cascaded down her shoulders, blue eyes flashing behind black-framed circular glasses, and a square face. She was pretty in a sexy librarian kind of way. A few years ago, I would have said she was out of my league. Now I was so used to being hit on as Omega that I had no idea what league I was in anymore. The Justice League, maybe, if I weren't such a loner. And if I were a comic book character.

Viola wore black boot-cut jeans and a tight blue sweater whose V-neck revealed a hint of cleavage and occasional flashes of a pink bra. I wore the Omega suit camouflaged as a high-necked red pullover, dark blue jeans, and brown dress shoes. Casual superhero chic.

It was not gentlemanly to look at Viola's cleavage. I discreetly did it from time to time anyway. Viola could be a disguised Rogue who had hidden weapons down there. If there was one thing I had learned over the past few years, it was that a Hero could never be too careful. The readiness is all, as Hamlet said.

"So this chick wanted to drink your blood? Is her name Dracula?" Viola asked incredulously once I'd finished telling her about Candace.

"No. Maybe Dracula's her ancestor. It would explain the vampire neck tattoo. I didn't stick around to find out," I said. Viola said something in response, but I barely heard her. I was distracted by someone who had caught my eye. As I always did when I was in a public place, I sat with my back against the wall where I could see all the entrances and exits. A tall guy with greasy hair wearing a heavy, buttoned-up winter coat had just walked in.

It was an overcast fall day. Crisp, but certainly not cold. Why then was this guy dressed like he was about to brave a blizzard? What was he hiding under that coat? On top of that, the guy looked nervous: he kept licking his lips, his skin was flushed, and his eyes moved from side to side like windshield wipers as he scanned the throng of people in the large coffeehouse.

If I had a Spidey sense, it would be tingling.

I fidgeted with the cardboard sleeve encircling my latte, using the movement to cloak me activating my powers. I gave the man in the winter coat a quick scan with my telekinetic touch.

I found nothing more threatening than back acne and the beginnings of a potbelly.

Feeling sheepish, I watched as the man spotted a woman

in the crowded coffee shop. He went to her, and they awkwardly shook hands. The man took his coat off, revealing a multicolored shirt that made me dizzy looking at it. Wearing it might have been a fashion crime, but it was not dangerous. Now I realized the nervous man was just a guy on a first date like me who had dressed inappropriately for the weather, not a bloodthirsty terrorist hiding a shotgun under his coat who was about to shoot the place up. I shook my head at myself. I was so used to looking for the slightest hint of danger as Omega that I was as nervous as a cat on a hot tin ro—

Someone touched my hand, startling me. I snatched my hand back. I refocused on what was in front of me. Viola's eyes were wide with a combination of alarm, concern, and a look that said *Don't make me pepper spray you*. I realized Viola was the one who had touched my hand. I also realized my fist was clenched and cocked back, ready to punch. Embarrassed, I brought my fist to my mouth and pretended to cough into it. Where was choking on a pumpkin spice latte when you needed it?

"What is your deal?" Viola demanded.

"What do you mean?" I asked, shooting for wide-eyed innocence and likely hitting busted instead.

"Ever since we sat down, you've been looking around like you're expecting someone to stab you to death. And just now, when I touched you, you reacted like I really did stab you."

"Sorry. I'm a little jumpy. I've had some brushes with violence since moving to Astor City." *You can say that again*, I thought. "Being from a small town originally, it's not something I'm used to. Just last night I saw a mugging. Four guys robbing an old man."

"That's terrible! What did you do?"

"I shouted at the muggers, ran toward them, and they got

spooked and ran off." Another lie. What really happened was they got spooked when I dove from the sky like a peregrine falcon. I roughed them up a little to teach them a lesson; I had little faith the overwhelmed and corrupt Astor City justice system would teach them anything other than how to be better criminals. Then I immobilized them with my powers and used my watch to call the cops.

"Thank goodness they ran off," Viola said.

"Why do you say that?" I asked, puzzled.

"Because if they hadn't, they might've hurt you."

"Oh. Yeah, I suppose they might have."

Viola leaned back in her chair. She crossed her arms as she looked at me probingly. "You're an interesting fella, Theodore Conley."

"Why do you say that?" I asked again. I was hardly a brilliant conversationalist. No wonder I had few friends.

"Let me count the ways. You ran toward four muggers and act like that's the most natural thing in the world to do when most people in the city would've just minded their own business or at least kept their distance and simply called the cops. Normally I'd assume a guy was lying about confronting muggers to try to impress me, but I get the feeling you couldn't care less about impressing me. I'm not sure if I should be offended by that, by the way. You seemed surprised at the thought the muggers could have hurt you. You're sizing up everyone who walks through the door like you might have to wrestle them later. You inherited a pile of money in your twenties, yet instead of partying 24/7 the way a lot of people our age would, you're giving a lot of it away. Your hands are as fidgety as a little kid's, yet the rest of you is as calm and still as a lake, with no wasted movement. At least on the surface. Despite your veneer of calm, you're wound as tight as a two-dollar watch, as indicated by how you overreacted when I touched your hand. And on top of all that, you go around quoting the Bible, which is not something people our age normally do."

Wow. Viola was both pretty and perceptive. I'd have to stay on my toes around her. If I kept carelessly running my mouth, it would be like hanging a sign around my neck reading *Hi, I'm Omega. I suck at keeping secrets.*

Instead of doing that, I shrugged. "What can I say? I'm complicated. I'm like an onion."

"Because you smell and you make girls cry?"

I smiled. "No. Because I have layers."

"I would have gone with a cake instead of an onion."

"The next time I need a better analogy, I'll be sure to give you a call."

Viola smiled back at me. Her teeth were perfectly straight and even. I wondered if she had worn braces. She flipped her hair over her shoulder. "I certainly hope you will," she said.

I realized Viola was flirting with me. She liked me. I was startled to also realize that I liked her too. The twin realizations made me nervous. Though it was irrational, it felt like I was cheating on Neha and dishonoring her memory by sitting here talking to another woman. Part of me wanted to bolt. Another part of me, the same part that kept glancing at Viola's cleavage, made me sit tight.

"So tell me, what makes you so complicated and onion-like?" Viola asked.

I shook my head. "I feel like I've talked too much as it is. Tell me more about you."

She did. Her last name was Simpson. ("No relation to O.J.," she said. "Imagine my relief," I said.) She was 24-years-old and a native of Portland, Oregon. She lived in Appalachian Springs, a suburb a short drive from Astor City. She had moved to this area after graduating college in Massachusetts to take a job as an associate editor at *Ms. M*, an online magazine for millennial women. She was working toward a master's degree in psychology at night at Astor City University. She wanted to be a psychotherapist. Her background and professional aspirations explained why she was so observant. I tended to scoff at psychologists because of how little I thought of the one I had been forced to go to when Mom died, but Viola made me want to reconsider my prejudice. Her father, a construction worker, died in a work-related accident a few years ago. Her mother had recently remarried a man who had hit on Viola the day he met her, and later drunkenly fondled Viola at their wedding. Viola was not a fan of her stepdad.

"I can't imagine why," I told her.

Viola saying her father had been killed prompted me to share that my father had been killed too, in my case during a Rogue attack. I left out that Iceburn had attacked because Millennium, Mechano, and Seer had dispatched him to kill me. The key to being a good liar, I had learned, was to tell as much of the truth as possible while omitting key facts. That way your story would appear to be true if someone ever checked on it. Also, there were fewer outright lies you had to keep straight. Who knew being a Hero would qualify me to teach a masterclass in lying? My parents would be so proud.

Somehow science fiction came up. Viola was as much of a fan of science fiction and fantasy books as I was. "Hence the weak eyes and the glasses," she said. Though my reading habits these days tended more toward books that would help me be a more effective Hero—current events, history, the latest scientific advances, that sort of thing—I still loved fantasy and sci-fi though I didn't have time for it much anymore. Talking about science fiction led to talking about *Star Trek*. I told Viola that *Enterprise* was my favorite of all the *Trek* series. She mocked me relentlessly at that admission.

"Hey," she said, "have you heard that Klingons make really colorful fabrics every day?"

"No," I said, puzzled. "Why is that?"

"Because today is always a good day to dye."

It took me a second to get it. Then I groaned. "How could you be so cute and yet have a joke so monstrously bad inside of you?" Too late I realized I had said out loud I thought she was cute. My dating skills were rusty. No, that's not right —*rusty* implies they ever existed in the first place.

"I am large, I contain multitudes," she said.

"Walt Whitman?"

"Yep."

"You make a terrible *Star Trek* pun one minute, then quote *Leaves of Grass* the next. You're one to talk about me being complicated."

"Most people just think I'm weird. And I probably am. I've yet to meet anyone who studied psychology who wasn't weird. It's a 'physician, heal thyself' sort of thing." Viola said.

"I don't think you're weird. I think you're interesting."

"So we're both interesting, we both understand the other's references, and we're both cute. We should get married or something."

We fell silent, both of us embarrassed. Or maybe I was just projecting how I felt onto Viola. As a future psychotherapist, she could probably tell me.

Viola said, "Speaking of *Star Trek*, there's a *Trek* retrospective at the Museum of Pop Art. I was going to check it out after leaving here. Since you're into the show too, do you want to go with me?"

"Does a Vulcan get pon farr?" I said.

Viola grinned. "FYI, I don't pon farr on the first date."

"Good to know."

The Astor City Museum of Pop Art was miles away on the

outskirts of the city. We headed toward Viola's car, parked a few blocks away. I did not own a car; it was all too easy to get around the city using public transportation, ride-sharing services, walking or, when I was Omega, flying. The tall buildings of downtown acted as a wind tunnel, augmenting the already brisk wind. It was chilly out. Gray clouds had blotted out the sun. Viola shivered, zipped up her jacket as we walked, and peered up. "It looks like it's about to rain," she said.

I sniffed the air. I got a whiff of Viola's perfume. Something floral. "Nah. Doesn't smell like rain. Plus the barometric pressure's all wrong. Maybe it'll rain in a few hours, but certainly no sooner."

"What, are you literally Rain Man?"

"You know puns and poetry, I know weather. I grew up on a farm, remember? The weather is far more important to a farmer than what kind of hoe he has."

"Did you just call me a ho?"

"No. But now I am." Viola tried to punch me in the shoulder. I saw it coming from a mile away and slipped it automatically. Her fist only hit air.

Viola's eyes widened. "Wow, you've got quick reflexes," she said.

I shadowboxed, deliberately making my movements far clumsier than they normally were. "Float like a butterfly, sting like a bee," I said. As I punched the air I silently chided myself for moving out of the way of her punch so fluidly. Playing the role of hapless was harder than it looked. I didn't know how Clark Kent pulled it off. Maybe it was the glasses.

On Allure Avenue, we walked toward a shady-looking dude. I only halfway paid attention to what Viola was saying as I gave the guy the suspicious side-eye until we passed him. I kept a lock on him for the next couple of blocks with my telekinetic touch, but he did nothing warranting further attention.

He was evidently minding his own business and wasn't planning on knocking someone upside the head.

Between this guy and winter coat guy in the coffee shop, maybe Isaac had been right that I needed to do a better job of taking the mask off. Not everybody was a criminal or a Rogue.

We climbed into Viola's car, a late model blue Honda Civic. She pulled out of the parking space and eased into traffic heading north on Hamilton Street. As we continued to talk as she drove, the guilt I had felt about going out with Viola started to ease out of me. Neha and I hadn't even been dating when she died; only in that imaginary alternate reality the Omega spirit had put me in had Neha and I dated and gotten married. And even if Neha and I actually had a romantic relationship in this reality, she was gone now. It wasn't like I was cheating on her. I had no legitimate reason to feel guilty. I was not doing anything wrong.

Viola made a right off Hamilton and onto Greene Street, a three-lane road. The speed limit was higher now that we were out of the downtown district. Viola's car accelerated. Traffic was moderate, as was the foot traffic on the sidewalks. It was the middle of a Saturday, after all. Things would be much busier tonight.

As we proceeded on Greene, Viola and I had a friendly argument about which *Star Trek* movie was the best. I threatened to jump out of the car in disgust when she said *The Voyage Home* was the best. She said she threw up in her mouth at my assertion that the 2009 reboot of the franchise was the best movie. I realized during all this that I was not at all nervous talking to Viola as I had been years ago when I talked to other girls. I wondered if that was because I was more confident thanks to my exploits as Omega, because Viola was a geek like me, or simply because I was not a kid anymore.

Regardless, Viola was fun, and I enjoyed being around her.

Maybe I was silly for living the life of a warrior monk, as Isaac had put it.

I was in the middle of thinking that perhaps Theo Conley could lead a normal life while Omega simultaneously led a decidedly abnormal life when a costumed Rogue fell out of the dark sky. Broken asphalt went flying when he landed directly in front of Viola's speeding car.

8

_____

"Oh my God!" Viola shrieked. She had the presence of mind to not try to swerve out of the way since we were boxed in by cars on either side of us. Instead, she slammed on the brakes. I choked on the smell of burning rubber.

No use. The Rogue was too close and we were going too fast. We skidded toward him like a bowling ball toward a pin.

Hairy fists the size of ham hocks pumped up, then swung down like a guillotine. They hit the hood of Viola's Civic with a terrific smash. The blow and our forward momentum sent us sailing into the air, tail end first, spinning end over end.

Viola screamed. The world spun like a kaleidoscope around us.

We landed with a smash on the street again, roof-side first. We skidded. Sparks flew. We slammed into a car, then another. The second impact slowed us, then brought us to a bone-rattling halt.

Viola and I hung upside down by our seat belts. The stench of gas and exhaust filled the air. Viola frantically ran her hands over her body, like a coked-up doctor examining a patient.

"I'm not dead," she said in wonder, almost to herself. "How am I not dead?" Even her glasses were still on, though they dangled from her nose since they were upside down.

"The Japanese know how to make cars," I said. Though true, Japanese engineering had gotten a secret assist from my powers. When we had gone airborne, I had encircled the car's passenger compartment with a force field. It had prevented us from being shaken like a martini while in the air, and from doing a pancake impersonation when we hit the ground. The car had crumpled around my field, leaving us completely unhurt. I had also stopped the car's air bags from deploying; they would have just gotten in the way. I had even kept Viola's glasses from falling off.

I fumbled for the seat belt release. "Sit tight. I'll see if I can get us out of here."

"'Sit tight,' he says. Where would I go?" She was surprisingly calm. I was impressed. Most people would freak out. Even my heart raced, and I'd been through this sort of thing before.

I unfastened my seat belt and slid off the seat onto the crumpled roof. I twisted around, feet facing the passenger side window. I kicked the closed window. My first two kicks only cracked the window more than it already was. The third kick, with an assist of my powers from a surreptitious finger flick, made the glass pop out of the frame like a contact lens out of a dry eye. I wiggled out feet-first.

I scrambled to my feet. My watch buzzed insistently. I glanced at it. A message from Augur. It read, "Rogue sighting on Greene Street in Astor City, Maryland." *No shit, Sherlock*, I thought.

In front of us was the SUV we had slammed into. Its rear

end was a crumpled ruin. We were surrounded by cars that had stopped haphazardly in the middle of Greene Street. Some had run into one another, no doubt to avoid my and Viola's failed flying Jetson car impersonation. Honking filled the air. People were getting out of their vehicles, gawking, pointing. Many had cell phones in their hands, pointed down the street, taking pictures and recording video of the Rogue who had started this mess.

I turned to look at him too. With one arm, he flipped an empty stopped car out of his way like it was made of cardboard. The car sailed through the air. It smashed against the stone façade of a building on the other side of the street. The sound was like a metallic thunderclap. The wreckage burst into flames with a whoosh. People screamed. Others cheered and applauded. Idiots. Some people acted like life was an action movie, with death and destruction merely a fun show.

The Rogue was Silverback. It was impossible to mistake him for anyone else. Over eight feet tall, he had an absurdly muscled, hunched-over body garbed in a brown and tan costume, arms that almost dragged the ground, long fangs sticking up from his lower jaw, and an ugly mug. I had run him out of town over a month ago and threatened to make his life a living hell if I ever saw him again. Before I had chased him out of Astor City, he'd been all about smash and grab robberies—bank vaults, armored cars, high-end jewelers, that sort of thing. Wreaking havoc in the middle of the street for no apparent reason was not his usual modus operandi. I wondered why there was a change in his behavior, and why he had gotten the courage to show his face in Astor City again.

It didn't matter. What did matter was that I stop Silverback before somebody got hurt.

Since so many others were already doing it, I lifted a hand to point at Silverback. I used the movement to mask activating my powers. Though Silverback was a nasty costumer, I had been able to subdue him back when I was merely Kinetic. He certainly was no match for Omega. I'd trap him in a force field and hold him until the authorities arrived. Silverback would be under control before I could say supercalifragilisticexpialidocious, though I didn't know what in the world would possess me to say such a thing.

Silverback turned slightly. He seemed to look straight at me even though we were separated by rows of stopped cars and a large stretch of the street. He stepped forward, moving through my invisible force field as if it didn't exist.

What the hell?

Then I tried to latch onto his body with my powers to immobilize him. Nope. No dice. Trying to hold onto him was like trying to hold onto a fistful of air.

Taken aback, I blinked in surprise bordering on shock. Maybe I should have said supercalifragilisticexpialidocious after all. My powers not working on someone hadn't happened since I had tussled with Iceburn years ago.

Silverback advanced implacably in my direction. Upright as he was now, he didn't move as quickly as he could when he dropped to all fours, much like the gorilla he took his name from. Silverback shoved and flung cars out of the way as he approached. The sound of rending metal and breaking glass filled the air.

I ducked down, peering through the car window I'd crawled through.

"We need to run," I said to Viola. I raised my voice to be heard over the pandemonium Silverback caused. "Can you unfasten your belt and crawl out this way?"

"I can try." She wrestled with the seat belt. Each second brought Silverback closer. I felt in my chest vibrations from the tremors Silverback's super-dense body sent rippling through the street with each step.

"Hurry!" I urged. If I used my powers to free Viola, it would be as obvious as a whore at a Boy Scout jamboree, though I'd do it if I had to. *Do it* meaning use my powers, not do the whore. What a time to channel Isaac's sense of humor.

There was a ripping sound. Viola's seat belt finally retracted, freeing her. She yelped, almost banging her head on the roof of the car when she fell onto it. Meanwhile, I tugged on the handle of the crumpled door so Viola wouldn't have to crawl through the window. It was stuck. The vibrations from Silverback's approach intensified. Stupid stubborn door. I gave my muscles a subtle assist from my powers. Too much. I staggered backward when the entire door ripped away from the car with a screech that made my teeth ache.

Viola crawled out and scrambled to her feet. I dropped the door on the street, hoping Viola hadn't noticed my feat of seeming strength. I had a *My strength is as of the strength of ten because my heart is pure* deceptive quip all ready to go. No need. Viola was too busy staring at the approaching monstrous Rogue to think twice about the door. Despite the tumult she'd been through, her glasses were still in place, again thanks to a subtle use of my powers. At least her glasses weren't immune to them. Too bad they weren't a Rogue.

"Run!" Viola exclaimed. She grabbed my hand, turned, and followed her own advice. I trailed after her. Her blonde hair streamed in my face. Her hand was warm in mine. *Who's saving whom?* I thought.

We dodged cars and darted left, off the street and onto the sidewalk. We pounded north. Others were running away from Silverback too, on both sides of the street. Still on his hind legs, Silverback moved to the left as well, advancing slowly yet implacably behind us.

Coincidence? Maybe. There were a lot of people running with us now. Silverback didn't have to be after us. He could have been after one of our fellow runners, or after no one in particular. Besides, he didn't know my secret identity. But why had he landed in front of Viola's car? Just another coincidence? And why had it seemed he looked right at me before he started moving in this direction? If you piled a bunch of seeming coincidences on top of one another, pretty soon you had a big pile of It Ain't Just A Coincidence.

I scanned behind us with my telekinetic touch as we fled. My mind was awhirl with thoughts of whether Silverback was really after me. The distracting thoughts almost made me almost miss it.

"Get down!" I yelled. I lunged into Viola, tackling her, driving her toward the sidewalk. Simultaneously, I extended my hand toward the people in front of us, activating my powers, knocked them all down like bowling pins. I twisted as Viola and I fell, taking the brunt of the impact on the meaty part of my shoulder. Viola fell on me. Pain lanced through my shoulder and down my spine.

The streetlight Silverback had ripped from its foundation and hurled at us whizzed over our heads with a high whistle as it spun like a boomerang. It curved to the right and smashed into two parked cars. Glass broke and metal twisted. One of the car's alarms started shrieking, adding a new layer of sound to the pandemonium.

I had to put a stop to this before someone got hurt. I also couldn't continue to use my powers without risking revealing who I was. I needed to change into my costume double-quick.

"C'mon, c'mon, c'mon," I urged. I pushed Viola off me, scrambled to my feet, and pulled her up after me. She was dazed. Her eyes looked unfocused without her glasses. The bent frames were on the sidewalk, their lenses smashed to pieces by our fall. If Viola ever learned about my powers, I hoped she'd forgive me for neglecting to keep her glasses affixed to her face this time. In my defense, I had a lot on my mind, including the streetlight that had nearly caved our skulls in. Better to lose your glasses than lose your head.

My ankle throbbed. I had twisted it when Viola had fallen awkwardly on top of me. I ran as fast as I could further up the block, pulling Viola with me. Silverback continued his inexorable advance behind us.

I turned left. I flung open the glass door of a tall office building, and pulled Viola inside after me. The sounds of the chaos outside faded slightly. A shiny stone receptionist's desk matching the shine of the floor was in the middle of the lobby, with an empty leather chair behind it. Two vases of fresh flowers sat on either end of the desk.

A man jumped at our sudden appearance. He was right inside of the door. He had been craning his neck, obviously trying to see down the street through the clear glass to spot what all the commotion was all about. He wore tight gray slacks, an equally tight white shirt, and dress shoes so shiny I could have used them to shave. Tall and thin, he had thick, wavy, slicked-back black hair and cheekbones that could cut glass. He was the poster child for the phrase "pretty boy." A thin headset was around his head. The receptionist, obviously. A waste of genes—he should have quit and become a model.

Now recovered from his startle, the man greeted us with a well-practiced smile. His cheeks were dimpled; his teeth were even and perfectly white. Of course they were. "Welcome to Myers Tower," he said. "I hope you're having a wonderful day. How may I help you?" Viola's clothes were askew, and her hair looked like she had just walked through a wind tunnel. Blood dripped down my face from a cut on my cheek. I wiped it away with my palm. Despite our appearance and the obvious uproar outside, this guy was saying *I hope you're having a wonderful day*? First impression? He was as ornamental as the flowers on his desk, and about as bright.

I ignored him. I'd already scanned the building with my powers. I said to Viola, "Go through the lobby, take a right, and then a left. There's another exit on the other side of the building. Once you're out and safe, call the cops. Take this—" I caught myself, almost saying *idiot*, "guy with you."

"But what about you?" Viola said. Hopefully later, when things calmed down, she wouldn't wonder how I knew where the other exit was.

"I'm going back out to see if I can help other people get away."

"I'll help too."

The tremors caused by Silverback's approach got stronger. "No offense, but it's obvious you can barely see without your glasses. You'd just be in the way. Now go."

Viola hesitated, looking like she was going to argue further. Then her face softened. She quickly kissed me on the cheek. "You're very brave," she murmured. She stepped away and jerked her head at the receptionist. "Come on, you heard the man, let's go."

"But I'm not supposed to leave my post," the guy protested. Like he was the Queen's Guard at Buckingham Palace or something.

Viola shot me an eye-rolling look. She said to the guy, "I'm sure your boss will understand. Let's go, Fabio." She grabbed his arm, and pulled him along as she half-walked, half-ran through the lobby. The guy followed behind her like he was a lost puppy. Cute but stupid.

The moment the two turned the corner and were out of sight, I dashed to the lobby's nearest door. I yanked it open, then slammed it shut behind me. The tiny room was dark and reeked of cleaning supplies. A supply closet. Of course I was changing into my superhero costume in a closet. Could I be more of a cliché? The only thing that might've been more clichéd was if I made the change in a phone booth. Assuming I could find one in this age of cell phones.

I'd ducked into this closet because, though I hadn't seen any security cameras in the lobby, I had little doubt a ritzy building like this one had hidden ones. Not changing into your Hero costume while on camera should be rule number one of the Hero handbook. Maybe, once all this was over, I'd write one. Unlike with my autobiography, I wouldn't be stupid enough to let my publisher name it. They'd probably name it something misleading like *Coming Out of the Closet*.

In seconds, my clothes melted and changed shape and color, reforming into my Omega costume. I skipped the cape this time. No need to dress to impress. I was going to an ass-kicking, not a wedding.

I laced my fingers and cracked my knuckles. "Time to batter Rogue butt," I murmured. I winced. After all this time, I still hadn't come up with a decent catchphrase.

Though probably my imagination, I felt the warmth of Viola's kiss on my cheek. She said I was brave. She was wrong. I wasn't being brave. Bravery was action in the face of fear. I wasn't afraid. I wasn't even nervous. I'd dealt with Silverback before. Though him not being affected by my force field was a new trick, I still had him thoroughly outclassed. Now that I was in costume and wasn't hampered by having to hide my powers, I would defeat Silverback easily. Though my powers apparently could not affect him directly, there were plenty of things I could do to him indirectly. Maybe I'd wrap a bunch of abandoned cars around his big body until he was immobilized and looked like the world's biggest Christmas present to the Astor City Police Department.

I smiled at the thought of wrapping a chrome fender around Silverback's neck like a silver bow. Maybe I'd hang around afterward, make a statement to the press, and take a few photos with fans. Though my modesty-is-a-virtue upbringing always rebelled at the thought of making a spectacle of myself, my publicist Margot had been nagging me lately about goosing Omega's Q Score. A Q Score was the measurement of the public's awareness of my brand and how they felt about it. The fact I even knew what a Q Score was showed how much I'd changed these past few years. Some of my merchandise deals were expiring soon, and Margot wanted more leverage to negotiate for more money. When I had suggested that we already made enough money, she had looked at me like I had sprouted a second head and it spoke an alien tongue. Maybe ginning up some extra publicity off of Silverback's defeat would get Margot off my back for a while. She was persistent as Chinese water torture.

Anyway, I was putting the cart before the horse. First I had to get out of this dark closet. Then I had to kick Silverback's butt from here to the top of the UWant Building. Then I'd worry about my Q Score, and maybe a few other letters of the alphabet while I was at it. Like *E*, for *Easy*.

After doing a quick scan with my telekinetic touch to make sure no one was in the way, I raised my personal shield and shot through the wall of the closet. I felt bad about the damage I caused, but a building like this one was surely insured. It likely even had a Metahuman damage insurance rider. A lot of business in big cities did. Rogue attacks weren't common, but they weren't exactly unheard of, either.

Drywall burst, bricks shattered, stone cracked, and wood beams broke in a cacophony of sounds. I burst through the building's outer wall. I skidded to a halt, hovering in the air a few feet off the ground. Screams, shrieks, and horns filled the air. People were still running. If anything, the chaos I'd left behind had increased. I twisted to look at Silverback.

Uh oh. I felt like Wile E. Coyote when he realized he had run off a cliff and was about to fall and break every bone in his body.

Silverback was no longer alone. Five additional Rogues were with him:

Mad Dog, in a garish green and maroon costume. No longer what Dad would call hard fat, Mad Dog was far leaner than when I had imprisoned him in The Mountain. He was still a big, muscular man, though. The red outline of a snarling dog's head was on his chest. His head was unmasked. I'd know his bald head and pig eyes anywhere, having seen them more times than I wanted to when I visited The Mountain. He had still been there when I last visited, with his Metahuman power of spitting energy balls neutralized by him being in the holding cell I had inherited from Avatar. He glared at me. Even this far away from him, I felt the intensity of his hatred for me. It radiated from him like heat from an oven. I wondered where he had gotten his costume from, though that was the least of my unanswered questions.

Elemental Man, aka Frank Hamilton III, aka Trey, aka Isaac's hated stepbrother. Trey had raped Isaac's younger sister, a horrific act that led to her suicide. Trey was a muscular man in a white, red, blue and brown costume, each color taking up a solid quadrant of his body. I wondered if the colors represented the substances he could manipulate and control, namely air, fire, water, and earth. Though there was a black domino mask around his eyes, the rest of his head was uncovered, which was how I recognized him even though I had not seen this particular costume before. He had the strong jaw, pouty lips, and classic features of a male model. And an ego to match unless he had a personality transplant since I'd last seen him. I had given him the nickname Hitler's Youth during the Trials because of his alabaster white skin, perfectly styled blonde hair, arctic blue eyes, and I'm-better-than-you attitude, all of which would probably have given Hitler a boner had he known Trey. I had defeated Trey during one of the Trials' tests. Because of that defeat, he had failed the Trials for the third time and was therefore forever barred from getting a Hero's license. According to Isaac, post-Trials Trey had told everyone who would listen I must have cheated because otherwise someone like me would have never beaten someone like him. He was wrong—I had beaten him fair and square. My cheating during the Trials had not come until later.

Brown Recluse, a tall, wiry figure in a brown and tan costume with the black outline of a spider on the front. He crouched down on all fours on top of an abandoned minivan. That pose, his costume's colors, and his long, spindly limbs reminded me of the arachnid he had taken his name from. His costume covered him from head to toe, except for his hands, which were bare. He was a former licensed Hero and Trials proctor who had been bribed by the disgraced Sentinels to smuggle a bomb into the Trials to kill me. For his crimes, he had been sentenced to serve time in MetaHold. I doubted he was out on work release.

Iceburn, in the same pitch-black costume with luminescent ragged lines running through it I had last seen him in. The costume covered him from head to toe. Iceburn's body glowed as if lit up from within. The half of his body that glowed orange-red generated heat and fire; the half that glowed light blue generated cold and ice. He too was supposed to be in MetaHold, serving multiple life sentences for killing my father, and killing and hurting others while he tried to kill me. He was also supposed to be paralyzed from the neck down. I had broken his back when we had last fought years ago. He certainly looked hale and hearty now, though. Maybe he had been taking vitamins in prison.

Last, but most definitely not least, Doctor Alchemy. His birth name was Ajeet Thakore. In addition to being Neha's father, he was one of the most prominent Rogues on the planet. He was as well-known as Avatar had been, but for opposite reasons: Avatar had been famous, whereas Doctor Alchemy was infamous. Some mothers kept their wayward kids in line by telling them Doctor Alchemy would come and get them if they did not straighten up.

Like Hitler's mustache, Doctor Alchemy's costume and appearance were instantly recognizable, and for similarly evil reasons. The only Rogue here in a cape, the flowing dark purple garment combined with Doctor Alchemy's imposing height and palpable physical presence made him seem almost regal. A slightly curved V-shaped piece of fabric rose from the neck of the cape to past his hair, serving as a dramatic back- drop to his head. The rest of his costume was a lighter shade of purple with black accents. His purple cowl exposed the top of his head and his mouth, nose, and chin, displaying his dark brown Indian skin, thick black hair, and a well-groomed shiny black mustache and beard. He had the same hooked Indian nose Neha and our son James had.

The tightness of Doctor Alchemy's costume highlighted the musculature of a fit man decades younger. Only touches of gray at his temples hinted at his true age. Thick gauntlets of a dull gray metal were around his wrists. A small tube extended from the top of each. A utility belt affixed with rectangular containers of the same metal as the gauntlets was around his waist.

"Howdy kid," Iceburn called out cheerfully. He had to shout over the din of noise from cars honking and people running and screaming. "You've gotten some fancy new duds since I saw you last. I like 'em. Blue suits you." Though I hadn't heard his self-confident voice in years, I had listened to it often enough in my nightmares when I relived the night he murdered by father. Hearing his voice again was like hearing a song you hated that had burrowed into your head like an earworm. "My colleagues and I are the Revengers. Because we're looking for revenge. Get it? A little too on the nose and dangerously close to trademark infringement, I know. My big buddy Silverback here wanted to call us the Super Fiends, but I said that was too cartoonish. I wanted to call us 'The Six Guys Who Are Gonna Kill The Hero Formerly Known As Kinetic Because He Screwed Them,' but that got voted down. Too wordy, they said.

"Silence," Doctor Alchemy ordered flatly. He spoke with a pronounced Indian accent in a tone that brooked no dissent. He stared daggers at me. His left arm was raised. The metal tube extending from his gauntlet pointed right at me, like the barrel of a gun.

My watch buzzed like a startled rattlesnake. I did not take my eyes off the Rogues to look. It was no doubt Augur informing me of more Rogue sightings. *Yeah, thanks for the heads-up,* I thought. *Too little, too late.*

I stared at the assembled Rogues—the Revengers, apparently—scarcely able to believe my eyes.

I hadn't been scared before.

Now I was scared.

9

I thought of calling for reinforcements. Myth, Truman, maybe even Ninja. I dismissed the idea as soon as I had it. If I could not handle six Rogues—even if one of them was Doctor Alchemy—then I did not deserve the Omega spirit, the Omega suit, or even the name Omega.

Questions tripped over themselves in my head. How were all these Rogues here, especially the ones who were supposed to be languishing in prison? I doubted they would tell me if I asked. Close-mouthed bastards. Besides, this was no time to ask a bunch of fool questions, not when facing this many superpowered threats and with so many people around who could get hurt.

So instead I reached out with my powers, before Iceburn had even finished speaking, trying to latch onto the bodies of all the new Rogues at once and immobilize them.

Nope. Trying to hold onto them was like trying to grasp wisps of smoke. They were as immune to my powers as Silverback had been. Add how they had managed to pull that little trick off to my list of questions.

Time for plan B.

All the bystanders with any sense were fleeing, putting as much distance as possible between them and us faced-off Metas. Meanwhile, many others stood around us, gawking and recording with their cell phones, like bystanders to a schoolyard fight. The problem was this fight was not between preadolescents who did not know how to throw a punch and could barely hurt each other, much less bystanders. This kind of fight promised to get bystanders killed.

I was vaguely tempted to leave the gawkers where they were in the line of fire, let natural selection do its work, and maybe raise the IQ of the gene pool a tad. But I knew I could not let a bunch of innocents get hurt or killed no matter how foolish they might be. So, I reached out with my powers, grabbing hold of everyone in the immediate vicinity. I yanked them all off their feet and flung them away from where I and the Rogues faced off. They cried out in surprise and confusion as they sailed through the air like dandelion seeds caught in a strong breeze. An instant later, I set them all back down on the ground far away from me and the Rogues.

I then threw up a large force field around me and the Rogues that was over half a city block large. It would not keep the Rogues in since they were somehow immune to my powers, but it would keep curious bystanders out. Now I wouldn't have to worry about innocents getting hurt. I just had to worry about me getting hurt, which was more than enough to fret about. I felt like I was about to be a part of the world's biggest cage fight.

Iceburn looked at how we all had gone from being surrounded by bystanders to being alone in seconds. "Nice trick kid," he said. "What do you do for an encore?"

I believed in showing, not telling. The words were still on Iceburn's lips when I launched myself at Doctor Alchemy. I zoomed toward him like a shot bullet, dodging a ball of energy

Mad Dog spat at me, then an icy blast from Iceburn. Though I had never faced Doctor Alchemy before, his reputation preceded him. He posed the biggest threat. He had fought Heroes like the Sentinels to a standstill, including Avatar. He had tortured and killed the Hero Wildside and God only knew how many others, both Meta and non-Meta. The main reason Neha had become a Hero was to try to prevent him from taking over the world.

A blast of concentrated wind like a mini-tornado hit me before I reached Doctor Alchemy. It took me by surprise. The wind blew me off course, forcing me back through the air. It slammed me against the front of a building so hard that its stone cracked and splintered behind and around me. My personal shield was up of course, or else my body would have been smeared across the side of the building like a bug hitting the windshield of a speeding car.

The blast of wind pounded me, roaring in my ears, drilling into me, pinning me in place, sucking the air out of my lungs. It was not *like* a mini-tornado as I'd thought before—it *was* a mini-tornado. The larger end of the funnel bore into my body. I gasped for breath. My lungs burned, feeling like they would collapse. I might as well have been blind with all the debris whipping around me.

Trying to swallow my mounting panic, I reached out with my telekinetic touch, groping for the source of the tornado. The tapered end of the tornado's funnel sprouted from Elemental Man's palms. Of course. I should have known. He had also attacked me with a twister during the Trials.

I had absorbed a good bit of kinetic energy from my impact with the building and from the continuing wind-blast. Though I still could not see, I shifted my eyes in the direction of where I sensed Elemental Man. I channeled some of the pent-up energy through my eyes. My eyes burned. Twin energy beams burst out of me. They shrieked through the cyclone, and found the Rogue generating it. They hit Elemental Man. The beams' concussive force blasted him off his feet. The mini-tornado pinning me against the building immediately dissipated into harmless gusts of wind.

Elemental Man sailed through the air. He landed on his back. Hard. But not as hard as he could have. He had generated an upsurge of wind to cushion his fall at the last second. Though no Hero, he had Heroic training. Some of the onlookers trapped outside my force field applauded. I didn't know if they applauded me or Elemental Man. If the former, I wouldn't let it go to my head. They would probably applaud if (when?) I got knocked on my ass too.

Elemental Man was down, but not out. I felt the same way —rocked, but still in the game. I peeled myself out of the small crater my shield and I had gouged into the side of the building. Gasping, my vision blurred, I tried to refill my lungs. I felt like a bug someone had stepped on.

A cloud of greenish-white gas engulfed me. My lungs, already burning, felt like acid was pouring into them. Choking, I had the presence of mind to hold my breath. It went against my body's natural instincts, like a swimmer not coughing after he has inhaled water. Knockout gas, or something more potent? My head swam, the world spun. I didn't know which way was up or down. Due to the green mist surrounding me, not having yet recovered from Elemental Man's attack, and now my spinning head, I couldn't see properly. I cast around with my telekinetic touch, looking for the source of gas.

Brown Recluse. He had leaped from the street onto a ledge above me. He was using his Metahuman ability to produce toxins to engulf me in a cloud of gas. The heavier than air gas billowed from his hands down onto me like fog from a fog machine.

I tried flying out of the cloud. Dizzy and disoriented, I succeeded only in slamming myself into the building again. I caromed off it like a cue ball. With friends like me, who needed these enemies?

Time to attack the source instead. Using my powers, I broke the stone ledge that Brown Recluse perched on, hoping to send him tumbling. Instead, he leaped onto me. I knew he was super-agile, but knowing it and seeing it in action were two different things. My personal shield useless against him, Brown Recluse wrapped his long arms and legs around me in an embrace that might be called intimate under different circumstances. His bare hands slid around my head, probing for bare skin, like a horny teen boy anxious to reach second base. I didn't think he was trying to feel me up or give me a facial. Trying to rub a deadly toxin onto my skin was more likely.

Still holding my breath, I bucked in the air like a bronco, trying to dislodge Brown Recluse. I closed the openings of the Omega suit's cowl with a thought. Just in time. Brown Recluse's hands brushed my now protected lips, right where bare skin had been an instant before. I was safe from his deadly touch. I had solved one problem, but added a new one —the Omega suit's thick, durable material now completely obscured my vision like I had been thrust into a dark cave. Breathing would be a problem, too, with my nostrils and mouth covered. Not that I had stopped holding my breath anyway because I was still engulfed in poisonous gas with the gas' generator clinging to my back like a deadly addiction. I'd heard of having a monkey on your back, but never a spider monkey.

Blood pounded in my head. I ached for breath like a

woman ached for her lover. I needed to breathe, especially since panic and exertion were depleting my body's already slim stores of oxygen.

Inspiration hit. If Brown Recluse wanted a piggyback ride so badly, I'd take him for a spin.

I began spinning in the air. Faster, faster, and faster I spun. In seconds I was going around and around like a top. So fast that I generated enough wind that the gas around me was dissipating. Brown Recluse shrieked in my ear for me to stop. *Yeah right,* I thought.

Brown Recluse's grip around me weakened, slipped, then fell away altogether. He was flung from me like a stone from a sling. His wail followed him like a jet's contrail. He careened into the window of a building across the street and smashed through it.

I slowed my spinning, then stopped. I wobbled as the world continued to spin without me. Super-equilibrium was not one of my powers. I re-opened my cowl and hastily took a breath. The air was fresh and clean. It was like drinking cool spring water after trudging through a desert.

A blast of energy exploded against my personal shield, rocking me. A Mad Dog energy ball. Another. Then another. Twin blasts of fire struck me, one from Iceburn, one from Elemental Man. Normally I would be able to absorb the energy from the blasts without batting an eye, but I had been through too much too quickly. An airborne SUV crashed into me, no doubt flung by Silverback. It was the last straw.

I fell from the air like a shot pigeon. I hit the roof of a van. Metal shrieked, plastic snapped, glass broke. The top of the van crumpled around me a stomped soda can. Then the flung SUV fell on top of the van, pinning me between it and the van.

Moments later, big hairy hands fished me out of the wreckage. Silverback held my limp body aloft with his huge hand around my neck. He shook me like a dog shaking a caught rat. My eyes were only half open.

"Never should have left town cuz of you. You ain't as tough as everybody thinks," Silverback rumbled. He poked me in the chest with a finger that felt like rebar. The fangs that jutted up from the bottom of his mouth like stalagmites made his voice almost indecipherable. Thick drool oozed from around them. *Oh Granny, what big teeth you have!* I thought hazily. His breath smelled like his mouth had never even heard of a toothbrush, much less used one. *Oh Granny, what bad breath do you have!*

My eyes snapped open.

"Wrong, stupid. I'm even tougher," I said. Though it was true I had been rocked, I had also been playing possum to catch my breath and to get close to one of the Rogues. I channeled some of the energy I'd absorbed from my recent impacts. I let it arc out of me, through Silverback's hand around my neck, and down through the rest of his body. There was the stench of burning flesh. Silverback howled in pain. It likely felt like I was electrocuting him. Silverback's clenched hand opened. He dropped me like a hot potato. I landed on my feet. I slammed my fist into Silverback's stomach. I really put my weight into it, not to mention a compressed blast of stored energy.

There was a loud pop, like a big firecracker exploding. Silverback flew backward as if he had been hit with a guided missile. His body arched up into the air. Then he fell dozens of feet away, hitting the street back-first. His big body skidded for a second, then began digging a shallow groove in the street. The street made terrific ripping sounds as Silverback barreled toward Mad Dog and Doctor Alchemy.

I had been aiming for them when I punched Silverback. Doctor Alchemy somersaulted out of the way in an incredible move that would have fit right in during the Olympics. Mad

Dog wasn't so fortunate. He was bowled over by Silverback and the ripped-up street. Mad Dog landed heavily on his side. I picked up a chunk of busted concrete with my powers and clocked him on the side of the head with it to ensure that he stayed down. He was immune to my force fields, but obviously not immune to an old-fashioned smack upside the head.

Silverback's barreling body came to a stop. Silence replaced the sound of his body tearing up the road. Dust hung in the air like fog. A mass of torn-up asphalt and dirt rose up behind Silverback's still and battered body like a headstone. *Here lies Silverback, KO'd by Omega,* I thought. *Rest in Pieces.*

"Who else wants some?" I exclaimed. Though it wasn't terribly catchy, maybe I was getting better at coining catchphrases. I hoped one of the spectators had recorded what I had done to Brown Recluse, Silverback, and Mad Dog. Exultation had replaced my earlier fear and panic. Six against one had been quickly slashed to three against one. Mad Dog was not moving. Silverback was also down for the count, as was Brown Recluse. I'd checked on the latter already with my telekinetic touch. He lay on the floor of the office suite he had been flung into, having been knocked cold by flying through its window.

Though I was not foolish enough to be cocky, I felt better about things. I was glad I had not called Myth, Truman, Ninja, or someone else for help. I did not need their help. I was Omega. I did not need anyone.

Doctor Alchemy's arms pointed in my direction. Two metal pellets the size of large caliber bullets shot out his gauntlets' tubes. They hurtled toward me. I tried to stop them, but couldn't. Whatever had made the Rogues immune to my telekinesis obviously operated on Doctor Alchemy's projectiles as well.

No matter. I had trained for combat relentlessly. Muscle

memory took over. I twisted to the side, dodging both missiles easily.

I was about to gloat about the mighty Doctor Alchemy missing when there were two small pops behind me. Then a giant whooshing sound. I was yanked off my feet. I was pulled back through the air, like a swimmer caught in a powerful riptide. Even trying to fly forward didn't work. I clawed the air, trying in vain to stop being pulled backward.

Debris from the street flew toward me, bounced off my shield, and then whipped past me with whizzing sounds. It felt like being caught on the business end of the hose of a giant, all-powerful vacuum cleaner. I glanced backward. I was being pulled toward a jagged hole that hung in the air like a helium balloon. About twice the diameter of a trash can lid, the hole floated several feet off the ground. The surface of the hole was so dark, it almost seemed to shimmer. Debris from the street flew into the hole. The debris disappeared as if it had never existed.

Doctor Alchemy had not missed after all. *Pride goes before a fall.* What a time to think of a Jamesism, one of the sayings my Dad had been so fond of using. The fact he was right did not make the Jamesism any less annoying.

Increasingly panicked, I dropped the massive force field I had maintained around me and the Revengers, hoping that jettisoning the mental distraction of holding the field in place would change my inability to stop being pulled toward the hole.

Nope. No dice.

My feet touched the surface of the hole. They meet with absolutely no resistance. The rest of my body followed, like I had been dropped off a bridge into a river.

I plunged into dark nothingness.

10

B efore my entire body was engulfed by darkness, my frantically groping, outstretched hands caught on . . . seemingly nothing, but definitely something tangible. I jerked to a stop, like a man falling from a building who grabs a ledge before hitting the ground. My arms and shoulders exploded in pain. They felt like they would rip free of my body as some invisible yet insistent force pulled relentlessly at me.

It was like being caught in a powerful wind tunnel. Only here—wherever here was—there was no sound of wind. There was no sound at all. I couldn't even hear my ragged breaths.

Darkness surrounded me. The only light came from the mysterious hole I had been pulled into and now apparently was on the other side of. I held onto the lip of the hole for dear life. It was like having fallen into a dark well, with my hands clutching the lip of the well's opening, only them keeping gravity from pulling me further down the well. In this case, a force far more powerful than mere gravity pulled relentlessly on me. It took every ounce of strength I had to hold on.

I saw Greene Street through the hole that my hands were on either side of. The street was blurry, like I viewed it through a dirty window. Trash, bits of building material, broken car parts, and other debris from Greene Street were still being pulled through the hole, slamming into my personal shield, bouncing off and past me as they traveled . . . where? I risked taking my total focus off of holding on to range outward with my telekinetic touch. Other than the debris streaming in from Greene Street, there was absolutely nothing here for as far as I could feel. It was like being in space, only without stars, planets, cosmic dust, light, or absolutely anything at all. A complete and total void.

Where was I? Why couldn't I fly out of here? The potions and other substances that Doctor Alchemy shot out of his gauntlets were said to be magic-based. Even with my prior interactions with Millennium, I was not sure I believed in magic. Some people thought what I could do was magic, and it most definitely was not. I had learned over the years that things which seemed fantastic at first usually could be explained by science and the application of reason. How, though, to explain where I was if it was not magic?

Magic or no magic, clearly the projectiles Doctor Alchemy had shot at me had done something. Created a bizarre illusion that seemed all too real? Ripped a hole through the fabric of reality? Opened a portal to another dimension? Something else entirely? I didn't know.

My hands slipped a touch, jarring me away from thoughts about where I was. Where I was wasn't important. Getting out of here before I slipped into oblivion was.

Except for my personal shield which stopped debris that shot out of the hole from clocking me over the head, my powers seemed otherwise useless. Only my grip on the edges of the hole kept me from being tossed deeper into wherever this was and perhaps being lost forever. I did not understand why my powers couldn't get me out of this. It did not matter. A caveman didn't have to understand how an acorn grew into an oak; it was more important for him to be able to climb that oak to escape a tiger.

Channeling my inner caveman, I strained, trying to pull myself out of here and back through the hole with naked brute strength. It was like doing a pull-up at the gym while someone incredibly strong simultaneously pulled on your legs.

At first, I did not move at all. Then, as I continued to strain, I slowly started to inch up. Or maybe it was forward. Hell, I could have been moving backward for all I knew. Direction seemed to have no meaning here. Except for the hole, there were no reference points in the inky blackness all around me. I did not know why my muscles could do what my far more potent powers could not, but I wasn't going to look a gift horse in the mouth. Maybe it had to do with the nature of magic. If it was magic.

Material sucked in from the other side of the hole continued to pound me. I struggled and strained, bringing my head increasingly closer to the hole. My muscles were on fire. They began to shudder. I was grateful the Academy had emphasized the importance of a Hero being in shape. Scrawny me never would have been able to pull himself up against the force that pulled at me. Not scrawny me was having a hard enough time doing it.

Finally, my head broke through the surface of the hole. My eyes were out of the hole. I was back on Greene Street. Though the day was still overcast, it was blindingly bright out here compared to how dark it had been in the hole. Straining, my body crept out of the hole bit by bit. My ears passed through the surface of the hole. Sound again. A cacophony of noise compared to the tomblike silence I had just left. Debris still pounded into me, bouncing off my shield and then into the hole. The parts of the street closest to the hole had been swept clean by the pulling force the hole generated, like the world's most thorough street sweeper had come along and worked his magic. Things outside of a maybe one hundred feet radius from the hole seemed to not be affected at all by it. Items within that radius but not super close to the hole were being pulled toward it, faster and faster the closer they got. The tires of a nearby hatchback squealed in protest as the small red car was dragged closer and closer to the hole.

Still straining mightily, I pulled myself out of the hole until I was free of it from the chest up. Suddenly, maddeningly, I hit the metaphorical wall. I stopped moving. My arms and shoulders shook like they were at ground zero of an earthquake. I was completely spent. As hard as I tried, I could not pull myself out further even the slightest bit. It was like trying to squeeze out one last bench press at the gym, but not being able to lift the barbell off your chest because your muscles were too fatigued.

At the gym, Isaac would be there to spot me, helping me lift the weight. He was not here to help me now. No one was.

A scream of pain and frustration escaped my lips. The part of my body that hung outside the hole started to creep incrementally back inside it despite my struggles. The icy hand of fear closed tighter around my feverishly beating heart. I knew that if I slipped back into the hole I would not have the strength or endurance to pull myself out again.

Part of a thick wooden sign zoomed over my head. The hole's pull must have dislodged it from a nearby business. The sign fragment smacked against the hole lengthwise, with the sign's length extending past the hole's circumference, covering the hole completely above where I struggled. Wood cracked in my ears as the hole pulled insistently on the stuck sign. It was almost imperceptible, but I felt a slight decrease of the intensity of the hole's pull on me.

Hope blazed like a rekindled fire within me. I pulled out several inches further.

Then, with loud popping sounds, the wood broke. The fragmented pieces were immediately sucked into the hole, uncovering it. I was jerked partially back into the hole, as if a giant had grabbed my legs and yanked me. While my head, neck, and shoulders were still free, I had lost all the progress I had made while the sign had been in place, plus more. One step forward, three steps back. The fire of my hope died down.

Died down, but it did not completely extinguish. I did not know why the sign partially covering the hole had the effect it did, but it most definitely had one. It gave me an idea.

I still had an iron grip on the sides of the hole. I risked moving my left hand slightly, activating my powers with the movement. My lessened grip on the hole made me slip further into it. Only my head was free now. I hoped the sacrifice was worth it.

I ripped the driver's side door off the red hatchback with my powers. I let the pull from the hole do the rest. I was too busy trying to not be swallowed by the hole like an ant being washed down a kitchen sink.

The door, free of the far heavier car, hurtled toward me like a bat out of hell. Right before it hit, I gave the spinning door a slight nudge with my powers to make sure it did not ram into me.

The door slammed into the hole above me with a crash and the shattering of glass. The glass was immediately sucked into the hole. The hard part of the door below the now empty window frame crinkled, shrieking in protest. But, it held. It partially blocked the hole. I felt the same lessening of the hole's tug that I had felt with the wooden sign.

Quickly, before the last of my strength drained away or before the door yielded to the hole's pull, I pulled myself almost completely free. I did not pull all the way out. I suspected if I did, I would simply be sucked right back in.

Now that I was out of the hole further, I could shift my grip more easily without risking plunging all the way into the hole. I moved my left hand, again activating my powers. This time I picked up the entire hatchback that was inexorably being dragged toward the hole. Its tires cleared the ground. Now airborne, free of the ground's resistance, the car shot toward me like it had been launched from a catapult.

Right when the car was about to slam into me, I yanked myself the rest of the way free of the hole. The underside of the rocketing car grazed me as it zoomed over me. The car smashed into the hole with a crash, like it had driven into a brick wall.

The pull from the hole instantly lessened. I fell to the ground. I released my personal shield, not because I wanted to, but because exhaustion and pain forced me to. My hands were cramping up after holding onto the edges of the hole for dear life. My arms felt like wet noodles set on fire.

I was underneath the car, which was suspended in midair. Loud crunching sounds assailed my ears as the hole sucked on the car like someone trying to suck an ice cube up through a straw. The front end of the car twisted, compressed, and partially disappeared into the hole, mangled by the force exerted on it. Glass and gasoline rained down on me. It was like being pelted by hail and drenched by a thunderstorm in a twisted nightmare. The gas got into my mouth and nose. I rolled out of the way, sputtering and choking.

The car shuddered, then stopped advancing into the hole.

Though there was still the sound of metal and plastic snapping, twisting and deforming, for now the car had plugged the hole, like a misshapen stopper shoved down the mouth of a drain. The car hung from the hole like a giant dart from a too small dartboard. The pull from the hole stopped, or at least it stopped pulling on everything except the car that was embedded in it.

My chest heaved with exhaustion and relief as I blinked gas out of my eyes. Unfortunately, this was not over. I still had three of the Revengers to deal with. The only things I wanted to deal with were a deep tissue massage to get the kinks out of my arms and shoulders, then a shower and a nap. You can't always get what you want.

11

I dragged myself to my feet. My arms and shoulders felt like lead weights nailed onto my torso with barbed spikes. The pain and the inability to easily move my arms told me I likely had torn muscles. Better torn muscles and alive than untorn muscles and dead.

I turned to face the remaining Revengers. They were further down the street, out of the range of the hellish hole. The perfect name for the thing then hit me: the hellhole. I was slow sometimes. No surprise I hadn't come up with a good catchphrase yet.

My eyes burned from the gasoline. My vision was blurry. I was lightheaded from overexertion and gas fumes. The Revengers' costumes were indistinct smears of garish colors.

"That all you got?" I called out to them. It was false bravado. My aching body belied my words. I was stalling, hoping to catch my breath before I was attacked again. My earlier cockiness had been knocked—no, sucked—right out of me by the hellhole. Wonderfully clever name, that. *If my Omega merchandise money ever runs low, I can get a side gig naming supervillain phenomena*, I thought. Then I thought that pain, exhaustion, and relief had made me slightly delirious.

I blinked hard. My vision started to clear. The time on the bank clock down the street told me I had been struggling with the hellhole for only a couple of minutes. It had seemed far longer than that. Time dripped like molasses in winter when you weren't having fun. I just invented that. First hellhole, now this. I was on a roll.

Doctor Alchemy, Elemental Man, and Iceburn were not alone. Four women and three men were on their knees, facing me, in front of the Rogues. I had a flashback from the hostages Amok had taken. Iceburn casually tossed a fireball back and forth between his hands like he was eager to play catch. I for one had no interest in playing. Neither did the people on their knees if the stricken and frightened looks on their faces were any indication. A little black girl wailed in fear, her arms wrapped around the neck of her kneeling mother. Her mother tried in vain to comfort her. It wasn't hard to figure out the Rogues had grabbed these people when I had dropped my force field that had cordoned the bystanders off. I bet these bystanders-turned-hostages wished they had run away when they had a chance instead of sticking around to gawk. I certainly wished they had.

"Submit Omega, or we will execute these people," Doctor Alchemy intoned in his heavily accented English. Both tubes from his gauntlets pointed at the kneeling people. If the situation weren't so screwed up, I might have been flattered the Rogues had thought there was a decent chance I would escape the hellhole. Why else take hostages?

If I were at one hundred percent, I could have whisked the hostages to safety with my powers. But thanks to the hellhole, I was far from one hundred percent. It was a supreme effort to move my arms and hands, and I needed the latter to use my powers. If I tried to use them to save the hostages, the Rogues would likely kill the kneelers before I barely moved.

On the other hand, if I surrendered, then what? Iceburn had said the Rogues were here to kill me. I took him at his word. As my conversation with Angel had made me realize, I was not afraid of death. I was however afraid of more people dying because of me. Not only the hostages, but also everyone else in the world if the major crisis the world faced the Sentinels had warned me about was true. If I surrendered to the Revengers and they killed me, what would happen to the world when the crisis hit and I was not around? My death would mean the Omega spirit would pass to someone else. What if that person was not ready to face the crisis? Hell, I didn't know if I was ready, and I had been struggling these past couple of years to get ready. Because of what was at stake, maybe my life was simply too valuable to give up in exchange for the lives of a handful of others. Weren't the lives of the many far more important than the lives of the few?

What if I surrendered and the Rogues killed the hostages anyway? And maybe, with me out of the way, they would not stop with just the hostages. There were far too many potential victims still on the street and looking out the windows of nearby buildings, watching the show. On the other hand, despite how crazy and homicidal Doctor Alchemy was, he had the reputation of being a man of his word.

"Shit," Elemental Man said, "the asshole is taking too long." He gestured upward, like a stage magician performing a feat of levitation. The asphalt under the mother and her crying child split open like an overheated hot dog. As I watched in horror, dirt from underneath the street rose, crawling up over the mother and child like an army of advancing ants. In seconds, they were completely covered. Their screams were cut off as if a switch had been flipped. The resulting mound of earth bore only a vague resemblance to two human beings, like a bad sculptor had amateurishly fashioned a girl and woman out of dirt.

"How long can the average person survive without air?" Elemental Man called out to me. "What's your precious Heroic training telling you? A few minutes without brain damage if you're calm and you've prepared yourself for the lack of oxygen. A lot less if you're not. My guess is these dumb cunts only have seconds." I wanted to wipe the smugness off his pretty boy face with a tire iron.

"You'll free the woman and the girl if I surrender? And you'll let everyone else go too?" I asked. My mind raced. There had to be a way out of this mess. I had been trained to believe there was a way out of any predicament, no matter how bleak it seemed. I just had to find it.

"Sure," Elemental Man said. I would sooner trust a spitting cobra.

"You have my word," Doctor Alchemy said. Him I believed more.

My mind groped for a solution that did not involve me or anyone else dying. It came up empty. I suddenly felt as deflated as a flat tire. It rankled to give myself up, especially to this lot: a rapist, my father's killer, and a homicidal maniac. But what choice did I have? Maybe it was true that the lives of the many were more important than the lives of the few, but I simply could not bear the thought of people dying because of me. Not again. Dad, Neha, Hannah . . . too many had died because of me already.

"Alright, I surrender," I said. I felt lower than a flea, and about as Heroic.

"Put your arms over your head, with your hands pressed together," Doctor Alchemy ordered. "If you so much as twitch a finger, everyone dies."

I did as he commanded. I moved slowly, both because my arms and shoulders were still on fire and because I was looking for an opportunity to get myself and everyone else out of this mess. Once my hands were over my head, Doctor Alchemy moved his hands away from the hostages, pointing them at me instead. Two projectiles shot out of the tubes attached to his gauntlets. It took every ounce of willpower to ignore my training and resist the instinct to move out of the way.

The projectiles hit my hands and exploded on impact. A black foam spread around my hands, wrapping around them like a boa constrictor. The foam hardened. In mere seconds, I could not do so much as wiggle my fingers. My fingers and hands were completely immobilized.

The first thing that surprised me was that I was not dead. I had assumed Doctor Alchemy would hit me with flesh-eating acid or something equally deadly and painful. Other than the initial sharp sting of the projectiles hitting my hands, my hands did not even hurt. Well, they did not hurt any more than they already had thanks to the hellhole.

The second thing that surprised me was that I was not able to use my powers. I could not activate them without moving my hands. As far as I had been aware, only I, Isaac, Neha, Athena, and the Old Man had known that. How in the world did Doctor Alchemy know?

"I surrendered like you asked," I said. "Now release the two you buried."

"Fuck you," Elemental Man said. Same old Hitler's Youth, as dishonest as the day was long. I started striding toward him. I wasn't the martial artist that Ninja was, but I had studied some savate. I would kick the crap out of Elemental Man until he freed his earth-bound prisoners.

Doctor Alchemy put his hand up for me to stop. "Let them go," he said to Elemental Man.

"Why? You've neutralized golden boy's powers already. There's nothing he can do to us. Let those two suffocate. It's just a nigger bitch and her crotch spawn. They don't matter. The world will be better off without them."

Doctor Alchemy lifted his arm again, pointing the barrel of his gauntlet at Elemental Man's head. He said, "I gave my word. Let them go. I will not tell you again."

Elemental Man eyed Doctor Alchemy's gauntlet sullenly and nervously.

"Fine," Elemental Man said, sounding like a petulant child. He lifted his hands again in the direction of the buried mother and child. The dirt covering them fell away like iron filings from an electromagnet that had lost its power. The uncovered woman blinked furiously and gasped loudly, hyperventilating. She clutched her child closer. As for the kid, she looked around with wide eyes, too shocked to start crying again.

"Go," Doctor Alchemy said to the hostages. Unlike Elemental Man, they did not have to be told twice. They scrambled to their feet and took off running. No one bothered to help up the mother, who was still freaking out. It took a helping—dare I say gentle?—hand from Doctor Alchemy to get her to her feet. She staggered after the others, carrying her shocked child.

Oh Omega, thank you so much for saving us from certain death! Now we'll return the favor and rush to your assistance. Said no one ever. The fleeing hostages were no different. They did not give me so much as a backward glance. *You're welcome*, I thought bitterly.

Iceburn, Elemental Man, and Doctor Alchemy walked toward me. This must be what it was like to face an advancing firing squad. I could run, and thought about it. But without my powers, I would not get further than a couple of steps before one of these Rogues cut me down. Besides, if someone was going to kill me, I was going to die facing him, not with my back to him like a coward. So, I stayed right where I was. On the upside, maybe I could break a bone or two with a couple of well-placed kicks before they killed me. The fact I had surrendered did not mean I was going to meekly submit to my fate like a lamb to the slaughter.

In the movies, a hero facing certain death has a quip at the ready. My mouth was dry, my brain empty. All my quips seemed to be out of stock. Like catchphrases and defeating a team of Rogues, I guess I was no good at them.

The Revengers surrounded me. Iceburn was about my height; the other two were much taller than I. They were close enough for me to smell Elemental Man's cologne. Who wore cologne to a Metahuman battle? The god-king of the pretty boy racist douchebags, that's who. He was to my side, closer to me than the other two. Arrogant and over-confident as ever. I eyed him with my peripheral vision. If my arms were fully functional, even with my hands bound, I was certain I could crush his windpipe with an elbow strike. Since they were not fully functional, I was fairly sure I could instead break his fibula with a well-placed kick. It would not kill him like a crushed windpipe might, but it would hurt like hell. I would take what I could get. Ever since Isaac had become my best friend, I had been especially sensitive to the use of the N-word. Not that I had been thrilled about it before Isaac had come along. Maybe a broken leg would teach Elemental Man to stop calling black people names, though I doubted it. It sure would make me feel better, however. I would be dead before I could turn my attention to the other two, but at least I would go down swinging. Kicking. Whatever.

"Kneel before your betters," Doctor Alchemy demanded. His eyes flashed maniacally. He was in front of me. Iceburn was to my right.

"Sure. As soon as you find me some of my betters, I'll kneel like a nun in church." Maybe I was better at quips than I thought.

"Mouthy asswipe," Elemental Man said. He threw a punch at my head. He telegraphed it almost as much as Viola had. I ducked, pivoted on my left foot, spun, and launching a kick with my right leg at his left quadricep, a couple of inches above his knee. My timing was off because of the stiffness of my arms and the fact my hands were bound together. Even so, my shin struck Elemental Man's leg like an axe chopping into a log.

Howling, Elemental Man went down like a felled tree. He grabbed his leg and writhed in pain. In my haste, I had hit his femur, not his fibula. I likely had not broken it because the femur was much stronger than the fibula, but I would take what I could get. The impact from the blow had made my teeth rattle; since he had been on the business end of the kick, it would take a while before Elemental Man was on his feet again.

Movement behind me. Iceburn. I turned. Made clumsy by sore arms and bound hands, I didn't move in time. He landed two blows on my back. Kidney shots, like the ones I had given Amok. Stunned, my body seized up. It felt like acid raced through my guts. A cry escaped my lips.

Iceburn grabbed me by the neck, making my back arch. He tried to force me to my knees. Through sheer pigheaded stubbornness, I willed myself to remain upright.

"You've handled yourself well, kid," Iceburn said into my ear. "I'm impressed. You've changed a lot since I last saw you.

Back then, I said you reminded me of me. Now you remind me even more of me."

"That hurts my feelings," I said through clenched teeth. It was hard to sound devil-may-care when it felt like your insides were trying to drip out of your anus.

Iceburn slipped a hand down my back. He pressed into where he had struck me. His hand got ice-cold. There was crackling and popping as ice formed on my back, spreading out from Iceburn's hand. Even through the protective layer of the Omega suit, it felt like being stabbed with a frozen dagger.

"Kneel like Alchemy said," Iceburn murmured in my ear. "He has a flair for the dramatic. It's not my style, but I work for him, not the other way around. The sooner you kneel, the sooner this will be over."

"Never!" I vowed through gritted teeth. "I'd rather die on my feet than live on my knees." That made no sense. I was going to die either way, but it was the first thing to spring to mind.

Iceburn pulled back slightly. He kicked me on the back of my legs, right behind my knees. My legs collapsed. I dropped heavily onto the hard street. Hot pain radiated up my legs, mingling with the icy pain in my back. It was with a herculean effort that I didn't fall over. I tried to rise, but couldn't. My body would not obey my brain, as if it belonged to someone else.

Panting, I looked up at Doctor Alchemy. He looked down at me the way an exterminator might look at a cockroach. Then he frowned, and turned to look at Elemental Man. He still twisted and cried with pain on the ground.

"Be quiet," Doctor Alchemy snapped. "Have some self-respect. You're whimpering like a mewling baby."

But Elemental Man did not stop. He raised such a ruckus, perhaps he had not heard the order. Doctor Alchemy frowned again in disgust. He raised his arm, pointing a gauntlet at Elemental Man. A projectile shot out of the gauntlet's barrel. It hit Elemental Man's body, exploding with a dull flash of light and a puff of smoke. His moans of pain stopped immediately. Elemental Man's writhing body froze in place, as if he were a movie that had been paused.

Doctor Alchemy turned back to me. He bent over me. His head blotted out the dim sun. With Iceburn holding me in place, Doctor Alchemy very carefully, deliberately, almost surgically, spit in my face.

This was not the first time I had been spat on. I had been bullied as a child, after all, and had tangled with some bullies whose go-to move was to spit on you. Even so, having a grown man spit on you was startlingly offensive. On my knees, unable to get up, in danger of toppling over, and without my powers, I felt as helpless now as I had when I was a bullied kid.

My mouth had been open and some of Doctor Alchemy's spit had gotten in. "Refreshing," I said, breathing hard, speaking with effort, "but if given the choice, I'd prefer water. You don't by any chance have some squirreled away in that Halloween costume of yours? I'm parched, and that little spritz from you isn't cutting it."

Doctor Alchemy acted as if I had not spoken. Water-hoarding bastard.

"You killed my daughter," he said. His tone was calm, almost conversational. He sounded as gentle as he had looked when he had helped that mother to her feet.

Sudden anger at his words gave me a surge of energy. Neha's death was a wound that had never healed. "No, I didn't," I said hotly. "The Sentinels killed her. I tried to save her."

Doctor Alchemy slapped me so hard my head spun

around.

"Lies!" he screamed. The calmness was gone, instantly replaced by maniacal rage. Spittle was on his lips; his eyes blazed with anger. He grabbed me by the throat. His fingers dug into me. "You let her die to keep us apart. You knew that once we were reunited, no one in the world could stand against us."

"You are what kept the two of you apart," I croaked. "Neha didn't want any part of your crazy schemes."

"How dare you speak her name!" Doctor Alchemy screamed in my face. He slapped me again, so hard I tasted blood. "You keep her name out of your filthy, lying mouth!" The third slap knocked me over. My head cracked against the pavement. My vision dimmed. I threatened to black out. Doctor Alchemy's swift kick to my side brought me back to full consciousness. My mind exploded red with pain.

Doctor Alchemy went berserk, kicking, stomping, punching me, all while screaming at me in a hodgepodge of English, Hindi, and Gujarati. Thanks to my time with Neha, I understood snatches of the non-English. Mostly curse words and racial slurs.

Immobilized by pain and by my hands being bound, I could not protect myself, much less fight back. The Omega suit protected me some, but not enough. Surely some bystander was recording this and would upload the footage to UWant Video. I wondered if the sales of my Omega merchandise would take a hit. It's strange the things you think about when you're being beaten to death.

It was only when I heard Iceburn's voice that I realized he had pulled Doctor Alchemy off me.

"Unhand me," Doctor Alchemy demanded, his eyes wild. Iceburn's arms were around his waist. Though not close enough to strike me anymore, he still angrily kicked the air. "You dare soil the person of the great Doctor Alchemy?"

"I signed up to kill the kid, not beat him to a pulp," Iceburn said. He sounded disgusted. If it hadn't been for the fact he had killed Dad, I might have been grateful. "Plus, you hear those sirens? They mean that the higher-ups you paid off in police headquarters couldn't stall anymore. And if the cops are on the way, another cape is likely not too far behind. Stop screwing around with the kid, finish him, and we'll collect the others and get out of here. I'm not going to prison again."

I heard sirens too, though I had supposed they were merely the product of wishful thinking and having my bell repeatedly rung. Iceburn's words explained why none of the authorities had shown up yet. It was not as though our fight had been quiet and in an out-of-the-way place. The good old Astor City Police Department, as corrupt as ever. One would think cops would love me since we were both on the side of law and order. One would be wrong. I'd heard through the grapevine that a lot of cops were none too happy about the Omega Effect. Crime being down meant lower budgets and lower pay.

Through eyes half-swollen shut, I saw the crazed look slide off Doctor Alchemy's face. He shrugged out of Iceburn's embrace. Doctor Alchemy tugged at his costume, smoothing its lines, making himself presentable, as if he was about to walk on stage and accept an award.

"You're quite right," Doctor Alchemy said, as calm as he been crazed moments before. He patted Iceburn on the shoulder with the demeanor of a man patting his favorite dog. "Ever the professional, as always. So unlike our comatose colleagues. There will be a place for you when I assume my rightful place as ruler of the world."

"Imagine my excitement," Iceburn said dryly. If Doctor

Alchemy noticed Iceburn's sarcasm, he gave no sign of it. Doctor Alchemy was one way one moment and so completely another way the next moment, that I wondered if he had a multiple personality disorder. I only wondered that vaguely, though. Mostly, I was past caring.

Get up! something deep inside of me said urgently.

You get up if you think getting up is so awesome, I retorted. But neither of us did. We couldn't. We tried.

Doctor Alchemy raised his arm and pointed a gauntlet at me. Lying under the business end of it, its barrel looked as big as a cannon's muzzle.

"Know that you are dying because of Neha Thakore. She was my princess, and would have been the world's. If not for you," Doctor Alchemy said. He sounded like a judge delivering a sentence. I supposed he was.

I looked up at Doctor Alchemy, unable to do more than twitch ineffectually and watch. If I were a superhero worth his salt, I would have something to say as last words. Something clever. Memorable. Quotable. Noble. Heroic. But absolutely nothing came to mind. It had been one of those days. Next time, I would have something ready.

Then I remembered:

Next time. Ha!

They say your life flashes before your eyes when you were about to die. I can report that nothing of the sort happens. Or at least it did not with me. Instead, I found myself wondering how the Revengers had gotten together, how the ones who had been in prison had gotten out, and how Iceburn was not paralyzed anymore. I thought of the great crisis the Sentinels had spoken of, and how I hoped the next vessel for the Omega spirit would be ready to deal with it. I thought of Angel, and hoped he would be able to turn his life around. I thought of Viola, and hoped she had gotten away safely. I thought of

Truman, and what he might have done differently if he rather than I was in this predicament. I thought of my son James and how very real he still seemed. I thought of Isaac, and how he wouldn't come up short if he needed memorable last words. He probably had a list of options written out and taped to his refrigerator, just in case.

And, I thought of the people who had entered the great beyond before me and that perhaps I would see again soon: Hammer, Mom, Dad, Hannah, and Neha.

I thought about how the last three had died because of me. I had failed them all. Just as I was failing the rest of the world now.

The world became an impressionist painting through my tears. I was thinking about how a real Hero would not cry when Doctor Alchemy shot me.

The blurred world faded away, and then was gone.

PART II

12

Eighteen Years Ago

Ajeet Thakore knew something was terribly wrong the moment he opened the door of his Wilmington, Delaware home.

The front door had been unlocked. That in itself was unusual. The Thakores did not live in a bad neighborhood, but it was not the best either. They were always careful to keep the doors locked to guard against casual thieves and junkies looking for a quick and easy score in their working-class neighborhood in the Ninth Ward.

Ajeet now stood in his living room. It had been ransacked. Normally it was as neat as a pin thanks to his wife's constant tidying. Chairs were turned over; upholstery had been cut open; holes had been bashed through the walls; books had been pulled off shelves and ripped apart. The family's Hindu altar in the corner of the room had been swept clean and smashed apart. The things normally on the altar littered the floor, torn apart or smashed: tinsel, colored lights, photos of family members both living and dead, and figurines of Hindu

gods adorned with swastikas, ancient Hindu symbols of goodness and prosperity that had been appropriated and warped
into symbols of hate by the Nazis.

The rich smell of curries, Indian spices, and cooked
vegetables did not assault Ajeet's nostrils and make his mouth
water the way the aroma had every evening after work since
his and Rati's arranged marriage twelve years before in their
native state of Gujarat, India. Theirs was a traditional Indian
marriage, with Ajeet working outside the home and Rati
working inside it. Ajeet could not remember a time he had
ever come home after work without the smell of a freshly
made traditional Gujarati meal to greet him, even when Rati
had been sick and he had urged her to stay in bed instead of
toiling over a hot stove. Rati took her wifely duties very seriously. It was but one of the many things Ajeet loved about her.
The absence of the smell of freshly cooked food was in its way
even more alarming than the disarray of the living room.

Was whoever had ransacked the living room still in the
house? Ajeet silently cursed the fact his Alchemist gauntlets
were locked away in his secret underground bunker beneath
the tool shed. Was there time to dart outside and get them?

No. What if Rati or their daughter Neha was in danger?
There was no time to waste.

Suddenly sweaty with anxiety, Ajeet's thick and heavy
glasses slipped down his nose. He pushed them back into
place. Ajeet reached into the pocket of his work slacks. He
pulled out the two metal pellets he always kept on himself in
case of an emergency, even when he was not wearing his
Alchemist costume. Ajeet called these pellets and the others
like them his alchemy cartridges. The size of a medium-sized
grape and not much heavier, each pellet was shaped vaguely
like a bullet, except each end was tapered, coming to a dull
point. Like a bullet's, the pellets' shape was for purposes of

aerodynamics, so they would go where Ajeet aimed them when he shot them from the cartridges in his thick gauntlets. Despite its small size, the pellet now in Ajeet's left hand contained enough gas to knock out a roomful of people; the other in his right contained enough explosive to blow through the toughest of bank vaults.

That was Ajeet's sole Metahuman power—he could make a container, regardless of its size, hold any amount of a substance. Years ago, when his powers had first manifested when he was a teenager in India, he had filled a thimble with several bathtubs full of water while barely increasing the weight of the thimble. Even all these years later, Ajeet had no idea how his powers worked. Did he open up a pocket wormhole in containers, allowing them to hold far more than their size would normally allow? Did he send the container's excess to another dimension? Create some sort of singularity in the fabric of space? It did not matter. The fact that his powers worked did. And, with the Philosopher's Stone, he could create a wide variety of substances with various effects to fill his custom-made metal pellets with.

Ajeet had not registered as a Metahuman with the federal government under the Hero Act of 1945 as he had been legally required to do when he immigrated to the United States with Rati and baby Neha a few years ago. In India, Metas had a habit of disappearing in the dead of night. It was an open secret the government kidnapped Metas to experiment on them, hoping to unlock the secrets of their powers. The United States' government was not nearly as corrupt as the Indian government, but why take a chance? As a result, Ajeet had kept quiet about his powers. Only Rati knew about them. He kept no secrets from his beloved wife.

So, technically, under the terms of the Hero Act, Ajeet was a criminal. A Rogue. The fact he used his powers to rob businesses as the costumed adventurer named the Alchemist made him more than just technically a criminal. Ajeet did not think of himself as a criminal, though. In his mind, he was just a guy who used his abilities and the substances formulated with the Philosopher's Stone to supplement his meager income as a chemical technician at Burke Pharmaceuticals. Nobody got hurt during his robberies. Ajeet made careful sure of that. Even the businesses he hit would be made whole by their insurance. No harm, no foul.

With dread increasing its icy grip around his heart as he stood in his vandalized living room, Ajeet struggled to flip the tiny latch on each pellet to arm them. His fingers were damp with sweat, clumsy with anxiety and fear. Normally the mechanism in the barrels attached to his Alchemist gauntlets automatically armed the pellets the instant they were fired.

Finally, his fingers quivering, he managed to arm the pellets. Now they would explode the instant they hit something. His throwing arm was not as accurate or as powerful as his gauntlets, but it would have to do.

Emboldened by the fact he could now defend himself, Ajeet stepped through the living room. His senses were heightened, alert to any hint of danger.

"Mother?" he called out for Rati in Gujarati. The only time the couple called each other by their given names was when they were cross with each other, which had only occurred a handful of times over the years. "Neha?"

No answer. No sound. No movement. The house was as still as a grave.

The kitchen was in the same state of disarray as the living room. As was the downstairs bathroom and the small dining room. As quietly as he could, Ajeet crept up the stairs to the sleeping quarters.

There was no sign of life in the upstairs bathroom. The

shower curtain had been pulled down, the lid to the commode's tank pulled off and broken, and the medicine cabinet emptied and torn off the wall.

There was also no one in Neha's room. A complete mess, it too had been searched sloppily and violently.

Ajeet found Rati in their bedroom. Like the rest of the house, the bedroom had been torn apart. It was not the only thing that had been torn apart.

Ajeet's world crashed down around him.

Rati lay faceup on the bed in a pool of her own blood. Her thick limbs were twisted, contorted, like a discarded puppet's. Her face was battered, obviously beaten. Her right eye was swollen shut. The other, unnaturally red, stared lifelessly up at the ceiling. Much of her long black hair had been ripped out. It was scattered in her blood like macabre confetti. Her traditional sari had been ripped from her body. Its fragments lay on the floor. The matching petticoat and short beige blouse she wore underneath the sari had been torn, almost to shreds, exposing Rati's plump flesh. As a traditional Indian woman, Rati valued gold jewelry. The rings, earrings, necklaces, and nose ring that she so loved and always wore had been stripped off her and were nowhere to be seen. Her skin, normally olive, was discolored, splotched brown, black and red. Her legs were spread. Her genitals, raw and bloodied, gaped open. She had been shot at least twice in the chest. With all the blood, it was hard to tell.

Ajeet fell to his knees, stricken, overwhelmed, light-headed, unable to breathe, unable to think, all else forgotten. The armed cartridges almost slipped from his limp fingers. The explosive one would have destroyed the room and much of the rest of the house.

Rati had been a rail-thin, raven-haired beauty when they had first met in India after their betrothal. Though Rati's figure had thickened and matured over the years, Ajeet had worshipped every belly roll, every stretch mark, every wrinkle, every gray hair, every lump of cellulite. They were mute reminders of the happy years they had spent together, and of the beloved child they had created together. To him, Rati always had been beautiful, a work of art made flesh.

Whoever had done this had mutilated that work of art. Defiled her. Desecrated her. Destroyed the only woman he had ever loved. The only woman he *would* ever love.

Ajeet sobbed so hard he almost choked. Fat tears rolled down his cheeks, hitting the wood floor like raindrops. Salty mucus bubbled out of his nose, dripping into his mouth.

The small sound of whimpering, like that of a wounded and frightened animal, pierced through his grief. Could it be? Sudden hope gave him wings. He flew to the bed, checking for a pulse.

Hope was dashed on the hard rock of reality. Rati's body was as cold and lifeless as it appeared.

Then who?

Neha. In his shock and grief over Rati, Ajeet had forgotten all about his 6-year-old daughter.

He called for Neha, loudly. No response. The whimpering continued. It came from inside the room, though he could not tell from where and he did not see anyone. His ears were stopped up. He blew his nose messily on this sleeve, clearing his nose and ears.

The closet! Ajeet flung the ajar door wide open. Whoever had searched the bedroom had not skipped the closet. The shoes and clothes had been yanked out and tossed on the bedroom floor. The closet seemed as bare as the soul of whomever had done this to Rati. Yet the whimpering was louder here.

Ajeet crouched down. He reached toward the back corner

of the closet, where the whimpering seemed to come from. His hand met with fabric and warm flesh, though his eyes still saw nothing but an empty corner. Whatever he had brushed against recoiled from his touch, shrinking in the other direction. The whimpering got louder. A child crying.

"Neha?" Ajeet said wonderingly, his mind awhirl, in shock, not understanding what was going on. Then what was happening finally penetrated his mind. It had been made dull and sluggish by the horror of seeing Rati.

Ajeet stood, stumbling over the debris on the floor. With trembling, grief-stricken hands, he disarmed the alchemy cartridges he carried before he dropped one or both and made an already horrific situation worse. Trying hard to not look at his wife, knowing doing so would overwhelm him again, he started shifting through the things strewn on the floor.

After several minutes searching, he found what he was looking for: another alchemy cartridge, this one of several he normally kept in the drawer of the bedroom nightstand. The drawer had been pulled out and emptied. This particular cartridge had rolled under the radiator. He knew it was the one he wanted because there was a raised code stenciled on each cartridge, similar to the bumps and ridges of braille, that told him the substance each cartridge contained. Without looking at or touching the stenciling, it would be impossible to tell what the cartridges contained as each appeared identical.

Ajeet took the found cartridge and picked up a drinking glass from the nightstand. Incredibly, the glass had not been knocked over and broken. He popped the cartridge open. He poured its neon green contents into the glass, careful to not let any of it spill on him. Despite how small the cartridge was, thanks to Ajeet's powers, the thick liquid inside of it filled the tall glass halfway.

Ajeet went back to the closet with the glass. "Drink this,

baby," he said in Gujarati, extending the glass to the still-whimpering presence in the closet. "It won't taste good, but you need to get it all down."

After a slight hesitation, something took the glass from Ajeet's hand. As if by magic, the glass lowered, and tilted. The whimpering disappeared. The liquid inside of the glass slowly drained out, seemingly disappearing into thin air.

Ajeet had realized Rati must have dosed Neha with some of his invisibility potion, which he had also kept a cartridge of in the nightstand drawer in case of an emergency. Rati must have done it to hide Neha from whomever had torn the house apart and brutalized her. Neha had just drunk the antidote to the potion.

The seemingly empty air in the closet's corner started to shimmer. Then, Neha's 6-year-old body hazily appeared, translucent at first, then more and more opaque with each passing moment. Soon, she was fully visible again.

With her olive skin, silky black hair, and deep-set brown eyes, Neha was a miniature version of her dead mother. Looking at that resemblance now made Ajeet's heart ache. The only feature of his the child had seemed to inherit was his hook nose. Neha's thin arms clutched her Lady Justice doll. She hugged the doll to her chest like it was a talisman. Lady Justice of the Sentinels had always been her favorite Hero.

Neha was dressed in a pink tee shirt and shorts. Her shorts were soiled. Due to his roiling emotions and the foul smell coming from his dead wife, Ajeet had not noticed until now the smell of urine and excrement in the closet. Neha's normally well-groomed long hair was wild and askew, but not as wild as her eyes. Her skin was pale. She looked both like a ghost and like she had seen one.

Despite his gentle urging, Neha would not come to him. She cowered in the corner, like a frightened animal. She would not even speak. A precocious and extremely bright child, normally it was hard to get her to sit still or be quiet. Neha was obviously in shock. Ajeet guessed she had watched what had happened to her mother through the slats in the closet door. She was traumatized by what she had seen.

Ajeet wanted nothing more than to curl up in the corner with his daughter and comfort both her and himself. Then hot anger bubbled up within him, breaking through the thick miasma of his grief. No! There was time for grieving later. First, Ajeet had to find out who had done this to his beloved. And why? Was it merely a simple robbery gone awry? Other than Rati's gold, nothing seemed to be missing, though it was impossible to tell for sure with the mess that had been made of the house. In light of how the house had been ransacked, had the vandals been looking for something? The Philosopher's Stone sprang to mind. Only a handful of people alive knew of its existence, though. Of those, only Rati and Ajeet knew it was hidden on their property.

Regardless of why someone had come into their home, the way Rati had been brutalized made no sense. Rati would not hurt a butterfly. Wherever she went, that place was better because of it. She did not have an enemy in the world. Quite the opposite. Everyone loved her. She was warm and open, whereas Ajeet was reserved and standoffish. The yin to his yang. Literally his better half.

Ajeet did not even think about calling the police. The fact he engaged in criminal activity as Alchemist did not factor into that. Rather, he knew the most the police would do would be to arrest his wife's murderers and put them in jail. Ajeet did not want them arrested. He did not want them in jail. He wanted them dead. He wanted to hurt them. Mutilate them. Brutalize them. Debase them. Treat their bodies as just so much meat. Just as they had done to his sweet, golden Rati.

Suddenly needing to hold his daughter close, Ajeet pulled Neha out of the corner. At first she resisted, clawing like a wildcat, pushing away from him, wailing at such a high pitch that his ears hurt. Then, abruptly, Neha dropped Lady Justice. She clutched her father as tight as her small arms would let her. She sobbed long guttural sobs that stabbed at Ajeet's already broken heart. Her tears dripped on his work shirt, where they mingled with his own.

They held each other for a long while. Adult and child, father and daughter, widower and orphan. Some helpless, desperate impulse made Ajeet sing her the Gujarati lullaby that Rati always sang Neha to sleep with. No. It was the lullaby Rati *used to* sing Neha to sleep with.

The song comforted neither of them. It made them cry all the harder.

Something deep inside of Ajeet darkened and hardened. Oaths and curses swirled in his fevered mind.

Wherever they were, whatever it took, however long it took, Ajeet swore to make the vermin who had done this pay.

On all the gods above, on his love for Rati, on their child's life, he swore it.

13

Eighteen Years Ago

After a while, it penetrated Ajeet's shell-shocked mind that sitting here in the closet with Neha was not doing her any good with her mother's stiffening body merely feet away. Equally important, sitting here was not doing Rati's murderers any ill.

Ajeet stood. Neha was still glued to his body like she was afraid he would suffer the same fate her mother had.

First, he went to the bathroom. He peeled Neha's soiled clothes off and threw them in the trash. He washed her, quickly but thoroughly. He put clean clothes on her he got from the garments that had been dumped on her bedroom floor. Throughout all this, Neha took absolutely no initiative. She was like a mannequin whose limbs he had to move for anything to happen. Aside from crying and sniffling, she remained completely mute, staring at her father with wild eyes.

With Neha riding his hip—she refused to walk, as if she had forgotten how—Ajeet left their white clapboard house.

He looked around carefully, suspicious of every shadow. It was fall, and the leaves on the trees around the house being mostly gone made it easy to see if there was anyone lurking around their suburban house. Everything around the house and on their street seem normal. Ajeet did not see anyone or anything that did not belong.

He hastened to the backyard where a dilapidated tool shed stood. Its wood had turned white and gray with age and weathering. Despite how run-down the exterior was, Ajeet kept the small building's interior neat and clean. It was neat and clean no longer. Tools, electrical components, and hoses had been pulled from their places on the walls and dumped on the warped wooden floor. Obviously the same people who had been in the house had been here.

With Neha still balanced on his hip—she started screaming whenever he tried to put her down—Ajeet bent over and pulled at a loose floorboard here, pushed another one there and then there, and then stuck his finger in a knot-hole in the corner. There was an audible click when the last step of the sequence was complete. A section of the wood in the center of the shed rose slightly and then slid to the side, exposing a metal hatch. Ajeet pulled the hatch open. Lights automatically came on in his underground bunker. It was hard to squeeze through the narrow opening with Neha attached to his hip, but Ajeet did it. He closed the hatch, which would trigger the floor above it to shift and conceal the entryway again. Ajeet climbed down the short ladder to the floor of the bunker. Its ceiling was just barely taller than he was.

Ajeet glanced around the cramped underground space. Its walls were made of concrete. The portable metal fabricator he used to construct his gauntlets and the cartridges they contained was in the far corner, as were the gauntlets themselves and a box of cartridges full of various substances. Other than those items, the bunker contained books, charts, beakers, test tubes, scales, measuring devices, other scientific equipment, and various chemicals. It looked like a chemist's lab, which was exactly what it was. Nothing had been disturbed. Clearly whoever had ransacked the house and the tool shed had not discovered this space. Ajeet was relieved to see everything was as he had left it, including the Philosopher's Stone.

Ajeet flushed with shame at the thought. *I'd give a thousand Philosopher's Stones to have Rati back*, he thought. There were not a thousand of them, of course. There was only one Philosopher's Stone, the stuff of legends that was all too real. It had been passed down to the firstborn male in Ajeet's family since time immemorial. Ajeet would eventually have given it to his own son, had the gods seen fit to bless him and Rati with one. His stomach twisted at the thought. That would never happen now. Neha would have to be both son and daughter.

Ajeet nose wrinkled as it always did when he entered his bunker. The smell of decades of urine and feces lingered here, as if it had been baked into the watertight concrete walls. Ajeet's bunker had originally been a septic tank, before Ajeet and Rati had even bought the property, back before the neighborhood had grown to sufficient size to justify it being linked to the city's sewage system. When Ajeet bought the house, he had seen the potential in the then-unused septic tank as a place to create the substances he used as Alchemist. He had hired a firm to pump the septic tank out. Then he had used a solvent he had formulated with the help of the Philosopher's Stone to scrub the septic tank completely clean. The substance had eaten away the residue of the waste material like a swarm of locusts feeding on a farmer's crops, leaving the concrete walls of the septic tank looking as clean as the day the tank had been built. A bit of the potent smell lingered, though, no matter what Ajeet did.

Ajeet peeled Neha off of him. She squirmed, clearly uncomfortable with the strange, smelly environment. Ajeet had never brought her down here before today. Ajeet's reasoning had been that what she did not know about, her childish tongue could not tattle about. Ajeet sat her on the hard floor next to a workbench. She promptly started wailing. She shrank against the wall, clutching a leg of the bench like it was a lifeline. Her wild eyes looked at Ajeet with hurt accusal, as if he was abandoning her. The look cut Ajeet to the quick, but he needed his hands free.

Ajeet tugged on a pair of tight lambskin gloves. He never wore gloves made of an artificial material when concocting a substance with the Philosopher's Stone. For reasons Ajeet did not quite understand, artificial materials wrought havoc with the substances created with the Philosopher's Stone.

He turned to the Philosopher's Stone, which lay on a wooden table. It was not a jewel as ignorant Hindu tradition said. It certainly was not a mere stone as even more ignorant Western traditions and legends said.

Rather, it was a book.

A massive and thick brown tome with many hundreds of pages, the Philosopher's Stone was about three feet long and two feet wide. Made of animal skin and parchment, it was written in an ancient Sanskrit dialect and suffused with an even more ancient magic. Its Sanskrit title roughly translated into *The Philosopher's Stone*. Hence the name that had been passed down through millennia of myths and legends. According to family lore, one of Ajeet's distant ancestors, a great and powerful alchemist, had written the book. That ancestor had memorializing in the book's pages a lifetime of scholarship, learning, and unlocking the secrets of the universe. According to a competing family legend, that distant ancestor had been nothing more than a thief and whore-monger who had stolen the book while its true author had been preoccupied between the legs of a member of the whore-monger's inventory.

Ajeet vastly preferred the former version of the story.

Regardless of the truth of the book's origins, application of the book's secrets had enabled Ajeet's ancestors to become rich and powerful. He was the descendant of a long line of kings, emperors, and conquerors. Even Ajeet's Gujarati last name of Thakore translated into *ruler*, a surname no doubt adopted by a literal-minded ancestor of Ajeet's who had possessed more power than he had imagination.

The problem was that the son of a great man was rarely great. Over millennia, the energy and initiative of Ajeet's family dwindled and faded. The family had grown softer with each passing generation, resting on the laurels of their ances-tors and coasting on their achievements rather than struggling to equal or surpass them. Inherited achievement threw cold water on the fire in the belly necessary for continued achieve-ment. Over time, Ajeet's family believed more and more they were rulers simply because they were Thakores and they deserved to rule by simple birthright, rather than them under-standing their power derived from and largely relied on the use of the Philosopher's Stone.

Inevitably, the power of the Thakores slowly faded over the course of centuries. Now, all that remained of the Thakores being rulers was their name. Ajeet's immediate ancestors had merely been small shopkeepers and struggling merchants. The ability to read the dead language the Philoso-pher's Stone was written in and the technical skill to create the substances it described were lost to dusty history. In fact, the last several generations of Ajeet's family had not even really believed the tales of the Philosopher Stone's power. They thought it was merely an old wives' tale, some long dead family storyteller's attempt to explain why a dusty old book of gibberish had been handed down from generation to generation.

Ajeet had believed the stories, though, when they had been told to him as a small child. They set fire to his imagination, appealing to his sense of adventure and desire to stand out. To be special. Ajeet's father Nanku gave him the Philosopher's Stone on his seventh birthday. Though Nanku had told Ajeet he was being gifted the book as part of the family's grand tradition and in recognition of the fact that Ajeet would soon become a man, in reality Nanku had given his son the book because he was too stingy to buy an actual gift and to get Ajeet off his back, who by that point pestered his father about the book day and night.

From that moment on, Ajeet had devoted his life to unlocking the book's mysteries. It was why he had studied ancient Sanskrit obsessively, ruining his eyes pouring over ancient texts. Growing up, he had spent countless hours and what little money he had traveling all over India, haunting dusty bookstores, libraries, and private collections with stacks of long-forgotten books sealed shut from disuse to teach himself the dead dialect the Philosopher's Stone was written in. It was why he had studied chemistry, earning a PhD in that field from Dharmsinh Desai University in Gujarat.

Ajeet had achieved some level of success with all his studying. He was the first Thakore in hundreds of years to understand enough of the Philosopher's Stone to make some of the simpler substances described in its pages: explosives, acids that would eat the toughest of substances, knockout gases, sleeping potions, the invisibility potion Neha had drunk, and others. Ajeet had not unlocked all of the Philosopher Stone's secrets, however. Not even close. There were tantalizing descriptions in the book of mind-blowing substances: love potions, a liquid that would transmute objects into solid gold, healing elixirs, beverages giving their drinker superhuman strength and endurance, gases that would turn people into stone, and so many others. Ajeet's understanding of ancient Sanskrit was not advanced enough for him to successfully make those more complex substances. Precision and exactness were all-important. Add an unnecessary extra gram of a component to a potion, and the drinker who was trying to heal himself would instead go mad, or his limbs would shrivel and fall off, or his blood pressure would increase so dramatically that he would explode, or something equally horrific. Mistranslate a formula, and the pebble you were trying to make impossible to pick up would collapse in on itself and take an entire city along with it.

It was beyond frustrating to Ajeet that he could not yet create the more complicated substances described in the Philosopher's Stone. He was convinced they held the key to him recapturing the glory of his illustrious ancestors, the ones who had made the world tremble at the sound of the name Thakore. Without those substances, he was stuck working in a low-status job, under the supervision of people far less educated than he. His doctorate from an Indian university was not respected here in the United States. Sometimes he regretted immigrating here, the so-called land of opportunity. Yes, there were plenty of opportunities if you were white and connected to the right people, but Ajeet was neither. His job as a chemical technician at Burke Pharmaceuticals had been the best one he could get to support his family. The whites he worked under made fun of him. Including his supervisor Oliver Meaney, a British national who, like Ajeet, had immigrated to America.

DARIUS BRASHER

Ajeet's coworkers didn't think he knew how they talked about him behind his back, but he did. They made fun of his name, his accent, his dark skin, his clothes, his coke-bottle glasses, and the way Rati's deliciously pungent cooking made him smell. They called him Apu behind his back, after the brown-skinned *Simpsons* character who spoke with a heavy Indian accent. Provincial dolts. Ajeet's family was conquering empires when their European ancestors were huddling in caves, picking lice off each other, and trying to master fire. He hated them. One day, he would show them who the superior was and who was the inferior. The contempt they showed for Ajeet and the resentment he in return had for them was one of the reasons he had used his powers and the Philosopher's Stone to steal as the Alchemist. In the Alchemist's all-black costume and ski mask, he felt powerful. Like one of his conquering ancestors.

Ajeet thought he had come up with a means of understand the Philosopher Stone's more complicated formulas. He was almost certain an elixir he had carefully concocted over the course of many weeks with the book's help would boost his intelligence immeasurably, allowing him to decipher the many secrets of the book that still eluded him. *Almost certain* were the operative words. He was not positive he had gotten the formula exactly right. He had made the mistake of telling Rati about the elixir. Whether or not he should drink it was one of the few things they had ever fought about. Rati had made him swear to not drink the elixir.

"It's too dangerous," she had said. Though it pained him to do so, he had given her his word he would not drink the elixir. The purple liquid, glowing with an inner fire, sat in a stoppered beaker next to the Philosopher's Stone. It had been there for weeks. Despite giving Rati his word, Ajeet had not had the heart to throw the substance out.

Ajeet pushed thoughts of the purple elixir aside. Trying to ignore Neha's incessant wails so he could concentrate, he opened the Philosopher's Stone, and got to work. He thought he could get the potion he had in mind right without consulting the book, but better safe than sorry. He could not afford to make a mistake.

Ajeet mixed the correct chemicals together in their proper proportions and in the proper order as dictated by the Philosopher's Stone. When he finished about half an hour after he had begun, he had a small wooden bowl about a quarter full of a mud brown liquid.

Ajeet took the bowl to Neha. She still sat clutching the table, still howling. Ajeet felt perverse pride at her lung capacity.

"Drink this baby," he said, trying to bring the bowl to her lips. "It will make you feel better." Neha swatted the bowl away, nearly spilling its contents. Ajeet cursed, making Neha cry all the louder. It was worse than nails on a blackboard. His pride in her lung capacity began to fade.

After much coaxing and soothing, Ajeet finally got Neha to swallow the contents of the bowl, though it took almost as long as it had to make the stuff. A few moments after she swallowed the potion, she stopped crying. Her breathing returned to normal. Her eyelids drooped, though they did not close completely. The potion was a mild sedative which also had a hypnotic effect.

Ajeet squatted on the floor in front of his now quiet daughter.

"Can you hear me baby?"

"Yes Papa," Neha said. Despite how sleepy she appeared, her voice was strong and clear.

"Can you answer some questions for me?"

"Depends on what they are." Neha's arch tone suggested

he had asked a stupid question. Sometimes he wished his daughter was not quite so precocious.

"When you were in the closet in Papa's bedroom earlier today, did you see what happened to Momma through the slats in the door?"

"Yes." The answer was devoid of emotion.

"Tell me all about it," Ajeet said. His throat was tight.

In an unemotional tone that suggested she was reciting what she had for lunch rather than how her mother had been gruesomely murdered, Neha told the story of what had happened. Though Neha's intellect was still maturing, already she had an eidetic memory. Ajeet had no doubt she had a genius level IQ, or close to it. With the shock of what she had witnessed blocked for now by his potion, Ajeet knew everything Neha told him was an accurate account of what had occurred. The details made Ajeet sick to his stomach, but he forced himself to listen to all of them:

Shortly after Ajeet had gone to work that morning, three men came into the house. *They must have picked the lock*, Ajeet thought, as he had not seen any sign of forced entry. Rati and Neha had been upstairs at the time. Rati had kept Neha home from kindergarten because she was coming down with a cold. Once Rati heard the home invaders, she made Neha drink Ajeet's invisibility potion. She had told Neha to hide in the closet and to not make a sound or come out no matter what she saw or heard.

Men wearing gloves had come upstairs, found Rati in the master bedroom, pointed a gun at her, and demanded that she tell them where the Philosopher's Stone was. Despite the gun pressed to her temple, she told them she did not know what they were talking about.

Two of the men searched downstairs while the third continued to hold Rati at gunpoint in the bedroom. The two men eventually came back upstairs and searched up there. When they found nothing, they returned to Rati, demanding again that she tell them where the Philosopher's Stone was. Again, Rati denied knowing what they were talking about.

At the suggestion of one of the men, two of them began to beat Rati with their fists and the gun. The third man tried to stop them. The other two mocked him and called him names for not being willing to do what needed to be done. They threatened to kill him for being "a weak bitch."

Neha watched it all happen through the slats in the closet door. She had been terrified. Nonetheless, she wanted to leave the closet and help her mother, but Rati had made her promise to stay in the closet, hidden and silent. Both her parents had emphasized the importance of obeying them and keeping her word. So she stayed in the closet even though she did not want to.

The two men continued to beat and torture Rati. They ripped her clothes off her, shamed and ridiculed her body, and pulled her long hair out of her head clumps at a time. Eventually, she passed out from all the abuse.

The man who initiated Rati's beating then unzipped his pants. "Either this curry cunt doesn't know anything about the stone, or she's too stubborn to tell us," he had said. "I don't know about you, but I'm gonna get something out of this."

He proceeded to rape Rati both genitally and anally. Neha did not know those words of course—she was too young to even know what sex was—but from her detailed description, it was clear that was what had happened.

Once the first man had his way with Rati, the other one who had beaten Rati took his turn. That was how the first rapist had put it after he had pulled out of Rati: "Time to take your turn." The third man again tried to stop the other two, but they said they'd shoot him if he did not stop his whining.

After the two men finished pleasuring themselves with Rati's unconscious body, the first rapist shot Rati twice in the chest. Then, all three left. Neha had wanted to come out of the closet then to help her mother, but she had promised to stay in the closet until her mother fetched her or told her to come out. Since her mother had done neither, Neha stayed in the closet for hours until Ajeet came home from work and found her there.

Ajeet was shaking with emotion by the time Neha finished telling him what had happened. Fury, pride, and sorrow swirled within him.

Fury for the obvious reasons.

Pride because Rati had refused to tell the men about the Philosopher's Stone despite the fact she knew exactly where Ajeet kept it and how to access this bunker. She had known what the Philosopher's Stone meant to him. By remaining silent, Rati had demonstrated how dedicated she was to Ajeet and his dreams of glory. It had been her final act of love and devotion to him.

Sorrow because Ajeet wished Rati had told the men what they wanted to know. Though the book was priceless, Rati was by far more priceless. He would set fire to the Philosopher's Stone if there was even a ghost of a chance doing so would bring Rati back.

"What did these men look like?" Ajeet asked Neha. It was an effort for him to not scream the words.

Neha told him. Incredibly, what she said made Ajeet's waking nightmare even worse.

Ajeet stood, dizzy, nauseous, the world spinning around him. He staggered back, hitting the concrete wall behind him. He slid to the floor, his legs unable to support his weight.

It's all my fault, he thought.

Ajeet knew the men Neha had described: Austin Miller,

Peter Lighthouse, and Bart Wood. Ajeet occasionally teamed up with the three white men to pull off robberies he did not think he could handle by himself. They were more ruthless than Ajeet was. Though they were not educated men, they had a toughness Ajeet had admired. They were, if not his friends, then certainly his comrades-in-arms, sharing a camaraderie forged by the crimes they had committed together.

Or at least Ajeet had thought they were comrades. What kinds of comrades did this to someone's wife? Truly there was no honor among thieves.

Two weeks ago, the four of them had robbed a bank. Flush with post-heist euphoria, Ajeet had gone out drinking with the three afterward. Drunk on beer and unaccustomed bonhomie—between his obsession with the Philosopher's Stone and his family life, Ajeet had no time for friends—Ajeet had let slip that the substances he used as the Alchemist were thanks to the Philosopher's Stone.

Now, Ajeet realized after listening to Neha, the three had decided to take the Philosopher's Stone away from Ajeet and use it for their own purposes. Little did they know they did not have the knowledge nor the learning to use it. Ajeet had not told them it was a book written in an ancient language. They probably thought it was the stone of legend, as easy to use as waving a magic wand. Thank the gods Ajeet had not told the three men that he had a child. If he had, they might have taken pains to find and kill Neha.

It's all my fault, he thought again as he slumped against the wall. *If it weren't for my peacocking, my drunken braggadocio, Rati would still be alive.*

Ajeet sat sprawled on the hard floor of the septic tank for a while, full of self-loathing and recriminations, barely able to move. Barely able to breathe. The heavy weight of guilt pressed against his chest.

Ajeet's mind slowly turned to the oath he swore to kill the men who had done this to Rati. Now that he knew who they were, he could find and kill them.

And yet, Ajeet was unable to get up. Unable to act.

He realized, to his great shame, that he was afraid. Fear paralyzed him. He had never hurt anyone before, much less killed someone. Despite his nocturnal exploits as the Alchemist, Ajeet at heart was a scholar. A scientist. Not a killer. Not a man of action or a conqueror like his ancient ancestors had been. Austin, Peter, and Bart were rough customers who made their living with their toughness and their fists. Austin in particular was formidable. He was an Alpha-level Meta with a touch of super strength. He was the ringleader of the three.

He was also the one who had suggested the men beat Rati, who had initiated her rape, and who had shot her in the chest.

The thought of those atrocities pulled Ajeet to his feet. His body felt like it belonged to someone else. He staggered to the wooden table the Philosopher's Stone rested on. If he could unlock all the book's secrets, he would not be afraid of Austin and the others. He would not be afraid of anyone.

Everyone would be afraid of him.

He picked up the beaker holding the purple elixir he had concocted, the one that held the promise of unlocking the rest of the book's potent secrets. That held the promise of unlimited power. That held the promise of vengeance.

Ajeet pulled out the beaker's cork. He hesitated at the strong smell of the elixir. If he had not gotten the intelligence-boosting formula exactly right, drinking the elixir could kill him. Or cripple him. Or drive him mad. Or any number of terrible prospects. Ajeet looked at Neha. She still sat droopy-eyed on the floor, staring straight ahead, looking at nothing. He was the only parent she had left. His and Rati's extended families were still in India. If something happened to him, what would become of Neha? Who would take care of her?

Besides, had he not promised Rati to not drink the elixir?

Ajeet shook his head. Rati was dead because of him. On her memory, on their love, on their daughter's life, he had sworn an oath of vengeance. Regardless of the danger, regardless of his fears, he had to satisfy that oath. He had to make things right. Or at least as right as they ever could be.

Ajeet upended the beaker and drank. The elixir was thick, almost oily, hard to swallow. Despite the consistency, the taste was not unpleasant. The liquid was mildly effervescent, like a flat soda.

The beaker was now empty. Ajeet waited, breathing heavily, not knowing what to expect.

For several long seconds, nothing happened.

The beaker slipped from Ajeet's hand when he doubled over. His thick glasses slid off his face. Both the glasses and the beaker hit the cement floor, shattering simultaneously.

Ajeet began to scream.

14

Eighteen Years Ago

Ajeet flung open the door of the roadside bar. It was almost as dark inside Roy's Tavern as the night was outside.

People turned to stare and conversations stopped as Ajeet strode through the windowless, smoky bar. Roy's Tavern off of Interstate 95 outside of Wilmington was frequented by bikers, truckers, and low-level criminals, all of them white men. Ajeet's dark skin would have stood out like a black man at a Ku Klux Klan rally even if Ajeet had not been garbed in his new purple and black costume. He had chosen black as an homage to his Alchemist costume. He had chosen purple partly as a nod to the color of the elixir he had drank days before. Mostly he had chosen purple because it was the color of royalty.

Ajeet casually dropped some of his alchemy cartridges on the floor as he made his way through the bar. Each cartridge hissed softly, unheard by the crowded bar's patrons over the rock music blaring over the sound system. Ajeet's long purple cape swished softly as he strode purposefully to the back of the bar. Three pool tables were there, all of them in use. Cigarette and marijuana smoke hung over them like a thin cloud.

Austin Miller was bent over a table, stick in hand, lining up a shot. Peter Lighthouse was there too, holding a cue and standing on the other side of the table, looking like he prayed Austin would miss. Bart Wood, lanky and balding, sat on a nearby stool, smoking a joint, blearily watching his friends' game.

Peter's prayers were answered. Austin missed. Austin cursed, and straightened up. He noticed Ajeet standing there, staring at him. Austin's mouth curled in amusement around the lit cigarette dangling there.

"Ain't it a little early for Halloween, buddy?" Austin said.

"Today's not Halloween," Ajeet said. "Today is Judgment Day. For you, Peter, and Bart."

"I don't know what you're talking about," Austin said. "And I don't want to know. So why don't you go back to whatever insane asylum let you out?" Tall and broad with his head shaved bald, Austin was an intimidating tough guy accustomed to pushing people around.

"I'm talking about Rati Thakore. You beat, raped, and killed her." Ajeet's voice was cold, calm, and implacable.

"I don't know what the fuck you're talking about," Austin said. Austin was such a convincing liar that had it not been for Neha's eyewitness testimony, Ajeet might have believed him.

"I recognize those gauntlets," Peter suddenly interjected. "Ajeet?"

Austin's eyes narrowed as he peered at the head of the man in the purple cowl before him. "Oh shit, it *is* Ajeet," he realized. He looked startled and guilty for an instant before he recovered his composure. "I didn't recognize you in the new getup. Where's the Alchemist outfit? Even aside from the duds, you look different. Bigger. Taller."

"Alchemist is dead," Ajeet said. "You three killed him, and I buried him. Only Doctor Alchemy remains."

"Look Ajeet, I don't know what you're going on about," Austin said. "Let's grab a beer and talk about it. Maybe I can help."

Bart had been watching this exchange from his perch on the stool across the room, slack-jawed, his mouth partly open, as high as a kite. With a fluid movement, Doctor Alchemy raised his arms and fired an alchemy cartridge into Bart's open mouth with the unerring accuracy of a latter-day William Tell. A split second later an alchemy cartridge from Doctor Alchemy's other gauntlet hit Bart's chin, cracking open at the impact. A mass of black that looked like an octopus made of tar exploded out of the cartridge, expanding and writhing like something alive. The black mass swallowing Bart's entire head in a blink of an eye, sealing in the unexploded cartridge in Bart's mouth.

Bart was off the stool now, stumbling, tripping, pulling furiously and futilely at the sticky substance that enshrouded his head. Shocked and stunned by what was happening, everyone nearby stared at Bart.

"Bart, I want you to know what is happening and why," Doctor Alchemy said in a loud calm voice as Bart continued to struggle. Flailing blindly, Bart bounced off the back wall. "Though you participated in the break-in of my house, you tried to stop these other two animals from molesting and killing Rati. You will die with the least amount of suffering when the over one hundred gallons of water I poured into the cartridge in your mouth explodes out of it."

As if on cue, the unseen cartridge exploded with a pop and a whoosh. Like a balloon filled with far too much water, the abrupt release of all that water made Bart's head explode. Bar patrons shouted in alarm and confusion. Those closest to Bart were suddenly drenched with water flavored with bits of Bart's brain, bones, and flesh. Doctor Alchemy lifted his cape and shielded his body from the downpour.

Bart's drenched, decapitated body was still upright and moving, responding to impulses sent by a brain that was no longer there. His heart, still pumping, sent blood spurting out like a geyser from the empty space between his shoulders. The headless body hit a pool table, bounced off, and fell to the floor. There it continued to twitch, adding bloody slickness to the already drenched floor.

"Jesus, Mary, and Joseph," Peter said, staring at Bart's body. His voice held a combination of awe, disgust, and fear.

"You will need more than just them to save you," Doctor Alchemy said.

Austin was the first of the onlookers to recover from stunned stillness. He swung the thick end of his cue at Doctor Alchemy's head. Quick as lightning, Doctor Alchemy reached up and grabbed the piece of wood rocketing toward his head, staying it well before it hit him. Doctor Alchemy twisted his wrist sharply and pulled, jerking the cue out of the hands of the super strong, powerfully built, and now very surprised man.

Doctor Alchemy took a step back. The cue began to whistle in the air as he twirled it like a majorette twirling a giant baton. Austin stared at the cue with disbelieving wide eyes as it danced in Doctor Alchemy's hands like something alive. Doctor Alchemy said to Austin, "It's amazing how much the human body's strength and agility increases when the mind operates at peak efficiency. But you're too dim-witted to know anything about that."

Moving like a striking snake, Doctor Alchemy jabbed the

thick end of the cue into Austin's gut. Austin grunted, doubling over. Doctor Alchemy cracked the other end of the cue over Austin's exposed back, breaking the cue in half and driving Austin to his knees. Without missing a beat, Doctor Alchemy spun, smoothly driving the jagged end of the part of the cue still in his hand through the throat of the man who had been creeping up behind Alchemy, intending to brain him with a beer stein. Blood spurted, spraying onlookers. The man clutched his throat and fell on a table. He was dead before he hit the floor.

"The next person who interferes suffers the same fate," Doctor Alchemy thundered. A few hard-looking men who had started to get out of their seats paused, reconsidered, and sat back down.

With Austin on the floor, temporarily stunned, Alchemy turned his attention to Peter. Panicked, Peter fumbled hastily through a leather jacket draped over a chair.

"You beat Rati. You were the second person to rape her. For that, I will expose your true nature," Doctor Alchemy said to Peter's back.

Peter turned, gun in hand. Doctor Alchemy shot him with an alchemy cartridge on the wrist of Peter's gun hand. The cartridge exploded on impact. Peter dropped his gun, screaming in pain.

The cartridge's explosion had left an electric orange splotch of liquid on Peter's wrist. Peter clawed at it, trying to wipe away the substance that scalded him like boiling water. The splotch spread out on Peter's skin like oil spilled on a lake's surface. In seconds, the substance covered his entire body. Peter's body glowed, lighting up the corners of the dim bar. Most of the bar's patrons averted their eyes from the light. Not Doctor Alchemy. He looked unflinchingly at Peter's illuminated body with grim satisfaction.

The glow of Peter's body extinguished like a lit match dipped in water. Those who had averted their eyes looked back at Peter. Or, what used to be Peter. In his place was a human-shaped mass of writhing, wiggling, squirming cockroaches. The chittering of the countless insects rivaled the sound of the still-blaring music.

Peter's roach-filled clothes slowly sank to the ground as the mass of roaches disentangled from one another and scattering in all directions. Grown men shrieked like children as the swarm of disgusting insects crawled on them like a Biblical plague. Doctor Alchemy smiled as the men swatted and stomped the roaches. He knew that a piece of Peter's consciousness and soul was in each insect. Peter would feel every slap, every stomp, every crunch of every insect body. The roaches that escaped the bar would fare no better as most would be eaten by birds, rodents, and other insects. As cockroaches did not balk at cannibalism, they would even eat each other. Peter would die not once, but thousands of times, sometimes at his own hands. *Mandibles*, Doctor Alchemy corrected himself silently.

"From ashes to ashes, from dust to dust, from vermin to vermin," Doctor Alchemy said to no one in particular. The men who were not trying to run out of Roy's Tavern in horror were too busy killing roaches to hear him.

The roach invasion had roused Austin. Struggling to rise from his knees, he smacked the bugs crawling on him, not knowing he killed or maimed his friend with each slap. Doctor Alchemy shifted smoothly to stand in front of Austin. He raised his arm again, pointing a gauntlet at Austin's chest.

"I have saved the worst for last," Doctor Alchemy said to him. "It was you who initiated Rati's rape. You who started beating her. You who shot her. And, though I cannot be certain, I suspect it was you who decided to break into my house to begin with. The other two would not even have a bowel movement unless you first gave them permission."

The roaches crawling on him forgotten for now, Austin looked up at Doctor Alchemy with dread in his eyes. Doctor Alchemy savored the look like a fine wine. Until tonight, no one had ever looked at him with fear before. It was intoxicating.

Doctor Alchemy shot Austin in the chest with an alchemy cartridge. Crimson red spread out on the front of Austin's tight shirt. Austin knelt there stunned for a moment. Then he looked down. He reached up, frantically patting his chest. Other than the sting of the cartridge's impact against him, he was unhurt. Whatever substance Doctor Alchemy had hit him with, it had an appetizing sweet smell, like that of a ripe peach.

The sounds of men frantically killing cockroaches throughout the bar dimmed. Some men stopped altogether, turning to look at where Austin knelt in front of Doctor Alchemy. Austin looked back up at Doctor Alchemy, clearly puzzled he was still alive.

"I hit you with a pheromone. Even as I speak, it's soaking into your skin, suffusing through your entire body. By itself, it's quite harmless," Doctor Alchemy said in response to Austin's unspoken yet obvious question. "However, it is not by itself. When I walked through the bar, I dropped alchemy cartridges that released a gas. Completely odorless and colorless, yet its effects are quite potent. Think of it as a love potion in gas form." With a strange, almost feral look on their faces, all the men in the bar had stopped what they were doing and were slowly walking toward Alchemy and Austin. They moved awkwardly, like zombies, as if they could not fully control their own movements. "On second thought, it is really more of a lust potion. All the men here have inhaled it. They are attracted to the pheromone you absorbed and now reek of. They will be unable to control their desire for you. They will feel compelled to mate with you. By force, I imagine, unless you are more of a fan of all-male gangbangs than I suspect you are."

The man closest to Austin reached out and touched his hair in a manner that could only be described as a caress. Austin slapped the man's hand away with a curse. Based on the feverish look on the man's face, Austin's touch had only inflamed the man's rapidly increasing desire.

Austin tried to stand. The men closest to him tackled him. They pulled him to the ground. His low-level super strength could not break him free of the men's combined efforts. They held his struggling body down as the rest of the men in the bar slowly walked closer and closer. Austin's eyes were wild, spinning in their sockets. He pleaded with Doctor Alchemy, talking so fast that his words were almost gibberish.

Doctor Alchemy continued to speak as if he could not hear Austin's begging. "I have inoculated myself against the gas, of course. I have no interest in mating with the likes of you. If one lies down with a dog, one invariably rises with fleas. I am too much a man of refined tastes and standards for that." As Alchemy spoke, men began ripping Austin's clothes off, exposing his hairy, heavily muscled body. Austin was screaming now, yelling for the men to get off him. For them to stop. No one listened. Doctor Alchemy certainly did not.

"When everyone's lust is slaked," Doctor Alchemy said, though it was unclear if Austin could hear over his own screaming and thrashing, "their compulsion will change. Did you know the black widow spider eats her partner after she mates with him? Sexual cannibalism, the phenomenon is called. As coincidence would have it, black widow venom is a component of the gas the people here have inhaled. To make a long and painful story short, after these men's sexual appetites have been satisfied, their stomach's appetites will take over. You are a big man. You have a lot of good meat on your bones. It is well-marbled too if your gut's size is any indication. I read that long pork is quite delicious if one has a taste for such things. Your friends most definitely do. Or at least they will. I wonder how long it will take them to rip you apart and consume you."

Doctor Alchemy sighed regretfully. "Alas, I cannot linger to find out. Time waits for no man, not even one such as I. I have a world to conquer."

Austin's blood-curdling screams trailed Doctor Alchemy as he walked back toward the bar's exit. Doctor Alchemy pushed patrons out of his way. They did not seem to notice. Their eyes shone with lust, focused only on reaching Austin.

When he reached the door, Doctor Alchemy turned back around to face the bar's interior. Roaches crunched underfoot. Austin screams now mingled with sobs. He was hidden from Doctor Alchemy's view by the tightening throng of men. The men on the floor with Austin grunted loudly with exertion and desire.

Doctor Alchemy's face had been cold, almost analytical until now. Now it twisted, turning feral and animalistic. His eyes danced maniacally behind his cowl. He shook a clenched fist at the backs of the lust-fueled occupants of the bar, none of whom paid him the slightest bit of attention.

He thundered, "Now you call me Doctor Alchemy. Soon you will call me king!"

15

_____

Ten Years Ago

Doctor Alchemy read the letter from his 14-year-old daughter Neha for the second time. He did not need to. His photographic memory had automatically memorized it during the first reading. However, his disbelief at the letter's contents made him doubt what his eyes had told him.

Written in Neha's clear, bold hand, the letter read:

Dear Papa:

As you know, I have disapproved of your behavior and your desire to rule the world for some time now. When I was younger, I went along with your plans and ambitions out of childish ignorance and a child's natural desire to please her parent. I even trained in the martial arts and studied history, strategy, and statecraft to prepare to take what you always called my "rightful place as the heir apparent to the Thakore Empire." Now that I am older, I see how misguided your objectives are and how evil the means you have chosen to achieve them are. The world does not need to be ruled, does not want to be ruled, and it certainly does not need to be conquered. You fancy yourself the world's savior, yet, it pains me to say, you are little more than a superpowered thug who has needlessly killed more people than you probably remember. And, just as important if not more so, I am deeply dismayed and disappointed by what you have done to mother.

In light of this, I am leaving home for good. I will not continue to participate in activities that are not only illegal, but immoral and misdirected.

Despite your many flaws, you have taught me well. Surely you know you will never find me unless I wish to be found. I do not so wish. I will never return to live with you unless and until you change your ways and seek the psychological help I have repeatedly urged you to get. The help that you so desperately need. Further, now that I have manifested Metahuman powers, I intend to devote my life to fighting you, to ensure that your plans of world domination fail.

Unless you see the error of your ways and get help to change your behavior, the next time we meet, it will be as adversaries.

Despite all you have done, I still love you.

—Neha

Nothing about the letter changed upon his second reading. Doctor Alchemy angrily waved the letter in Rati's direction. She sat feet away on a throne that was the golden twin of Doctor Alchemy's diamond one in their palace's throne room. She was radiant in her ornate sari, numerous jewels, and gold crown. Over two dozen of their subjects stood silently and meekly before the dais on which the thrones rested. The palace was hidden in the jungle of an otherwise uninhabited island in the Indian Ocean.

"Can you believe this, Mother?" Doctor Alchemy exclaimed incredulously. "After all we're done for that ingrate of a child, she spits in our face. We've been nursing a viper in our bosom."

Rati said something.

Doctor Alchemy snapped, "Well of course the letter is well-written. Neha is a near genius. She is my daughter after all. What did you expect, that she would write it in crayon with only one syllable words and sign her name with a smiley face?"

Doctor Alchemy's face grew contrite as he listened to his wife again. He wore his full costume, minus the purple cowl. A gold crown matching Rati's was on his head.

"You're quite right, Mother," he said, chastened. "There is no need for me to take that tone with you. I apologize." Doctor Alchemy's eyes fell on the letter again. "My emotions got the better of me. That daughter of ours makes me so mad. Where did we go wrong in raising her?" He shook Neha's letter in his fist again. "Not only did that ungrateful whelp write these insults and lies, but she stole one of our jets. She even disabled the jet's transponder so we cannot track where she went. Our forefathers had the right idea about a woman's place. We never should have taught that girl to read, much less how to pilot a plane or about electronics. What's more, our ambitious Judas was not satisfied with a trifling thirty pieces of silver—she took with her a considerable sum of cash, gems, and precious metals from our vault. How in the world she got into the vault is beyond me. Turned into a gas with her powers and seeped into it, probably. If I had known we harbored a traitor in our midst, I would have made sure the damned thing was airtight. Thank the gods, Mother, that only you and I know where the Philosopher's Stone is hidden, else Neha might have taken that too. What kind of daughter steals from her father the things he worked his fingers to the bone to steal? An atrocious one, that's what kind. Kids these days."

Overcome by fury, Doctor Alchemy crumpled Neha's letter into a ball. He threw it on the gem-encrusted marble floor. He rose and stomped on the wad of paper repeatedly. His long cape made swishing sounds as it bounced up and down. His ornate crown slipped off his head and fell to the floor with a clatter. It spun on its edges like a dropped coin.

Doctor Alchemy pointed at Rati. "I'll tell you the first thing we did wrong in raising that quisling. We never should have bought Neha that Lady Justice doll when she was a toddler. The blasted thing was a bad influence. It made perverse notions of right and wrong seep into her. To make matters worse, we later bought her a doll in the likeness of that sanctimonious do-gooder Avatar. Well actually, I stole it because I'd be damned if I spent one red cent on that overgrown Boy Scout, but that's not relevant to the larger point. Eh? What's that Mother?"

Doctor Alchemy listened intently.

"Yes, yes, I know Neha says the Avatar one is an action figure. She thinks the term makes the toy sound cooler. But she can't fool me—the beastly thing is a doll. Both the Avatar and Lady Justice dolls are nothing but Hero propaganda in toy form. Their insidious presence in our home has twisted Neha's mind. Turned her against us." He snorted indignantly as he paced. "Licensed Heroes. Rogues. Hah! The most ironic titles ever. They're not heroes. *We're* the good guys. *They're* the bad guys. I am trying to save humanity from itself, to bring the world peace under my leadership. These so-called Heroes are agents of the old world order. Of the status quo. The same status quo that's produced every war, every genocide, every inequitable class system, every institution of slavery, every murder. Including yours, Mother. Thank the gods I was able to formulate a potion to resurrect you. The Philosopher's Stone said that resurrection was one of the few things under the sun that was impossible, but my genius combined with the other secrets I unlocked in the book's pages made the impossible possible."

Doctor Alchemy shook his head at frustration at the thought of Heroes. They had foiled so many of his plans over the years: His attempt to detonate a bomb in the Earth's atmosphere that would have scattered mind-control gas around the world. His ploy to take the place of the United States' President after Doctor Alchemy had drunk a potion that transformed him into the chief executive's doppelgänger. His plot to establish a base on the Moon from which he would launch massive rocks to pelt the Earth with, an idea Doctor Alchemy had cribbed from Robert Heinlein's *The Moon Is a Harsh Mistress*. His scheme to poison the Chinese president, blame it on Germany, and start World War III, with Doctor Alchemy ready to pick up the pieces once the major countries of the world destroyed each other. His attempt to neutralize the Metahuman gene of every superpowered person on the planet. Except for his own, of course.

Those were but a few of Doctor Alchemy's schemes and plans Heroes had thwarted. Heroes had even broken up the cult he had started, with himself as god and chief prophet with power of attorney over all the cult members' assets. Those sacrilegious supers had the nerve to call his Promise of Peace and Prosperity Church a "sham religion," and had sicced the United States' Internal Revenue Service on him for tax evasion. *Freedom of religion,* Doctor Alchemy thought bitterly. *What a joke.*

"I'll destroy every last Hero and do-gooding Meta on the face of the Earth if I have to. Erase them from existence," he vowed. His eyes were wild. "I'll start with those goddamned toys. Where's my manservant? Boy! *Boy!!* There you are. Gods damn it, snap to it when your king calls you. Maybe a kiss from my whip will quicken your step. Go to Neha's room. Find her Hero dolls. Have them burned. Bury the ashes. No, wait. On second thought, swallow the ashes, defecate them out, and then bury that. Serve those filthy bastards right. I will whip your back to ribbons if I catch you calling the Avatar doll an action figure. And make a note: Remind me to research the effectiveness of a Doctor Alchemy doll as a propaganda tool. Further, should I decide to start production on one, remind me to order some A/B testing on which sells better: One with a kung fu grip, or one without." Doctor Alchemy hesitated, frowning as he thought. "Blast it! Also remind me to order A/B testing on if the doll will sell better if we call it an action figure."

The white, almost elderly manservant—Doctor Alchemy's former boss Oliver Meaney from his old chemical technician job at Burke Pharmaceuticals—wordlessly shuffled out of the throne room toward the palace's living quarters. Like all Rati's and Doctor Alchemy's subjects, the manservant wore tight black pants and an emerald green top with a bright pink sash worn diagonally across his chest. Doctor Alchemy changed the look and color of his subjects' clothes when he got bored with their old look. The female subjects' tops were all cut to expose their cleavage. Doctor Alchemy enjoyed looking at them much as a person might enjoy looking at a beautiful flower. He never touched his female subjects inappropriately, however. He had always been and always would be faithful to his golden Rati. All other women, no matter how beautiful, paled in comparison to her.

Doctor Alchemy frowned slightly as he watched his manservant retreat from the throne room. Doctor Alchemy picked up his fallen crown and placed it back on his head at a jaunty angle. He resumed his seat on his diamond throne. He was careful to pick his cape up before he sat. He draped the purple garment regally over an arm of the glittering throne. Doctor Alchemy firmly believed a ruler should look and act like one. One should honor the proprieties.

"Have you noticed our subjects are not as quick to leap to obey our commands as they normally are?" Doctor Alchemy asked his wife. The identically garbed subjects who comprised Doctor Alchemy's honor guard were arrayed in formation before the twin thrones. They did not move or speak. Subjects were to be seen, not heard, unless Rati or Doctor Alchemy spoke to them first. They were all armed with high-tech projectile weapons. The Gulf Coast Guardians had caught Rati and Doctor Alchemy off guard when the Hero team invaded their previous palace last year. Doctor Alchemy and Rati had barely escaped in time. Since then, Doctor Alchemy made sure his subjects were always armed. He would not be caught napping again.

What kind of asinine name is Gulf Coast Guardians anyway? Doctor Alchemy thought, annoyed. *What is it with Heroes and their childish obsession with alliterative names? Have they no dignity, no self-respect? Do I call myself the Awesome and Astonishing Almighty Alchemist?* He paused, cocking an eyebrow. *Actually, that's not half bad.*

He shoved the thought aside. He spoke again to his wife. "Perhaps it is time to give our subjects another dose of my obedience potion. I look forward to the day when our right to rule is recognized universally and it is not necessary to constantly make fresh batches of the potion."

Doctor Alchemy sighed loudly, thinking of that glorious day. He had so much left to do to make it a reality. He said, "'Uneasy lies the head that wears a crown.' A good line, that."

Doctor Alchemy thumped the arm of his throne with sudden fury.

"Too good for an Englishman like Shakespeare to have

come up with it on his own," he snarled. "That thieving plagiarist must have stolen it from an Indian writer. The only thing the British are good at is theft. They'll steal the fillings out of your mouth if you speak slowly enough. Rapacious Limey bastards." The people in the room had heard all this before. The British were a particularly sore subject for Doctor Alchemy. He would never forget or forgive how they had colonized and exploited his Indian forebears. He often daydreamed of sinking the British Isles once he assumed his rightful position as world ruler. It was no accident that his chief manservant was a Brit.

Doctor Alchemy's mind shifted back to Neha's letter. Its words popped up again in his mind's eye like lines on a computer screen.

"What in the world did that brat mean when she wrote 'I am deeply dismayed and disappointed by what you have done to mother'?" Doctor Alchemy asked his wife. "Would she prefer if I had let you stay dead? What kind of daughter would wish that on the woman who suckled her at her breast?" Rati did not answer. It had been a rhetorical question anyway.

"'Superpowered thug.'" Doctor Alchemy scoffed at Neha's words. "'Needlessly killed more people than you probably remember.' Lies, all lies. I am a conqueror, not a thug. Was Alexander the Great a thug? Was Napoleon? Was Hitler? Was Genghis Khan? Was William the Conqueror?" Doctor Alchemy paused, remembering the latter's nationality. "Bad example. William *was* a thug. Disgusting Englishman. I would not be the slightest bit surprised if the reports of his conquests weren't all lies, anyway. He probably just took the credit for something an Indian did."

Doctor Alchemy shook his head in dismay at the unfairness of the world.

"And I haven't needlessly killed anyone. Everyone I have

killed needed killing either because I was defending myself, my family, or they were trying to prevent me from imposing peace and order on the world. From ushering in the world's first true golden age. Contrary to Neha's lies, I remember every person I've killed." The names scrolled past like a readout in Doctor Alchemy's mind. Starting with the men he had killed in Roy's Tavern years ago, he recited them all aloud. The recitation took a couple of minutes to complete.

The room fell silent once Doctor Alchemy finished. The recitation had taken the wind out of the sails of his anger. Sadness replaced it. With Neha gone, Rati was all he had left. It was him and Rati, alone, against the world. The palace was full of their subjects, of course, but they did not matter. Their subjects were little more than cattle, dumb brutes who could not be trusted to rule themselves. Just like the rest of the world.

Look at the mess the world is in due to the cattle foolishly believing they can govern themselves, Doctor Alchemy thought. *Why can't the world understand I am its savior? Why does the world and its so-called Heroes resist submission to my rule? It is further proof of their foolishness, their utter incapacity to take care of themselves.*

Doctor Alchemy chewed at a knuckle in frustration. He started to tear up. Neha was his only daughter. She had so much potential, so much promise. He loved her deeply despite everything he had just said about her.

Neha abandoning him and Rati and rejecting his cause pushed Doctor Alchemy to the edge of despair. If he could not make his own daughter see his glorious vision for the world, how could he ever hope to make the rest of the world see it?

Doctor Alchemy slammed his fist on the armrest of his throne again. He blinked away his tears.

"No! No! I will not let Neha leaving deter or distract me

from my mission. Even without her here, Mother, we will save the world by ruling it. Just you and me. As it was meant to be. As it was destined to be."

Rati spoke. Doctor Alchemy smiled lovingly when she finished, reached over, and patted her warm hand.

"Don't fret, my love," he said. "I realize now that Neha leaving is merely a phase. Nothing more than adolescent rebellion. Teen girls are as temperamental as weathervanes. When she matures more and sees how much better things will be for the world under our leadership, she will relent and return to us. She will again take her rightful place as the heir to our glorious empire."

The throne room fell silent again. Doctor Alchemy turned his mind's considerable horsepower to his latest plan for world conquest. The first thing he would have to do, he thought, would be to construct a new lair. Maybe in a volcano. He had always wanted a lair in a volcano. With Neha gone and vowing to stop him, this palace and its location had been compromised. Doctor Alchemy had far too many enemies who would love to know his whereabouts. He was a wanted man in . . . how many countries now? He had lost count.

He stroked his beard thoughtfully. Visions of his future empire danced in his head. His honor guard stared at him blankly, unthinkingly waiting due to the potion in their systems for their lord and master to give them a command.

Rati sat motionlessly and silently on her gold throne. Thanks to Doctor Alchemy's resurrection potion, her flesh was as warm, voluptuous, and whole as it had ever been. As her husband schemed and planned and plotted, Rati's eyes stared straight ahead into nothingness. They were vacant, still, and lifeless, just as they had always been ever since she was murdered eight years ago.

16

Two Years and Several Months Ago

She was dead. Neha, his beautiful and brilliant baby, the only person he loved other than Rati, was dead.

With a hard lump in his throat, Doctor Alchemy sat in his lair and replayed the footage captured from the U.S. Central Intelligence Agency's satellite for the umpteenth time, hoping and praying what it showed was some sort of trick. Some sort of mistake. The footage was months old. Doctor Alchemy had escaped from a Chinese prison for so-called crimes against the state and returned home days before. When he escaped, he had already served six months of a life sentence. Doctor Alchemy would rather have stayed in prison longer—his plot to overthrow the Chinese government had been coming along nicely, and masterminding it from a Chinese prison had been the perfect cover—but when he heard Neha had been killed in the United States months ago, he had broken out of prison the same day he was informed. He had made his way back here to his Pacific Ocean volcanic lair where Rati and their subjects eagerly awaited his return.

He had been unwilling to rely on secondhand information—he just had to find out for himself if the horrific news his informers had told him was true.

The spy satellite footage Doctor Alchemy watched was not supposed to exist, of course. By law, the CIA was prohibited from turning its satellites' attention to domestic soil to spy on American citizens. Then again, someone like Doctor Alchemy was not supposed to be able to hack into the CIA's satellite feed. Things rarely worked the way the government publicly said they did.

Doctor Alchemy watched the footage closely yet again. He sat in the Monitor Room, nestled deep in his lair. Only his manservant was with him. That man stood in the corner, silent and motionless. He faced the wall and awaited an order, just as he always did when he accompanied his master. A bank of television monitors about seven feet tall was in front of where Doctor Alchemy sat on his throne, a smaller and more comfortable version of the diamond one in the Throne Room. Each monitor had different angles of the satellite footage on it, slowed down so it advanced frame by frame.

The footage showed the Hero Omega bursting out of the roof of Sentinels Mansion in Maryland accompanied by Neha, beaten, bound, gagged, and wearing her Smoke outfit. The two took off flying toward Astor City. Right outside of the city, the shackles around Neha's arms and legs exploded with terrific force. She was incinerated. Omega was thrown clear of the explosion. He survived the blast, apparently able to erect a force field to protect himself from the massive explosion. After flying around for a while in what seemed to be a search for any trace of Neha, he flew back to Sentinels Mansion.

Doctor Alchemy punched a button. The footage paused. The monitors bathed his tear-streaked face in their still light. It was no trick, he reluctantly concluded. No special effects wizard's attempt to mislead. No mistake. Doctor Alchemy had longed feared that something bad would happen to Neha if she foolishly continued to associate with Heroes and if he was not there to protect her. Now his nightmare had been made all too real.

She was gone forever. After Doctor Alchemy blew the footage up and digitally enhanced it, it showed no trace of Neha remaining after the explosion. Doctor Alchemy would not be able to give her the same life-restoring potion that had resurrected his beloved Rati. There was simply nothing left of Neha to give the potion to.

Doctor Alchemy had eyes and ears everywhere, particularly in the Metahuman world. Through them, he had followed Neha's adventures since she had run away from home years ago: the petty larceny she had resorted to when the funds she had stolen from him had run low; the period during which she was homeless; her entering and then graduating from Hero Academy first in her class; her Apprenticeship with that meddling fool Amazing Man alongside of Kinetic and Myth; and her taking a job as head of security for Willow Wilde, the inane reality television star. While Doctor Alchemy did not agree with Neha's life choices—her decision to enter Hero Academy had made him sick to his stomach, just as her graduating from it first in her class had filled him with a perverse pride—all her bad choices would simply have been water under the bridge if Neha had come to her senses and resumed her rightful place at his and Rati's side.

Now that would never happen. The reconciliation between him and Neha he long anticipated would one day occur now never would.

How would he tell Rati? She would be devastated. Their only child, their love made flesh, gone. And why? For what? A stupid spat between idiotic Heroes?

The sorrow smoldering in him ignited, turning into white hot anger. He clutched the side of his throne so tightly that the metal and wood under its comfortable leather exterior cracked and splintered with loud screeches and pops. The soft leather had been fashioned from the skin of some of his enemies.

I'll kill them all! he silently vowed ferociously, not trusting himself to speak. *Everyone responsible for Neha's murder will die a horrible death.*

He punched buttons on a panel on his throne. News articles about Omega's confrontations with the Sentinels sprang onto some of the screens. More punching. A few minutes later, supposedly confidential reports from the Heroes' Guild's internal investigation into those confrontations sprang onto the other screens, including witness statements from everyone involved.

Doctor Alchemy let the information wash over him as it sped by on the monitors faster than a normal human would be able to follow. Fortunately, Doctor Alchemy was no normal human. With his enhanced intelligence, he could absorb and synthesize information far faster and more efficiently than human cattle could.

In minutes, he had absorbed all available information about Omega's conflict with the Sentinels that had culminated in Neha's death. Doctor Alchemy seethed with newfound anger. Neha had not been the primary target of the bomb that killed her. The explosive had been incorporated into the metal that bound Neha to kill both her and Omega, formerly Kinetic, after he supposedly turned over the so-called Omega weapon to the Sentinels. Both he and Neha knew too much about the Sentinels' crimes and had to be eliminated, according to the full confession Seer had later made.

Doctor Alchemy now had his list of people who were

involved in Neha's murder and who therefore had to die: Mechano, Seer, Millennium, Omega, Myth, and Truman Lord.

Doctor Alchemy immediately crossed Mechano off his hit list. *One good thing about Omega's run-in with the Sentinels is that he destroyed Mechano,* Doctor Alchemy thought. *Though I would have preferred to do it myself. On the bright side, with Mechano gone, the Heroes' Guild's computer firewalls are out-of-date and laughable inadequate. Arrogant fools.*

Seer Doctor Alchemy had dealt with before during past confrontations with the Sentinels. Those myopic meddling Metas! The self-described "Earth's greatest Heroes" had thwarted several of his brilliant schemes over the years. The day he captured Wildside of the Sentinels and then skinned him alive was one of Doctor Alchemy's fondest memories. Doctor Alchemy stroked the soft side of his throne, almost aroused at the thought. Wildside's skin was one of the hides that composed the throne's supple leather. When he broke into MetaHold and killed Seer, he thought, perhaps he would also skin her and use her pelt to reupholster a piece of furniture. The footstool of his sitting room, perhaps.

Then again, maybe not, he chided himself. Seer's skin was albino white, tinged with blue. Her skin's color would clash with the rest of his and Rati's furnishings. Tacky.

Millennium would be a thornier knot to unravel. He was an Omega-level Meta. Heroes like him and Avatar had given Doctor Alchemy fits over the years. Moreover, no one seemed to know where Millennium had disappeared to after Omega chopped off his hands in Sentinels Mansion. The Heroes' Guild and other authorities had searched the planet for him, to no avail. Ineffectual ignoramuses! Doctor Alchemy resolved to devote some of his own considerable resources to locating Millennium. Once he did, he would find a way to defeat and kill the formidable magical Metahuman. Just as every problem had a solution, every Hero—no matter how powerful —had a weakness.

Speaking of which, he thought. Doctor Alchemy pulled up additional footage of the murderous stripling Omega, the first Omega-level Hero to come on the scene in decades.

According to his confidential and private Heroes' Guild file that was no longer either thanks to Doctor Alchemy's hacking abilities, Omega's birth name was Theodore Conley. He went by Theo. *Hah!* Doctor Alchemy scoffed silently. *Theo* was the Greek word for god. What kind of god would let this happen to his daughter?

Omega had let Neha die. He was as much to blame for Neha's death as the Sentinels were. More so actually, because he was supposed to be Neha's friend and comrade. You were supposed to protect the ones you loved, not let them be murdered. *Look at how I've protected my beloved Rati over the years,* Doctor Alchemy thought.

Scenes recorded by news crews and amateur videographers of young Theodore's exploits both under his current alias and that of Kinetic filled Doctor Alchemy's screens. Almost immediately, Doctor Alchemy noticed that the Hero's hands and fingers always moved when he activated his telekinetic powers. *A weakness I can exploit?* He filed the thought away for later contemplation. He also noticed that Theodore was more powerful as Omega than he had been as Kinetic. He was beginning to realize his potential as an Omega-level Metahuman. As such, he posed a threat to Doctor Alchemy's plans for world domination. Destroying him would kill two birds with one stone: avenge Neha as well as take a powerful Hero off the global chessboard.

Doctor Alchemy also made a mental note of the men and women Omega had battled in his short career as a Metahuman. Perhaps he would enlist some of them in destroying

Omega. Doctor Alchemy smiled grimly. The thought of hoisting the young Hero on his own petard appealed to the Rogue's sense of poetic justice.

Myth, aka Isaac Geere, had to die as well. Though he had not been on the scene when Neha died, he should have been. Like Omega, he was supposed to have been Neha's friend. Therefore, he was as culpable in her death as Omega was.

He would also kill Truman Lord for his participation in the events leading to Neha's death. Doctor Alchemy had met Lord years before. Even before his involvement in Neha's death, the Heroic detective's infantile sense of humor had been enough to make Doctor Alchemy want to kill him. "Hey Doctor Alchemy, can you turn Flint, Michigan's drinking water into gold?" the gun-toting nuisance had the temerity to ask when they had crossed paths. The only thing Doctor Alchemy hated more than a joke was a joke he did not understand. It would give him great pleasure to rid the world of that incomprehensible irritant.

Doctor Alchemy shut off all the computer screens. He was plunged into near darkness. He sat for a while on his throne, brooding. As much as he wanted to rush out and start crossing people off his hit list, he could not do so immediately. With him being out of circulation for so many months in China, the ship of his burgeoning empire had listed without his sure hand on the tiller. Despite her many virtues, Rati was not a capable administrator. She seemed incapable of taking any initiative without him present. As a result, the influx of new subjects was down to a trickle. Research and development of the technology his plots and schemes relied on had ground to a halt—his potion-controlled subjects were great at blindly following his orders, but terrible at independent thought and creativity.

His income was also down. Several crime lords around the

world who were supposed to regularly pay tribute to him had refused to do so in his absence. Even sales of the Doctor Alchemy action figure with its kung fu grip—distributed through a perfectly legal toy company whose board of directors did not know he owned a controlling interest in it—were down. With him in jail, Doctor Alchemy had not been in the headlines lately. The public had turned its attention to the latest villain of the week. They apparently needed constant reminders of his exploits for merchandise sales to remain brisk. Fickle fools!

In short, Doctor Alchemy had to get his multifaceted empire back in order before turning his full attention to the murderers who destroyed his family. Plus, he had some new ideas regarding his final objective of world domination while he had been in the Chinese prison. He would set them in motion before turning his attention to his hit list. He estimated it would be several months if not longer before he terminated the lives of those on his list.

No matter, he thought. *Revenge is a dish best served cold.* He especially looked forward to snuffing out young Theodore. With all the power he had that he should have used to protect his darling daughter, Doctor Alchemy blamed him the most. Some Hero he was. Doctor Alchemy felt a surge of impatient anger at the thought of postponing his vengeance on the boy.

With effort, he smothered the emotion.

I will be calm. I will be thoughtful. I will be patient, Doctor Alchemy mused. *I am a man of towering intellect, determination, and resolve unlike any Theodore has ever dealt with. When I do finally move against him, I will disembowel him mentally, physically, and spiritually. He will die screaming my name. He will rue the day he ever heard the name Neha Thakore.*

Fresh grief almost overwhelmed him. Neha. His bright, golden girl. He would never feel her embrace again, never again bathe in the warmth of her smile, never again delight in the quickness of her mind. The reconciliation between him and her he had long dreamed of was now impossible. She would never join him in his quest to bring the world peace and order.

Sick at heart, Doctor Alchemy stood.

"Come boy," he said to his manservant. The man had grown old in Doctor Alchemy's service. His face was wrinkled and lined, and sported scars from Doctor Alchemy correcting him over the years. If Doctor Alchemy had not rescued him from his humdrum life at Burke Pharmaceuticals, he undoubtedly would have long retired from that job by now. Doctor Alchemy, however, was as young and fit as ever thanks to secrets gleaned from the Philosopher's Stone.

He did not feel young and fit now, though. Now he felt as tired and world-weary as a broken-down old man.

With a suffocating feeling of dread, Doctor Alchemy slowly walked through the gilded walls of his lair, toward the Throne Room where Rati patiently awaited him. He did not know how he would find the words, but he would inform Rati of their tragic loss.

And, what he planned to do to all the people who caused it.

With his mind preoccupied with grief and thoughts of vengeance, Doctor Alchemy did not even notice the bows of his subjects as he swept past them through his sprawling, opulent lair. His manservant shuffled after him like a beaten old dog.

17

One Week and Several Days Ago

Jason Sydney lay in his bed in the medical ward of MetaHold. The country's primary prison for housing Metahuman criminals was on Ellis and Liberty Islands in New York. The Statue of Liberty had been on Liberty Island before the Rogue Black Plague destroyed it decades ago. The islands through which millions of immigrants had once streamed into America with dreams of freedom and a better life now imprisoned hundreds of superpowered criminals with similar dreams of freedom and a better life.

Cute, Jason thought about the prison's ironic location, not for the first time since he had been imprisoned here years ago. *The government is not good at much, but it sure as hell excels at irony. Just look at the buzzwords it puts into laws' names. Any time a bill has the word "freedom," "liberty," or "rights" in the name, that bill is for sure designed to take away freedom, liberty, and rights.*

Jason had plenty of time to think about Orwellian doublespeak. Paralyzed from the neck down, he was unable to do too much else other than think. Reading, watching television, being occasionally chauffeured around the prison in a wheelchair, and thinking about better days were pretty much the extent of Jason's activities. He could not even move enough to adjust his gray and white prison gown, which had somehow gotten bunched up so it exposed most of his gaunt legs.

Jason knew Bella would take care of his gown. Bella was his favorite prison nurse. She was in his room now, preparing to move his broken body to help him avoid getting bed sores. The voluptuous raven-haired woman always seemed to leave undone the top couple of buttons on her white uniform, permitting Jason a nice view of her ample cleavage when she bent over him. He was pretty sure she exposed herself on purpose because she felt sorry for him. It certainly was not because she was attracted to him. With his muscles atrophied from years of disuse, Jason looked like a Holocaust survivor. He felt like he was held together with bubble gum and baling wire.

And, of course, the miracles of modern medicine. The machines and electronics that kept him alive clicked, beeped, and whirred as Bella prepared to turn him. He could not even shit or take a piss without mechanical assistance. He was a far cry from the robust and powerful Metahuman assassin known as Iceburn he had once been. As Iceburn, he had struck fear in the hearts of people when he appeared.

Even Jason's fire and ice powers were gone, nullified by the field that permeated the medical ward and all the prisoners' cells in the facility. After all this time without them, Jason still felt the absence of his powers, like a missing tooth his tongue kept probing for out of habit.

Bella turned. Jason got a quick glimpse of her overflowing pink bra through a gap in her uniform. Glee mixed with frustration in Jason. It was like looking at a delicious meal he would never be able to eat. His junk was as useless as his arms and legs. Even so, the fact he could no longer drive a car did not mean he could not admire a beautiful one when it sped past.

"You're doing the Lord's work," Jason said to Bella. Her plump face dimpled into a smile. Her fleshy upper arms jiggled as she fussed with bottles of his medication. Jason had always liked big girls. In his heyday, when he was an obscenely high paid assassin who attracted gold-digging women like moths to a flame, he had shoved skinny super-models out of the way to get to bigger women like Bella.

Bella's smile and the rest of her froze like someone had pressed *pause* on her body. The noise from the medical devices in the room, which were as familiar to Jason as his own heart-beat, froze as well. The sudden silent stillness was both eerie and startling.

Two empty halves of a small metal canister lay on Jason's chest. They had not been there an instant before. It was as if they had magically appeared. "What the fu—?" Jason exclaimed, trailing off when he spotted him.

Doctor Alchemy. The Rogue had appeared in full costume and cowl as if out of thin air to the left of Jason's bed. Jason would have jumped in surprise if he could have. He recovered almost immediately. Jason was pleased to see that, even after all this time in bed, he had not lost reflexes honed from years of being faster than the other guy.

"What's up, Doc?" Jason said. "What brings you to this neck of the woods? If you brought me a get well soon card, you should've saved your money. I won't be getting well soon. Or ever, for that matter." Despite Jason flippancy, the purple and black garbed Rogue made Jason nervous like few people did. Jason had pulled a few jobs for Alchemy back in the day. Though Alchemy's word was good and he had always paid up like he said he would, he was erratic. Erratic was one word for it. Crazy was another. Alchemy would act and sound like a university don one minute, and foam at the mouth and spout vulgarities the next. If he wasn't nuttier than peanut brittle, he might be able to conquer the world as he always blathered it was his destiny to. Jason trusted him about as much as he'd trust a dog that had been known to turn and bite without warning. It flashed through Jason's mind to say something to trigger Alchemy's volcanic temper. After years of lying in bed unable to even wipe his own ass, there were days when death looked like a blessing.

"Iceburn," Doctor Alchemy said in greeting. "Aren't you going to ask how I penetrated the security of one of the most secure facilities in the world to visit you?" He sounded like a kid who hadn't been asked *Who's there?* after the kid said *Knock, knock*—disappointed and faintly offended. Jason noticed Alchemy still spoke in a thick Indian accent. Jason had often wondered if the accent wasn't at least partly a put-on. Alchemy seemed to want everyone to know his ancestry. Jason had once seen him beat a man senseless who mistakenly referred to him as Hispanic.

Jason would have shrugged in response to Alchemy's question if his body could make the movement. "I just assumed it was more of your magic."

Doctor Alchemy drew himself up to his full imposing height. "What I do is not magic," he huffed. "I am a man of reason and science. It only appears to be magic because it is so much more advanced than anything others are privy to. As Arthur Clarke said, 'any sufficiently advanced technology is indistinguishable from magic.'" Alchemy's face screwed up in sudden anger. "Infernal Brits! Why must they be so eminently quotable?"

Same old Doctor Alchemy, Jason thought. The thought had

barely passed through Jason's mind before Alchemy's face calmed again, like a summer thunderstorm that had abruptly come and just as abruptly had gone.

"The reason why that zaftig nurse and everything else appear frozen is because they are." Alchemy said it in the manner of a professor lecturing a particularly dense student. "Before entering the facility, I doused myself with a substance allowing me to slip outside the normal time stream. Because of that, everything around me froze, or at least seemed to from my perspective. After that, it was a simple matter to gain admission to the prison, liberate a frozen guard's key card, and use it to make my way to you. I used one of my alchemy cartridges to douse you with the same substance, pulling you into the same time stream I am in to permit us to talk. The substance is quite toxic if used long-term—meddling with time tends to disrupt organic matter as it goes against the natural order of things—but I can assure you I will not be here long."

Jason was curious despite himself about why Doctor Alchemy wanted to talk to him. He said, "You say you want to talk. So talk." He motioned slightly with his head at the surrounding prison. "I'm a captive audience, after all."

Doctor Alchemy frowned. "Is that a joke? Puns are beneath me."

"They're not beneath me. Not much is. I have to take my pleasure where I can find it these days."

"I have a job for you."

Jason was surprised. "Unless the job involves me lying flat on my back and not wiping my own ass, I'm not qualified."

"I want you to help me kill someone. Someone you have dealt with before. You were previously hired to assassinate him. Theodore Conley. You knew him as Kinetic. He goes by Omega now." Jason had never heard of Omega before. If he had access to the news, perhaps he would have. The only television channels he was allowed access to were filled with mindless entertainment. Thanks to countless hours of watching Telemundo, Jason was fluent in game show Spanish. In the unlikely event he was made the host of a Spanish version of *Wheel of Fortune*, he was ready.

"What've you got against my old pal Theo?" Jason wondered why Theo had changed his code name. He doubted it was for the same reason Jason had changed his own alias several times over the years—to evade the authorities. Jason remembered Theo as a superpowered Cub Scout who might graduate to Eagle Scout one day if he applied himself.

"Omega killed my daughter."

Jason was surprised again. "I didn't even know you had a daughter, much less that she was killed. That doesn't sound like Theo at all. I accidentally offed Pappy Conley while trying to kill Theo, yet Theo did not in turn kill me when he had me at his mercy. He showed more restraint than most would in a similar situation. Certainly more than I would've."

"Whether it sounds like him or not, he did it. I am assembling a team of Metas who have confronted him before to help me subdue and kill him. You are the first person I've approached, both because I have had successful dealings with you in the past and because you have something that may prove useful. Parts of your last fight with Theodore were captured by Washington, D.C.'s city surveillance cameras. In reviewing that footage, I noticed you wore a suit that seemed to immunize you from Theodore using his telekinesis directly on you. Such technology would be useful in a future battle with him."

Jason was still dubious that the kid he had dealt with years ago could kill anyone. The Theo he had known had eaten too steady a diet of American apple pie, Bible verses, and aw-shucks, down-home values for that. Jason kept his doubts to himself. Alchemy was not fond of being contradicted. Instead Jason said, "That suit was destroyed in my last confrontation with Theo."

"Come now. Do you really expect me to believe a consummate professional such as yourself with a well-deserved reputation for preparing for all eventualities did not have spare suits salted away somewhere? I could reverse engineer the technology and incorporate it both into my own clothing and that of the other members of the team I am assembling."

Doctor Alchemy was right. Jason did have spare telekinesis-proof suits that he had gotten from his then-secret employer, whom Jason had not even known at the time had been Mechano of the Sentinels. Mechano had retained Jason through a series of intermediaries so that the Hero's connection to Theo's assassination would be hidden. The suits Mechano had designed were stashed in various hideaways. Jason had not volunteered information about them when Theo had turned him over to the authorities. Just as Jason had not volunteered information about the millions of dollars he had squirreled away in safe deposit boxes and offshore accounts under various names. Those concealed millions had gone untouched when the federal government had seized Jason's assets to make restitution to the families of the people he had killed over the years. The victims the authorities knew about, at any rate. There were others, so many that Jason had lost track. Jason was still a very wealthy man thanks to his hidden assets. Not that all that loot was doing him any good while trapped in a prison bed.

Jason wasn't about to volunteer to someone as erratic as Alchemy the things he had hidden. He avoided Alchemy's question about his suits. "Though Theo's older now than when I tangled with him, not all that much time has passed.

Surely he's still just a hayseed from South Carolina. He had his hands full dealing with just little ol' me. Why would someone like you need my or anyone else's help in taking him out?"

"His power level has increased exponentially since your encounters with him," Doctor Alchemy said. He seemed sheepish. It was a look Jason was not accustomed to seeing on Alchemy's normally supremely confident face. "I am not certain I can defeat him on my own." The sheepish look faded, replaced by a slightly crazed one. "Besides, I seek to not merely defeat Omega," he spat. "I'm looking to humiliate him. Embarrass him. Shame him. Who better to help me do that than people Omega defeated in the past and have an ax to grind against him? As the light fades from his eyes, he will realize that the seeds sown in his past have grown into a bitter harvest that have choked the life out of him.

"And you certainly have an ax to grind," Alchemy added, glancing down at Jason's frail, broken body. "Look at you—a once proud, powerful man brought low by that murdering Meta. I will pay you handsomely for your assistance, of course. A craftsman like you deserves to be compensated for his efforts."

"How much?" Jason asked. Greed had roused itself like sexual need within him. Though he had plenty of money socked away, old habits died hard.

Doctor Alchemy told him. Jason whistled at the number. That amount of money would buy—or at least rent—plenty of voluptuous vixens. Not that either renting or buying a bunch of busty babes would do Jason any good in his current condition, he thought. It would be like a crippled man buying a fleet of bicycles.

"What say you?" Doctor Alchemy asked impatiently.

"There are other MetaHold inmates I need to visit before the time freeze wears off."

Jason did not hesitate. "No," he said.

"No?" Alchemy frowned.

"No," Jason repeated firmly. "I'm not going to lie and say the thought of getting out of this oversized cage isn't appealing. But, I went into this business knowing the risks. I did not expect to spend my life killing people, then grow old and die peacefully in my sleep. I got paid a lot of money to do a very illegal, very dangerous job, and my employers expected results. Normally I got them. But as good as I was, I knew it was only a matter of time before I ran into someone who was better. That person would put me down, just as I had put down so many others. I didn't expect that person to be a wet behind the ears farm boy from Nowhereville, South Carolina, but life rarely turns out the way you expect. I had a good run. Theo ended it fair and square. The better man won. And to continue with my honesty kick—all these meds must've addled my brain because I never told the truth so much in one clip before—I gotta admit that I kinda liked the kid. I've known a lot of people with powers over the years. Far worse people than Theo have had them. If he's using them to help people instead of enriching himself like so many others do— me, for example—I say good luck and godspeed to him. Who am I to piss in his Wheaties? I had my shot and flubbed it."

Jason had researched Theo and his family before he confronted the kid years ago. Jason had spent a lot of time staring at MetaHold's ceiling and thinking about how different his own life might have been if his parents had loved him the way Theo's had. Jason had never met his own father, and he wished he never met his mother. His earliest memory was of her beating him. His last memory of her was her beating him when he was 15-years-old, right before he turned her into solid ice and then shattered her body into bloody ice shards with a fireball. It had been the first time his powers had manifested.

Jason's mouth twisted into a slight smile at the thought of his mother. Remembering her bloody bits was the only time she ever made him happy. "And even if I was inclined to help you, I'm still a cripple. Outside the confines of this prison I imagine my powers will return, but a cripple with superpowers is still a cripple." Jason shook his head. "Most people would say that what I did for a living was wrong. Certainly the judge who sentenced me to multiple life sentences thought so. Shit, maybe she and the rest of them are right. How the hell would I know? I never thought too much about wrong and right. I just lucked into superpowers and used them the best way I knew how to make a buck. Maybe that makes me a bad guy. Compared to someone like Theo, I suppose I am. But whether I was a good guy or a bad guy, what I was—what I took pride in being—was a professional. Paid well to do a job well." He looked down at his useless body. "I can't do a professional job like this. I won't even try."

Jason took a breath. He didn't think he'd talked this much in one stretch the entire time he had been in MetaHold. Doctor Alchemy's wordiness was rubbing off on him.

"So again, the answer is no. The *only* thing that would even tempt me to change my mind is if you waved a magic wand and gave me my arms and legs back. For them, I'd help you. As much as I liked the kid, I still gotta look out for number one."

Alchemy had remained uncharacteristically quiet during Jason's monologue. "I cannot say I am terribly surprised to hear you say that," he said. "In your own way, you are a man of honor. You always have been. It is why I trusted you in the past when I needed to eliminate someone I could not spare the time to take care of myself. It is part of the reason why I did you the honor of coming to you first."

Alchemy fished in his utility belt as he spoke. He pulled out a clear vial, several inches long, filled with a florescent yellow liquid. He held the vial out in front of Jason's eyes.

"What this?" Jason asked. "Something to quench my thirst after my long speech? You think of everything."

"I took the liberty of reviewing your medical records before coming here. The security of MetaHold's computerized medical records is even more laughable than that of the Heroes' Guild. This," Alchemy said, shaking the vial, "is a healing potion specially formulated for you."

Alchemy smiled with smug pride, like a new father might.

He said, "Or you may prefer to call it the magic wand that will give you your arms and legs back."

18

One Week and Several Days Ago

Anastasia Wyoming, once known as the licensed Hero Seer, sat on her cot in her cell in MetaHold. She wore the gray and white jumpsuit all MetaHold inmates did. She silently counted brushstrokes as she ran her brush through long hair so white that it seemed to almost glow.

234, 235, 236, 237, 238 . . . This life of confinement was not as exciting as her life as a Hero on the Sentinels had been. Not even close. Then again, what was? Not even the President's job was as exciting as being a Sentinel. Anastasia knew that for a fact. She had gotten an inside look at the mostly dull life of the occupant of the Oval Office years ago, back when Avatar was still alive, long before Anastasia had been imprisoned, disgraced, and had her Hero's license revoked.

Back then, Anastasia had taken turns with the other Sentinels guarding the chief executive when it was rumored Doctor Alchemy planned to assassinate her. Nothing had come of the threat, though, other than the President's right wrist breaking. Doctor Alchemy did not break it. He had never made an appearance at all. Anastasia herself had broken the President's wrist when the President had grabbed her ass. Anastasia not seeing the grope coming with her precognition had confirmed the Sentinels' long-held suspicion that the President was an unregistered and closeted Metahuman with the ability to dampen others' powers. The bruise the President left on Anastasia's ass had also confirmed their suspicion that the President was a closeted lesbian. A particularly aggressive one at that. "Tall, thin, and pale is just my type," the President had murmured about Anastasia's body while trying to stick her tongue down Anastasia's throat. Fending the President off without hurting her too badly had been like fending off an octopus.

444, 445, 446, 447, 448 . . . Anastasia focused on her brush-strokes, tuning out the chatter, howls, and yells of the prisoners who filled the cubical concrete cells near her own. She was aiming for two thousand strokes, which would beat her all-time record. She had to kill time somehow. She still had twenty years left to serve before release. Already no spring chicken, Anastasia would be elderly when she finally got out, unless she got an early release for good behavior. Or unless she succumbed to temptation and implemented one of the several escape plans she had contemplated. Unlike most of the Metas here, she was not a common crook. MetaHold had not been designed with people of her unique set of skills in mind. She was a Hero. Or at least she had been. Unlike her cape and license, her years of Heroic training and experience could not be stripped from her. Since the moment she had stepped foot into MetaHold, her mind had instinctively formulated ways to break out:

Mechano had done the initial design of the cells at Meta-Hold. Though Anastasia certainly was not an engineer like her robotic former teammate had been, she had paid enough attention over the years to him bragging and droning on about his technological achievements that she had a rough understanding of how the Metahuman power dampening field in her cell worked. She would just need a strip of metal to punch a hole through the ceiling to access the field's circuit boards. Perhaps a fork or knife smuggled into her panties or, safer still, her vagina—*ouch!*—so the guards would not find it when they searched her leaving the mess hall. That piece of metal, bent out of shape to bridge the appropriate parts of the dampening field's circuits, could be used to short the field out. With it gone, Anastasia could then use her telekinesis to rip a hole from the cell ceiling all the way through the top of the prison building, fly through the hole, and be a state or two away before the prison could scramble guards in armored flying suits to stop her.

Or, she could use her prison laundry job to slip out of the facility. The laundry truck came twice a week—to pick up dirty laundry, and then again to drop off the freshly laundered clothes. It would make a lot more sense for laundry to be done on site by the prisoners themselves. Anastasia knew the laundry contract was pork, a favor to a powerful United States Senator from New York who had a nephew in the laundry business. The nephew's truck driver was a creature of habit, always taking a three-minute smoke before getting back in his truck and driving off. It would be a simple matter for Anastasia to slip under the truck while the driver was away getting his nicotine fix. She could cling to the truck's long undercarriage, flat as a board, until it left the MetaHold facility. The truck was wide enough, Anastasia was skinny enough, and the guards who checked under outbound vehicles were sloppy enough that they would not see her. By the time her supervisor in the laundry department noticed her absence, she would be long gone. Out of boredom and curiosity, she had practiced the hanging under the truck maneuver by clinging to the underside of her cot. She had increasing her grip strength over the course of several weeks until she was certain it could be done.

Or Anastasia could escape from MetaHold using any number of other ploys and strategies her agile mind had presented her with. She had escaped from worse spots than this during her Heroic career, usually because a Rogue had put her into one.

And yet, Anastasia had not lifted a finger to escape. She would serve every minute of her time. She deserved to be punished. She knew that now.

523, 524, 525, 526, 527 . . . Anastasia felt the weight of someone's gaze. She looked up. Directly across the corridor was another cell. Through the nearly transparent front walls of the cells, she saw that the big man in the opposing cell glared at her. Leviathan. As meaty as a professional wrestler, but a lot less smart. He stared daggers at Anastasia as she continued to brush her hair.

Leviathan shifted now that he saw Anastasia looked back at him. He started humping his cell's transparent front wall while making choking motions with his hands. He was pantomiming what he would do to Anastasia if he had the chance. Anastasia winked at him and blew him a kiss. Deprived of his super strength by the prison's dampening fields, she knew Leviathan would be in for a nasty surprise if he did somehow manage to get his hands on her. Just as the Rogues who had jumped her in the yard during the first month of her incarceration had gotten a nasty surprise. They were laid up in the infirmary for two weeks afterward. Anastasia's willowy build was deceiving.

Anastasia was not popular among her fellow inmates.

After all, most of them were in MetaHold because a Hero had captured them. Many had been subdued by the Sentinels themselves, including Chaos, the Omega-level Rogue who was held in his own special section of MetaHold. The inmates would happily take their anger toward Heroes generally out on Anastasia specifically. Also, they thought she was a snitch because she had confessed to the crimes she, Mechano, and Millennium had engaged in. If there was one thing the inmates hated more than a Hero, it was a snitch. Snitches got stitches. Even the prison officials hated her. She was a disgraced Hero, after all.

Because she was so hated by the rest of MetaHold, Anastasia was forced to keep to herself. Even her cell, which was large enough to accommodate two inmates, she occupied alone. After at first giving her a series of cellmates, the prison's administrators had thrown up their hands at the constant fights between her and her cellmates, and decreed she would be housed alone going forward.

Being reviled by everyone around her wore on Anastasia's soul, like the steady drip of Chinese water torture. She was heartbreakingly lonely. It was like being a child on the Sioux reservation she had grown up on all over again. Because of a genetic mutation, she had been born with white hair, milky white eyes, and alabaster white skin tinged with blue instead of shiny black hair, brown eyes, and mahogany skin like her relatives. The Sioux kids she grew up with called her Paleface, Fish Belly, or Ghost when they had bothered to speak to her at all. Once Anastasia became a Hero in her early twenties, she finally felt like she had found her true people and a place where she truly belonged. That was all gone now.

And yet, despite how awful her prison life was with its disgrace, loneliness, hatred, and lack of freedom, Anastasia knew she deserved every bit of it.

810, 811, 812, 813, 814 . . . Anastasia had not always felt that way. Before she was in MetaHold, back when she still had her precognitive powers, she saw the dark hell the world would plunge into if a competent carrier of the Omega spirit was not available to help stave off that future. Seeing what the future could be had made it all too easy for Anastasia to justify what she, Mechano, and Millennium had done to Theodore Conley and others. They had tried to kill Theodore multiple times, hoping that someone more suitable to be the vessel for the Omega spirit would take his place once he was dead. Their attempts on Theodore's life had resulted in the death of his father James, and the deaths of many other innocents in an Oregon wildfire set by their agent Iceburn to flush Theodore out of the sanctuary of Hero Academy. The three Sentinels had killed the young Hero Smoke both to cover their tracks and in their last attempt to kill Theodore. They had done things a young and idealistic Anastasia would never have imagined her older self would do.

All in pursuit of the greater good, the three Sentinels had told themselves. *The ends justify the means,* were the words they had comforted themselves with when they violated their Hero's Oaths time and time again. With a bleak vision of a possible future in her head, Anastasia had participated in all of it. *Was it so terrible,* she had thought at the time, *that a few should die to save the many?*

Both awake and asleep, Anastasia used to dream of the future. Its possibilities, when it was far in the distance; its certainties, when it was close by. But when she arrived at MetaHold and her powers were shut off by the facility's dampening fields, her precognitive dreams of a dark future had turned into nightmares of an all too real past. Every night when she first arrived in MetaHold, she had relived the terrible things she and the other Sentinels had done. Constant nightmares had plagued her, haunting her with all the people who were dead because of her and the Sentinels.

Finally, she could not stand it anymore.

She had then confessed to each and every crime the Sentinels had committed. That confession led to the revocation of her Hero's license and the imposition of her twenty-year prison sentence for felony murder and other charges. Only the fact that Anastasia took full responsibility for her crimes, the judge had said at her sentencing, stopped him from giving her life in prison.

Though all the evils she and the other two Sentinels had committed still haunted her, at least she was able to sleep at night now.

1025, 1026, 1027— Anastasia's silent count was interrupted when something hit her in the chest. Startled, she dropped her brush.

Or rather, the brush should have dropped with Anastasia's hand no longer on it. Instead, the brush hung in the air like it rested on an invisible shelf.

Anastasia looked down to see what had struck her in the chest—a small metal cartridge, broken in two. A chill ran down her spine. Only one person used cartridges like this. It was as distinctive as a fingerprint.

"Hello Seer," Doctor Alchemy said.

Her heart pounding, Anastasia looked up. Doctor Alchemy stood at the front of her cell, having appeared there as soundlessly as the ghost kids had once called her. The nearly transparent front cell wall that only the guards could open with their keycards was gone. The always noisy cellblock was now as still and quiet as a grave. The sudden silence was deafening. Across the hall, Leviathan was frozen in place. His erect manhood pressed motionlessly against the clear wall of his cell.

The Sentinels had foiled Doctor Alchemy's fiendish plots many times in the past. Anastasia could not imagine he was here to ask how prison life was treating her. Especially since she had been involved in the death of his daughter Smoke. The fact Doctor Alchemy held one of the guard's futuristic-looking guns stoked her fears. Doctor Alchemy was as dangerous as a rabid dog, and equally as predictable.

"Guards!" she called out sharply. She got up from her cot.

"They cannot hear you," Doctor Alchemy said in his thickly accented voice. "They are frozen in time. It is quite a long story. Though it is interesting and further demonstrates my genius, it is one that I do not have time for." The gun was at his side, pointing at the floor. Even so, Anastasia's muscles tensed up. She wondered if she could disarm him before he raised the gun and shot her. She knew he was faster and stronger than she. Still, she had to try. She eyed the distance between them.

Perhaps reading the expression on her face, Doctor raised a placating hand. His other hand, the one with the gun, was still down at his side. "Before you do something rash, know that I come in peace," he said.

"Since when did you ever come in peace?" Anastasia asked. She would never forget how he had butchered her teammate Wildside. She wished she had her powers. What-ever Doctor Alchemy had done to the rest of the prison, it had not affected the cell's Metahuman dampening field. She thought that if she feinted to the left and then spun to the right, she could make him spoil his first shot and give her the chance to disarm him. He would still have his gauntlets full of those alchemy cartridges, however. *One problem at a time,* she chided herself. Trying to make it look casual, she took a step toward him.

"Do not come any closer," Doctor Alchemy said sharply,

though he still did not lift the gun. She froze. *So much for being casual,* Anastasia thought. "As I said, I come in peace. I am putting together a team. A team of Rogues. I want you on it."

"I'm not a Rogue."

With a look of incredulity, Doctor Alchemy waved his free hand at their surroundings, as if to say *Look where you are*.

"Okay, technically I am a Rogue," Anastasia admitted. "But whatever you have in mind, I'm not interested."

"Wait until you hear my proposal," he said. "The team I am assembling is of Metas whose lives were ruined by Theodore Conley. As someone in this penitentiary because of him, you certainly qualify."

"I'm not here because of him," Anastasia said. "I'm here because of my own actions."

"How very heroic of you to take responsibility for it. 'Heroic' with a small *h*, of course, since the Guild took your Hero's cape away from you." Anastasia couldn't tell if Doctor Alchemy was mocking her. "My team of Rogues and I are going to kill Mr. Conley for what he has done to us all. Are you sure you will not reconsider? I am after all offering you a get out of jail free card. Your fellow inmates Iceburn and Brown Recluse have already taken me up on my offer. Both are wasting away in here because of Theodore, just as you are."

Anastasia thought both men deserved to be in and stay in prison. Iceburn had tried to kill Theodore and had killed several other people along the way. Brown Recluse had planted a bomb in the Trials that was meant to kill Theodore. Anastasia's testimony that the Sentinels had paid him to do so led to him being convicted. But Anastasia did not say any of that to Doctor Alchemy. She knew he was crazy. Saying the wrong thing could set him off. Angering someone with a gun when you did not have one yourself was not the best survival strategy.

It flashed through Anastasia's mind to pretend to go along with Doctor Alchemy's scheme. Once she was out of Meta-Hold, she could warn Theodore of the looming threat against him.

No, she thought fiercely. *Enough lies. Enough hidden agendas. Enough going along with a present evil in pursuit of a future good. That's what landed me in this cell to begin with. Besides, I can tell Warden Sakey about Alchemy's plot. He can get word to Theodore.*

"I said I'm not interested, and I meant it," Anastasia said firmly. "Go away. I was in the middle of beating my hair brushing record. You made me lose count. Now I'll have to start all over again."

Doctor Alchemy sighed deeply. "A shame. Ending young Theodore would be easier with another former Hero on board." He shook his head sadly. "You can take the girl out of the cape, but apparently you cannot take the cape out of the girl."

Doctor Alchemy dropped the gun. It clattered on the hard cell floor. He kicked it toward Anastasia. It skittered across the cell, coming to rest a few feet from her, much closer to her than it was to him.

"What's that?" Anastasia asked, puzzled, still afraid to move.

Doctor Alchemy smiled. "A gun."

"I know it's a gun. What's it for?"

"Shooting people."

Anastasia felt a surge of irritation. "I'm not interested in playing games with you."

"Nor I with you." Doctor Alchemy's dark eyes glittered. "What I am interested in is killing you for your role in the murder of my daughter."

"I won't join your revenge squad, and now you want to kill me?" Anastasia shook her head in disbelief. Talking to Doctor

Alchemy was like talking to the wind—you never knew when it was going shift on you.

"No, I always wanted to kill you. If you helped me with Omega, I would have waited until he was dead first. Since you will not help, I have moved killing you from the back-burner to the front-burner."

"I'm ashamed of the part I played in the death of your daughter," Anastasia said honestly. "I deeply regret it. I'm so sorry for your loss. I think about her every day and how I wish I'd done things differently."

"Too little too late. Your cowardly act against my daughter has already signed your death warrant. Now it is time for me carry out the sentence." Doctor Alchemy hit a button on each of his gauntlets. They fell off his wrists and clanked onto the floor. "If you were a man, I would have struck you down the moment you refused to help me against Omega. But, since you are a woman and I grew up being taught that women are to be protected and cherished, I will not murder you in cold blood. It is so hard to shake the teachings of one's youth, no matter how outdated. Hence me removing my gauntlets. And, hence the gun on the floor. One of us is going to shoot the other with it. Whoever gets to it first lives. Whoever does not dies. Kill, or be killed. Since my reflexes are faster than yours, I even made the gun stop closer to you than it is to me. It is all really quite sporting of me, don't you think?"

Doctor Alchemy's eyes danced with madness, both the anger kind and the crazy kind. They burned into Anastasia's.

He flicked a finger toward the gun.

"Try to pick it up," he said.

"No," she said firmly. "I have too many people's blood on my hands already. I don't want to add yours to the list."

"I did not want to eat the heart-healthy oatmeal my wife directed our servants to make me this morning for breakfast.

Yet I ate it anyway. My daughter did not want to die. Yet she died anyway, thanks to you and other self-styled Heroes. We often must do things we do not want to do. This situation is no different. Pick the gun up."

"No," Anastasia said again. She didn't want to die, but she didn't want to be responsible for Doctor Alchemy's death either. A Hero did not kill. Being trapped in this cell all this time had reminded her of that. Could she incapacitate this homicidal maniac with her bare hands before he killed her?

"Perhaps you need a countdown to get you into the proper mindset," Doctor Alchemy said. "We will both reach for the gun on the count of five. It will be like an old-fashioned duel. We are like cowboys with a beef against each other in a Western. Well, actually we are both two different kinds of Indians, you are not even a boy, and there are not any cows within fifty miles of this place, but you know what I mean."

Doctor Alchemy put his arms straight down at his sides. He waggled his fingers. His Indian accent disappeared, replaced by a Western twang. "This here town ain't big enough for the both of us, Tex. If you're still too lily-livered to go for your piece on five, ready or not, here I'll come anyhow. One."

"Don't make me hurt you," Anastasia warned.

"Tex, that's mighty power of positive thinking of you. Two."

"Don't do this."

"Three."

Anastasia dove for the gun, not waiting to hear *four*.

Moving like a cobra, Doctor Alchemy sprang forward. He scooped up the gun before Anastasia laid hands on it, then leaped into the air to avoid Anastasia's diving body, like a second baseman avoiding a runner sliding into base.

Empty-handed, Anastasia skidded to a stop on the cold, hard floor. Breathing heavily, she twisted around. She stared into the gun's big barrel.

She had thought before that being imprisoned in Meta-Hold was what she deserved because of all the people who died because of her and the other two Sentinels. Now she realized *this* was what she truly deserved: An eye for an eye. Blood for blood. To die by the sword just as she had lived by the sword.

Doctor Alchemy looked down at Anastasia. "Tex, I ain't even get to five. You dealt me dirty and you still couldn't get it done. Disappointing. Oh well. Partner, I beat you unfair and unsquare. To the victor belong the spoils. This is the way your world ends—not with a whimper, but with a bang."

A satisfied Cheshire cat grin slowly spread across Doctor Alchemy's face, like that of a kid finding what he wished for under the Christmas tree.

"Bang," he said.

Then the gun said it too.

19

Five Days Ago

Thad Wilson shook his fanged head in disgust as he contemplated breaking into the vending machine. From plucking armored cars like fat Christmas geese to shaking down a soda machine. How the mighty had fallen.

"This is humiliating," he said aloud, though he was alone. He was on the second floor of a community college's fitness center. He did not know what town he was in. Bumfuck Nowhere, USA as far as he was concerned. An empty yoga studio was to his left; a weight and cardio room was down the stairs further to the left. A ratty couch and a smattering of chairs stained by generations of sloppy students surrounded a low table behind him.

Thad, who went by the street name of Silverback, wiped spittle off his chin with a forearm. The long fangs that extended up from his lower jaw where a normal person's canine teeth would be made it impossible for Thad to close his mouth completely. He therefore drooled constantly, and had ever since the fangs sprouted out of his mouth at fourteen when his Metahuman powers manifested.

Thad caught a vague reflection of himself in the shiny red plastic of the vending machine he stood in front of: big brutish body in soiled jeans and wrinkled tee shirt, hairy arms corded with muscle, low sloping forehead, and slightly hunched back. All that combined with his fangs and the drooling made people think he was stupid. He was not. He was not the sharpest knife in the drawer, but neither was he the dullest.

He felt stupid now, though. With all his super strength, all the cool shit he had done, all the hot women he had banged, all the daring big money heists he had pulled over the years as Silverback, he was reduced to this.

Thad watched his reflection shake its big head in disgust again. *Fuck you Omega,* he thought fiercely.

Thad gave one final glance around to make sure he had not missed any surveillance cameras. Then, he shoved his meaty hand through the metal part of the machine that surrounded the lock. The metal scrapped his super-tough skin but did not pierce it. The metal screeched in protest as Thad closed his fist. He flexed and pulled. The machine's lock ripped free of the machine. Part of Thad hoped the thumping music coming from the gym below would conceal the racket. The rest of him did not care.

Thad pulled the now unsecured door open. He grunted in disapproval at the interior. He hadn't noticed before that the stupid machine did not accept bills. The only money inside was coins. Thad pulled out the metal money bin. He shook it, eyeballing the coins and feeling their weight. Around seventy dollars. Maybe as much as ninety. Clearly the serviceman had not come around to collect the coins lately. Once Thad emptied the thin plastic cylinders still in the machine that contained the coins the machine gave out as change, he'd probably have around a hundred dollars. *My lucky day,* Thad thought sarcastically. *It's goddamned humiliating.* Thad had dropped far more money than this on the ground when escaping from a bank heist and had not thought twice about it. Those had been good times. All over thanks to Omega.

Fuck you Omega, Thad thought again.

Not feeling like heading back to his RV parked outside, Thad pulled a cola out of the open machine. He felt a fresh surge of disgust when he saw the cola was not even a major brand name like Blast.

America's Heartland my ass, he thought. *The whole place smells like cow patties. More like America's Fartland.*

Thad giggled about his cleverness as he opened the can of soda and quickly downed it. He dropped the empty can on the floor and grabbed another from the machine. He leaned on the machine, relaxing. It shifted against his weight.

Where am I anyway? he thought. *Nebraska? Kansas? Colorado?* One of the rectangular states in flyover country full of nothing of significance and nobody who mattered. Driving aimlessly in his RV, Thad had lost track. He had been on the road now for how long? A month? A month and a half? He had lost track of that too. He was in a nothing college in a nothing town in a nothing state in the middle of nowhere.

As Thad finished his second drink and started on his third, he heard the conversation of people climbing the stairs. They appeared. Two young women, likely students here based on their age. They were sweaty and in workout gear. They fell silent when they saw Thad. They stared at him and the open vending machine. Thad stared right back. A primal hunger rose within him. Though these women were not Thad's type —he was into big city sophistication, striking faces, thin bodies, and improbably large breasts, whereas these women were Midwest plain and plump—Thad had not been with a woman since leaving Astor City. Unfortunately, he did not have the money to pay for the kind of woman he was into. He always had to pay. Thanks to his freakish appearance, it was rare that a woman of the caliber Thad liked hopped on his dick for free. Not that he would be able to find the kind of woman he was into of either the free or paid variety out here in the boondocks.

The women exited the building, though they kept peering at him through the glass doors. One of them pulled out a cell phone and dialed a number. Calling the campus police probably. Thad stayed where he was against the machine and opened another soda. By the time those hillbillies put down their donuts and remembered where they had stashed their guns, Thad would be long gone.

Or maybe he wouldn't. Thad suddenly felt stubborn and cantankerous. Maybe he'd stay right here and dare the cops to arrest him, he thought. Putting some small-time fuzz in their place would make Thad feel better.

Thad sighed. He was looking forward to tangling with a couple of Barney Fifes. His life really was in the crapper. God how he missed Astor City! Astor City had been perfect for a guy like him. It was big enough that there were lots of high-priced brothels with plenty of hot-tailed talent to choose from. It was big enough that there was lots of easy money to fund his hooker habit and the rest of his lifestyle through bank robberies, armored car heists, cleaning out high-end jewelry stores and other businesses with a ton of cash and valuables, and shaking down rich douchebags with more money than the good sense to hire decent security. Astor City was also small and corrupt enough that Thad knew which cops and judges were on the take so that he could wiggle out of charges when he got caught. Until recently, did not get caught often. Even though the world's most famous team of Heroes had been right outside the city, the Sentinels had been more concerned with big fish like Black Plague and Doctor Alchemy than about small fish like him. For a long time, operating in Astor City had been like being a kid in a candy store owned by your indulgent daddy.

Until the hero Kinetic had changed his name to Omega, his look, and his power levels a couple of years ago. Ever since then, that damned Hero had seemed to be everywhere. Thad did not know how the always meddling Omega found time to sleep or take a dump. Maybe he didn't need to.

Thad opened another soda. If he had to choose between a plentiful supply of soda and a plentiful supply of money and whores, Thad would choose the latter. *Fuck you Omega,* he thought yet again. Empty cans littered the floor around him. It started to look like the bottom of a recycling bin.

As Thad drank, he brooded about the day Omega had banished him from his beloved Astor City.

———

THAD STOOD ON TOP OF A SEVEN-STORY APARTMENT BUILDING IN southwest Astor City dressed in his brown and tan Silverback costume. His binoculars were trained on Davis Street below. It was shortly after two in the afternoon. He had been up here waiting for thirty minutes. He was not impatient yet. The armored car should be passing through the residential neighborhood below shortly according to his informant in the armored car company. Thad had promised the informant a small cut of the money Thad stole. So the timetable was right, or else the informant would walk away as empty-handed as Thad.

Thad was on top of the tallest building in the small neighborhood to avoid being spotted by the handful of residents who were at home. Thad had chosen to hit the armored car in this working-class neighborhood because, in the middle of a workday, not too many people were around. Also, traffic was light. Thad liked to minimize the risk of people getting hurt during the jobs he pulled. Thad liked money, not hurting people. Also, people getting hurt drew too much heat from the authorities. Though Thad had bought his way out of trouble in the past, not all cops and judges were for sale. Damn their honest hides! The minority of people who wouldn't play ball puzzled Thad. What kind of fool turned down free money?

A blue and gray metal box on wheels came into view about a mile up on Davis Street. Thad smiled, baring his fangs. *Right on time,* he thought. He loved armored car drivers who stuck to their schedules. It made Thad's job so much easier. Thad put the binoculars down. He did not need them now that he knew exactly where the armored car was. He would retrieve them later, long after the job was over.

Thad waited on the edge of the roof until the armored car was almost directly below. The vehicle drove slowly, obeying the neighborhood's low speed limit. When the moment was right, Thad jumped off the roof. He dropped like a stone. He felt himself grinning. This part was fun, like an especially exciting roller coaster.

Seconds later, he slammed into the pavement, right in front of the armored car. The street cratered. Thad bent at the knees, absorbing the force of the impact. He twisted at the waist, shielding his vulnerable eyes, trying to let his absurdly muscled and dense back take most of the impact. The armored car slammed on brakes, swerving.

Too late. The car plowed into him with a teeth-rattling thump. Thad was shoved backward. He leaned forward, pushing against the slowing truck. He broke up pavement, furrowing the street, like he was the business end of a farmer's plow.

Finally, he and the truck slid to a halt. Dust from the street and smoke and steam from the armored car's accordioned engine rose up in a thick, choking fog. Thad's body ached from the crash and the jolt of his legs being pushed through the street. He knew his aches and pains would soon fade thanks to his super-fast metabolism.

Thad clambered out of the depression he had cut into the plowed-up street. The air stunk of burnt rubber, asphalt dust, and engine oil. He glanced through the impact resistant windshield of the stopped armored car. The head of the guard on the passenger side was down. He did not move. Unconscious. The driver squirmed, rattled but still awake.

Thad hustled to the driver's side. He thrust his hands into the thick metal of the door. He squeezed. Metal balled up in his thick fists. He pulled hard. Squealing in protest, the door ripped away from the vehicle. Thad was about to fling the door away like it was the lid to a can of beans when he saw the still-conscious guard fumble with his sidearm. Thad raised the door like a shield. Bullets thudded off its metal as the panicked guard shot at him. Thad's thick hide could withstand bullets, but they would've hurt like hell.

Hollow clicks. The guard had emptied his magazine. Thad dropped the door, stepped forward, and grabbed the guard who was now scrambling for his radio. Thad ripped him out of the truck, right through his fastened seat belt. Thad chopped the flailing guard with a flat palm on the side of his neck. The guard went limp as a tissue.

Thad laid the comatose guard on the ground. Gently, because he did not want to hurt him. The guard had just been doing his job, just as Thad was doing his. Thad rushed around to the back of the truck. He had a narrow window before the

Five-O arrived. A passing driver or some nosy resident had probably already called them. It was cheaper and easier to avoid the cops altogether than it was to pay them off.

The harsh sound of tearing metal filled the air as Thad ripped open the vehicle's thick back double doors. Labelled bags of money from area businesses the armored car company made bank deposits for lay inside. It was a sight for sore eyes. Thad's mouth watered and his manhood hardened at the thought of all the rich food and expensive whores this money would buy. Though Thad had stolen a lot of money over the years, he spent it almost as quickly as he made it. He lived hand to mouth, and his cash reserves were running on fumes. This money would refuel Thad's money tank nicely.

Thad hopped into the vehicle. He grabbed a couple of empty heavy-duty bags that were stowed there. He started filling them with the smaller bags of money. If a bag jingled too much when he picked it up, he left it behind. Thad was interested in paper money that crinkled, not coins that jingled.

In less than a couple of minutes, Thad had as much money in the two bags as he could comfortably carry. He slung them over his shoulders, feeling like Santa Claus bogged down with presents. *Ho, ho, ho* was right. Soon he'd shower some deserving hos with the cash, but only if they were both naughty and nice.

Thad hopped back down to the street. Approaching sirens wailed.

Time to blow this popsicle stand, Thad thought. He squatted, preparing his powerful legs for the jump. From here he would hop from building top to building top like a frog jumping on lily pads until the police and the scene of the crime were but a distant memory.

Thad leaped into the air. Wind rushed past him, making him squint. This was almost as fun as falling.

Unexpectedly, Thad sailed right past the roof of the six-story building he had been aiming for. He continued straight up into the sky, far past where his well-calculated jump should have taken him. Startled, Thad almost dropped his hard-earned money.

What the hell?! he thought, confused and panicked. After years of practice, jumping from building to building was as natural as banging hookers. Surely he had not misjudged his jump by this much. He rose in the air like a balloon.

Flailing now, Thad spotted a speck above him. As Thad continued to rise, the speck expanded into a man. Dark blue costume, cowl-covered head, white cape, and matching white symbol on his chest that looked, Thad always thought, like a circle drawn by a retard.

Omega. *Fuck!*

Thad slowed to a stop in the air in front of Omega. Now Thad realized he was being held in the air by Omega's powers. Thad stopped flailing. He had unfortunately encountered Omega several times before. He knew trying to fight against Omega's hold on him would do no good.

"Howya doin' Omega? Nice weather we're having."

Omega's arms were folded. A booted foot tapped the air impatiently. Everything about the guy read *annoyed*.

"Silverback," Omega said, "I'm about sick of you."

"Why?" Thad said, his feelings hurt. "What did I do?"

Omega looked pointedly at the bags of money slung over Thad's shoulders. In his surprise over being pulled high into the sky, he had almost forgotten about his loot.

"Oh," Thad said. Omega was close enough that Thad could hear him over the gusting wind, but unfortunately far enough away that Thad couldn't throttle him.

"Yeah, *oh*. Do you know how many times I've captured you either while or immediately after you've robbed someone in the past year and a half?"

Thad's brow furrowed in thought. As a live in the moment kind of guy, he did not have the best of memories. "Four times?" he said, hoping he was not overestimating the number.

"Try seven."

"That many?" Thad was impressed by how diligent and hard-working he had been. He was single-handedly making America great again.

"Yeah, that many. I catch you, the police take custody of you, and then miraculously they'll let you go, no doubt after you've greased the right palms. And those are just the times I've been around to catch you. There have been other times you've gotten clean away because I was otherwise occupied at the time. Like I said, I'm sick of both you and this catch and release thing we have going on. I've got more important things on my plate than having to deal with you every turnaround." Omega had a Southern accent. Thad hated that this country bumpkin thought he could lecture him.

"You could always stop catching me," Thad suggested hopefully.

"Yeah, that's not going to happen."

"A guy can dream."

A smile flashed on Omega's lips before an annoyed frown replaced it again. Omega said, "Madness is continuing to do the same thing over and over and expecting a different result. Me turning you over to the authorities only to have you go free shortly thereafter is exactly that—madness. Considering that, I have a proposition for you."

Finally! After all this time dealing with Omega, Thad thought he had found in him one of the rare honest men. The fact Omega now had his hand out restored Thad's faith in humanity. "I'll give you two thousand," he said.

"What?" Omega said, startled.

"Alright, alright, you drive a hard bargain. Five thousand. But between paying off you and my inside man at the armored car company, you're really cutting into my profit margin. You've gotta leave me something to live off of. I'm the one who stole the loot and took all the risks."

Omega shook his head. "I don't want your money."

"What?" It was Thad's turn to be startled. Thad's eyes narrowed suspiciously at Omega. *What sort of dirty Commie doesn't want money?* he thought. *It's downright un-American.*

"I said I don't want your money. Instead, I want your crimes to stop. Though it's not hard to see you take pains to not seriously hurt anyone, eventually you'll slip up and get someone killed. It's bad enough you're taking money that doesn't belong to you, but I definitely won't stand for someone to get seriously hurt because of your shenanigans. I'd tell you to go straight and get a regular job like everybody else, but you and I both know you're not likely to do that."

"Who'd hire me looking like this?" Thad demanded incredulously, pointing at his prominent fangs. He wiped some drool off his chin. "The circus? I'm no circus freak. I'm a small businessman."

Omega sighed.

"Look man, I'm not entirely unsympathetic. I don't have fangs, but I have an idea of what it's like to be different and have people judge you for it. But it's my job to protect people. Because of your antics, you're a ticking time bomb who's going to get a bunch of people hurt sooner or later. So here's my proposition—you leave town. Better yet, leave the state. When you're outside of your network of corrupt cops and judges, maybe you'll be less likely to rob people because you'll know you'll wind up behind bars where you belong. And if you take a chance anyway and pull another job that I hear about, know that I will find you and turn you in."

Thad thought about that. He had a sweet thing going in Astor City. He had no interest in abandoning it. "And if I don't leave?"

Omega floated a little closer, though he unfortunately remained outside of Thad's throttling range.

"Then I'll drop everything else I have going on," Omega said, looking straight into Thad's eyes earnestly, "and make you my pet project. I already know your name is Thad Wilson. I also know where you live, your favorite cathouse, your favorite call girl, and your favorite place to eat. Don't look so surprised—you've been booked often enough that discovering your real name wasn't hard. Finding out the rest was only barely less easy. Every step you take, I'll be there. I'll become your little blue shadow. You won't be able to make a move without me knowing about it, or have a bowel move-ment without me smelling it. The moment you do so much as litter, I'll hand you over to the police. They'll likely let you go free again, but hand you over to the cops enough times and eventually you'll run out of bribe money or we'll stumble across a member of Astor City's finest who takes his oath to serve and protect seriously. And if that doesn't work, I've got a secret place of my own where I stash Rogues the law can't seem to deal with. I've already got somebody cooling his heels there who would just love the pleasure of your company. And there's not so much as a change jar to steal from there."

"You . . . you . . . you wouldn't dare," Silverback sputtered. "That's illegal."

Omega barked out a laugh. "Are the bags you stole full of cash or irony? So, what's it going to be? Leave Maryland forever, or stay and get me as your personal Big Brother until you're behind bars for good?"

Thad thought about it. His interactions with Omega in the past indicated Omega always did what he said he would do.

Thad made his decision. *Goddamn these do-gooding Heroes,* he thought. *They make it impossible for a fella to make a dishonest buck these days.* "All right, you've gotta deal. I'll leave the state. I'll need to keep this cash, though. Starting over seed money, you know."

"No," Omega said. "Hand it over."

"But—"

"No," Omega said firmly.

Thad grunted in resignation. "I think I liked you better when you were Kinetic. You were less of a hard-ass back then."

What little Thad could see of Omega's face suddenly looked world-weary. He looked like he had lost his best friend and didn't have a friend left in the world.

"I think I liked me better too," Omega said. "I think I did too."

———

A FEW DAYS AFTER THAT CONVERSATION WITH OMEGA, THAD had used his dwindling funds to buy an RV in cash. He had one final romp with his three favorite escorts in Dog Cellar before he bought the RV because he had his priorities in the right place. That last bit of fun with Bambi, Maserati and Ebony was the main reason why he had so little money left when he bought the RV.

The three hookers were his favorites in the whole city. He called them the Neapolitans. He had named them after the ice cream because Bambi was vanilla pale, Ebony was chocolate brown, and Maserati had strawberry red hair, with her carpet matched her drapes. The Neapolitans did not come cheap. Thad thought they were worth every penny. It had been a tearful farewell at the end of Thad's last session with them. At least on Thad's end it had been tearful—the girls had looked somewhat relieved when he told them he was leaving town. He was convinced it was because they were not used to guys who were as good in the sack or as enthusiastic as he was. They were probably happy to get some rest. Bless their sexy little hearts.

Thad initially was going to steal the RV, but then remembered what Omega had said. Thad did not want to travel across America while looking over his shoulder, waiting for that buttinsky Hero to nab him for vehicular theft.

RVing was the safest way to travel since Thad was pretty sure there were some outstanding warrants for his arrest. He didn't want to risk showing identification to buy a plane, train, or bus ticket. Besides, because of how he looked, he drew too much attention on public transportation. If Thad wanted a bunch of strangers staring at him, he would go ahead and join the circus like he had told Omega.

After loading the RV with his few possessions, Thad had driven out of Astor City aimlessly, going nowhere in particular. He had grown up right outside of Astor City, and Maryland was the only home he had ever known. He had a vague notion to go to California. Free online porn had nearly killed California's once-thriving porn industry, and Thad had heard that many former porn stars now worked as escorts. Since a bunch of them were on his sexual bucket list, maybe he would wind up there.

Thad had earned eating and gas money while he made his way across the country by knocking over small gas stations, mom and pop shops, and other low hanging fruit that did not have security cameras. Thad thought that surely news of such small fry being robbed would not make its way back to Omega.

Thad had stolen millions over the years. He had also spent millions, mostly on wine, women, and song. And not in that order. The millions he had spent was why he had no assets other than some clothes, the RV outside, and memories of good times and sexy women. As he stood in the fitness center and drank stolen sodas, he did not regret one cent of all the money he had squandered. He had lived life to the fullest. The only thing he regretted was so quickly abandoning the good life. With every mile he had driven further from Astor City, Thad had grown to dislike Omega more and more.

Now, that dislike was full-blown hate. Thad had half a mind to go back to the RV right this second, drive back to Maryland, and kick Omega's meddling ass once and for all. Who the hell did that guy think he was?

Thad avoided hurting people. With Omega, he would make an exception to his rule.

Instead, stewing in humiliation and frustration, Thad opened a can of fruit punch. He had drunk all the colas in the machine. It was time to switch things up. Ah, the exciting life of an exiled Rogue. Besides, his diet had been crap the past few days, mostly burgers and greasy fries from fast food joints, so he thought he needed the fruit punch's vitamin C.

Thad chugged the fruit punch. He belched, then let out a long sign of resignation. He knew all his self-talk about kicking Omega's ass was just that—talk. The annoying Hero had been a handful when he had merely been Kinetic. Now, as Omega, he was simply too powerful. Of the times he had tangled with Omega, Thad had bested him exactly zero times. If he went back to Astor City, Thad knew he would merely extend his perfect losing streak.

Thad drank and drank and drank, crunching and dropping each can when he was done with it, and then reaching for a fresh one. Twisted aluminum surrounded him. He wondered why Barney Fife and his dumber cousin had not shown up yet. Maybe they had forgotten where the fitness center was. They probably couldn't find their unwiped asses with both hands and a bloodhound. Stupid cops for a stupid school in a stupid town in a stupid state.

All the liquid he drank soon had the usual effect. He dismissed the idea of looking for a bathroom. *Screw this dumb school,* he thought. He pulled his penis out and took a leak in front of the vending machine. His pee hit the empty aluminum cans around him on the floor with a pitter-patter that made Thad's heart ache with nostalgia. It reminded him of the sound a hard rain made when it hit the streets and buildings of downtown Astor City.

Thad was standing there, homesick, with his penis in his hand, daydreaming of how much fun it would be to twist Omega's head off his neck, when a swirling oval mass of gray and white blinked into existence a few feet away. About the size of a large doorway, looking at it was like looking at the roiling clouds of a thunderstorm.

Doctor Alchemy stepped out of it.

Startled, Thad dropped his fruit punch and his streaming penis. Punch and pee soaked through his shoes and wet his hairy toes.

Doctor Alchemy's cape swirled around his costumed body. He looked at Thad's wet shoes, the open vending machine, the empty cans arrayed around Thad's feet, and Thad's hairy exposed manhood. Doctor Alchemy's nose wrinkled at the smell of Thad's urine.

"I see things are going well for you, Silverback," Doctor Alchemy said.

"Never better," Thad said sarcastically. His initial surprise was fading. He had dealt with Alchemy before. Alchemy had hired Thad a few times in the past when he had needed muscle. Thad tucked himself back into his jeans. Then he reached inside the vending machine and grabbed another fruit punch. He waved it at Alchemy. "Want one? They're free."

"No thank you. I am perfectly capable of manufacturing my own poisons. Plus, I have seen with my own eyes where your hands have been."

"Suit yourself. More for me. What're you doing here, anyway?"

"Looking for you."

Thad was surprised again. "How the hell did you find me?"

Doctor Alchemy turned and pointed at a security camera mounted over the ratty couch. It pointed right at the vending machine. *Fuck!* Thad thought. He didn't know how he had missed it before. Then again, casing a place had never been Thad's strong suit. He was more of a smash, grab, and run like hell type of robber. What if Omega happened to see the footage of him breaking into the vending machine?

Fuck Omega, Thad thought for the umpteenth time. Even so, he resolved to make this his last drink before hitting the road again. Silently cursing Omega was one thing; having Omega follow through on his threat to be Thad's 24/7 chaperone was quite another.

"My underworld informants told me Omega had driven you from Astor City. They also told me you were none too happy about it," Doctor Alchemy said. Thad wondered who he had to thank for wagging her lips about him: Bambi, Ebony, or Maserati? Probably Bambi. Thad had never been able to figure out the thoughts that ran around behind her cold and mysterious blue eyes. He had a sudden suspicion that Bambi's name was as fake as her boobs. *You can't trust anybody these days,* he thought. *If pillow talk with a hooker ain't sacred anymore, what is?*

"So?" Thad said. He was still in a foul mood. He couldn't muster the will to be polite despite the fact he knew Alchemy was both powerful and crazy as a loon. *What the hell is a loon, anyway?* Whatever it was, he felt like punching one.

"So, I had my Monitor Room's computers scan for any sign of you. When they got a ping from this school's security feed, I decided to pay you this visit and talk to you about Omega."

"And what's that thing?" Thad pointed to the swirling mass of whatever in the hell it was that Doctor Alchemy had stepped out of.

"That?" Doctor Alchemy waved dismissively at it with a gloved hand as if to say *This old thing?* "That is a dimensional aperture. It allows me to travel from one place to another in the blink of an eye."

"Cool," Thad said. He wanted to add that Doctor Alchemy should step back into his dimensional aperture thingie and leave him alone, but he didn't dare. He knew how touchy Doctor Alchemy could be. Thad was in a foul mood, not a foolhardy one.

"Years of intense study and sweat equity to bend the laws of time and space to my will, and all you can say is 'cool.'" Doctor Alchemy rolled his eyes heavenward. "Gods, save me from these philistines." Thad didn't know what philistines were. *Maybe they're related to loons,* he thought. Doctor Alchemy said, "But I'm here for your brawn, not your intellect. Am I correct in assume you are no fan of Omega's?"

"I hate his guts," Thad said frankly. Visions of Omega's decapitated body danced through his head, followed by images of Maserati, Ebony, and Bambi (if that really was that loose-lipped bitch's name) dancing naked. He missed them desperately.

"With your help, I plan to rid the world of Omega for good. With him out of the way, you can return to your lavish and sybaritic lifestyle in Astor City instead of . . ." Doctor Alchemy glanced around disdainfully, "this."

Thad did not know what sybaritic meant either, but he knew what lavish meant. It meant no more RVs, no more knocking over vending machines, and no more getting hard over plain Jane Midwesterners. He could be with the Neapolitans again.

Thad tossed his half full can of fruit punch over his shoulder.

"I'm listening," he said.

20

Antonio "Mad Dog" Ricci hated his life. He did not have much of a life, but what little life he had, he hated.

He hated being trapped in the hollowed-out middle of a mountain, which was in turn in the middle of nowhere. No, not merely *a* mountain. *The* Mountain, Omega's lair. Antonio hated that name too. The place had first been Avatar's mountain retreat, now it was the Boy Blunder's. Antonio thought Heroes, with all their training and fancy suits and holier-than-thou attitudes, should be able to come up with a more imaginative name for a mountain retreat than The Mountain. Then again, Heroes were not supposed to hold men against their will without due process. Heroes were not the morally superior paragons they pretended to be, clothed in bright colors and righteousness. They were just like him, Antonio thought —people who did what they wanted to the people they wanted to do it to when they wanted to do it simply because they could.

Antonio hated his cubical cell, which he had been confined in for over two years. The Mountain's rock composed the floor and the back wall, and thick glass comprised the remaining four walls. The glass was unbreakable. Antonio knew that because he had literally spent weeks when he had first arrived here trying to break it. Antonio's efforts had not produced so much as a scratch.

Antonio hated that his Metahuman powers to spit energy balls from his mouth were gone, suppressed somehow by the cell he was in. Maybe if he had his powers back, he could've busted out of here long before now. And maybe if pigs had wings, they'd be pigeons. Antonio knew you had to play the hand life dealt you even if you hated that hand with a white-hot passion.

Antonio hated the food he had been forced to live off of since being brought here: canned food, dehydrated food, raw fruits and vegetables, and dried meat. What he would have given for a taste of one of his grandma's cannoli! The thought of biting into its crispy sweet shell, and having it crack open to ooze soft cream in his mouth made him drool. His MeeMaw was for all intents and purposes his mother since she had raised him when his biological drug-addled mother had abandoned him when he was just a baby. MeeMaw had been old and ailing when Antonio last saw her. He wondered if she had died while he was trapped here. The thought both saddened and enraged him.

Antonio hated that he lived like an animal, with where he urinated and squatted mere feet from where he choked down his lousy food. It was worse than being in prison. At least in prison he had someone to talk to. Not to mention drugs and girls if you had the right connections or bribed the right guard. Antonio was in a position to know, having spent a lot of time in confinement, especially when he was a kid. If his MeeMaw had been his mother, the juvenile justice system had been his father. However, he had not gone back to prison for any real length of time once he got out of the joint at twenty-one after a four-year stretch for arson and slinging dope. During that prison stint, Antonio had hooked up with the Esposito crime family. After his release, he had become one of the crime family's enforcers, putting his aggressive tendencies and Metahuman powers to good use. Though Antonio had done plenty of things as a mob enforcer he should have been locked up for, the Espositos protected their own. Whenever Antonio had been nabbed for something after associating with the Espositos, the vast tentacles of the crime family had reached out, bribing officials, intimidating witnesses, doing whatever needed to be done to free one of their best enforcers.

Until now. As far as Antonio knew, absolutely no one, much less the Espositos, knew he was trapped in The Mountain. Other than Omega, Antonio had not seen another living soul since he had been brought here.

Antonio hated that he had not been with a woman since that bastard Omega had kidnapped him from where he had been holed up in Italy, waiting for the heat over Hannah Kim's death to cool before he returned to the United States. Be with a woman? Ha! Hell, at this point Antonio would give his left nut just to lay eyes on a woman again. Long ago, Antonio had first asked then later begged Omega to bring him a laptop filled with porn, or at least some girlie magazines.

"You're in prison, not on a Vegas vacation," Omega had said. Sanctimonious prick.

Omega had given Antonio a steady supply of books, though, to occupy his time and help him while away the otherwise empty hours. With nothing much else to do, Antonio had grown to love reading. He was especially a fan of Westerns, thrillers, and—God help him—romance novels. The once-feared enforcer for the Esposito crime family had become a goddamned bookworm who loved a well-crafted story ending in a happily ever after.

Antonio hated that, too.

And, most of all, Antonio hated Omega. Theodore Fucking Conley. The Blue Bastard. The Heroic Hick. The Telekinetic Turkey. The Caped Cocksucker. Antonio had come up with a lot of nicknames for Omega during his imprisonment. The idle mind truly was the Devil's playground.

Omega had told Antonio his real name the day he had imprisoned Antonio here. Omega had also shown Antonio his face that day, and was not shy about continuing to show Antonio his face during his periodic visits to The Mountain. The fact Omega did not keep his secret identity hidden from Antonio told Antonio more eloquently than words ever could that Omega expected Antonio to never leave this place.

Antonio hated everything about Omega—the self-righteous speech he had given Antonio when he had first brought Antonio to The Mountain, the fact he thought he had the right to imprison Antonio, his costume, his hick Southern accent, the cocky way he walked . . . everything. Antonio especially hated the fact he was glad to see that caped asshole when Omega made one of his periodic visits to The Mountain. Not only did Omega's appearance mean Antonio would get some new books to read, but it also meant he would have someone to talk to, however briefly. Talking to the man Antonio hated was better than having absolutely no one to talk to at all.

Antonio's one-man prison and the man who had put him in it were not the only things Antonio hated.

He also hated himself.

Antonio had killed his girlfriend Hannah. If he had a mirror, he would not be able to bear looking at himself in it out of shame and self-loathing. He had not meant to kill Hannah. He had loved her.

Antonio had been enraged years ago when Omega and his friend, both in disguises, had braced him in his apartment and tried to force him to break up with Hannah. They had threatened him. Omega had beaten him. That wasn't something Antonio had been used to—he was used to being the hammer, not the nail. When Antonio later went to Hannah's condo to find out if she had sicced Omega on him, things had gotten out of hand. He had beaten her. He had hit her plenty of times in the past—Hannah liked it rough, and Antonio had been more than happy to oblige her—but nothing like this. He had lost his temper when Hannah lied to him about not knowing anything about the men who had broken into his apartment and beaten him. He lost his temper a lot back then. It was why he had gotten the nickname Mad Dog.

Furious, Antonio had spat one of his energy balls at Hannah. Hannah's body had been thrown backward, slamming her into a wall. Antonio had watched, horrified, as his energy ball bored a hole right through the woman he loved.

If Antonio could take it all back, he would have. Antonio had relived the moment he killed Hannah every day since it happened. When he closed his eyes, he could still smell the stench of her charred flesh.

When it came to women, Antonio knew you couldn't listen to what they said. What mattered was how they behaved. They all said they wanted a nice guy, but they all chased after bad boys. Guys like Antonio. It was only after their looks faded and they could no longer attract the bad boy did they settle down with the nice beta boy they had turned their noses up at years before and give him unenthusiastic, starfish sex every couple of months after he begged and pleaded.

As a bad boy, Antonio never had to beg. As a result, he had

been with a lot of women over the years. More than he could remember. Hannah had been the only woman he gave a damn about, though. The only woman he had ever loved.

And, the only woman he had ever killed.

Antonio had killed men before, of course. When he was a young man, he had killed for fun, simply because he could thanks to his powers and unusually strong body. After hooking up with the Espositos, he had become more disciplined, killing because they had told him to. Because someone needed to die.

Now Antonio had a different reason to kill someone—revenge. Revenge for caging him like an animal. Revenge for stealing what should have been some of the best years of his life. Revenge for making him feel weak and powerless.

Hannah had been the last person Antonio had killed. He intended Omega to be the next person he killed.

Antonio's fiery hate for Omega was the only thing that kept him from slitting his wrists with the jagged lid of one of his food cans out of loneliness, boredom, and self-loathing. The thought of killing Omega gave his mind something to focus on other than images of Hannah's limp and lifeless body with a hole burned through it.

The problem was, Antonio did not know how or when he would be able to kill Omega. He could not break out of his cell. Antonio had spent literally weeks of time proving that inescapable fact to himself. Escaping the times Omega opened the cell to feed Antonio or clean the cell had proven impossible as well. Omega always used his powers to keep Antonio completely immobilized until he left the cell and resealed it.

Nonetheless, Antonio clung to the belief that one day the opportunity to kill Omega would present itself. That belief was the one thing that kept Antonio from sliding into isolation-induced madness or offing himself.

In anticipation of the happy day he had an opportunity to kill Omega, Antonio did everything he could to keep his mind and body busy. When the opportunity for vengeance finally presented itself—and Antonio told himself every day that it would, repeating it like a mantra—he did not want to be a broken shell of a man, unable to capitalize on the opportunity. So, every day before and after eating breakfast, Antonio did exercises in his tiny cell. Bodyweight squats, Turkish squats, regular pushups, handstand push-ups, crunches, sit-ups, running in place, shadow boxing . . . Antonio had lost track of the countless types of exercises he did before settling down to read for the rest of the day.

Slowly, over the course of many months, thanks to Antonio's exercise regimen and the lean diet Omega fed him, Antonio got into the best shape of his life. The belly he had all his adult life disappeared, replaced by a trim waist and washboard abs.

Antonio was as ready as he ever would be for when the opportunity to kill Omega presented itself.

And then, one day, it did.

Four Days Ago

ANTONIO HAD JUST COMPLETED HIS TWO HUNDREDTH TURKISH squat of the day when he saw something unusual. A swirling mass of gray and white that looked like a miniature oval thunderstorm had formed in the middle of The Mountain, near where the overturned neutronium spear had split the rock floor open.

Mid-squat, Antonio straightened up and stared. Breathing hard, his mouth was agape with surprise and exertion. He wiped the sweat off his brow and blinked several times, thinking maybe he had overexerted himself and that he was hallucinating. No matter how hard he blinked, though, the swirling mass did not disappear.

A costumed man with a purple cape draped around him stepped out of the swirling mass as if it were a doorway. Since Antonio had only seen Omega here, for a split second he thought it was the Hero in a different costume. Then Antonio realized this guy was taller, leaner, and browner than Omega. He looked vaguely familiar, like Antonio had seen him before. On television, or something.

Then his memory supplied Antonio with a name. He got excited.

"Doctor Alchemy!" Antonio shouted. "Hey! Over here!"

Doctor Alchemy had been gazing around at the items in the vast cavern like a visitor to a museum. He looked in Antonio's direction for the first time. He approached Antonio's cell. His long purple cape swirled behind him. He stopped before the transparent front wall of Antonio's cell.

"And whom might you be?" Doctor Alchemy asked. Antonio did not know how the technology in the clear glass that imprisoned him worked, but it somehow enabled him to hear what was said outside its thick confines. Doctor Alchemy's voice was heavily accented. First Omega with his hillbilly accent, Antonio thought, now this guy with his foreign accent saying *whom*. Did anybody ever come to this godforsaken place who spoke regular goddamned American?

"My name's Antonio," he said, wisely keeping his thoughts to himself. His voice was scratchy from disuse. He wiped sweat off his brow again with the back of his hand. "Hit that gold switch right in front of you and let me out of here, would you?"

"Perhaps in due time. But first, tell me where we are."

"The Mountain. It's a retreat in the Himalayas for the Hero who goes by the name Omega. He got it from Avatar."

"That certainly explains the Avatar artifacts that decorate this cavern. I even see over there in the corner the bottle of poison I tricked Avatar into drinking that turned him into stone and nearly killed him." Antonio looked at where Doctor Alchemy pointed. He only vaguely made out a bottle resting on a stand. Doctor Alchemy must have eyes like a hawk's. "A happy memory. It would be happier still if it had actually killed him." The costumed Rogue signed regretfully. "This being Omega's lair that he inherited from Avatar does not, however, explain your presence." Doctor Alchemy's eyes surveyed Antonio's cell. "Nor why you seem to be incarcerated here."

"Omega's got a beef with me, so he locked me up here. I ain't done nothing to deserve it."

"Except mangle the English language," Doctor Alchemy said dryly.

"Huh?"

"Never mind. I see that I scatter pearls before swine." Antonio didn't know what Doctor Alchemy was talking about. If there had been pearls around here somewhere, he was sure he would have spotted them long before now. Maybe Doctor Alchemy had seen some with his eagle eyes.

Antonio said, "Like I said, just hit that switch right there."

"Not until you tell me why you are imprisoned here."

"I told you, I ain't do nothing."

"Yes, I know. You were walking down the street with a song on your lips and pureness in your heart, helping little old ladies cross and handing out hundred-dollar bills to the homeless, when Omega flew by, scooped you up, brought you here, and tossed you in this cage." Doctor Alchemy shook his head in obvious disbelief. "Despite his many flaws, Omega would not toss a man behind proverbial bars for no reason. Lie to me again and I will leave you where you are. Let us start anew: Why are you here?"

Antonio was not about to squander the first chance he had to escape this hellhole. So, he started talking. He initially intended to leave out the part where he killed Hannah and was going to pin the blame on someone else. But, under Doctor Alchemy's intense and perceptive gaze, he realized that would be a mistake. Besides, Antonio knew enough about Doctor Alchemy to know he had plenty of blood on his hands too.

Before Antonio knew it, he had told Doctor Alchemy the entire truth behind how he wound up in his cell, including the fact he was a Meta. He even told him he intended to kill Omega once he got out. Once he started talking, it was hard to stop. It had been so long since he had someone to talk to.

Doctor Alchemy smacked his fist into his palm once Antonio had finished. "When I break the law, I get an all-points bulletin," Doctor Alchemy snarled in frustration. "When a Hero breaks the law, he gets a book deal. There really is no justice in this world. The whole system is rigged against us hard-working Rogues. No justice, no peace."

Antonio didn't say anything as Doctor Alchemy continued to rant. He was afraid to. Doctor Alchemy had been calm and cool moments ago, but now there was foam at the corners of his mouth as he paced and gesticulated in front of Antonio's cell.

With a visible effort, Doctor Alchemy calmed down some-what after a few minutes. "Omega's illegal detainment of you explains the hate you have for him. That hate is what attracted me here. Once I located Silverback, it was child's play to use his blood to formulate an elixir to point me in the direction of others who hate Omega. First Elemental Man, now you. Hate has a distinct energy signature, you know."

"Elixir? Silverback? Energy signature?" Antonio was confused. "I don't understand."

Doctor Alchemy smiled condescendingly. "No, I do not suppose you would. The only thing that matters is that I am here and that I too want to kill Omega. I have assembled a team of other Metas who want to accomplish the same objective. Join us. Surely you must know you have no chance of defeating Omega alone. If you agree to throw your lot in with us, I will let you out."

Antonio did not hesitate.

"I'm in," he said.

PART III

21

***

Now

Slowly my eyes opened. Bright lights shining in my face felt like icepicks jabbing into my brain. I squinted, relieving the stabbing sensation somewhat. I ached all over. I felt like I had been beaten like the proverbial redheaded stepchild.

No, I did not feel *like* I had been beaten. I *had* been beaten, both in the literal and the figurative sense. By Doctor Alchemy and his band of not very merry men. What had they called themselves?

My sluggish mind slowly provided the answer: The Revengers. Stupid name. Not that they had asked me. They had not wanted my opinion. They had wanted me to die.

Why, then, was I still alive? A teensy part of me regretted that I was, considering how much pain I was in.

The last thing I remembered was Doctor Alchemy spitting in my face and blaming me for Neha's death. There was a lot of that going around because I blamed me too. He had

245

pummeled me until Iceburn had pulled him off. Then Doctor Alchemy had shot me with one of his alchemy cartridges, presumably to send me to the sweet hereafter.

But I wasn't in the sweet hereafter. I was in the here and now. According to the little I could see through squinting, half-blinded eyes, *here* was a square room with unadorned beige walls, a table against the front wall on which rested various metal implements, a sink against the same wall, and twin bright white lights that shone down on me from the ceiling like spotlights. There was no doorway.

I did not understand why I was here. Wherever here was. I had been completely at the mercy of the Revengers. I should be dead.

I didn't like it. Not the being alive part. That part suited me just fine. I didn't like the *why* I had been kept alive part. The Revengers keeping me alive could not possibly bode well for me. I doubted they had spared me to give me a Hero of the Year award.

Still squinting against the bright lights, I tried to shove thoughts of all the nefarious reasons why I was still alive to the side. It did not matter. The pain I was in did not matter. The mere fact that I was alive mattered. As long as you were alive, things could get better. South Carolina's state motto was "Dum Spiro Spero." *While I breathe, I hope.* As long as this Carolina boy was still alive and kicking, there was hope for a better—and hopefully less painful—tomorrow.

The problem was I was not kicking. As my mind slowly pulled off the heavy blanket of unconsciousness, I realized I could barely move at all.

I looked down at myself, and forced my eyes to open wider despite the too bright lights. Ricky Ricardo started playing *Babalú* in my head, beating on the inside of my skull like it was his conga drum. I winced, cursing all the *I Love Lucy* reruns I had watched as a kid.

My body slowly came into focus. I stood spread-eagle within a tall, chrome-colored metal ring that was not much wider than the length of my feet. It and I were in the center of the plain room. A large drain covered by a stained grate was directly below me. The grate could've been discolored by rust; it just as easily could've been blood. Unsurprisingly, I still had my Omega suit on. It only changed forms or disappeared when I consciously willed it to do so. From the ankles down, some sort of thick, hard substance encased my legs. It looked like I wore casts like the ones people got when they broke their feet, only this substance was black rather than white like casts usually were. My waist had a tight ring around it of the same metal as the larger ring I stood inside of. Horizontal rods attached the ring around my waist to the larger one.

The result of the ring around my waist and the casts on my legs was that I could wiggle my body slightly, but not much else. My splayed legs were perfectly straight; I could not bend my knees even slightly.

None of that was a problem. I was an Omega-level telekinetic. I'd break free of these restraints faster than I could say *Harry Houdini*. I activated my powers.

Or at least I tried to.

Nothing happened. The burning in my hands that had been present ever since my powers first manifested years ago was still there, but I could not access my powers.

My still-sluggish brain was confused. I looked up. Like my legs, my arms were straight with no bend at the elbow, and spread out at a 45-degree angle from my torso. From the middle of my forearms up, my arms were encased in the same hard black substance as my lower legs were. Thanks to the tightness of the substance, I could not so much as twitch my fingers.

So *that* was why I could not activate my powers. As Doctor Alchemy had proven when I had surrendered to the Revengers and he had shot my hands with that black foam, without being able to move my hands, I was as powerless as a non-Meta.

With my arms and legs spread out and with the giant ring around my body, I probably looked like Leonardo da Vinci's *Vitruvian Man*. *Vitruvian Man*—the name sounded like that of a Meta. Maybe that guy had superpowers, but for all intents and purposes, I did not. Not like this. It was beyond frustrating. It was like knowing you had the means to illuminate a pitch-black room you were lost in, but you could not turn on the lights even though you knew they were there.

Yeah, dum spiro spero. I was just a guy from South Carolina with no powers, breathing and hoping something terrible was not about to happen. Because that was how it felt —like something terrible was about to happen. Why else was I God only knew where trussed up like a Thanksgiving turkey? Everybody knew how well that turned out for the turkey.

But you're not a turkey, I thought. *You're a highly trained licensed Hero. And there's more to being a Hero than simply having superpowers. Batman doesn't have superpowers, and he'd get out of this contraption lickety-split.* As soon as I finished that internal pep talk, my subconscious started playing devil's advocate. *Batman trained for years in the art of escape. If there was an Escape 101 class at the Academy, we somehow missed it. And besides, Batman's not even real.*

Sometimes I wondered whose side my subconscious was on.

I shook myself as much as the contraption allowed me to, hoping to jar something loose. If an ant was crawling on my stomach, I doubted I moved enough to shake it off. The contraption did not move at all.

I racked my brain for a way out of this thing. As my Debbie Downer subconscious had pointed out, the Academy had given me zero training in the fine points of escape artistry. If I somehow managed to get out of here, I'd write the headmaster and recommend an addition to the curriculum.

I wished Ninja was here. In addition to the fact that misery loved company, I knew she was an accomplished escape artist. Maybe, if I had taken her up on her team-up offer, she would have taught me enough about escaping from restraints that I would not be stuck in this mess.

I let out a long breath of frustration. My chest hurt. Cracked ribs, or something more internal? I put the pain and thoughts of Ninja on the backburner. Wishing things were other than they were was not getting me free. What was that expression? *If wishes were horses, beggars would ride.* Clearly that proverb had been coined in the pre-jet age, because who'd wish for a horse when he could wish for a Learjet? Regardless, I had neither a horse nor a Learjet. Ninja was not here, and she had not taught me anything other than the fact she could knock me on my butt. Also, my Academy training was providing no help.

What else you got, brain? I had a faint recollection of reading a Hardy Boys novel as a kid in which one of the characters had escaped from being tied up by flexing his forearms while he was being tied, making the ropes loose enough when he relaxed his muscles that he could shimmy free. Had that been Frank or Joe Hardy? I couldn't remember. Maybe it had been their trusted chum Chet or even their good buddy Biff. It didn't matter. Unlike the villain in that Hardy Boys novel, whoever had imprisoned me here had not had the decency to revive me first so I could flex my muscles à la the Hardy Boys and escape. Things never work out in real life the way they do in novels.

That scene from the Hardy Boys book gave me an idea, though. I looked over at my outstretched right arm. The Omega suit covered me from head to toe, including my hands. Maybe if I removed the suit's fabric from my hands, the newly formed space, however tiny, between the black stuff trapping my hands and my hands themselves would be enough to get the job done. I just needed to move my fingers the slightest bit to trigger my powers.

I held my breath. My suit melted away from my hands with a thought. I could not see it happen because the black substance blocked my view of my hands. But I felt the slight tickling on my skin I always did when I either retracted the suit into my body or changed its appearance.

However, before I could move a muscle or so much as think, the black substance around my hands contracted further around my flesh, simultaneously with the retracting of the Omega suit into my body. Despite the Omega suit no longer being around my hands, I still could not wiggle so much as a pinkie finger.

Crap! I was sure my ploy would've worked. Not only was I no Batman, I was proving to not even be an escape artist on the level of the Hardy Boys. Or even Chet.

I dredged my pounding head for another idea. I came up empty. I wished I had spent less time as a kid reading the Hardy Boys and more time reading Houdini biographies, boning up on getting out of restraints. Youth really was wasted on the young.

Then I realized I did not need to free myself if I summoned someone else to free me. My brain was definitely firing on fewer cylinders than usual. I moved my aching head to look at my left wrist, where I usually wore my communicator watch with its built-in, handy-dandy panic button. If I hit it, it would send a SOS to Isaac's twin watch. If there ever was a time to hit the panic button, it was now. I had hit it once before, back when I was still the Old Man's Apprentice and a blonde woman in a bank in D.C.'s Chinatown had nearly blown my head off by planting on me a Mechano-designed explosive. Thanks to me hitting the panic button, the Old Man was able to get Doctor Hippocrates to heal me in time instead of me bleeding to death in Rock Creek Park after the bomb exploded in my face.

Double crap! My watch was gone. Unfortunately, the GPS in it only activated if I hit the panic button, so I could not expect Isaac to find and rescue me unless I hit the panic button first. The watch had been designed that way so its wearer would have privacy. I was in such a fix that I would happily have traded privacy for safety. I didn't know how I would have hit the panic button being bound the way I was, but I would have thought of something.

My watch had no doubt been removed by whomever had trapped me here. I had a guess who that whomever was based on how the substance around my hands had shifted like something alive to keep my hands immobilized.

Surely it was Doctor Alchemy. He was the last person I had seen before awakening here. Plus, the black stuff around my hands and feet was like the black foam Doctor Alchemy had shot onto my hands to neutralize my powers on Greene Street. It was probably something he had formulated using the Philosopher's Stone book Neha had told me about.

I reluctantly shelved thoughts of escape for now. Maybe a brilliant plan to free myself would occur to me once my brain started working better. I wondered how long I had been unconscious. I moved as much as I could in my restraints and flexed different muscles. Pain greeted me like an abusive spouse. Though unwelcome, the pain did give me an inkling of how long I had been out—a day, maybe two at the most, had passed since I fought the Revengers. I had been beaten and battered more than once over the years, and knew how my body felt during every stage of healing. It was an occupational hazard of Heroing. Maybe, if I escaped from this room and after the existential crisis the Sentinels warned of passed, I would take up something less dangerous. Coal mining, or perhaps shark wrestling.

I was thinking about how I would rather dig coal than be stuck in this contraption when, over to the far right of the wall I faced, the wall dilated with a barely audible hiss, exposing a circular doorway I had not known was there. Two women entered, both white, one with curly blonde hair, the other with straight brown hair. They had slight smiles and unfocused looks on their faces, almost like they were high on something. A thick choker made of a gray metal encircled their necks. They each wore long, bright turquoise dresses. There were yellow sashes around the middle of the dresses. The outfits had low scooped necks exposing the women's cleavage. Their garish outfits and the pleasantly dazed looks on their faces made them look like extras on a science fiction movie set. In fact, their outfits reminded me of the dress the Deanna Troi character on *Star Trek: The Next Generation* wore before the show's producers stopped gratuitously flashing the actress' flesh and let her wear a traditional Starfleet uniform.

"Who are you? Where am I?" I demanded. My throat was sore; the words came out hoarsely. The women ignored me as if I had not spoken. The blonde one raised a hand to her choker and tapped it.

"Your prisoner is awake, my lord," she said.

"I will be there shortly," responded a voice from her choker. Doctor Alchemy. My chest tightened. Having deduced that a homicidal maniac had imprisoned me was one thing; knowing it for a fact was quite another.

The two women moved to stand in front of me, with their backs against the wall. They stared straight ahead. They still had a slight smile on their unfocused faces. They reminded me of the people I had run across in my Heroic career who had been high on heroin. Though Neha had not spoken much about her life with her father before she ran away as a teenager, she had told me that he surrounded himself with a group of people he referred to as his subjects. Like he was the King of England or something. I assumed these were two of them.

"Is Doctor Alchemy holding you against your will?" I asked the two women.

No response.

"If you help me get out of this thing, I can help you. I'll protect you from him." *Like you protected yourself from him?* something within me asked. My negative nellie subconscious again. I guess it didn't believe in positive thoughts and you-can-do-it affirmations. Maybe it needed to read some rah-rah self-help books.

Unfortunately, my subconscious was the only thing talking to me. The women just stared straight ahead with the same weird smile on their faces. Though they faced me, it did not feel like they were looking at me. More like they looked *through* me. It was a blast from the past. Before I became a Hero, girls habitually ignored me. But now more than my teenaged ego was at stake.

Time passed. How much, I could not be sure in the windowless room. I was still trying to get the women to help me or at least to acknowledge my existence—if my hands and body had been free, perhaps I would have tried mooning them—when the door dilated again.

Doctor Alchemy strode in. *The Imperial March* started playing in my head. I knew how Luke Skywalker had felt when Darth Vader had first walked in.

And here I was, trapped and defenseless, without a lightsaber or powers, Jedi or otherwise.

22

Doctor Alchemy did not have on his cape, cowl, or gauntlets, though he was otherwise in full costume. A futuristic-looking gun that looked like it could blow a hole through a steel door hung from his utility belt.

This was the first time I had seen Doctor Alchemy's bare face. Angular, arrogant, and brown with piercing dark eyes, his face looked like a predator's. If I were a deer, my instincts would tell me to run. Hell, I wasn't a deer and my instincts told me to run.

I was surprised to see Doctor Alchemy was not alone. If he had come in with the other Revengers, I wouldn't have been. None of those Rogues were with him, though. Rather, Doctor Alchemy came in pushing a bejeweled wheelchair. The gems it was encrusted with glittered under the bright lights of the room. The chair appeared to be made of gold, though I assumed it was merely gold-plated as it would be too heavy to push if it were solid gold. Because of the gold and the jewels, the chair looked more like a throne than it did a wheelchair for a disabled person. A plump Indian woman wearing a sparkling red and gold sari sat in the wheelchair. I recognized her from pictures Neha had shown me. It was Neha's mother Rati. She didn't appear to have aged a day in all the years since the pictures Neha had shown me were taken.

I didn't understand. I thought Neha's mother was dead, murdered by men who had broken into the Thakores' home almost twenty years ago.

I got a better look at Rati as Doctor Alchemy rolled the chair directly in front of me. Though Rati's flesh looked natural, she was completely still. She did not breathe or blink. Her eyes were as lifeless as a doll's. She had looked lifelike at first glance, but I now realized she was as dead and inanimate as a wax flower. I began to understand what Neha meant when she had obliquely and disapprovingly mentioned what her father had done to her mother. I decided it would be wise to not point out to Doctor Alchemy the dead elephant in the room. As mercurial as he was, who knew how he would react.

With my attention consumed by Doctor Alchemy and the disturbing corpse of his wife, I did not realize at first that another person had come in after Doctor Alchemy. An elderly white man with sad eyes and a fringe of white hair around his otherwise bald head had shuffled in after the Thakores. He stood in the corner of the room, with his eyes facing the wall, like a naughty child in time-out. He wore pants and a tunic that were the same color as the dresses of the women against the wall. He had the same choker around his neck they did.

Here I was, immobilized, powerless and spread-eagle, faced by two live women who stared into forever, a dead woman who stared at nothing, an old man who stared at the corner, and a Rogue who stared at me with venomous hate. If mama had told me there would be days like this, I wouldn't have believed her.

When a situation arose I did not know how to handle, I often thought of four letters: WWAD—what would Avatar do?

How would Avatar play this? I asked myself. Cool, calm, and confident with a hint of cocky, I decided.

"I was just telling the ladies that I would help them pass the time by juggling," I said to Doctor Alchemy. "Now that you're here, you can help. It turns out I'm fresh out of balls. You got any I can borrow?"

Doctor Alchemy stepped forward wordlessly. He slapped me with an open hand, so hard that my head twisted to the side. I tasted iron. My ears rang. The blow did my pounding head no favors.

I spit out a mouthful of blood. I turned my head back to face Doctor Alchemy. "Slapping someone who can't hit you back? Looks like you don't have any balls either. How about knives? I'm not picky. I can juggle them just as easily."

"I did not bring you here to listen to your feeble attempts at wit," Doctor Alchemy snarled.

"A shame. I've got plenty more attempts where that one came from. Why did you bring me here, then? To spruce the place up some? Mission accomplished." Channeling my inner Avatar had turned me into a smart-ass. How smart could I be, though, if I couldn't figure a way out of this predicament? "Where is here, anyway?"

"You are in my volcanic lair. As for why, I brought you here to kill you."

"Didn't you try to do that in Astor City? Yet I'm still very much alive and kicking." I remembered the restraints on my legs. "Well, not so much the kicking part. More like alive and twitching. I hope to be kicking again shortly, though. One should always dream big. What makes you think an assassination attempt will work this time?"

"A quick death is too good for the likes of you," he said. "In Astor City I merely hit you with a substance that simulated death so the Revengers would think I had killed you. I never intended you to die so easily. I brought you here so my beautiful wife can bear witness to your humiliation and death for killing our blessed daughter Neha."

A hot surge of anger got the best of me, sweeping away my faux Avatar-like calmness. "How many times do I have to tell you I didn't kill her? I loved her. I tried to save her."

Doctor Alchemy slapped me again, on the other side of my face. Fresh pain exploded on my face. At least my bruises would be symmetrical.

"How dare you say you loved her," he said. He stuck his face into mine, so close that his facial hair almost grazed me. His breath was hot on my face. His eyes glittered like brown topaz. The fact he was completely calm rather than snarling as he had been before made him all the more terrifying. "A man who loves a woman protects her. With all the power you possess, you should have found a way to ensure Neha's safety. Look at the lengths I went to bring my beautiful Rati back to life after her murder. You did not love Neha. The fact she is not alive today proves you did not."

Doctor Alchemy stopped, cocking his head toward his wife, as if he was listening to her. "You are exactly right, Mother," he said after a few seconds. "Omega let Neha die to prevent the three of us from reuniting. He knew the world would not be able to stand against us once the Thakore family was together again." Doctor Alchemy shook his head in disgust. "And they say I'm the villain."

I didn't say anything. What was there to say that would change this madman's mind? Doctor Alchemy was even crazier than Neha had said, crazier than his reputation and exploits indicated. He treated his long-dead wife as if she were still alive. He even thought she talked to him.

And, there was another key reason why I did not argue with him: Part of me thought he was right. A Hero as powerful as I should have found a way to save Neha's life. The failure to do so would haunt me until the day I died. It seemed that day would come much sooner than I would have guessed just a week ago.

Doctor Alchemy said, still calmly, "Everyone who had a hand in Neha's murder will die. Unfortunately, despite using my formidable resources, Millennium is nowhere to be found. Mechano you have already destroyed. Seer died at my hands a few days ago in MetaHold. I used this gun, as a matter of fact." He patted his sidearm affectionately. "I kept it as a trophy. Perhaps I will use it to shoot you in the head just as I did with her.

"But, before the happy moment of ventilating your insignificant brains arrives, Mother and I will have the satisfaction of seeing you betray your friends just as you betrayed Neha by letting her die. You will tell me Myth's real name and where I can find him. Then I will kill him for his involvement in Neha's death. You will go to your grave mortified, broken-hearted, knowing you betrayed everyone who was foolish enough to call you friend.

Doctor Alchemy's words shocked and confused me. Seer was dead? Though I wouldn't cry myself to sleep over her death—that pale-skinned bitch had helped kill Neha and nearly killed me—it was still a surprise. If MetaHold had informed me Doctor Alchemy had killed Seer, maybe I would have been better prepared for him. Then again, the Department of Metahuman Affairs and the rest of the federal government were hardly known for their sparkling efficiency. That inefficiency was probably why the USDMA hadn't contacted me when Iceburn and Brown Recluse escaped MetaHold.

I was also confused by how Doctor Alchemy did not already know Myth's true identity. Elemental Man was Isaac's stepbrother. Surely he had told Doctor Alchemy everything he knew about Isaac, especially since he and Isaac hated one another. If Elemental Man had been loyal enough to Isaac to not spill his guts to Doctor Alchemy, I was almost sorry I had kicked him in the leg in Astor City. Almost.

Regardless, if Doctor Alchemy had not gotten information about Isaac out of Elemental Man, he sure as hell wasn't going to get it out of me. Isaac was my best friend. There was no way I would betray him. "Myth has nothing to do with this," I said. "He wasn't even there when Neha died."

"Exactly!" Doctor Alchemy said triumphantly, as if I had just confessed Isaac had assassinated John F. Kennedy. "Like you, he professes to have been Neha's friend. Yet he was not even loyal enough to her to attempt to rescue her from the Sentinels. Instead, he idiotically let you face them alone. And Neha paid the price for your and his foolishness. For that, he will die. Just as you will once you tell me what I want to know."

"Well it looks like I'm going to live forever then. Because I'm not telling you anything." Back in WWAD mode, I wrinkled my nose. "Except to say you need to pop a breath mint. For someone who calls himself doctor, your halitosis and bedside manner leave a lot to be desired."

Doctor Alchemy smiled broadly at his wife like I had just told him he had won the lottery. "You see, Mother? I told you the prideful young fool would not tell us without prodding."

Doctor Alchemy walked over to the table against the front wall. He returned holding a long piece of flexible metal that looked like a knight's chain mail, only with bigger holes between the links of metal. His other hand held an open straight razor like you'd find in an old-fashioned barber shop. The business end of the razor gleamed ominously under the room's lights.

"No thanks. I shaved a couple of days ago," I said. "I'm

going for that stubbly, ruggedly Heroic look." It was much easier to sound tough than to be tough. Despite my bravado, I felt like I was about to pee my suit.

Doctor Alchemy smiled sadistically. "Your fear belies your words. It's so palpable, I can almost smell it."

"Nah. That's your halitosis. Fear and bad breath smell a lot alike. It's an easy mistake to make."

"You're right that I'm going to give you a shave," Doctor Alchemy said as if I had not spoken. I guess he was not big on constructive criticism. "Only it is not your hair I will shave. Tell me Theodore, have you heard of death by a thousand cuts?"

"No. But hum a few bars and I'll try to sing along." I noticed he had used my real name. I didn't ask how he knew it. I had bigger and more pressing problems than my secret identity no longer being a secret.

"Also known as lingchi and the lingering death, death by a thousand cuts is a method of torture invented by the Chinese," he said, again acting as though I had not spoken. He had everything ass-backward—he heard things his wife did not say, and didn't hear things I actually said. "An ancient and glorious culture, the Chinese. Not as ancient or as glorious as that of us Indians, of course, but no one is perfect. Except for my beautiful Rati." He waved the chain mail in my face. It rustled like a rattlesnake. "First I will wrap this around your flesh. It has holes that, when the metal is wrapped tightly enough, your skin will protrude through. I will then use this razor to cut your flesh, literally skinning you one tiny bit of flesh at a time. The process is quite excruciating. Or so the people I have subjected this to have told me with their screams of agony." Doctor Alchemy's face took on a thoughtful cast as my skin crawled. "I wonder how long you will last before you break and betray your friend Myth?"

He paused, again tilting his head toward his wife's lifeless body. "A few minutes, you say Mother? You give young Theodore insufficient credit. I think he will withstand my gentle ministrations at least a couple of hours. He does fancy himself to be a Hero, after all. Surely his ego and self-image will bolster his willpower for that long."

Doctor Alchemy's face suddenly twisted, becoming wild and feral. He got in my face again. "I will break you," he hissed. "I will make you betray the person you hold dearest. Just as you betrayed the person my wife and I held the dearest. But when you break, when you do betray Myth, your ordeal will not be over. Far from it. I will continue to slit bits of flesh off you. If I proceed carefully enough, slowly enough, you will live through the process of me slicing your skin away bit by excruciating bit. If the torment you will experience can be called living. I will make you pray you had never been born. You will rue the day you slid out of you mother's diseased vagina. You will curse your father's name for impregnating her with his defective sperm." Flecks of saliva flew out of his mouth, hitting my face. Spit bubbled out of the corners of his mouth. "At first, you will hate me for what I will do to you. But once I have finished, once I have peeled your skin away like a rotten apple's, you will thank me with love and gratitude in your voice when I finally deign to give you sweet release from your agony."

The room fell quiet as Doctor Alchemy let all that sink in.

Then I smiled gamely.

"Sounds like fun," I said. "Let's get started."

Doctor Alchemy stepped back, recoiling as if it was I who had slapped him for a change. He looked surprised, an emotion I was unaccustomed to seeing on his face. I had only seen supreme confidence, loony bin craziness, or a combination of the two.

Then, Doctor Alchemy chuckled. The chuckle grew until he was laughing like a hyena. The maniacal laugh reverberated off the walls. Doctor Alchemy doubled over with laughter, clutching his wife's lifeless shoulder to keep from falling over. The whole scene was bizarre. It was like watching a remake of *One Flew Over the Cuckoo's Nest.* "Now with extra crazy!" the tagline would read.

Eventually, the Rogue's laughter faded. He straightened up.

"Mother, I begin to understand what our daughter saw in young Theodore. If I did not hate him so much, I might actually like him." Still chuckling slightly, he wiped tears of laughter from his eyes with his costume's sleeve. "Since you are so eager to begin Theodore, we shall do so at once. But first I need you to tell me how to remove your costume. We tried to remove it while you were unconscious, but proved unable to do so. We tried cutting it off you. We used every solvent available to me to dissolve it. We even tried to burn it off, but could not do so much as singe it."

It was my turn to laugh. "You really expect me to make it easier for you to do your tai chi on me?"

"Lingchi," Doctor Alchemy corrected, stomping his foot in irritation. I knew he had called it lingchi, but I was being deliberately annoying. The prospect of being tortured to death did not put me in the best of moods.

"Tomato, tomahto," I said. "I don't care how you say it. Right now, I'm too busy relaxing and staring at this wall to find the time to help you torture me. Ask again later and maybe I'll be able to squeeze you in. I think I have an opening on my calendar the first day of never."

Doctor Alchemy frowned slightly. Then he drew the big gun hanging from his belt. I thought he was going to shoot me with it. I knew the Omega suit could withstand a traditional

263

bullet, though it would still hurt like hell. This gun did not look like it shot traditional bullets, though.

Instead, Doctor Alchemy stepped over to the blonde standing against the wall.

"What's your name?" he asked her. She was young, probably no older than I.

"Tiffany, my lord." She spoke to him the way a devout Christian might speak to Jesus.

"Ah yes, I remember now. I liberated you from your humdrum existence just a few weeks ago, during my raid on Fort Knox. You were a clerk there."

"Yes, my lord." She seemed thrilled he remembered her. Her adoration of Doctor Alchemy was that of a dog to her master. If she had been a dog, she would be wagging her tail gleefully.

"You may stop calling me 'my lord.' Though I know it's protocol, everyone here knows who their master is." I most certainly didn't, but Doctor Alchemy hadn't asked me. If he had, he wouldn't like the answer. He said to Tiffany, "And you're married. I recall ordering you to surrender to my treasury your engagement and wedding rings. Any children?"

"Two. A four-year-old girl and a two-year-old boy."

"And you love them?"

"Yes, very much."

"Do you love me more?"

"Oh yes, certainly." From her tone, it was like he had asked her if water was wet.

Doctor Alchemy stroked Tiffany's cheek affectionately, like a father touching his child.

"Of course you do." He handed her the futuristic gun. Now that he had established how much Tiffany loved him, I expected him to tell her to threaten to shoot me. I steeled myself. If the Omega suit could not stop the bullet, being shot was still a heck of a lot better than being sliced to pieces.

"Shoot yourself in the head," Doctor Alchemy told Tiffany.

"No!" I cried.

Too late. Like a dog eager to perform a trick, Tiffany smiled broadly as she raised the gun to her temple. She pulled the trigger. The blast in the enclosed room was deafening.

Blood, brains, and bone splattered the beige wall behind Tiffany. The gory result looked like a madman's abstract painting. Tiffany's body, missing most of the top of her head, toppled to the floor. The dull thump of her impact mingled with the clatter of the fallen gun. Streams of Tiffany's blood began trekking across the gently sloping floor toward the drain under my feet. The smell of blood, strong and metallic, filled the air. My stomach churned, threatening to spew. Bitter bile rose into my mouth.

Neither the other woman nor the old man in the corner had flinched during all this. Only Doctor Alchemy moved. He bent over and retrieved the gun. Blood coated its muzzle.

"I knew this gun would come in handy again. How clever of me to have held onto it," Doctor Alchemy said. Then he glanced at Tiffany's oozing body. "Look at the mess you made, my dear. I have half a mind to reanimate you and make you clean it up. I suppose it's not worth the time and trouble. There's plenty more like you." He handed the gun to the other woman. She took it with the same dumb smile on her face Tiffany had. "What do you say, Theodore? Shall we perform emergency brain surgery on this one too? I have nearly five hundred other subjects here who would be happy to be operated on if this second procedure isn't a success."

I wanted to curse him, to threaten him, to tell him what I was going to do to him. No, what I really wanted to do was break free of my bonds and do unto him as he had done unto Tiffany. But what good would cursing or vain struggling do?

Instead, without a word, I let the Omega suit withdraw into my body. It tickled slightly as it always did. Now I was as naked as a newborn. Goosebumps rose on my bare skin from a combination of a chill in the air, anger, revulsion, shame at being naked in front of others, and lots of fear. I could have expelled the suit from my body instead of absorbing it, but I wasn't about to risk Doctor Alchemy getting his hands on it. He was dangerous enough as it was. Also, if I expelled it from my body, I had no idea if I could absorb it again. It was not like the Omega suit had come equipped with an owner's manual.

Doctor Alchemy clapped his hands with glee when he saw the Omega suit was gone. "Ah, the first operation was a success after all. Splendid!"

He walked slowly around me. He stroked his beard thoughtfully as he inspected my naked body. His gaze lingered on my genitals. "I would have thought an Omega-level Hero would be more . . . impressive." It was all I could do to not pee on him. Only the thought he might take his anger out on his so-called subjects instead of on me stopped me. "Never meet your heroes, as the saying goes. They will disappoint you every time. Be a dear and make sure the suit does not reappear, will you Theodore? I would hate to have to perform even more operations. I do so love my subjects and would hate to lose more of them. But know that I do not love them as children. You murdered the only child I will ever have. I love them more like pets. Speaking of which, this particular pet is dripping blood all over my nice clear floor. Boy, come clean up this mess Tiffany's making. Be sure to save her neck communicator. It is a very valuable piece of technology."

For the first time since entering the room, the elderly man in the corner stirred. Moving slowly, he got a big piece of plastic from the table and unfolded it to reveal a bag. After first taking the metal choker off Tiffany's neck, the old man struggled to slide the bag over the literal deadweight that was her body. During this, a spatter of blood went flying. The blood landed on Rati.

Doctor Alchemy's face darkened like a thunderstorm. Cursing the old man's clumsiness in several different languages, Doctor Alchemy started slapping, punching, and kicking him. Unlike the remaining woman, who seemed to view everything through a filter of near euphoria, pain, fear, and resignation swirled on the old man's face as he meekly and wordlessly bore Doctor Alchemy's blows. He did not try to protect himself, much less fight back. The part of me that was a trained professional noted almost clinically how differently the old man reacted to Doctor Alchemy's treatment than the women had. The rest of me was outraged. Watching a woman blow her own brains out had surprisingly not blown my outrage circuits.

"Stop it! You're hurting him!" I cried, though I feared speaking up might just make matters worse. How I hated a bully. I shook with impotent rage in my restraints.

Finally, Doctor Alchemy stopped cuffing the old man, more because the storm of his anger seemed to have passed rather than because of my protests. He carefully wiped Tiffany's blood off his wife, probably not trusting his subjects to do the job right. The old man—I refused to think of someone his age as 'Boy' even though that was all Doctor Alchemy called him—resumed his efforts to bag Tiffany's body, though he moved even more slowly than before thanks to the blows inflicted on him.

While the man finished bagging Tiffany's body and then struggled to drag her out of the room, Doctor Alchemy had the remaining woman soak the chain mail-like strip of metal and the straight razor in a liquid antiseptic. "It would never do for you to get an infection and die sooner than I intend you to," Doctor Alchemy told me. Thoughtful. Then the woman rubbed some foul-smelling ointment all over my body. The ointment burned slightly, but not unpleasantly, rather like Vicks VapoRub. Using a hose attached to the sink's faucet, she washed the ointment off me. The water gurgled into the drain under me, carrying with it the ointment and all the hair on my body. When she finished, I was completely hairless. Even my eyelashes were gone. Until that moment, I had not realized you could see your eyelashes. I had never noticed them before because I had been so used to seeing through them every moment of the day.

The woman used a towel to dry me completely off. She even scrubbed my genitals and between my butt cheeks. There was no sexual overtone to the woman's intimate touch. It was clinical, like being poked and prodded by a female doctor during a physical. First Neha, then that stripper in Areola 51 when I'd gone to consult with Cassandra, now this. This was only the third time in my life a woman had touched my genitals, though I had dreamed about it lots of times. Real life never lives up to your wet dreams.

Doctor Alchemy clapped his hands together and rubbed them in anticipation after the woman had finished prepping me. That was how he put it—*prepping me*. Like he was about to perform surgery on me. Then again, I suppose he was.

"Where do you think I should begin, Mother?" Doctor Alchemy paused, presumably listening to the answer from his wife. "The genitals? You always want to start with the genitals. You really are not fond of the male bait and tackle, are you Mother? Considering what happened to you, your blood-thirsty tendencies are understandable. I am not at all sure the genitals are the best place to start, however. That portion of the male anatomy is very sensitive. One should build up to it. It should be saved for the end. It is the crescendo, the pièce de résistance. The rich dessert at the end of a sumptuous meal."

My flesh crawled during this bizarre one-sided exchange. I absolutely loved it when people talked about me as if I were not even in the room. I especially loved it when they were talking about carving my bits and pieces into bits and pieces. I felt like the Thanksgiving turkey I had thought about earlier. *Would you like white or dark Omega meat, Mother?*

Doctor Alchemy snapped his fingers.

"I know. We will let random chance decide where I shall begin. That is fair, don't you think Mother? Maybe fortune will smile on you and fate will decide on Theodore's genitals after all."

Doctor Alchemy began to sing, poking one of my body parts with each word:

> Eeny, menu, many, moe
> Catch Omega by the toe
> If he hollers, don't let him go,
> Eeny, meeny, miny, moe
> My Mother told me
> To pick the very best one
> And you are it.

I let out the terrified breath I had been holding. On the word *it*, his index finger had moved off my penis and landed on my right thigh. Not that having the skin peeled off my thigh seemed like a fun time, but it was better than Doctor Alchemy doing a Lorena Bobbitt impersonation on me further north.

Doctor Alchemy looked at his wife, his finger still pressing into my hairless thigh. "So close, Mother. A shame. It just goes to show you cannot always have exactly what you want. Not

even us. If we could, our daughter would still be with us."
Doctor Alchemy's face clouded over and looked despondent.
Under different circumstances, I would have felt sorry for him.
It was impossible to feel sorry for him, though, with his finger
almost brushing my genitals and with a beaten old man
scrubbing a young mother's blood and brains off the wall.

Doctor Alchemy turned away from me. He peeled his
costume's gloves off, pushed his sleeves up on his wiry forearms that were corded with lean muscle, and started to thoroughly wash his hands at the sink with soap and water. No
doubt still guarding against me getting infected and dying
prematurely. Considerate. He happily whistled as he scrubbed
his hands. The tune was familiar, but I could not quite put a
name to it. His mood had already changed for the better. His
moods seemed to be ever-changing, constantly shifting like a
weathervane in a storm.

Doctor Alchemy dried his hands, still whistling. Too few
people had jobs they enjoyed; normally I liked seeing
someone look forward to work. Not today.

Doctor Alchemy picked up the sanitized chain mail and
straight razor from the table. He approached me. The sharp
edge of the razor gleamed under the bright lights. I finally
recognized the tune he whistled. It was that old song *Mack the
Knife*. Of course it was.

Doctor Alchemy wrapped the chain mail around my thigh,
fully encircling it with the flexible piece of metal. He latched it
into place. It was tight around my flesh, like a tourniquet.
Small nubs of my skin poked out of the holes in the metal.
They reminded me of the little plastic bubbles on a roll of
bubble wrap.

Doctor Alchemy brought the open razor toward the nubs
of my skin which stuck out of the metal. I thought about how I
had hurt Amok to get him to tell me what I wanted to know,

just as Doctor Alchemy was going to hurt me now. My encounter with Amok seemed like forever ago. Karma apparently had a long memory. And, she most definitely was a bitch.

I shivered, and not just because of the chill in the air. I won't lie—I was scared. My knees felt weak. If this infernal contraption wasn't holding me up, my legs might have buckled in fear.

In addition to that, I was boiling mad. Mad at what Doctor Alchemy was about to do to me, certainly. But, even more intensely, I was mad that Doctor Alchemy had a bunch of subjects that really were just his mind-addled slaves. I was mad at how Doctor Alchemy treated the elderly man who again stood in the corner, with his face to the wall. Most of all, I was mad that Doctor Alchemy had made a young mother shoot herself in the head to get me to remove the Omega suit. Two young children would grow up without a mother. Just like I had.

Before Doctor Alchemy's razor touched my flesh, I said to him, "Somehow, some way, I'm going to free myself. And when I do, it won't matter that you're a grieving father. I'm going to put a stop to you once and for all. You're a monster."

Doctor Alchemy looked up from my thigh. His teeth flashed white in his dark face as he grinned at me with fiendish glee. He was enjoying himself immensely. "Mighty bold talk for a hairless bound man about to be skinned alive. I appreciate your spunk, if not your grasp on reality."

He looked back down at my thigh. The razor hovered over me.

He said, "Remember that old commercial? 'How many licks does it take to get to the Tootsie Roll center of a Tootsie Pop?' The answer is an average of three hundred and sixty-four. I have done studies. Now I am wondering how many cuts it takes to get Omega to betray his friend and then die. Let's find out."

Doctor's Alchemy's tongue poked out of the corner of his mouth as the razor descended. He reminded me of a child focusing mightily on his coloring book so he would get a drawing just the right shade of red.

The razor kissed my flesh. It swept away chunks of my bubbled-up skin. Blood welled up, and began to stream down my hairless leg, hot and wet. It dripped into the drain, no doubt mingling with Tiffany's blood.

I looked away and clenched my teeth. No matter how much it hurt, I resolved to not give Doctor Alchemy the satisfaction of hearing me scream.

My spirit was willing, but my flesh was weak. I did not hold out for long. Certainly far less than a minute.

I started to scream.

23

O ver the course of many sessions spread over several days, Doctor Alchemy peeled my right leg like a potato.

"I have to proceed carefully. Slowly," he said conversationally as he worked on the skin right above the black substance that still bound my leg. He sounded like an artist working painstakingly on a painting rather than the latter-day Torquemada he actually was. "If I remove too much skin at once, you might bleed to death. That would be most unfortunate. You will die when I allow it, and not a moment sooner."

I was upside down as Doctor Alchemy explained this to me. Blood from my leg had dripped into my nose and partially clotted, making it hard to breathe. I was forced to breathe from my mouth. I tasted my own dripping blood. From time to time I spat it out. It was soon replaced by more. I felt like Sisyphus, doomed to roll the same boulder up the same hill over and over for eternity.

Eternity was exactly the right word. It felt like Doctor Alchemy had been slicing into me forever.

Unbeknownst to me until Doctor Alchemy had flipped me

upside down days before, the ring I stood on was actually two separate rings, one inside the other. The one nestled on the inside that I stood on could be spun on its horizontal axis a full three hundred and sixty degrees. It was so my blood did not pool from standing still and upright for too long, Doctor Alchemy had told me days before when he had rotated me for the first time.

I had largely lost my voice thanks to all the screams forced out of me. The most I could do now was whimper. Even whimpering felt like a betrayal. My mind wanted my body to remain stoic. Silent. Indifferent. Like a rock. Perfectly Heroic in the face of fear, pain, and evil. WWAD. Unfortunately, my weak body had other ideas. I whimpered like a run-over puppy.

My only refuge over the past few days was the fact I passed out from time to time from the pain. Even unconsciousness was but a temporary respite. When I passed out, Doctor Alchemy waved one of his alchemy cartridges under my nose that emitted a green gas that would awaken me for a while until my body was overwhelmed by the pain again. He had also forced me to drink an elixir preventing me from having a heart attack or otherwise dying from the pain and stress.

As Doctor Alchemy worked on me, my right leg felt like someone had taken a giant George Foreman grill, closed it on my leg, and was searing it. The pain was unbearable. It was hard to think, hard to focus, hard to do anything other than whimper.

When people's bodies underwent severe trauma and pain, like when sharks bit their limbs off, their bodies went into shock, largely shielding them from the pain. I had even read about one woman who had felt intense euphoria when her arm had been bitten off by a shark. I felt no euphoria, though. No numbness shielded me from this pain. I felt every bit of it.

The elixir Doctor Alchemy had given me that also stopped me from having a heart attack made sure of that.

Frankly, I would have been glad to have a heart attack. All the pain I was in and had gone through had burned away my earlier resolve to escape so I could bring Doctor Alchemy to justice. The only thing that was left was the desire for sweet release, an extended stay in the black pit of nothingness I descended into every time I passed out. I now understood why old people whose bodies were failing often seemed eager to die. There comes a time when death seems a blessing, a warm embrace that will swaddle you in its arms, kiss all the aches and pains and troubles away, and make everything better forever.

There's a way out of this, said something deep within me. *Just tell him what he wants to know. Tell him about Isaac. Sooner or later, you're going to crack. You're not strong enough. You never have been. Dad, Hannah, Neha . . . the history of your life is the history of you not coming through in the clutch. If you tell him now, he'll have mercy on you and end this. You're extending your suffering for nothing.*

That siren song was still playing in my head when I became faintly aware through my haze of pain that Doctor Alchemy had flipped me right-side up again.

"Ta-da!" he said triumphantly. "Mother, have you seen a better skinning job in your life?"

I pried my eyes partially open. Despite my best efforts to stop it, my head lolled listlessly between my shoulders. The movement made my body look like it rocked back and forth. Though it was hard to focus on it, the skin had been completely removed from my right leg down to where the black substance affixed my leg to the ring. My leg did not look real, more like a crazy sculptor's rendition of a leg. *Omega's Flayed Leg, 21st Century, rendered in blood and muscle,* the museum plaque would read. I've always hated modern art, and I hated it more now. What I would have given to be looking at a nice non-bloody portrait of a bowl of fruit instead.

"Yes, I agree, Mother. I too am surprised Theodore has not told us about Myth before now. He is tougher than he looks. Or stupider, though I would not have thought that possible. I cannot decide which. Perhaps both." Though Doctor Alchemy was right in front of me, his voice seemed like it came from far away. My head kept rocking back and forth, like a metronome keeping time to the rhythm of my whimpering. Worst song ever.

"Tell us what we want to know, Theodore," Doctor Alchemy's voice said. Or maybe it was the voice in my head again. Or maybe it was his wife's voice. Maybe I was going crazy too. Or maybe Doctor Alchemy had been the sane one this whole time and unceasing pain had battered down the walls of my preconceptions and finally let me see that. I wasn't sure. I wasn't sure of much anymore. "The sooner you tell us, the sooner this will all be over."

I was sick of all the voices telling me to give in. I was sick of the pain. I was sick of being here. I just wanted it over.

With a monumental effort, I lifted my head and held it upright.

"I'll talk. I can't take this anymore," I said hoarsely. It hurt to speak. I wondered if all my screaming had ruptured my vocal cords. "Myth's name is . . ." My voice lowered to a mumble.

"Eh?" Doctor Alchemy said. His face was alight with sadistic glee and triumph. "I cannot hear you."

"Hard to talk. Come closer."

Doctor Alchemy's head loomed in front of me like a mountain.

"Myth's real name is . . ." I whispered into his approaching ear. When it was close enough, I mustered all my strength. I bit down on his ear as hard as I could. His blood spurted in my mouth.

Doctor Alchemy yelped in pain and surprise. He jerked his head away. He clutched his bloody ear. His other hand lifted the bloody razor he had been using on me. He looked like he wanted to slit my throat with it. Any other time over the past few days I would have been thrilled to have him do it. But now my show of defiance gave me a fresh burst of energy.

I spit his blood out. It was nice to have blood other than my own in my mouth for a change. A bizarre thought, that. Instead of merely drawing blood, I had hoped to take a chunk out of Doctor Alchemy's ear à la Mike Tyson. Bound and bloody beggars can't be choosers.

I whispered harshly, "Myth's real name is Mister None of Your Goddamned Business. He lives at 6969 Go Screw Yourself Avenue. You want me to write it down, or can you remember it?"

Still looking like he was about to slit my throat, Doctor Alchemy just stared at me for several long beats. His normally brown face was mottled red with rage.

Finally, he lowered the red razor.

"You will rue this insolence," he hissed. I didn't have a witty retort ready. My earlier speech had taken all the wind out of my sails. My head sank down between my shoulders again.

Doctor Alchemy slammed the razor down on the table. Still glaring at me, he went to his wife's wheelchair. She had been present during every one of these skinning sessions, staring straight ahead into eternity. According to the one side of their conversation I could hear, she had immensely admired her husband's work on me. Bloodthirsty bitch.

His ear still bleeding, Doctor Alchemy wheeled his wife toward the door.

"Wait, where are you going?" I croaked weakly. I still wasn't able to lift my head. "I was looking forward to you starting on the other leg. One's red, one's still white. I hate being mismatched."

Ignoring me, Doctor Alchemy and his wife left the room. The old man in the corner, who I now knew was Doctor Alchemy's manservant who accompanied Doctor Alchemy everywhere in the lair, shuffled after the couple.

The door snicked shut behind the three. All-consuming agony and I were alone again. *Hello pain, my old friend.* With a friend like this, who needed enemies?

I was proud of the fact I had found the stones to mouth off to Doctor Alchemy. It was not a victory on the level of escaping and bringing Doctor Alchemy to justice, but it was the best I could manage right now.

I would have felt like more of a badass had I not already started whimpering again.

I would have felt like even more of a badass than that had it not been for the fact that, right before I came to my senses and mustered the will to bite Doctor Alchemy's ear, I had been about to tell him everything I knew about Isaac.

24

"What's your name, sir?" I rasped to Doctor Alchemy's manservant. The *sir* part was because my parents had raised me to show my elders respect. The *what's your name* part was because I felt it only right that I should know the name of the man who was wiping my butt.

Doctor Alchemy had forced me to drink water and some sort of nutritional supplement the past few days. "I would not want you to die of thirst," he had said the first time he had forced me to drink. "I am not a barbarian." That's what he thought.

The water and nutritional shakes had their inevitable effect. Urinating I could handle on my own. Doing it standing up was one of the advantages of being a man; the drain underneath my feet did the rest. Having a bowel movement without soiling myself was tougher.

That was where Doctor Alchemy's manservant came in handy. Literally, unfortunately for him, since he had to clean me by hand. I had been faintly aware of him coming in several times before without Doctor Alchemy to clean me off, but today was the first time I was cogent enough to speak to him. Though I was still in terrific pain, I was more lucid today than usual. Maybe it was because Doctor Alchemy had not sliced any more off of me since I had mouthed off to him. I had not even seen him since then. How long ago had that been? Days? A week? There was no way to know. Each moment seemed as painfully identical as the last. Perhaps my earlier display of stubbornness had made Doctor Alchemy give up on skinning me.

Not even I believed that one.

I felt the manservant behind me pause in wiping me clean when I asked him his name.

"Oliver," he finally said. I was surprised he answered. I had never heard him speak before. Then again, I had either been out of it when Oliver had been here before or Doctor Alchemy had been here too. Doctor Alchemy's subjects spoke to him only when he spoke to them first.

Oliver moved from behind me and toward the sink. In one hand was a bucket contained my waste he had cleaned up. In the other was a filthy towel. Nice work if you can get it. Between my blood and my waste, the room smelled like when my father and Uncle Charles slaughtered my uncle's pigs when I was a kid. Though I had been marinating in this stench, I still was not used to it.

Oliver covered the bucket with a lid. Then he washed the towel out in the sink. The stream of water from the faucet turned brown as it ran through the towel. Oliver was doing all of this with his bare hands. He did not seem the slightest bit disgusted or revulsed by it. Rather, his face held only resignation and weariness. There were heavy bags under his eyes. His lower lids drooped down, exposing redness. Ectropion. I knew the word for droopy eyes, but not how to get the hell out of here. Clearly I had studied the wrong things.

My brain was working in slow motion. Even so, seeing the look on Oliver's face now made me remember how he looked when Doctor Alchemy had hit him after he spilled Tiffany's blood on Rati. The look on his face then and now contrasted dramatically with the way Doctor Alchemy's other subjects looked. They looked like pampered indoor dogs eager to perform tricks for their master. Oliver looked like an abused dog chained up outside in the rain.

"You're not like Doctor Alchemy's other . . . subjects," I rasped. I had most called them *slaves* before I caught myself. Sometimes calling a spade a spade was not the diplomatic thing to do. "You don't seem happy like they do."

Oliver's droopy eyes flicked toward me before returning to his chore at the sink.

"My lord gives me a lower dose of his obedience potion than the other subjects get," Oliver said. He had a slight British accent. His voice was almost as hoarse as mine, though probably from disuse instead of from screaming like me. Though you never knew with someone like Doctor Alchemy. "He wants me to understand how he treats me unclouded by the narcotic side effects of his potion."

"Why?"

"My lord was once my employee. He believes I mistreated him when he was in my employ. Now he treats me the way he says I treated him." Oliver said all this unemotionally, like he was reading from a script someone else wrote.

"Where is he?" Not that I chomped at the bit to see him again. Each time he cut me increased the chance of my resolve slipping again and me telling him about Isaac. I had no intention of betraying him, but the near miss before had taught me my determination was chipping away with each slice of Doctor Alchemy's razor.

Oliver paused, obviously thinking. It looked like he

thought with effort. Thinking did not seem like something he did very much anymore.

"He did not tell me to not tell you, so I shall," he finally said. "His scheme to topple the political order in Australia and install one of his puppets as prime minister requires his personal attention. I expect him to return in a few days."

I didn't feel a surge of hope. I was too far gone to still be hopeful. "I see how he treats you, Oliver," I said. "You've got to free me so I can help you and everyone else."

Oliver shook his head firmly. "My lord expressly forbade me to help you escape. I cannot do anything that would betray him or his wishes."

It was a good thing I had not been hopeful, else my hopes would have been dashed. Nonetheless, my mind raced. That's overstating the matter. My mind was too hobbled by pain and exhaustion to race. More like it sped up a little as I thought about what Oliver said. *He did not tell me not to tell you, so I shall,* he had said. Apparently he could do things if Doctor Alchemy had not expressly forbidden them. Maybe it was because Oliver was on a lower dose of the obedience potion than the others were. Then again, maybe not. It did not matter. What mattered was if I could use this to my advantage.

After some thought, I said, "When Doctor Alchemy brought me here, was I wearing a watch?"

Oliver thought about it so long I thought he had forgotten the question.

"Yes," he eventually said.

"Where is it now?"

"My lord retains a keepsake from each of his exploits. He stores them in the Trophy Room. The watch is there."

Since Doctor Alchemy had forbidden Oliver from helping me, I could not tell him I wanted the watch so I could hit its panic button. Instead I said, "My father gave me that watch.

He's dead now. It's the only thing of his I still have. I'd like to see it one last time before Doctor Alchemy kills me. Can you bring it to me?" Maybe all the practice I had gotten lying since developing my powers had not been an entirely bad thing.

Oliver mulled that over.

"I have two sons. Harry and Jack. They're both older than you. I have not seen them since I started in the service of my lord eighteen years ago. I have no idea if they are still alive or dead." His droopy eyes stared off into the distance while he spoke. The sadness he wore like a cloak increased in intensity. Finally, his eyes met mine. His pale blue eyes were rheumy. "I will bring you your father's watch. My lord did not say I could not."

"Thank you, Oliver," I said. And I meant it.

Oliver finished cleaning up. He slowly shuffled toward the door, still carrying the bucket of my waste. His back was rounded and hunched over. Earlier, I had thought it was not possible for me to hate Doctor Alchemy more than I did when he was slicing into me. I was wrong. Watching Oliver struggle toward the door and thinking of what Doctor Alchemy had put him through and the years he had stolen from him, I hated the Rogue even more now.

The door dilated open. Oliver paused in the open doorway. He turned to face me. There were tears in his eyes. "You are the first person to call me anything other than *boy* in almost twenty years," he said. Then, he turned and left.

Chalk up one for common courtesy. Who needs superpowers when you've been brought up with manners? I thought fuzzily through the pain. It seemed to be increasing now with each passing moment. My heart raced. Maybe that elixir Doctor Alchemy had given me before was wearing off.

I didn't know how long it would take Oliver to fetch my watch. Maybe he had to wipe a cellblock full of other prisoners' butts before he got around to it. I would wait for him. It was not as though I was going anywhere.

I was still waiting when I fell asleep. Or maybe I passed out from the pain. These days, it was hard to tell one from the other.

25

W hen I regained consciousness and opened my eyes, I saw my watch. It sat on its side on the edge of the table. Good old Oliver.

That was the good news. The bad news was that I was alone, and the table was against the wall on the other side of the room. Nineteen or twenty feet, maybe? It might as well have been twenty million feet for all the good the watch was doing me over there when I was over here. So close, yet so far away.

I swallowed the bitter taste of despair. I was better off with my watch in the room than I had been when it hadn't been here. I just had to figure out how to use it. I forced my sluggish brain to think.

Maybe I should wait for Oliver to return, and I could get him to open the watch face and push the panic button for me. I dismissed that thought. Doctor Alchemy had instructed him to not do anything to help me escape. Surely if I asked him to press the panic button, he'd realize I was trying to get him to violate Doctor Alchemy's orders. I could hear the lie now: *It was my father's dying wish to have you push that red button inside the watch. Why's that, you ask? My old man loved himself some red buttons. It was almost a fetish.* Despite all the practice I had gotten lying since becoming a Meta, I was not accomplished enough to sell that one.

I felt hot. I was sweating despite the low temperature of the room. Was I getting a fever? A fever plus a leg that had been peeled like a carrot. Could life get any better? Maybe I had gotten an infection despite Doctor Alchemy's precautions. Since my own waste had dripped on my exposed right leg several times, I would not be surprised. It would be mighty embarrassing if I had survived all this only to be finished off by an infection caused by my own waste. People would talk. *Hey Joe! Did you hear about Omega, the Hero who brought down the Sentinels? He died. No, he wasn't killed in battle. Turns out he shit himself to death.* Imagine what that news would do to sales of the Omega dildo. They'd probably go completely limp.

Okay Theo, focus. The watch. The panic button. What to do, what to do, what to do? If I had a bunch of popsicle sticks, I could eat them, tie the leftover wooden sticks together, extend them toward the watch, pop the face open, and hit the panic button. Simplicity itself. Except I didn't have popsicles, the desire to eat a bunch of them, anything to tie the sticks together, and no free hands to do all the necessary work. Other than those niggling little details, it was a brilliant plan.

Okay, smart aleck, you got a better idea? I said to myself.

I blinked sweat out of my eyes and thought hard about it.

Nope, I admitted.

Fantastic.

I stewed on it for a while. If I were a cowboy instead of a superhero, I could lasso the watch and drag it to me. But I did not have a rope or the free hands or the skills to use it. Not being able to use my hands really put a crimp in my escape plans.

What I needed was a way to lasso the watch without using my hands. Struck by sudden inspiration, I stuck my tongue out. Damn it. Not nearly long enough.

I shivered, suddenly both hot and cold. Yep, I was definitely feverish. My mind, already clouded by pain, had been made foolish by fever. Trying to reach the watch with my tongue was silly, I realized. It was a shame I did not have a blue whale's tongue. Weighing three tons, dozens of people could stand on a blue whale's tongue. It would be plenty long enough to reach the watch. A whale's tongue! A whale's tongue! My kingdom for a whale's tongue! In my mind's eye, I could see the whale's tongue lolling out to reach the watch. In my imagination, the tongue was white, though I had no idea if a blue whale's tongue was white in real life. Truman's Hero sponsor to the Trials was a guy named Zookeeper, based in Atlanta, Georgia. If I visited the Peach State and asked him about the color of a blue whale's tongue, I bet he'd know. Actually, maybe not. Whales were kept in aquariums, not zoos. It was a shame I didn't know a Hero named Aquariumkeeper. Just as well. He'd probably be as lame as Aquaman. I mean, talking to fish? Really? What kind of lame power was that? Almost as lame as a telekinetic who couldn't pick up a watch within eyeshot.

A thought spurred by the image of a whale's white tongue skittered past my mind's eye, just out of sight. The thought felt important. I concentrated, trying to coax the now-hiding thought back into sight. *Here thought. Here thought, thought, thought.* The thought jumped into view. I grabbed it by its neck and shook it.

That was it! I didn't have to have a whale's tongue. I already had something long enough to do the job.

For the first time since the day Tiffany shot herself, I triggered the Omega suit. Instead of using it as I normally did to form a protective layer around myself, I sent a tendril of it out of my neck, like when I formed a cape with it. Only this time the suit extended from the front of my neck rather than its nape. I stretched the suit out toward the watch on the table.

Like the finger of a Metahuman with elasticity powers, the suit's tendril snaked through the air. It reached the table, then the watch. It came into contact with the watch. Damn it, too hard. The tendril shoved the watch, pushing it even further away from me.

I swallowed my frustration, tried to ignore how crappy I felt, closed my eyes and concentrated. Concentrating was tough when your leg throbbed so painfully you couldn't stand it and when you increasingly felt like you were being set on fire while standing in the middle of a freezer.

More carefully this time, I again extended the Omega suit's slender tendril toward the watch. Though the Omega suit was a part of me, using it like this was not like using my fingers. More like poking something with the tied together popsicle sticks I had wished for earlier.

With my eyes still closed, I gently probed the watch with the Omega suit. I groped for the tiny buttons on the side of it. Pressing the first and third buttons simultaneously twice would open the watch's face and expose the panic button.

Even if I was healthy, hitting the buttons would have been difficult to do with the Omega suit, like trying to tap two tiny buttons with broken fingers encased in thick mittens. Now that I was at far less than one hundred percent, the task seemed impossible. Sweat poured off me, making my right leg hurt even more as the salty liquid dripped down my exposed flesh. I started blacking out again. Dark unconsciousness beckoned seductively. It had become as welcome as a lover since Doctor Alchemy had begun slicing into me. My concentration on the watch and the Omega suit waned as I turned toward its embrace. Who needed a girlfriend when you had unconsciousness to love and hold you?

No! I forced myself away from the brink of beguiling blackness. Who knew when Doctor Alchemy would return? I did not trust anymore that I was strong enough to not tell him about Isaac. This was my best and maybe only chance to call the cavalry and escape. I refused to let Isaac down the way I had let Dad, Hannah, and Neha down.

Only pigheaded stubbornness kept me trying to mash the buttons as unconsciousness pulled at me ever more insistently.

It took me many tries, but I finally hit the buttons. The watch face sprang open.

Finally! How dare this stupid thing keep me from my lover's arms. Cock blocker.

I almost retracted the Omega suit and let myself pass out. Then I remembered the whole point of getting the stupid watch open in the first place. Annoyed by the further delay, I hit the red panic button in the center of the open watch. The watch flashed twice then snapped shut, indicating it was broadcasting its emergency signal. About damned time. Didn't it know my longtime lover awaited me with open arms? It was probably jealous because I had not asked it to join us.

Relieved all the delays were over, I quickly retracted the long tendril of the Omega suit back into my body, like a roll-up window blind that had been yanked on.

Now, where were we? I eagerly asked the bewitching blackness that was so anxious for me to join her again. My second interracial relationship. My second relationship period.

I embraced her, she embraced me, and we fell into the darkness together.

26

I weaved in and out of consciousness for a while. How long, I didn't know. Hours certainly. Maybe days.

During that time Oliver came in to give me something to drink, and to clean both me and the soiled floor. My stomach rebelled at having something in it. I projectile vomited the water and nutritional supplement back up, giving Oliver even more to clean up. I might have been impressed at the force and distance of the spew had I been in my right mind. I had thrown up so hard my stomach muscles were sore. If vomiting were an Olympic event, I would have won gold for sure. Curling was an Olympic event, yet vomiting wasn't. Unfair. I bet curlers never had sore stomachs after they competed.

I spent a lot of time after I hit the panic button praying. It was the first time I had prayed in a while. God and I had not been on good terms since Neha's death. When the Sentinels captured her, I had prayed that He help me rescue her safely. When He didn't, I had been as angry at Him as I had been at myself. People said He worked in mysterious ways, but the mystery of why He let someone like Neha die while letting villains like Millennium and Doctor Alchemy live was beyond me. Mom, Dad, Hammer, Hannah, and Neha. As far as I was concerned, God had a lot of explaining to do.

But, because there was nothing else I could do after hitting the panic button, I prayed. I prayed partly for myself. I would have to be far saintlier than I was to not want to escape the agony I was in. But mostly, I prayed I could escape so I could protect the world in my capacity as the vessel for the Omega spirit.

Dear God, I prayed, *if you let me get out of this, I promise I'll do everything I can to protect Your people.*

God did not answer. Not the first time that had happened. In fact, it seemed He did not answer more often than he did. I wondered what I had done to piss Him off so. Maybe it was because I could not kneel as I prayed. Who knew God was such a stickler for formality?

When God stubbornly refused to answer my prayers and Isaac did not show up, I convinced myself Isaac was not coming. Doctor Alchemy said I was in his volcanic lair. Maybe I was too deep in it for the watch's signal to penetrate to the wider world. I had no idea how the watch's emergency signal worked; maybe it had a range outside of which it did not function. I was a Hero, not an engineer. Since I was still stuck here, I was not even much of a Hero. When I got out of here, maybe I'd take up a profession more in line with my talents. Considering how well I vomited, I'd see if professional bulimia was a thing.

When I got out of here. Hah! That prospect looked less and less likely. The Omega spirit had done a crap job when it chose me. Somebody else would have to save the world. I was not up to the task. I could not even save myself.

Feeling like the world's biggest loser, I started to cry. That in turn made me feel like the world's biggest crybaby. The only good thing about Isaac not showing up was that no one was here to witness my humiliation. The tears were hot on my even hotter cheeks. I was burning up. Some small part of me realized my emotions were so volatile because of all the pain I was in with a healthy dollop of being sick on top. *If you're so smart, how come you haven't gotten us out of this mess?* the rest of me told that part. Pain, sickness, and despair combined in a potent cocktail, making me feel in my more lucid moments like I teetered on the edge of madness.

I had a sudden thought. Ice cold fear gripped my stomach, drying my tears. What if I had played into Doctor Alchemy's hands by hitting the panic button and trying to summon Isaac? Since Doctor Alchemy had not gotten what he wanted to know out of me, maybe he had tricked me into getting Oliver to help me retrieve my watch so I could summon Isaac. Maybe Isaac was walking into a trap. Maybe Isaac was already here, captured by Doctor Alchemy, and was being tortured right this second just as I had been.

Then I thought that if Doctor Alchemy had known about the panic button, he could have hit it himself instead of duping me into doing it. The thought did not make me feel better. He probably had some deviously inscrutable plan in place and him tricking me into summoning Isaac was but a part of it. And even if this was not all a part of Doctor Alchemy's plan, he had wanted to get out of me how to locate Isaac. After resisting ratting on Isaac all this time, now I had gone and done something to serve him up on a big silver platter by calling him here to rescue me. I was not the world's biggest crybaby. I was the world's biggest fool. On top of still being the world's biggest loser.

Just as fervently as I had wanted Isaac to rescue me before, now I just as fervently prayed he would not come. I wouldn't wish what Doctor Alchemy had done to me on my worst enemy, much less my best friend. I hoped Isaac stayed far, far away.

I was slipping in and out of consciousness and vacillating between wishing Isaac would come and praying he never would when, suddenly, he did.

———

Isaac floated through the front wall. His body was translucent, letting let me see right through him. He was in his ghost form. He wore his Myth costume, a form-fitting, full-body black number with light blue bands on the wrists and ankles. Its black cowl covered Isaac's face from the nose up. A ferocious-looking, blood-red dragon was emblazoned on his chest.

By now, I was not the slightest bit surprised to see him. I had been visited by a bunch of people already, including Avatar, Omega Man, Hanna, Mom, Dad, Neha, and our son James. I suspected they all had been fever and pain-induced hallucinations, unless the Last Trump had sounded and they had risen from the dead. It was just my luck to be trapped in a supervillain's lair when the biggest event in the history of ever happened. I had missed the Big Bang too, for reasons I could not remember. Darn my luck!

Isaac's ghostly form solidified. He looked at me aghast. His horrified eyes roved over my naked and bloody body. His nose wrinkled at the smell in the room, a heady mix of vomit, blood, waste, and sickness.

"Sweet Jesus," he murmured in a low voice, "what in the world have they done to you?"

"I don't have to explain myself to a hallucination," I rasped weakly. "Or an apocalyptic zombie."

"What are you talking about?" he asked, still in a low voice.

He shook his head. "Never mind. It doesn't matter. Sorry it took so long for me to come. Not only is this place in the middle of nowhere, but it's infested with hundreds of armed goons. I had to wait until the coast was clear to sneak in here undetected. Let's get you out of this thing."

"A hallucination can't free me. Dad already tried. You trying to say you're better than my Daddy?" Isaac didn't answer. Rude. Hallucinations these days. Clearly the products of bad imaginary parenting.

Isaac bent over and poked experimentally at the hard, black substance around my legs. His hand grazed my left leg. I felt his touch. I had not felt Neha when I had asked her to kiss me one last time. She had passed right through me like the figment of my imagination she had been.

"You're real," I whispered, startled.

Isaac didn't say anything, still busy examining my restraints. He didn't say *Yeah, real handsome* or *real hot* or *real good* or any number of other goofy jokes he normally would have made. I must have been a real mess and looked a fright if he could not muster a single joke.

Isaac's body glowed briefly, and shimmered. In seconds, a massive green-gray monster with sharp canines for teeth and the musculature of Mr. Olympia stood where Isaac had been. An ogre. The ogre grabbed the ring I stood on, near were my feet were attached. Its massive muscles bunched and flexed. The ring tore apart with the sound of rending metal, freeing my feet from the ring, though they were still encased in the black substance. Isaac broke the metal ring around my waist. Then he stood up straight and ripped the metal ring apart where my hands were attached. I went sprawling across Isaac's broad shoulder. For the first time in countless days, I was in a position other than ramrod straight. Fresh pain ran through my body like an electric current.

I was crying again, tears of pain and relief and feverishness.

"I didn't tell him about you. I swear I didn't. I wanted to, but I didn't," I blubbered. I said it over and over, like a rosary prayer. My right leg felt like it was burning into ashes. Pins and needles the size of spears stabbed me up and down my body.

Isaac tried to shush me, to no effect. He gently lay me down on a clean part of the floor. His ogre body glowed and shimmered again. When the glow disappeared, an animal the size of a large bear stood in the ogre's place. I had no idea of what Isaac had transformed into, but whatever it was had black matted hair and looked like what would result if you crossed an ape with a sloth. It had thick, sharp claws on its paws that were about the length of a ruler. Isaac used those claws to carefully slice into the black substance around one of my feet. It crumbled into a fine black dust once Isaac's claws breached it. In seconds, my hands and feet were free again.

The ape-sloth shimmered, and Isaac's human form appeared again. He looked down at where I lay on the floor. "Can you use your powers?" he asked.

"I didn't tell him about you. I swear I didn't. I wanted to, but I didn't."

Isaac sighed. "Kinda what I thought. Sit tight. I'll be back in a second."

Isaac became translucent. He walked through the front wall again, leaving me there to babble on the floor. Soon, he was back.

"The coast is clear for now," he said. "Let's get you out of here." He bent down, picked me up, and slung me over his shoulders in a fireman's carry. Being jostled and the fresh surges of pain it brought partially roused me from my stupor.

"We can't leave," I said weakly. I was bleeding on Isaac's

costume. I wondered if he knew a Hero with dry cleaning powers. "We have to save Oliver. And Tiffany. We'll start with what's left of her in the drain. And all the others. I don't want to fail again."

"You're sick and hurt and not in your right mind," Isaac said firmly, still in a low voice. After all the racket he had made freeing me from the ring, surely Doctor Alchemy's minions wouldn't raise an eyebrow at a regular volume conversation. I tried to tell Isaac that, but the words wouldn't come out. With me draped over his shoulders, Isaac turned back toward the wall he had just walked through. "You have a raging fever. I'm no doctor, but you look like you have the mother of all infections. You're in no condition to save anyone. I'm getting you out of here and getting medical help. We can come back later."

"Goddamn it, put me down. Coward. If you won't help me save Doctor Alchemy's slaves, I'll do it by myself. I'm Omega. Those Rogues got the drop on me before, but never again. Here I come to save the day," I cried. Or at least I tried to say all that. It came out as gibberish. It was just as well. *Here I come to save the day* was Mighty Mouse's line; I'd hate for him to sue me for copyright infringement. I tried to twist out of Isaac's grasp, but I barely moved. I tried instead to activate my powers to free myself, but could not concentrate enough to do so. My friends, my body, and my mind were all betraying me.

The world became draped in a fine gray mist. Isaac half walked, half floated through the front wall. I stopped cursing Isaac's cowardice long enough to say goodbye to my former accommodations. I started mentally composing my UWant review. My stay in Hotel Horror had been interesting, but all in all I would not recommend it to my friends.

With Isaac in his ghostly form and me riding shotgun on his shoulder, we alternated moving through solid rock and broad, brightly-lit, ornately decorated corridors that would not look out of place in Buckingham Palace. Isaac paused and ducked back into the rock once when he spotted a patrolling armed guard. The guard was dressed in the turquoise uniform with a yellow sash that Doctor Alchemy seemed to favor. The guard did not raise an alarm. He must not have seen us. Isaac proceeded once the guard moved on.

Soon we passed through a final rock face. We were outside. It was nighttime, but a crescent moon and a canopy of bright stars provided plenty of light. The night lights reflected off a large body of water off in the distance ahead. A dark mountain loomed up behind us. It was where we had come from. Sand was under Isaac's feet. Thin vegetation was around us. The distinct smell of salt water was in the air. I was thirsty. I wondered if Oliver would be coming along soon to give me some water.

"Be sure to hold on tight, now," Isaac said. I did not answer. I was too busy cursing him for not helping me save Doctor Alchemy's slaves.

Isaac glowed again, his form twisting and transforming under me. Before I knew it, I sat astride a four-legged animal. It had the head, forelegs, and impressive antlers of a large male deer, but the wings and hindquarters of a multicolored bird. *A Peryton*, my mind told me. I knew what the hell a Peryton was, but not how to move my body parts correctly or how to use my powers to go back and save everyone. My knowledge was mighty spotty.

The Peryton trotted forward, beating its wings powerfully. *This is no time for a horseback ride,* I thought. *Stagback ride,* I corrected myself. No, that wasn't quite right either. *Birdback ride?* Whatever. Regardless of what kind of animal ride it was, I wanted off. I made no effort to hold on. Not that I could have anyway, with my body being as uncooperative as it was.

Before Isaac went airborne, I slipped off his back. I handed heavily on the sand on my side. I barely felt the impact. Free of Isaac's constraints, now I could go back and save Doctor Alchemy's slaves. "Here I come to save the day," I cried again, getting a mouthful of sand. Mighty Mouse's doing, no doubt. A mouse was but a cuter version of a rat, and everyone knew you couldn't trust a rat.

Isaac trotted in a tight circle back around to me. Though I tried, I couldn't move from where I lay. His form shimmered again as he regained his human form. "That's my mistake," he said. "You're too far gone. We'll have to do this another way. This is likely going to hurt, so I apologize in advance."

Isaac began to transform again. This time his form swelled to several times his normal size. The bird he turned into looked like an eagle, only this eagle was bigger than a bull elephant. A roc.

The roc lifted its taloned foot and placed it over me. *Stuck between a roc and a hard place,* I thought. The thought would've made more sense if the sand been hard. It was not. It was softer than any bed I could remember. After I saved Doctor Alchemy's subjects, perhaps I would come back here and take a nice long nap. I resolved to never sleep on anything but sand for as long as I lived. I wondered if mattress companies knew about sand. They probably did and deliberately kept the public in the dark about the benefits of sleeping on sand. Conspiracies were afoot everywhere.

The roc closed its talons around me, gripping me tightly. It hurt like hell, but I did not mind. Pain was my old friend. Pain was the only friend around who wasn't carrying me in the wrong direction when there was work to be done and people to save.

The roc beat its massive wings, blowing up debris from the ground the way a helicopter's rotors would. The roc launched itself into the air, carrying me with it.

We rose high in the sky. The rushing wind made me shiver. How could I be so cold and yet so hot at the same time? Now that we were airborne, I saw that we had flown off an island with a volcano in the center of it. White smoke puffed lazily out of a huge crack in its summit. As the roc flapped its massive wings, soon the island was but a speck of black in the ocean. The water reflected the light of the moon and stars, making it look like a sea of quicksilver.

Heroes ran toward danger, not away from it. I was thinking I would not share with Isaac any of the credit for rescuing Doctor Alchemy's slaves because he was too eager to flee when I slipped in Isaac's talons, almost plunging into the shimmering quicksilver below. Isaac grasped me harder, my old pal pain embraced me tighter, and I passed out again.

27

The same scene played over and over, like a horror movie set on a loop.

I stood next to a waist-high stone bier on which a naked corpse lay. A bright light from above lit up the bier and the surrounding area. Thick gray mist swirled beyond the cone of illumination cast by the light. I was dressed in my full Omega costume, including my silver-white cape.

I was not alone. Avatar, in his red cape and iconic gray and blood-red costume with the stylized red *A* on its chest, towered over me on my right. Omega Man, almost as tall as Avatar, was on my left, garbed in his famous yellow and blue costume, its cape held in place with an ornate silver clasp wrought in the shape of an omega symbol. Dad, dressed in the only suit he owned that he wore to weddings and funerals, stood directly across the bier from me. Neha and Hannah were on either side of Dad, both in somber black dresses.

All six of us pointed accusing fingers at the battered and bloody corpse on the bier.

"You failed us again, Theodore Conley," we accused the corpse. We were joined by countless voices from the surrounding mist, voices that represented everyone in the world. Deafeningly loud, the world's voices accompanied us like a Greek chorus.

I was the corpse on the bier. Lying face-up, my eyes were closed. I was still bloody and battered from my encounter with the Revengers and the torture sessions with Doctor Alchemy. Naked and mottled with hues of white, pink, red, and black, I looked as far from heroic as anyone could possibly look. I looked more like a boy than a man, and simultaneously more like a mangled piece of meat than human.

"You failed us again, Theodore Conley," I and everyone else intoned once more. "You failed us again, Theodore Conley." With each repetition, the gray mist grew thinner and thinner, while the light shining overhead expanded, getting brighter and brighter, dispelling the mist like the sun chasing away a morning fog.

The light banished the remainder of the gray mist. With accusations of failure still ringing in my ears, my eyes snapped open. I sat up on the bier. I and the rest of my accusers faded away.

I BLINKED, BLINDED BY THE BRIGHTNESS OF THE ROOM. I WAS sitting up in a bed. Not my own. The room was spartan, antiseptic, full of medical equipment, and contained five other beds that were identical to the one I was in. The other beds were empty.

A hospital room. Hospital rooms all had the same depressing sameness to them. I had been injured enough over the years to know one when I was in one. While I wasn't stoked to awaken in a hospital room, this was a vast improvement over lying dead on a cold stone slab while also standing over myself and joining the world in chiding my corpse over what a failure I was. I hoped that had been a fever-induced dream rather than a premonition.

I wore a plain white short-sleeved shirt and shorts. I ran a hand over my head. I found stubble there despite the hair removal ointment Doctor Alchemy's subject had used on me. Obviously, my hair was starting to grow back. I pulled off the thin sheet that covered my legs. My right leg was no longer skinless, raw, and bloody. Other than it being discolored, like I had gotten a deep tan from my groin to my ankle, my leg looked normal. Hairless, but normal. An intravenous line ran from my arm to an IV bag dangling from a stand on the side of the bed. A thin electronic monitor was taped near where the IV line entered my arm.

All further evidence I was in a hospital room. Maybe I should be a detective instead of a Hero. I could apprentice under Truman. He could teach me to escape a Rogue's clutches without help.

I was tired and weak. Even so, while I did not feel up to running a marathon, I felt worlds better than I had when in Doctor Alchemy's lair.

I was not alone. I had been so busy taking stock of my body, I had not noticed before. Maybe I didn't have the talent to be a detective after all. First escape artist, now detective. I was crossing a lot of potential careers off the list.

"Where am I?" I asked the man. My voice was weak and hoarse. I coughed, trying to clear it.

"The medical bay in the Guild space station," the man said. Standing just a few feet away, he examined a machine that beeped and pinged. Since it looked like the big brother of the electronic sensor on my arm, I assumed the sounds it made meant I was still alive. Good. It had seemed touch and go there for a while.

The medium-sized man examining the machine wore a blue and orange costume that was composed of pants and a loose-fitting tunic rather than the tight costume most Heroes favored. His mask had a white caduceus emblazoned on its forehead. Doctor Hippocrates. I had seen him many times before. Not only had he been the chief physician when I was at the Academy, but he had healed me after Mechano's bomb exploded in my face in Washington, D.C. Hippocrates had also healed Isaac after Iceburn collapsed a building on him, Neha, and me during our Academy days. Among his other powers, he could boost and accelerate the body's capacity to heal itself.

"How did I get here?" I asked him.

"Myth brought you here. He said it was the safest place for you since there were some Rogues after you. After he brought you here, he went and found me. I was doing some work in South Sudan at the time. I told him I was too busy to tend to you. He said he'd knock me out and drag me here if I didn't come voluntarily." Doctor Hippocrates shook his head in bemusement at the recollection. "Though I don't enjoy being threatened, it's a good thing he was so insistent. Though the doctors here had done all they could, you were at death's door when I arrived. After taking care of the nasty infection you had, I performed a skin graft to replace the skin on your leg. That's why your leg looks the way it does. I've also accelerated the healing process for all your other injuries. You've been here almost a week."

"Where's Myth now?"

"Standing guard outside the door. He's been there every day while you've been healing. Said somebody would come in here to attack you again over his dead body. In light of how he threatened me, I believe him. You're lucky to have such a loyal friend."

I couldn't argue with that. I remembered how Isaac had

rescued me from Doctor Alchemy's clutches despite my foolish insistence we stay to rescue the Rogue's drug-addled subjects. Now that I was more clear-headed, I knew I had not been in any condition to rescue anyone. But now that I was on the mend, I would have to go back and liberate Doctor Alchemy's followers. "How much longer do I need to stay here?" I asked.

"It'll be several more days before you're one hundred percent well again. To be frank, you'll look like you're wearing a one-legged stocking the rest of your life thanks to the skin graft, but you won't die." Doctor Hippocrates shook his head at me. "At least not yet. This is the second time in just a few years I've treated you for life-threatening injuries. You need to be more careful. The next time, you may not have a friend handy to shanghai me into service."

A wave of exhaustion washed over me. I lay back down.

"I'm not in the be more careful business, Doc," I said. As soon as the words came out of my mouth, I wished they hadn't. Narrowly escaping death apparently made me sound like a swaggering douchebag.

I closed my eyes and thought while Doctor Hippocrates puttered around in the room. He was right. How many times had I narrowly avoided death since developing powers? So often, I was not certain of the number.

A cat had nine lives, and it did not have the responsibility of saving the world.

How many more did I have?

28

A few days later, I had my Omega suit on while in the space station's Promenade. I had spent most of my time the past few days exploring the station. The time I had spent recovering from my injuries was the first time I had been inside the space station. As a kid, I had read countless science fiction books about space and space stations, and now adult me was on one. If I were here under different circumstances, I'd be squealing like a little girl.

Doctor Hippocrates had cleared me to leave the medical bay. Even so, I wheeled around with me a portable stand from which dangled an IV bag, with the line running from it still embedded in my arm. The clear bag contained my final round of antibiotics. Doctor Hippocrates had already weaned me off the painkiller he had been dosing me with. My right leg throbbed, though the pain was mostly gone thanks to Hippocrates accelerating my body's healing. My grandma used to swear she knew it was going to rain when her arthritic knee throbbed. I wondered if I'd be able to predict the weather with my throbbing leg. It remaining off-white and pain-free would mean the coast was clear; it throbbing and turning blood-red would mean a severe thunderstorm with a sixty percent chance of a Rogue attack.

The low hum of other Heroes' conversations washed over me as I stood alone in the Promenade. It was a glass, chrome, and metal area that gleamed like the set of a science fiction show. Despite that, the couches and comfortable chairs that were scattered around the area and the Heroes who socialized in it made it feel more like a fraternity house than a *Babylon 5* episode.

Being surrounded by people who carefully ignored me made me feel like I was in high school again. Unlike in high school, I did not much mind being ignored now. I was too busy looking down at Earth.

That was not quite true. I looked down at a projection of Earth. Though the ceiling to floor glass I stared at appeared to be a window to space, it was in fact a projection screen that showed what would be visible if what I looked at really was a window. The space station was too heavily armored for there to be actual windows. After all, the Guild had built it as a precaution against another alien invasion after the V'Loth had attacked the world in the 1960s. I remembered the attack and me foiling it as if it had happened yesterday even though I had not really been there. As I often did, I thought of Neha, our son James, and our lives together as a family. Though none of it had happened, it still seemed real, like a vivid dream I had been awakened from and never would be able to return to.

One of the perks of my powers was they allowed me to go into space for short periods. During a previous jaunt into space months ago, I had seen the space station from the outside. It looked somewhat like a bicycle tire with a thick rod shoved through the center where the spokes met. The circular Promenade I now stood in was the rubber of the tire, the spokes housed the Guild's administrative offices and the medical bay, and the thick rod in the center of the spokes contained the machinery and electronics that kept the space station going, including the facility's armaments.

The existence of the space station was a secret known only to licensed Heroes. It was cloaked so it could not be detected from the planet or spotted by conventional satellites. I didn't like keeping something this big from the public, though I understood the reasoning behind it. If the public knew we Heroes maintained a giant space station bristling with weapons, many would fear we used it for some nefarious purpose. Considering how Heroes like Mechano, Seer, and Millennium had treated me, I could sympathize with such paranoia. Even paranoids had enemies.

There was a low hum and then a click behind me. I glanced back to see a willowy woman in a form-fitting olive costume step out of one of the station's matter transportation chambers. They were recessed into the Promenade's curved inner wall. The female Hero peeled her mask off as the door of the transportation chamber clicked shut behind her. She looked at me, glancing down at my Omega suit. Her eyes widened. I didn't know her, but obviously she recognized me. She took a tentative step in my direction, thought better of it, and instead turned to join a nearby group of Heroes congregated around a cluster of couches. The Heroes there carefully avoided looking directly at me, yet kept glancing at me out of the corners of their eyes. I didn't need super hearing to know they were talking about me. Though there was no rule saying they could not come up to me, it was bad form up here to approach a Hero you didn't know. We Heroes got enough of that from civilians down on Earth. The Guild space station was supposed to be a place we could take our masks off, both literally and figuratively. To ensure privacy, there was no electronic surveillance in the Promenade, and Heroes recording or photographing their fellow Heroes was strictly forbidden. Even so, unlike most of the Heroes now socializing on the Promenade, I had not removed my mask. I had no reason to believe any Heroes were out to get me other than the three corrupt Sentinels. But why take a chance? A cat who sat on a hot stove wouldn't sit on a hot stove again, but it was also leery of sitting on *any* kind of stove again. Once burned, twice shy.

Feeling like the elephant in the room, I turned back to look at Earth again. Despite hours of wandering the Promenade the past few days, I had not gotten used to Heroes treating me like I was a combination of a rock star and the only tiger in a roomful of cats. To have a group of people I once viewed as larger-than-life figures treat me like I was the one who was larger-than-life was a bizarre. Omega was famous in the general population, but even more so among Heroes. With Millennium's license having been revoked, I was the only Omega-level licensed Hero. Heroes knew better than anyone what that meant. Plus, I was famous for having exposed the corruption in the Sentinels' midst.

All the Heroes up here were why Isaac had brought me here to recuperate. He had thought that if there was anywhere in the world—or off the world in this case—where I would be safe from another Rogue attack, it would be in the Guild's secret space station. But even if the Revengers came after me here—Brown Recluse knew of the space station since he had been a Hero and might have spilled the beans about it—Isaac figured me being surrounded by a bunch of other Heroes would make Doctor Alchemy and the other Revengers think twice. Not only was the space station an alien early-warning system and battle station, but it was also the Guild's official headquarters and unofficial clubhouse. The Guild's ornate building in Washington, D.C. was more a public relations front and tourist trap than the headquarters it pretended to the public to be.

Matter transporters like the one the olive-garbed Hero had stepped out of were how Isaac had brought me here after taking me from Doctor Alchemy's lair. There were transporters in regional Guild offices scattered across the world. After flying me from Doctor Alchemy's volcanic island, Isaac had carried me to the closest landmass, in this case South America. He used a matter transporter in Chile to beam us to the space station.

Isaac had been relieved to get the call from my watch's panic button. After the Revengers attacked me in Astor City, Isaac had watched footage of the attack a bystander had uploaded to UWant Video. Isaac had been looking for me ever since Doctor Alchemy disappeared with my body. He had recruited Truman and a few other Heroes to look for me too. Until he got the distress call from my watch's panic button, he thought I was dead.

He had very nearly been right.

I looked down at the blue and white orb I was supposed to protect. Literally billions of people relied on me though they did not know it. Ignorance was bliss.

Death did not frighten me. My encounter with Angel and my suicidal thoughts unearthed by the wine I drank the next day had taught me that. But, the thought of dying before I had fulfilled my supposed purpose of protecting the world below did more than frighten me. It *terrified* me. Too many people had died because of me already. Dad, Hannah, and Neha. I had no interest in adding more to the list. Three people were three too many.

North America was below. I could reach out and put my finger on the spot where I'd grown up, give or take a few hundred miles. From a small farm to a space station looking down on that farm in a few short years. If I had not lived it, I would not have believed it. Heck, I *had* lived it, and I still barely believed it.

I was beginning to understand why the Trials were so bloodthirsty, with several Hero candidates getting seriously hurt or killed like Hammer had been. Until now I had thought the Trials were needlessly violent and perhaps indicative, like Seer, Mechano, and Millennium were, of a cynical disregard for the sanctity of human life in the ranks of the Guild. I still thought that. It was absurd that Hero candidates were taught to not kill, yet the administrators of the Trials had no problem putting those same candidates in situations that could kill them. It was like a parent telling her children, "Do as I say, not as I do." But now I was also starting to think that the official purpose of the Trials was not just empty words. The Guild said the purpose of the Trials was to make sure potential Heroes were hardened enough to withstand whatever a dangerous world threw at them. Fresh off the farm me would have broken both physically and mentally under Doctor Alchemy's tender mercies. Yet Heroic me had not broken. I had bent a little maybe, but I had not broken. I was scarred and humbled and questioning the way I had gone about things since I had become Omega, but I was still standing.

Still staring at the world below, I said, "I've been thinking."

"You've been thinking about how creepy it is when you know who's approaching without looking around?" Isaac asked. "You were less creepy when you didn't have your powers." He came up alongside of me. His freshly shaved brown head glistened under the Promenade's lights. He had barely let me out of his sight since bringing me to the space station. Normally I would chafe being under someone's watchful eye. After what I had been through with Doctor

Alchemy though, I did not mind. It was like have a guardian angel.

"I'm creepy?" I said. "You're the one who's been my shadow the past few days."

"You're calling a black man a shadow? Really? Your moonshine-drenched racist roots rear their ugly head yet again. You white-privileged, cis-hetero, patriarchy-enabled, micro-aggressive male monster. Next you'll be calling me a spook."

"I'm not sure how insulted I should be by what you just said because I didn't understand it."

"Don't worry about it. Nobody does."

Unmasked and out of costume, Isaac wore only jeans and a tee shirt. It was an Omega tee shirt, one of the U.S. made official ones I had licensed rather than one of the Chinese knockoffs some enterprising intellectual property pirates were making a bundle from. His shirt was the same color blue as my costume, with a white Omega symbol on the front of it. On the back of it Isaac had written in black marker, *I saved Omega, and all I got was this lousy t-shirt.* The saving me part was true enough, but the rest wasn't—he had bought the shirt himself months ago. I most definitely had not given it to him. I wasn't so full of myself that I gave people Omega brand swag. It would be like giving out selfies as Christmas presents.

"I've been thinking," I repeated. "And not of names to call you, so cancel your and Jesse Jackson's boycott of my Omega merchandise. I've been thinking about what a fool I've been."

"Well, hallelujah. I've been thinking the same thing for ages now." Isaac hesitated. "Um, what exactly have you been a fool about? There's so much to choose from."

"I've been thinking about the crisis the Sentinels warned me about. I thought that with my powers and the Omega suit, given enough time and training, I would be able to handle anything that was thrown at me. And after Neha died, I wanted to handle it alone. I didn't want someone else I cared about to get hurt because of me." As I spoke, I continued to look at the world I was supposed to protect. The longer I looked at it, the more I felt its weight on my shoulders. "Despite all my powers, despite the suit, despite all my training and preparation, I still got my ass handed to me by a group of Rogues. If it hadn't been for Doctor Alchemy not killing me immediately when the Revengers defeated me so he could torture me and get information out of me about you, I'd be dead right now."

Isaac shook his head. "I still don't buy that."

"What do you mean?"

"I mean that Trey knows my real name and my code name. If you know both, finding me is a snap. There's no way he didn't share that information with Doctor Alchemy."

"What makes you so sure of that?"

"Because if the shoe was on the other foot and Doctor Alchemy was targeting Trey, I'd drop a dime on him so fast it would make his blonde head spin," Isaac said matter-of-factly. His usual jovial demeanor made it easy to forget just how intensely he hated Trey because of what Trey had done to his sister. "If I'd do it to him, do you really think that lowlife would hesitate to do it to me? I think Doctor Alchemy tortured you because he wanted to, not because he really was trying to wring intel out of you."

I had to admit that made sense. Me thinking when I was in Doctor Alchemy's clutches that he didn't know where Isaac was seemed silly now that I was relatively unhurt and could think clearly. Being tortured clouded one's thinking. Who would've guessed? "You're saying I went through all that for nothing?"

"Not nothing. You got a real cool leg-length scar out of the deal. It's even cooler than mine. Lucky duck. Everyone knows chicks dig scars." Isaac's teeth flashed in a grin as he rubbed the jagged scar on his forehead from our run-in with Iceburn years ago. Then he sobered. "But before you start sulking again about the fact you got captured—"

"I don't sulk," I interjected indignantly.

Isaac rolled his eyes. "Please. You're so good at sulking, you should list it on your resume under 'special skills.' You sulked when Hannah died, you sulked when Neha died, and you've been sulking since you've been back in your right mind after Doc Hippoc fixed you up. And I'm here to tell you to stop it. Just like with Hannah and Neha, you did the best you could do under difficult circumstances. As far as I'm concerned, you showed what kind of man you are when Doctor Alchemy sliced and diced you. Though Doctor Alchemy probably already knew how to find me, you didn't know that at the time. You kept your mouth shut about me even though you could've cut your torture short by spilling your guts. And, when I came to fetch you, instead of being eager to get away like most people in your shoes would've been, all you could talk about was staying to rescue the people Doctor Alchemy has enslaved. So instead of sulking, you ought to congratulate yourself on how well you held up and performed."

I shook my head. "I don't feel like I deserve congratulations. How am I supposed to handle that major crisis the Sentinels warned of if I can't handle a motley crew of Rogues?"

"In your defense, one of those Rogues is Doctor Alchemy. Though he's a toy short of a Happy Meal, his power is nothing to sneeze at."

"The fact Doctor Alchemy is crazy makes him defeating me worse. Imagine what terrible things he would be able to do if he wasn't nuts." I shook my head. "It's made me re-think things. Maybe I've been going about this world-saving thing all wrong. Despite all my power, I'm just one dude. I can't be Omega 24/7. I still have to eat and sleep."

"And have a personal life," Isaac interjected. "I'd hate for the best man speech I've been working on to go to waste."

"And have a personal life," I reluctantly admitted, thinking of Angel and the *Richard Cory* poem. All work and no play made Theo a suicidal boy. That made me think of Viola. Isaac said she had gotten safely away from the carnage Silverback caused. Isaac had told her I was out of town on business, which was why she hadn't heard from me. "There's a limit to how much I can accomplish alone. Even with working myself to a frazzle in Astor City and the surrounding area, it's not like crime has dropped to zero. And it's not as though there's been an Omega Effect in the rest of the country. It's become obvious to me why so many prominent Heroes band together to form teams."

I continued to look at the slowly turning Earth. Thick clouds were clumped at the top of it, making the planet look like it had on a white hat worn at a rakish angle. If the title weren't already taken, I'd ask my publisher to change the name of my autobiography to *As the World Turns*. Unlike in a soap opera, I would not miraculously come back to life in the next episode if I bought the farm.

"I've come out of all this with more than just a cool scar. I've also come out of it with a realization: Thinking I can save the world all by myself was an arrogant mistake. Being up here has only reinforced that realization," I said. "Despite the fact the other Heroes up here treat me like a celebrity they're too shy to approach, merely being around them gives me a feeling of comfort I haven't had since you, Neha and I used to hang out together. If our prehistoric ancestors went their own way and tried to do everything alone, lions and bears and other predators bigger and stronger than us would've killed humanity off eons ago. Humans never would have become the world's apex predator if it had been every man for himself. We got to where we are as a species because we learned to work together. Man is a social animal, I think, who feels the most comfortable when he belongs to a tribe. For a lot of people, that tribe is their family and friends. For others, it's their favorite sports team, which is why you see grown men wearing another man's jersey, slathering on face paint in their team's colors, and braving frigid weather during football season. For others, their tribe is their town, or their state, or their country."

I shook my head. "I don't have any of that. My parents are the only family I had who gave a damn about me, and they're both dead. Until the Academy, I didn't have many friends. I never cared much about sports, and care less now that I can do things elite athletes can only dream of. And I'm certainly proud to be an American, but being the vessel for the Omega spirit forces me to care about more than just what is going on within our borders.

"The only tribe I really have is you and other Heroes. It was a mistake to let my grief over Neha's death make me turn my back to that tribe. Because I grew up a loner, my first instinct was to go it alone again. That was dumb. If I hadn't been acting alone, maybe the Revengers never would have defeated me and nearly killed me. I can't let that happen again. There's too much at stake. If there's one thing I've learned from the Revengers' example, it's that there's strength in numbers. That a group of people can accomplish things one person can't alone. If I'm going to save the world, I'll need all the help I can get. Plus, the Revengers are still out there, not to mention Millennium and God only knows who and what else. And with the Sentinels disbanded, there's a power vacuum that needs to be filled before some enterprising group of Rogues does it."

Isaac said, "If you want to start fighting crime with me again by me letting you become my sidekick, no need to be coy and hint at it in some big speech. Just say so. How do you like the name Kid Myth?"

"Here I am being vulnerable and admitting I was wrong, and all you can do is make jokes."

"You're surprised? You have met me, right?"

"Sometimes your mouth makes me regret it." My smile belied my words. The truth of the matter was I wouldn't have Isaac any other way. "What do you say? Are you up for being the founding member of a new superhero team? I know it'll be a burden with your obligations at Pixelate, but you wouldn't be the first Hero to juggle a job and being a member of a team."

Isaac looked embarrassed. "Yeah, about that. I kinda got fired from Pixelate. And by kinda, I mean I most definitely was."

"Fired?" I was surprised. "What for?"

"As you pointed out, I've been up here watching your every move for well over a week now. Employers tend to frown on their employees not showing up for long stretches of time. My boss left me a voicemail several days ago telling me to not come back in. She was quite snippy about it." Isaac shrugged. "I've been skating on thin ice with her for a while now anyway with all my unexplained absences. Rogues don't always have the good grace to wait until after business hours to be thrashed, you know."

"Why didn't you say something before? I know how much you loved that job."

"Because you'd blame yourself for me losing my job. You're a master at sulking, remember?" Isaac shrugged again.

"On the upside, I seem to be between jobs. I'd love to get the band back together again. It'll be just like old times. The problem is money. My landlord doesn't accept goodwill generated by fighting alongside Omega as a form of payment. And I sure as hell won't take money from you, so if you were about to offer to pay me, you can forget about it. Like I told you the last time we talked about money, I'm not interested in being your sugar baby. All the money in the world wouldn't make me put out for you. You're not my type." Isaac shook his head. "Plus, putting together a superhero team is not as simple as it is in the movies. You don't join hands, cry 'Avengers Assemble!' and call it a day. There are all sorts of things to be considered: liability insurance, where we'd be headquartered, how we'd pay for everything we'd need, getting approval from the Guild, and a bunch of other things I probably don't even know about. And, most importantly, there's the small matter of who else would be a member. No offense, but saving the world calls for more than just a dynamic duo. Even when half of that duo is as awesome as me."

"I've been mulling all that over the past few days. What you call sulking, I call thinking. I've got some ideas." My mouth was dry. I was tired. I had talked more in the past few minutes than I had in the past few days. "But can we talk about it later? I want to just enjoy the view for a while."

"Sure thing."

We stood in companionable silence. Maybe the medication Doctor Hippocrates had me on made me maudlin, but I was so grateful Isaac was in my life. And not merely because he had rescued me.

"At the risk of you making fun of me," I said, "I want you to know how much I love you."

"I love you too."

We watched the world continue to turn. I felt warm inside. Like I had come home after a long absence.

"Does this mean we're gay now?" Isaac said, breaking our silence. "Not that there's anything wrong with that. It's just that if we are, I thought I should let Sylvia know."

I sighed. "You just couldn't let it lie, could you?"

29

Isaac and I sat at the clear heptagonal table in the Situation Room of Sentinels Mansion, located on the outskirts of Astor City. In a nice change of pace from the other two times I had been here, Heroic homicidal maniacs weren't trying to kill me. Then again, the day was young. The way things were going lately, I might be fighting off the entire Guild by dinnertime. If I had learned anything the past few years, it was to expect the unexpected.

Expect the unexpected. Maybe that would be the motto of the new Hero team Isaac and I were forming. *Expect the unexpected* sucked as a battle cry, but that was unsurprising since I had come up with it. "Time to batter Rogue butt" and "Who else wants some?" were the less than glittering gems I had come up with when facing the Revengers. Coining catchphrases clearly was not my strong suit. I was an ace at alliteration, though.

Both Isaac and I were in full costume. So was Ninja, who wore her usual loose black costume that covered her from head to toe, leaving only a slit exposing her Asian eyes. As she always did, she gave the impression that if she held perfectly still, she would be hard to spot, even in this well-lit room.

Like Isaac and I, Ninja sat in a tall, silver-colored chair, except hers had a red glowing katana emblazoned on the front and rear of the back rest. It was the chair the Sentinels had reserved for her. Since the Sentinels were defunct and she could sit wherever she wanted, I guess old habits died hard. Isaac was in Tank's old chair. As for me, I sat in Doppelganger's chair, the one with the black and white pattern on its back that looked like a Rorschach inkblot test. I saw déjà vu in the inkblot. I never thought I'd set foot in this hateful place again.

The other four Sentinels' empty chairs were around the table. I had almost sat in Mechano's chair until I had realized whose it was. I wanted nothing to do with that murderous bucket of bolts, so had sat here instead. The temptation to take a dump in Mechano's chair might have gotten the better of me.

The mansion was different than the last time I had been here. For one thing, no one was trying to kill me. For another, Sentry had been deactivated. Sentry was the computer system the Sentinels had used to monitor the world for signs of trouble. As the massive computer system was covered by a thick tarp, it made the Situation Room look like it was about to be painted. Also, the Situation Room and the rest of the mansion were emptier than I remembered, like a dead man's house the contents of which were gradually given away or sold. Ninja had donated a lot of the artifacts in the mansion to museums, including the Lockheed Model 10 Electra Amelia Earhart had disappeared in and the painting *Starry Night*. Isaac, thanks to his Heroic training and former employment, knew something about the art world. He'd told me there was a spirited argument among art experts as to whether the Sentinels' painting was the original Van Gogh or if the one on display at the Museum of Modern Art in New York City was. My money was on the former, but what did I know? I had never graduated past the finger paint and stick figure stage of artistic achievement.

The supposedly extinct flock of passenger pigeons I saw the first time I visited the mansion had been donated to the Smithsonian National Zoological Park in Washington, D.C. There was talk of breeding that kit to repopulate the pigeons in the wild. I knew a group of pigeons in flight was called a "kit," yet I could not come up with a good catchphrase. Knowing obscure words and stringing them together cleverly were obviously entirely different skill sets.

"When we last saw each other and I suggested an association, you told me to go pound sand," Ninja said, making me stop thinking about pigeons. As a result of all I'd been through, my thoughts had been awfully flighty lately. *Pigeons. Flighty. Hah!* "Now you're here, hat in hand, making the same proposal you rejected out of hand not too long ago. What's changed?"

"I've eaten a healthy serving of humble pie with a side-order of crow since we last spoke," I said. Crow? Huh. What was my obsession with fowl lately? Focusing my birdbrain, I sketched out to Ninja what had happened with the Revengers and Doctor Alchemy.

When I finished, Ninja said, "So you've come to the realization that you can't do everything by yourself?" The fabric around her mouth twitched. "If I were a smaller person, I might be tempted to say I told you so."

"We're looking for a partner, not a gloater," I said. It sounded snappish, and I suppose it was. This was the room I had rescued Neha from before the metal that bound her had exploded. Sitting here dredged up unpleasant memories that were never too far from the surface to begin with.

Isaac raised his hands placatingly. "No one enjoys rubbing in how right he was more than I do, but now's not the time nor the place. Let's be frank, Ninja. Actually, I'll be Frank; you don't look like you have a penis. We need each other. As the last standing Sentinel and one of the beneficiaries of Mechano's fortune, you have resources Omega and I don't. The kind of world-class team Omega and I have in mind that can be ready for any and everything is going to take cash, and lots of it. We're envisioning something along the lines of the Sentinels. Minus the plotting against other Heroes and killing innocent people part. Plus, you're a more experienced Hero than either of us. Your experience as a Hero at the highest levels will surely prove useful."

"That explains why you need me," Ninja said. "It doesn't explain why I need you."

"Because associating with us gives you back some of the credibility you've lost," I said bluntly. "Your name is mud in the public's eyes because you're a Sentinel. Helping us can rehabilitate your image. Plus, there's the not so small matter of potentially helping us save the world."

Ninja regarded me thoughtfully with unblinking eyes. "You surprise me Omega. I was under the impression from our last conversation that you'd sooner trust a snake than a Sentinel."

"Honestly? Being in this room again makes my skin crawl. But like Myth says, you have resources that we will likely need. And, you knocked me on my butt and disappeared even though I was looking for you. Not too many people can do that. You may prove useful. The thought of working with a Sentinel hardly makes me jump for joy, but I'll do what I need to do to ensure the world's safety." I thought of how Avatar had kept The Mountain a secret from the Sentinels, as well as the fact he had hidden the Omega weapon there. "I'm under the impression Avatar had qualms about working with some of the Sentinels too, but he did it anyway in pursuit of the greater good. If something's good enough for Avatar, it's good enough for me. Besides, it's not like we're broaching this with you without carefully checking you out first. Other than questionable judgment in former colleagues, you're as clean as a hound's tooth. Plus, Truman Lord vouches for you." *You could do better,* Truman had said about Ninja, pointing at himself with a twinkle in his eye. *Then again, you could do much worse. Be hard not to if I'm the standard you're judging everyone else by. And be sure to tell Ninja she was your second choice. I've yet to meet a woman who didn't love hearing that.*

Ninja cocked an eyebrow at me. "Clean as a hound's tooth?" she repeated.

"Omega's from the South originally," Isaac said. "He says folksy stuff like that all the time. Bless your heart. Fixin' to go to the store. I suwanne. Sweatin' like a sinner in church. Grocery buggy. You get used to all the colloquialisms after a while. It's part of his charm. Have him tell you about chitlins sometime." Isaac shuddered. "Now the thought of that stuff is something you don't get used to."

"What we're proposing is a trial run," I said. "If we work well together, we can continue our association. If not, we'll shake hands and go our separate ways.

The room fell quiet as Ninja considered our proposal.

"At the risk of Omega accusing me of being a stalker again, I took a nice long look at you Myth right around the time I was checking Omega out since I knew you two were friends," Ninja said. "Both of you seem to have your hearts in the right places. As you say, it appears we need each other. And if Seer was right about you Omega, you're the key to whatever crisis the world will face. A professional goes where there's work to be done. Being near you promises lots of it. To make a long story short, I'm in." She hesitated. "And in the interest of engendering trust, I'll even reveal my secret identity to you."

Isaac and I glanced at each other.

I said, "Your legal name is Chie Sato, though you've gone by the nickname Shay ever since your first-grade teacher in Oregon mispronounced your Japanese name. You're divorced with no kids. I'd say how old you are, but my grandma told me to never reveal a woman's age. You live in the northeastern quadrant of Astor City in the Silver Sable subdivision."

"You've got a real nice house," Isaac added. "I love what you've done with the master bath. You'd think pink and gold wouldn't work together, but they do."

Ninja's eyes were wide as she sat in stunned silence. It was the first time I had ever seen her taken aback. Batman never would have been caught flat-footed like this, I guess she wasn't him after all. I said, "Like I said, we checked you out pretty thoroughly before contacting you."

"Apparently," Ninja said dryly, recovering.

Isaac clapped his hands and rubbed them together. "Now that that's decided, let's talk about the most important thing of all—our team name. The Sentinels is out, of course. Too much baggage. We need something both descriptive and that's got pizzazz. Now I'm just spitballing here, but how about Myth's Legends of Tomorrow?"

"No," I said.

"The Mythcreants?"

"No," Ninja said. The fabric around her mouth twitched.

"The Mythadventurers?" Isaac suggested hopefully.

"No," both Ninja and I said.

30

"I've always wanted to own a jet," Isaac said. "Ever since I was little. Who says dreams don't come true?"

"This is not your jet," Ninja said. "Since it used to belong to the Sentinels, it's my jet now. You're just a passenger. I bet you're one of those guys who sleeps with a woman once and then thinks he owns her."

"I know it's hard to not think about sex when someone as handsome and dashing as I am is around. Even Omega's heterosexuality succumbed to my charms the other day when we were on the space station. But try harder to keep your mind out of the gutter and on our mission to defeat Doctor Alchemy. As a martial artist, you should be more disciplined. Besides, I already have a girlfriend. She doesn't share well with others."

"Imagine my disappointment," Ninja said.

Ninja piloted the jet using an oversized joystick which stuck up between her legs. Its design looked like a video game had inspired it. Sensors, gauges, buttons, switches, and flashing lights densely dotted the cockpit in front of her. Wisps of clouds streaked by the cockpit windows as we zoomed through the air.

Isaac sat next to Ninja in the co-pilot's chair. Both he and I had our costumes and cowls on because Ninja did not know our secret identities. Even with his cowl hiding most of his features and though he was trying to be cool about it, I knew Isaac well enough to know he was as excited to fly in a Sentinels' jet as a kid was to sit on Santa's lap. The Sentinels had been *the* Hero team before their disgrace.

I sat in one of the five wing-back chairs behind Ninja and Isaac. Unlike Isaac, I was not as excited as a kid in Santa's lap because, like so much of the Sentinels' technology, this state of the art jet had been designed by Mechano. I didn't need to check my list twice to know he had been far naughtier than he had been nice.

We weren't in Santa's lap, but we were in the lap of luxury. The leather chairs we were strapped into were as soft as a baby's bottom. They vibrated ever so gently as the jet ripped through the sky at an absurd speed. Behind the Sentinels' seven chairs was a long couch that hugged one side of the jet's cabin; a small conference table with a holographic projector in the middle of it was on the other side. Everything was in shades of tasteful browns and ivory.

While the inside of the jet looking like something out of a braggadocious rap video, its outside looked militaristic. With its V-shaped design, the black jet looked like the smaller, chubbier cousin of the United States' B-2 Spirit stealth bomber. The distinctive S-shaped golden logo of the Sentinels was on the bottom of each of the plane's wings. The jet's various armaments made it a flying fortress.

The fact I was in a flying fortress, the fact I had use of my powers again, and the fact two other Heroes were with me did not make me any less nervous to be flying towards Doctor

Alchemy's lair. No, "nervous" did not quite explain the hard knot forming in the pit of my stomach. Scared was more like it.

The average person thought Heroes were fearless. Maybe some of the dumber ones were. I for one was always nervous when I headed into potential combat. More so when I had been fresh out of the Academy, less so after I donned the Omega suit, and even less so than that as I became adept in the use of my enhanced powers. However, my skirmish with Doctor Alchemy and the Revengers had taught me that, despite all my power, I was not invulnerable. I was more nervous now sitting here rocketing toward Doctor Alchemy's lair than I had been the first time I went on patrol with the Old Man.

According to Isaac, who had been far more aware of his surroundings than I when he had flown us off Doctor Alchemy's island, the island was located within the Ring of Fire, named that because it was the Pacific Ocean basin where a lot of earthquakes and volcanic eruptions occurred. The three of us intended to capture and bring Doctor Alchemy to justice if he was there when we arrived; we would merely liberate his subjects if he was not.

I was a jumble of nerves with a healthy scoop of fear on top because Doctor Alchemy had to know I was coming. After what he had done to me, surely he did not think I would let him roam around scot-free. The only ace in the hole I had was that I was not returning alone. Capturing Doctor Alchemy was one of the reasons Isaac and I had recruited Ninja. She had fought him before. Against someone as vicious and erratic as he was, we figured we'd need all the help we could get. We would have to track down the other Revengers too, but Doctor Alchemy was first on the to-do list because he was dangerous in a way the other Revengers were not.

In addition to being afraid for myself, I was afraid of what Doctor Alchemy might have done to Oliver. Isaac and I had left my communicator watch on the table of my torture chamber. Since Oliver had been the only person who visited me in Doctor Alchemy's absence, Doctor Alchemy would deduce Oliver had brought the watch to me. I shuddered to think of what Doctor Alchemy might have done to the old man as punishment. I prayed we would be in time to rescue him from the vicious Rogue's clutches. Or I should say *try* to rescue Oliver. The Revengers defeating me had severely shaken my confidence. I was deathly afraid that instead of liberating Doctor Alchemy's subjects, we would instead add three super-powered ones to their number.

We were getting closer to the island's coordinates. It felt like going back to an alley where I had been jumped and beaten half to death, not knowing if my muggers would still be there when I arrived. Theo the farm boy would never have dreamed of deliberately going back to the scene of where he had been peeled like a peach. Theo the Hero wasn't overjoyed by the idea, either. But, as the Old Man had been fond of saying, "A Hero runs toward the danger that a regular person would run from." Sometimes I wished I hadn't paid so much attention to his lessons.

"We're here," Ninja said. She tilted the joystick down and back. The low hum of the jet's engines changed in pitch as we slowed and lost altitude, dropping below the cloud cover. The ocean burst into view. It glittered like a blue sapphire in the sun. We hovered above the ocean, still high in the sky.

We stared through the cockpit windows. "According to the coordinates you gave me Myth, Doctor Alchemy's island should be right there." Ninja pointed through the cockpit window at the water below. Nothing was there. Not a speck of land marred the blue vista. Water was as far as the eye could see. "Are you sure you got the coordinates right?"

Isaac looked at her like it was a stupid question. She did not know him like I did. Despite the fact he would likely sit up in his casket and crack jokes at his own funeral, he knew his business. I said, "If this is the spot Myth says he rescued me from, then this is the spot he rescued me from."

"Then why is there nothing to see here but the deep blue sea?" Ninja demanded. "Nothing's showing up on radar or the jet's other sensors either."

"It's gotta be here," Isaac insisted. "An island doesn't just jump up and disappear like a guy caught in bed with someone else's wife."

"No, it doesn't." I unbuckled my seat restraints and shrugged out of them. "I'll go outside and use my telekinetic touch to see if I can find anything."

"Why can't you do that from here?" Ninja asked.

"It's easier if I do the scan with nothing around me. Why do you think I go to the top of the UWant Building all the time?"

"I thought it was because you wanted to look taller," Isaac said.

I ignored Isaac from long ingrained habit. I went to the center of the cabin, near the conference table. Drawing on the fifty-cent tour Ninja had given us before we took off, I hit a button on the panel mounted on the side of the table. The circle I stood on dropped down like an elevator car. It lowered me into a gleaming cylindrical chamber under the cabin. The opening overhead to the cabin closed with a hiss. My ears popped as the chamber equalized the air pressure between the chamber and outside the jet. Then the circle I stood on dropped open like a trapdoor. I fell out of the chamber, down toward the glittering water below. I caught myself with my powers, and levitated a few dozen feet under the hovering jet. The opening I dropped out of sealed shut behind me.

Okay, that's actually pretty cool, I thought despite my reflexive prejudice against anything Mechano related. Sometimes it was hard to not give the devil his due.

The wind whistled like a distant train as it whipped around me. The jet hovered silently, held up by a propulsion system I probably would not understand if I studied it for a decade. I was a chastened Hero and torture survivor, not an engineer. I lifted my hands in what Isaac would call my best zombie impersonation, activated my powers, and reached out with my telekinetic touch. I scanned the area below where Doctor Alchemy's island hideout was supposed to be.

I wasn't at all surprised to find the island right where Isaac said it would be. Though I still could not see it with my eyes, thanks to my powers, it rose up out of the surrounding water like an enormous rocky kraken in my mind's eye. Doctor Alchemy had obviously done something to render it invisible both to the naked eye and to the jet's sensors. I had no idea how he pulled it off. Some sort of super-advanced stealth technology maybe, or something else altogether. Again, I was no engineer. Maybe he had simply terrified it into invisibility.

I was about to activate the earbud communicator Ninja had given me to tell the others my discovery when my powers shrieked for my attention.

Two invisible objects had left the island's surface. They shot toward us like bats out of hell.

SAMs—surface-to-air missiles. I didn't have to be an engineer to know they were on their way to blow us to bits.

31

I hastily erected a force bubble around both the jet and me. The first missile slammed into it. The missile exploded on impact. The second one did the same an instant later. Fireballs engulfed us. The inferno competed with the sun in brightness.

But only for an instant. I sucked up the energy from the blasts like a thirsty sponge, ending the light show almost as quickly as it had begun. The explosions would have deafened me had I not been careful to make sure the force field was completely impermeable. Not even sound waves had penetrated it.

I swooped down toward the island, still maintaining the force bubble around the motionless jet while I erected my personal shield around myself. Ninja said something in my ear. She sounded awfully calm for someone who had almost been blasted out of the sky by invisible weapons. Then again, this was not her first rodeo. My mind otherwise occupied, her words barely registered.

In seconds, my telekinetic touch found what I was looking for below: two mobile SAM batteries, one on each side of the invisible island. The batteries looked a bit like dump trucks, only instead of them having a dump bed, missiles stuck up like pins in a pincushion on a mechanized platform on either side of an operator's chair. Each battery was manned by a two-person crew, one man, one woman, all dressed like the people I had encountered in Doctor Alchemy's torture chamber.

Despite the fact they had just shot at us, I knew they were as much victims of Doctor Alchemy as I had been. I was careful to not hurt them when I yanked them away from the SAM batteries. I flung them through the air like discarded wads of paper. Once they were far enough away from the batteries, I channeled the energy I had absorbed from the missile explosions. A blast of energy lanced out of my eyes, striking the first battery. It exploded into a raging bonfire with a boom they might have heard in Atlantis. I turned my head slightly. The second battery followed the first one into noisy, fiery oblivion.

I did not detect any other threats on the island's surface. I activated the earbud transmitter. I guided Ninja and the jet toward a flat part of the beach surrounding the island's volcano, not far from where the fire of one of the destroyed SAM batteries raged. Once the jet and I descended close to the island surface, the seemingly empty space the island occupied shimmered, like the air above a patch of highway on a hot day. Silently, the island appeared in the middle of the ocean as if by magic.

The jet and I landed on the beach between the water and the burning SAM battery. The other fire was on the other side of the island; black smoke from it rose above the island's tree line. I looked around. This was my first time seeing the island in the light of day.

The air was humid and warm, but not uncomfortably so. The tang of salt water was in the air, mixing with the acrid smell of burning rubber and plastic. I stood on sand as black as Doctor Alchemy's heart. The black sand beach was so wide, I wouldn't be able to throw a rock across it from the edge of the water to where it ended at the tree line. Thanks to my earlier telekinetic touch recon, I knew this beach of black sand surrounded the entire large island like a thick black snake eating itself. The ocean gently lapped at one side of the beach; tall palm trees like upside down giant feather dusters lined the other side. Beyond the trees was a thick tangle of vegetation. Past that loomed the volcano, green with vegetation at its base, black and brown with rocks as it climbed high into the air. White smoke puffed slowly but steadily out of its top. Cawing seagulls circled overhead.

If it weren't for the smell, sight, and sound of the fires from the SAM batteries and the knowledge this was the home of a notorious Rogue and his gang of mind-controlled minions, this place would be a latter-day Garden of Eden. If I ran across any snakes here, I knew not to eat any apples it offered.

Ninja and Isaac exited the jet from a ramp telescoping from its side. It noiselessly retracted back into the jet as soon as they dismounted. The scabbard slung diagonally across Ninja's chest was empty. She had her katana in her hand and at the ready. Her eyes were vigilant, alert for any sign of danger. Isaac was more relaxed. Unlike Ninja, he knew I'd never let them land much less disembark had I not been certain we were in no immediate danger.

"I've never seen an all-black beach before," Isaac said. His eyes twinkled behind his cowl. "It's much prettier than an all-white one. Something else the racist white power structure and global conspiracy has been keeping from us. The Rothschild family's doing, no doubt. I wonder why the sand is blacker than I am."

"They're tiny basalt fragments, probably from the

volcano's periodic eruptions," Ninja said in a clipped tone. All business, quite the contrast from how casual Isaac was. She glanced at the burning SAM battery, then looked pointedly at me. "Subtle. If Doctor Alchemy is home and didn't already know we were here, he surely does now."

"Maybe you'd prefer if I had let them blow you to kingdom come."

"Easy, Omega. I was commenting, not criticizing." It didn't sound like it. Regardless, she was right. I could have neutralized the SAM batteries without being so noisy about it. I had used a sledgehammer when a scalpel was more appropriate. Being on this island again was affecting my judgment, making me trigger-happy.

Isaac surveyed the volcano with his hands on his hips. He pursed his lips thoughtfully as he looked up at it. "That thing's huge. And everything looks different in the light of day. I don't think I can find my way back to Doctor Alchemy's lair in there without a sign pointing the way that reads 'Abandon hope all ye who enter here.' And Omega's communicator we left behind has been deactivated, so that's no help. Omega, can you . . ." he trailed off, wiggling his fingers in front of himself like a magician.

"I've already tried my telekinetic touch," I said. "The rock in the volcano is too dense for me to penetrate."

"Some might say the same about my head, especially when I'm stymied like I am now." Isaac shook his head. "If you two have any bright ideas on how to find Doctor Alchemy's lair without me wandering around inside the volcano like a ghost whose house has burned down, I'm all ears." He glanced up at the bright sun. "Let's hurry. I won't be able to pass the brown paper bag test if I stay out here much longer. If I'd known, I would have brought sunscreen."

"Way ahead of you," I said. With a tiny gesture from me,

one of the people who had manned the nearby SAM battery lifted off the beach and came sailing toward us like he dangled from a clothesline I was pulling on. The other three SAM personnel were sprawled out on the black sand, unconscious thanks to me carefully applying pressure to their carotid arteries while the jet landed. I had tied their hands and feet together with vines so they would not make nuisances of themselves when they woke up. The one floating toward us I had kept conscious but immobilized on the off chance we needed to question someone. Despite the mistake I made in so sloppily destroying the SAM batteries, I was not a complete Heroic neophyte.

I set the man down on the sand. The brown-haired, nondescript man stood immobilized, held upright and still by my powers, though I did free his head so he could speak. He did not. He just stared at us with the same hazy, slightly euphoric look on his face Doctor Alchemy's other subjects had. He had on the black pants and turquoise tunic with a yellow sash tied around the waist Doctor Alchemy's other male subjects wore.

Isaac waved a hand in the man's face, snapping his fingers right in front of the man's eyes. The man did not blink and kept the same vacant look on his face. It reminded me of the dumb look my Uncle Charles' cows used to give me when I approached their pasture—they had known I was there, but could not have cared less.

"This guy looks as high as a giraffe's vagina," Isaac said.

"Colorful," Ninja said.

"That too," Isaac said, eyeing the man's outfit.

"We're more likely to get straight answers out of a crack addict than this guy," I said, disgusted. So much for being pleased with myself for preserving someone for questioning.

"Not so fast, young Padawan," Isaac said. His form glowed

and shimmered as it always did when he underwent one of his transformations. His body lengthened and widened. When the shimmering stopped, a strapping, bare-chested, pale white man with shoulder-length strawberry-blonde hair and wearing a green and black tartan kilt stood before us. Young, handsome, and long-limbed, he was taller than Ninja and I by a considerable amount. He glowed a very faint reddish-yellow, yet not like how Isaac glowed from every pore when he transformed. This man's glow was more like a halo. A smooth black stone the size of my fist was in a mesh bag hanging from the man's belt. A broadsword far longer and thicker than Ninja's katana was in his meaty fist. The sword's blade had its own whitish glow separate and apart from the nimbus around the man. A spear hung diagonally from his back, held in place with a leather strap across his hairy chest. The shaft was wooden; the tip was covered by a brown leather bag tied shut at its opening by a rawhide cord. A thick red liquid oozed from the bag in a serpentine line down the shaft. Blood, from the looks of it.

In his new form, Isaac lifted his sword and held it against the immobilized man's throat. The sword's glow spread to encompass the man's body, like a burning candle igniting an unlit one.

"The mighty Fragarach compels you," Isaac rumbled in a voice much deeper and richer than his usual one. His voice had an almost musical quality, like resonant notes played on an organ. "Is Doctor Alchemy on the island now?"

"Yes," the man said immediately, though his voice sounded reluctant, like he didn't want to answer.

"Where is he?" Isaac asked.

"When I last saw him, he was in the throne room."

"And how do we get to this throne room from here?"

The man gave us instructions and directions, interrupted

occasionally by clarification questions from Isaac. Once Isaac wrung all the information he could out of the man, he removed his sword from the man's throat. The white glow around the man disappeared like a doused flame. I used my powers to choke the man unconscious. Then I tied him up with vines my powers yanked from the vegetation in the distance.

By the time I finished, Isaac had turned back into usual self. I had never seen him use that form before, but it had been awhile since we had been out in the field as Heroes together. "Who was that and how did you get this guy to spill his guts?" I asked.

Isaac shrugged modestly. "Lugh Lamfada from Irish mythology, though he's probably better known as Lugh the Long-Armed. His sword is named Fragarach. The Answerer. It's like Wonder Woman's Lasso of Truth. Only without the bustier. I don't have the rack for it."

Newfound respect was in Ninja's eyes as she looked at Isaac. "You're far more impressive than how you come across," she said.

"That's the worst compliment I've ever gotten. You're just mad because my sword was bigger than yours. Clear case of sword envy."

"Come on, let's go," I said, impatient to get this expedition over and done with. Were lambs similarly eager to head to the slaughterhouse? I knew my pessimism was the wrong attitude to confront a Rogue with. The Academy and the Old Man had pounded a can-do attitude into me, not a can't-do one. Being captured and tortured had a way of shaking one's confidence.

I led the way off the beach, past the line of palm trees, and into the thick vegetation. Tall, thick, and jungle-like, the vegetation swallowed us. It plunged us into gloom like we had entered the belly of a beast. Only the buzzing and chirping of insects and the faint scurrying of animals in the underbrush marred the silence of the jungle.

Following the directions of the man Isaac had questioned to the letter, we avoided a passel of boobytraps that we surely would have triggered had we not known of them. The force field I had up probably would have protected us, but you could never be too careful when dealing with someone like Doctor Alchemy. Deadfalls, land mines, poisoned darts, arrows tipped with explosives, proximity detectors that shot lasers . . . we dodged them all and more thanks to the intelligence gleaned from Doctor Alchemy's subject. We could not fly because going airborne would have triggered alarms in Doctor Alchemy's lair. He likely already knew we were here thanks to my stupid pyrotechnics earlier, but why surrender even the possibility of having the element of surprise?

After a while, it felt like we tromped through the vast jungles of darkest Africa. I kept the thought to myself. Isaac would accuse me of being racist.

I was starting to wonder if we would stumble upon Doctor Livingstone before we found Doctor Alchemy when suddenly, we were here.

Here was a black rock face at the base of the looming volcano. Isaac moved tangled vines out of the way, revealed a numeric keypad recessed into the rock face. Isaac started punching in the seven-digit access code he'd gotten from Doctor Alchemy's subject. It then dawned on me why the numbers had seemed familiar when the man had recited them—they were the day, month, and year Neha had been born.

A fresh wave of guilt washed over me. Despite everything else he was, Doctor Alchemy was still Neha's father. Him blaming me for her death was understandable.

I pushed the thought away as soon as I had it. Doctor

Alchemy's anger and grief were no excuse for all the people he had hurt over the years. He had to be stopped.

Isaac hit the last digit of the code. A section of the rock face disappeared, as if it had never been there. A large corridor was revealed that wormed its way deep into the volcanic rock. Except for the first few feet, the corridor was pitch-black. Doctor Alchemy could be standing in there with a bazooka pointed at our heads and we wouldn't know it.

With my heart in my throat, I probed the dark corridor with my telekinetic touch. No bazooka, and no Doctor Alchemy. Never was I so relieved to not find the person I was looking for.

Ninja's katana began to glow as if it burned with a pink flame. Knowing it could cut through anything when imbued with her Metahuman power, I was careful to keep my distance. Ninja stretched her katana tentatively into the corridor, dispelling some of the darkness.

"Do you have to be in contact with your sword to pull off that sparkler trick?" Isaac asked in a low voice.

"No. I just have to be near it. But what good is a sword without an arm to wield it?" Ninja answered, also in a low voice. "I'll go first and light the way. Keep your eyes peeled."

Isaac said, "Be my guest. I'm a firm believer in gender equality. Plus, I learned from every horror movie ever made that the black guy who's the first to go into the dark and scary place is the first to die a horrible death."

Ninja ignored Isaac as if he had not spoken. She was learning. She stepped into the corridor. I followed, and Isaac brought up the rear. Once we were all inside, the rock wall reappeared behind us, cutting off all the light from outside.

Ninja's sword was our only source of illumination as we crept along. After a bit, the corridor began branching off into different corridors. Without hesitation, Ninja led us first this way and then that, following the directions the man tied up outside had given us. Even with those directions, it felt like we were making our way through a maze. There were still no lights.

As we penetrated deeper into the lair, the walls of the corridor changed from being bare rock to being ornately decorated with stonework, gemstones, and elaborate friezes and murals featuring Doctor Alchemy vanquishing various foes and posing heroically. The gemstones glittered with reflected pink light like thousands of demons' eyes as we went deeper and deeper into the lair. We passed numerous closed doors to various rooms. Other than us, all was still and quiet. We did not encounter a single soul.

"The last time we were here," Isaac whispered in my ear, almost making me jump, "this place was lousy with people. Well-lit too. Now it's as dead and dark as a tomb. I don't like it. Reminds me of our Academy days when we went into that vacant building after Iceburn. And that didn't turn out so well for Team Us. Why do I get the feeling we're walking into a trap again?"

"Probably because we are," I whispered back. Though I still didn't sense anyone in the corridor or any surveillance devices, I couldn't fight the feeling we were being watched. The hairs on the back of my neck stood up.

"Fantastic," Isaac said. "Good pep talk."

After what seemed like an eternity, we arrived at the ornate double doors that were the entrance to Doctor Alchemy's throne room. I had never been to the Taj Mahal, but I imagined this was what the main entrance to that fantastically expensive building looked like—huge, made of precious metals, and decorated with a fortune of jewels.

The man Isaac had questioned said there would be guards posted. They were nowhere to be seen. Like the walls of the corridor we had traveled through, these doors and the walls around them were immune to my telekinetic touch.

Ninja and Isaac looked at me. I was startled when I realized they looked to me for guidance. Maybe Avatar or Omega Man would have inspirational words to share, or a brilliant battle plan to sketch out. Me? I had nothing. Unfortunately, neither the Omega spirit nor the Omega suit had come with an owner's manual full of strategic wisdom. If I got out of this place with my neck intact, maybe I'd end the no guidance cycle by jotting down some thoughts for the next vessel of the Omega spirit. *Don't be foolish enough to return to the scene of the torture crime* would likely be on top of the list.

For lack of a better idea of how to proceed, I reached to pull the doors by their ornate handles. Both doors silently swung toward me before I laid a hand on them. I jumped out of their way. My racing pulse roaring in my ears. I blinked against the bright light pouring from the other side of the doors.

"Well, well, well, Mother," Doctor Alchemy's strong voice rang out confidently. "I spy with my little eye three trespassing Heroes about to die."

32

The three of us darted cautiously yet quickly into the throne room, ready for anything. Ninja was in the middle, moving in her usual agile way. Isaac and I were on either side of her. We spread out to avoid presenting a single target.

Doctor Alchemy and his wife were directly ahead of us on the other side of the huge room, at the end of a red carpet running from the doorway to them. They sat on thrones resting on a platinum dais. Crowns that would have made a British monarch green with envy were on both of their heads.

"I really should have killed you before, Omega," Doctor Alchemy said. The room was so large, his voice echoed. "Alas, my desire to prolong your suffering and my flair for the theatrical gave you an opportunity to escape. It is like something a Bond villain would do. I do so hate acting the stereotype. Especially one invented by a loathsome Brit." A smug smile slowly spread across Doctor Alchemy's masked features. "On the other hand, you are once again in my clutches. And, you were thoughtful enough to bring your fellow daughter-killer Myth with you. And the redoubtable Ninja to boot. It is an absolute embarrassment of riches, Mother. I hardly know whom to kill first. Diwali has come early this year. Diwali is akin to Christmas, Omega, since I cannot imagine you know. As unlettered white trash, how culturally literate could you possibly be?"

While Doctor Alchemy blathered on, I took a careful but quick survey of the room, hyper-alert to any threat. Though the Thakores' thrones were of matching size and shape, hers was golden; his was made of a translucent, almost transparent, substance. I would have thought it quartz had I not known his towering ego would never let him sit on such a base substance. Diamond, maybe, but I had never before seen so much of it in one place. Doctor Alchemy had his usual costume on, including his gauntlets and utility belt. His purple cape was draped over the armrest of his throne. Rati Thakore had on a rich, shoulder-baring sari, and fairly dripped with gold jewelry. Above their heads hung an enormous chandelier that spanned the entire area of the dais below it. The chandelier dangled from the high ceiling by thick cables. The chandelier's light, refracted by innumerable crystals, made it look like countless tiny spotlights illuminated Doctor Alchemy and his wife.

The lush red carpet that ran the length of the room was trimmed with gold. The floor it rested on was a bluish-purple stone. Lapis lazuli, maybe, polished to such a shine that it glistened like it was wet. On the walls were more bejeweled murals of Doctor Alchemy performing spectacular feats. Famous stolen paintings were also on the walls, with Doctor Alchemy's face painted over the original subjects' faces. The ceiling was covered with gold leaf.

Caligula's palace would seem tasteful and modest compared to Doctor Alchemy's throne room. Yet despite the distracting garishness of the room, it was impossible to miss the fact that there were dozens of Doctor Alchemy's subjects lined up in staggered rows on both sides of us. As if we had rehearsed it, Isaac and I shifted our stances to face the throng of subjects closest to each of us while still keeping a wary eye on Doctor Alchemy. Though the men and woman all had sidearms, they were holstered. Their bodies pointed straight ahead toward us three Heroes, but their heads were all turned to look at Doctor Alchemy and his wife. The subjects looked at the enthroned Thakores with rapturous expressions, like devout Christians witnessing Jesus' resurrection. It was creepy and unnerving.

The only person in the assembled throng who did not have that worshipful look on his face was Oliver, Doctor Alchemy's manservant. He was at the front of the subjects, on my side of the red carpet. He had a resigned look on his face, as if he knew how crazy Doctor Alchemy was, but was powerless to do anything about it. Unlike when I had last seen him days ago, his wrinkled old face and hands were mottled red, black, and blue. I shuddered to think of what the rest of his body looked like under his uniform. Obviously, Doctor Alchemy had deduced Oliver had a hand in my escape, and he had punished Oliver accordingly.

"That's quite far enough," Doctor Alchemy said sharply. His ominous tone and something about the way his hand fondled the top of his utility belt made us stop advancing toward him. We halted roughly in the middle of the large room.

"Surrender yourself before someone gets hurt," Ninja demanded of Doctor Alchemy.

The room was silent for a moment. Then Doctor Alchemy's laugh broke the silence. The echoes of it reverberated around the room. "'Surrender yourself before someone gets hurt,'" he repeated mockingly in a high-pitched impersonation of Ninja's voice. "You're deep in the bowels of my lair, surrounded by almost a hundred of my faithful subjects, within spitting distance of hundreds more, accompanied only by two adolescent Heroes, and armed merely with a glowing pigsticker. I admire your chutzpah if not your grasp on reality. Hobnobbing with godlike beings when you were on the Sentinels has gone to your head, making you think that you too are godlike. You are not. You are but a somewhat agile pre-menopausal woman with questionable tastes in companions. You will surrender to me, not the other way around."

"Three Heroes against one Rogue with delusions of grandeur and a bunch of his coked-up followers?" Isaac sniffed. "I like our odds."

"It is no wonder my daughter graduated ahead of you in your Academy class, Myth," Doctor Alchemy said, shaking his head in sorrow. "For you really are not particularly bright, are you? Even with all of your abilities arrayed against us, Mother and I have two things in our favor that make all the difference: The brains to know you would be coming, and time to prepare for your arrival. You Heroes are all too predictable. Once I discovered Omega had escaped, I knew he would eventually return with his sanctimonious lips thirsting for justice. I also deduced he would bring help since I defeated him so handily before. The island's surveillance cameras showed he had escaped in the clutches of a giant mythological bird that is not supposed to exist. So, it was not hard to guess one of the helpers he would return with would be you, Myth. Ninja's appearance I will admit is more of a surprise. I imagined Omega would enlist the aid of someone more formidable—Amazing Man, perhaps—but one must not look a gift horse in the mouth. Killing you Ninja will be much more satisfying than killing Amazing Man. Your teammates were responsible for my daughter's death, after all. Plus, you and the Sentinels have been quite the thorn in my side over the years. It has warmed the cockles of my heart to watch your team's fall from grace.

"Knowing you would come back, Omega, I had time to get ready for your return. You no doubt have already determined that everything in this room is immune from your telekinesis. With a mind such as mine, repurposing the anti-telekinesis technology of Iceburn's suit was child's play." Unfortunately, he was right—I'd determined the moment the doors had swung open that trying to latch onto anything in this room was like trying to grab a phantom. My powers would only work on myself, Ninja, and Isaac. Otherwise I would have immobilized Doctor Alchemy long before he subjected us to this self-congratulatory ear-beating.

"When I became aware you were on the island, I assembled this welcoming party for you," Doctor Alchemy continued pompously. "Complete with party favors. Each one of my devoted subjects you see here has an alchemy cartridge in his or her mouth. If you do not surrender, I will push this lovely button on my belt," he caressed the button fondly, "and each cartridge will explode, taking my subjects' heads with them. Boy," he said, snapping the fingers of the hand that didn't hover near his belt, "open your mouth and stick out your tongue so my guests will know that I am not bluffing."

Oliver complied. One of Doctor Alchemy's cartridges lay on his tongue.

Doctor Alchemy's eyes flicked back over to us. "You and I both know you will surrender. You will not risk innocents being killed. As I said before, you Heroes are all too predictable."

"You expect us to believe you would kill your own people?" Isaac asked incredulously. Despite what I had told him about

Doctor Alchemy, hearing about what he was capable of and seeing what he was capable of were two different things.

Doctor Alchemy shrugged carelessly.

"Why not kill them?" he asked breezily as his adoring subjects gazed up at him. "There are plenty more where these came from. People breed like rabbits. A handful less will not matter. That is the difference between people like you and people like me. 'Protect the innocent! Succor the weak! Help the afflicted!' are your nauseating shibboleths. What you are too stupid, shortsighted, and tenderhearted to understand is that the weak, the afflicted, and the innocent do not need to be protected. They need to be led. Guided. Ruled. Or else their little monkey minds will lead them into mischief. It is why the world is in its sorry state. Overpopulation. Political unrest. Climate change. The threat of nuclear war. Half the planet eating itself to death, and the other half starving to death. All this and more caused by humanity left to its own unreasoning devices. It needs a ruler to bring an end to all that and to usher in an era of peace and prosperity. It needs me. History will show that I am the true hero, and you and your ilk standing in my way are the true villains. Omega, you and Myth already showed your villainous colors by letting our beautiful, beloved daughter and successor to my throne die. She would be alive and by our side today if she had not been beguiled down the wrong path and fallen into your bad company."

Mentioning Neha triggered his volatile temper. He slammed his fist down on the side of his throne. His crown became slightly askew due to the impact. A finger on his other hand was on the button on his belt. "I tire of this pointless colloquy. You swine lack the wit to comprehend my glorious vision," he snarled, his face abruptly red with rage. "Surrender, or you will have even more lives on your miserable consciences."

Things had not worked out so well the last time I had surrendered to Doctor Alchemy. I had seen this movie before and had not been thrilled with the ending. Fortunately, seeing Doctor Alchemy and his lifeless wife side by side like this had given me an idea of how to rewrite the ending. I remembered what I had thought after I had destroyed the SAM batteries—that the situation called for a scalpel, not a sledgehammer. My eyes darted to Ninja's glowing sword that would cut through anything.

"All right," I said. "We surrender." Isaac's eyes shifted from Doctor Alchemy's subjects to stare at me, shocked that I would give in so easily. I shot him a look back that said *Trust me*. His lips tightened, but he nodded almost imperceptibly. He didn't like it, but I knew he'd back my play.

"Are you mad?" Ninja murmured. She hadn't seen the look I had given Isaac. She still had her glowing sword in front of her, not taking her eyes off Doctor Alchemy. "If we don't stop this maniac, who will?"

"I'm not going to let all these people die," I said.

"Of course you won't. Because you're a H . . . E . . . R . . . O," Doctor Alchemy said, drawing the word out, saying it mockingly. He leaned back in his throne, supremely confident and self-assured. He was calm again, his mood already having shifted. "As are you, Ninja. You are cut from a different cloth than your erstwhile teammate Mechano. Though perhaps more jaded than your young compatriots, I know you will not let a slew of people die on your watch either." He pointedly fingered the button on his belt again. "Now drop your sword before I lose my temper and all these lovely people lose their heads. That's a good girl. Kick it away from you, out of reach. I have seen what you are able to do with that thing." Ninja's sword, no longer glowing, glided down the red carpet, coming to a stop about midway between us and the twin thrones.

"Now kneel before your king," Doctor Alchemy thundered, leaning forward, his eyes blazing. "Lace your fingers behind your head. If any of you use your powers or so much as twitches, my loyal subjects will suffer for it."

I had sidled close to Ninja before kneeling. "What do your powers tell you Doctor Alchemy's weakness is?" I murmured, referring to her Metahuman ability to sense an opponent's vulnerability.

"His wife," she immediately whispered back. It only confirmed what I had already thought. I had not forgotten how Doctor Alchemy reacted when Oliver accidentally splattered his wife with blood.

"Get ready to activate your sword on my say-so."

"Done," she whispered, thankfully not asking a bunch of fool questions. Her experience in high pressure situations was showing itself again.

"Now which of these three shall we kill first, Mother?" Doctor Alchemy was saying as we whispered. Though one hand still hovered near the button on his belt, his other arm pointed at us. We looked up the barrel of one of his gauntlets. "The situation calls for flesh-eating acid, don't you agree? Painful but, alas, relatively quick. I learned my lesson from the last time. As much as we would enjoy prolonging their suffering, we cannot have them escape again. Omega we will save for last. Of those here, he is the most responsible for Neha's death, so it is only fitting for him to suffer the most by witnessing his friends' death. What's that? Ladies first, you say? Of course, how boorish and ungentlemanly of me to not think of it myself. You always were the soul of courtesy, Mother." Doctor Alchemy's gauntlet shifted to point at Ninja.

"Neha and I were more than just friends," I said, the words tumbling out in my haste. "We were lovers."

Doctor Alchemy blinked in surprise. His eyes shifted from Ninja to me. "Your lies won't save you now."

"I'm not lying. We slept together more times than I can count. Don't believe me? She had a mole on her right breast, right under the nipple. And she had a birthmark that looked like a crescent moon on her upper thigh, right under her—"

"Lies! Lies! All lies! Don't listen to him Mother." His eyes were horrified. I had accurately described Neha's mole and birthmark. Though Doctor Alchemy's gauntlet still pointed at us, his other hand shifted away from his belt and pressed against his dead wife's ear, shielding her from my words. The scene would have been funny had it not been so deadly serious.

I said, "The truth is it was easy to get Neha to spread her legs. She was the town bicycle—everyone got a ride. We passed her around the Academy like she was a joint." It made me sick to talk about Neha like this.

Doctor Alchemy leaped to his feet. His face was livid with rage. His eyes burned as he pointed at me accusingly. "How dare you sully the good name of my chaste daughter! You're a filthy, lying cur."

Whatever it took, I had to goad him away from his wife. Sick at heart, praying Neha would forgive me, I said, "It's that whore you raised who's the filthy one. She was quite a piece of ass. Not as good as a white girl, of course, but not bad for an Indian girl when nobody better was available. Any port in a storm."

Doctor Alchemy's face was almost as purple as his cape. He jumped off the dais and strode toward me with murderous intent. "Death by acid is too good for the likes of you. I'll squeeze the lies and the life out of you with my bare hands."

His subjects temporarily forgotten in his rage, his hands were nowhere near the button on his belt.

"Now Ninja!" I cried.

Her katana blazed pink as she exerted her power on it. Due to my own power, it sprang up and forward, off the red carpet, like a striking snake. Doctor Alchemy twisted to the side, dodging the darting blade easily.

I expected as much. I hadn't been aiming for him anyway.

The sword zoomed into the air, toward the high ceiling. The glowing katana, thanks to Ninja's power, ripped through the thick cables holding the massive chandelier up like they were wet toilet paper. The crystals of the chandelier tinkled as the massive fixture fell.

Doctor Alchemy's head twisted around.

"No!" he screamed, realizing now he had not been my target. With superpowered reflexes, he sprang back toward the dais.

Too late. I had lured him too far away from it.

The chandelier slammed into the thrones with a crash that rattled my teeth. Pieces of the chandelier went flying. I lifted my forearms to protect the exposed parts of my face. Shrapnel bounced off the Omega suit.

Once debris stopped bouncing off me, I cautiously lowered my arms. Doctor Alchemy stood on the dais. The two thrones, massively heavy, were still upright.

Rati Thakore's body was not. It was twisted to the side of the battered gold throne, pinned under the heavy metal structure of the massive chandelier. Doctor Alchemy grabbed the broken chandelier and heaved, using strength no ordinary man possessed to pull the heavy chandelier off his wife's body. More crystals tinkled as they fell off the chandelier and hit the dais and the stone floor.

Doctor Alchemy picked up his wife's twisted body. Her

head fell off her neck. Her eyes seemed to stare at us as the head dropped. When it hit the dais, the head smashed into pieces, spraying dust and tiny fragments, like it was a glass ball full of sand.

The decapitation seemed to trigger something within Rati's body, as if it was a house of cards whose foundation had been knocked down. While Doctor Alchemy clutched his wife, stricken and horrified, her body literally disintegrated. Like the sands of an hourglass, bits of her trickled through his fingers. In seconds he was shin deep in tiny bits that had once been her, like a child playing in a sandbox.

Doctor Alchemy's hands shook like unfallen brown leaves in a harsh winter wind. He fell to his knees. He ran his quivering hands through the strange material that had once been his wife.

"You killed Mother," he moaned in shock and disbelief. The words came out in a hoarse whisper as he stared wide-eyed at the thick dust surrounding him. Fat tears began to run down his cheeks.

Isaac sprang forward, his form shifting as he hurtled toward the dais. By the time he bounded onto it, he had transformed into his shaggy, round-shouldered werewolf form. Claws like razor blades slashed forward and down. Isaac ripped Doctor Alchemy's utility belt off him. Another slash of claws. Doctor Alchemy's broken gauntlets hit the floor, then skittered across the throne room when Isaac kicked them far away.

Doctor Alchemy did not seem to notice he had been disarmed. His arrogance and belligerence had been ripped away like his belt had been. His whole world seemed myopically confined to the dusty debris that surrounded him.

"You killed Mother," he said again, louder this time. Tears streamed down his face. His face contorted into a mask of pain and grief, like everything he cared about in the world was shattered and gone. I was embarrassed, feeling like a voyeur watching the anguish of a widower at his wife's funeral. I wanted to look away, but I forced myself not to. Some instinct told me I needed to see this. Doctor Alchemy's subjects, some of their faces bloodstained from shrapnel, still stared at Doctor Alchemy with their usual euphoric looks.

His daughter was dead. Now he realized his wife was dead. Even surrounded by adoring subjects, he had no one. After all Doctor Alchemy had done to me, after all he had done to everyone, I felt profoundly sorry for him. Tears formed in my own eyes.

"You killed Mother! You killed Mother! You killed Mother!" he repeated over and over. He seemed to shrink in on himself like a collapsing star as he vainly tried to hold onto his wife. The echoes of his wails reverberated off the walls, mixing into a cacophony of torment and woe.

"You killed Mother!" he howled, louder and louder until I didn't think I could stand it. His bloodshot eyes were vague and unfocused, as if he was looking through all of us and into the past.

"You killed Mother!"

After a while, it didn't seem like he was saying it to us at all.

"You killed Mother!"

After a while, it seemed like he was saying it to himself.

33

I stared at the framed sketch of my son James that was over the mantelpiece in my Astor City apartment. Now that I had seen Doctor Alchemy up close and personally, I knew that James' gently hooked nose he shared with his mother was in fact an inheritance from his maternal grandfather.

It was days after we had taken Doctor Alchemy into custody. He currently was in a Metahuman containment camp in Melbourne, Australia. A boatload of nations around the world were wrangling over who would get the first crack at trying him for his various crimes. I hoped whoever wound up with him gave him the psychiatric care he needed. Me feeling sorry for him despite all he had done had not faded. Isaac had accused me of being a "bleeding heart liberal," but his eyes had been damp like mine as we watched Doctor Alchemy cry over his wife.

Before we called the authorities, Isaac had turned into Lugh the Long-Armed again and used Fragarach to compel Doctor Alchemy to tell us where he had hidden the Philosopher's Stone. It was now at The Mountain. Considering all the mischief Doctor Alchemy had caused with it, I did not want the book to fall into the wrong hands. I was by no means certain I was the right hands, but I would have to do. I trusted myself more than I did government officials. I had plans to beef up security at The Mountain in light of Mad Dog's escape and the fact I had the Philosopher's Stone there. I previously thought Avatar had kept so many relics from his adventures at The Mountain out of an uncharacteristic vanity. Now I realized they were likely all there because he had not known what else to do with them. Some books were best kept unread.

I still hadn't told Isaac I had imprisoned Mad Dog at The Mountain. In all the hurly-burly, Isaac had never raised the issue of how Mad Dog had reappeared after all this time. I knew I had to fess up soon. Teammates really ought not keep secrets like that from one another.

For that was what we were—teammates. "No man is an island," Ninja had said a while ago on the roof of the UWant Building. She was right. I had needed Isaac's and Ninja's help to take down Doctor Alchemy. I could use their help rounding up the rest of the Revengers and bringing them to justice. Not to mention Millennium, who as the only other active Omega-level Meta was the mother of all loose ends. I would probably also need Ninja's, Isaac's, and others' help to protect the world against the threat the Sentinels had warned me about. A burden shared was a burden lifted.

I had some thoughts on who those others might be, but that was a bridge I would cross later. As was what our team name should be. The Mythfits—Isaac's most recent suggestion —just would not do.

My eyes shifted to look at Neha's picture on the mantel, then back up to look at James. I thought of how Doctor Alchemy had collapsed when he saw the reality of his dead wife. She had been dead for years, yet he had clung to a fantasy world in which she wasn't. Living in that fantasy world had twisted and distorted his mind, making him into a monster. My son James was as much of a fantasy as Rati was. I saw in Doctor Alchemy a dim reflection of the emotionally broken person I might become if I did not let go of the past and my grief and deal with reality as it really was.

Despite vivid memories of my married life with Neha and of our life with our son, that life was as fake as Doctor Alchemy's wife. I had to let it go. Just as I had to let go of the guilt I carried like a millstone around my neck over Neha's death and the fact I had not reconciled with her before she died.

I remembered something my father often said, one of his Jamesisms: "The past can be the wind in your sails. It can also be an anchor." Though Dad would have said he was just a simple farmer, he seemed wiser with each passing day. Children rarely appreciate their parents until they were gone.

I let out a long sigh. I took James' picture down. I went to the bedroom, opened my dresser's bottom drawer, and put the picture inside. I hesitated, then slid the drawer firmly closed. Maybe one day I would throw the picture out instead of merely putting it away. Today was not that day. Baby steps.

The past was dead and gone. All any reasonable person could do was learn from the past, embrace the present, and prepare for the future.

I went into another room, grabbed my cell phone, and dialed a number. Someone picked up. After we exchanged pleasantries, I said to Viola, "I was calling to see if you'd be interested in going out again."

"That depends," she said.

"Depends on what?"

"Depends on whether a Rogue will attack again." I practically felt her smile through the phone.

I smiled back.

"I can't make any promises."

The End

If you enjoyed this book, please leave a review on Amazon. Even a simple two word review such as "Loved it" helps so much. Reviews are a big aid in helping readers like you find books they might like.

ABOUT THE AUTHOR

Darius Brasher has a lifelong fascination with superheroes and a love of fantasy and science fiction. He has a Bachelor of Arts degree in English, a Juris Doctor degree in law, and a PhD from the School of Hard Knocks. He lives in South Carolina.

Email: darius@dbrasher.com
Patreon: www.patreon.com/dariusbrasher

facebook.com/dariusbrasher

twitter.com/dariusbrasher

amazon.com/author/dariusbrasher

Made in the USA
Middletown, DE
24 September 2020

20521806R00217